HUNTER'S MOON

J. MOLLY B.C.

ISBN: 069272771X
ISBN 13: 9780692727713
Library of Congress Control Number: 2016914233
J. Molly B. C., Staten Island, NY

Publishers note:
The names and characters in this book are fictional.

Cover art by: Steven McCole - Artist - whelk7@aol.com
Editor: Steven McCole

A message to the reader:

Enjoy this journey.
There are more of us than you think)O(

To John
For granting me time, peace & support so that I could write this book.

Hunters Moon)O(

A Grey tale wrapped around the phases of the Moon.
The naked truth about perception, aligned within the journey of a Solitary
Witch who prefers to fly on her own terms. She discovers a matrix of eclectic Witches who bend the Rede and its laws. Within this surreal odyssey,
she hones her esoteric, unusual traits and learns to fly against the grain. The
realms within this book are about perception and truth, with a plethora of
imbedded messages for the reader to discover.
All will be revealed.

The Moon had always captivated Mia. Every night, just before bedtime, she would stare out of her bedroom window, searching across the night sky for her majestic glow. She longed to Know the wonder of All of her. On some nights, the Moon's luminescent rays would kiss her eyelids and wake her from a sound sleep. She'd rush to the window to greet her, whispering inquisitive words of curiosity and ask for clarity and guidance regarding her current perception of goings on within her world. She knew that the answers would come to her in their own time. The Moon had always left her feeling star struck and sanguine.

As a child, thunderstorms had terrified her. Their approaching, cryptic warning signs had always sent her cowering into her mother's bedroom, until the one night when she had been forced to ride out the storm, alone. By the next morning, her perception had significantly changed and from that moment on, they had empowered her. The warning signs of an approaching storm would promptly send her outdoors to watch, feel their energy and absorb the feral symphony of unbridled power. On occasion, she would escape to the beach, just to watch the combined symphony of the storm, enhancing and merging with the ocean's raging glory, inevitably allowing their phenomenal power to seduce her Spirit. This entity had always reset her and left her feeling invincible.

During her late teenage years, her undiscovered, Empathic trait had been misdiagnosed as anxiety. For many years, she had believed this diagnosis to be the underlying cause of her symptoms, until she had come across some information in a magazine that revealed otherwise, thus challenging this theory and beginning her research. She read everything that she could get her hands on, leaving no page unturned. As she began to understand herself, her discoveries on Empathic traits, in comparison to her symptoms, began to make sense.

Over time, she avoided of crowds and steered clear of negative people. Her known traits were inclusive of Empathic abilities, dream interpretation as well as other forms of Divination via her path. She synched her life around the phases of the Moon and the Rede, seldom straying outside of her small Circle. She considered the Moon, hers, as with everything else that she had embraced wholeheartedly, her name and demeanor were precisely what it had meant - mine.

She discovers a matrix of eclectic Witches who bend the Rede and its laws. Within this surreal odyssey, she hones her esoteric, unusual traits and learns to fly against the grain. The realms within this book are about perception and truth, with a plethora of imbedded messages for the reader to discover. All will be revealed.

PERCEPTION is the most debatable entity, yet, there is no right or wrong in its results. The results change as new information is received and processed. Therefore, perception is infinite. For example, the way a person processes art or music is dependent upon how a person has seen and experienced their world, inclusive of the surrounding Elements of a person's upbringing. The original intention of a piece of art or song was based on the life experiences of the creator's journey. When the same piece of art or music is presented to the world, each individual senses their own perception, based on their life experiences, thus having a different meaning and different results. As a person gains additional life experiences, the way they look at the art and music, changes. The way that you saw colors as a child, were limited to primary shades, until you were shown the limitless hues derived from each of those colors. It is ok to make a decision based on the facts that you have so far, however, always leave yourself open to possibilities that have yet to present themselves.

CHAPTER 1

WHITE, BLACK AND GREY

"*Five PM on a Friday has got to be one of the most euphoric endings to a work day, ever!*" Mia thought to herself as she walked home from work. This evening was to be a new experience for her. She had met some people at a fair the previous weekend. They seemed to share similar interests, and they extended an invitation to her for a Samhain celebration.

On the day of the fair, Mia had noticed that two people had been glancing at her for a while. They had noticed her necklace and decided to approach her, one with her hand extended. "Hi. My name is Ceridwen. People just call me Kerry. This is my friend Faeryn." Ceridwen stood about five foot three, with reddish brown hair and hazel eyes. Faeryn was about an inch shorter, with mousy blonde hair and light brown eyes. "My name is Mia." Mia shook their hands. "Those are unique names. I've never heard them before." "My name is spelled with a C but it's pronounced as K. We noticed your necklace, that's why I came over to you." We wear similar ones." Ceridwen pulled her necklace out from under her shirt to show her. It was a small Pentacle necklace with a white Moonstone in the center. Ceridwen extended her hand to touch Mia's necklace and Mia quickly covered it with her hand. I'm sorry I don't let anyone touch it." "I understand. I love the Triple Moon phases on yours." "Thank you." Mia, instead, extended it to show her the front and back. "The symbol is behind the Moonstone." "Mia do you socialize with anyone like us or are you Solitaire?" Mia smiled. "No, I don't and yes, I am. I don't really know many people like me. " Ceridwen smiled. "We are having a party this Friday. There will be food, drink, music and some wear costumes as well. There will be a Samhain ritual as well and you can meet others there who are like us. Would you like to attend?" "I don't have a costume." "No worries. Wear whatever you want Mia. A few people go to the extreme and others don't dress at all." "I'll come up with something. Where is it being held?" "It's not far from here. I'll write the address down for you. So you'll go?" "Yes. It sounds like fun." Ceridwen pulled a piece of paper from her pocketbook, jotted the name and address down and handed it to her. "Thanks." Faeryn placed her hand on Mia's shoulder. "We'll see you there. Nice meeting you Mia." "Same here and thanks for the invite." "You're welcome."

Ceridwen and Faeryn walked to the far end of the fair grounds. Ceridwen pulled out her cell phone to send a text to Theron. "Are you there and sitting down?" "Yes, Kerry. What is it?" "I found her. She will be attending Friday."

On the evening of the party, Mia arrived home from work, hopped in the shower and then quickly dried her hair. Given her limited time to find a costume, she had chosen to be a black cat. She purchased the ears, tail, whiskers, a black body suit and tights. Due to her modest disposition, in addition, she had chosen to wear her pleated black skirt because she had felt that the costume alone, was not appropriate attire because it was way too revealing for her taste. She laid the costume out on the bed, made herself a cup of coffee and returned to the bathroom to begin her makeup process. She planned on doing her eyes in a "cat eyes" style. It had been a long time since she had done this technique and she needed to give herself some extra time in case she messed up and had to start over. She turned the radio on and immediately recognized the song that was in mid-play. It had been in her dream the night before. ♪...*Making waves across my time...*♪ She recalled images of her dream from the prior night. Since it had been the second time that this song had presented itself to her, she felt that it was time to decipher it and try to reveal the veiled, personal message to her. The only images that she could recall were of the familiar people that surrounded her. She couldn't feel their aura or see their faces. It was as if they were in a parallel universe. She interpreted these messages to be the people who she would meet at the party. Leery as she always is and dependent on the vibes that she felt, she would try to an extent, to make new friends. Her roommate and friend, Sebastian, was out with friends. She texted him a picture of herself in full costume.

"Hi Sebastian. U like? I'm kinda nervous." She finished her coffee and checked through her purse to ensure that she had everything that she needed. Sebastian replied. "U look perfect Mia! Love the eyeliner! Please socialize and try to have a good time. If U need me, shoot me a text me and I'll come get you." He knew how she was and was thrilled that she was making an attempt to socialize. "OK and TY!"

She called a cab, grabbed her things and waited on the front stoop. When the cab arrived she felt startling warmth through her body. It actually caused her to break out in a sweat. She chalked it up to nerves and focused on the cab driver. She climbed into the car and the driver reiterated the address to her. She replied. "Correct." She pulled out a tissue and her mirror, blotted her forehead and then checked to make sure that her makeup didn't streak. The house where the party was being held was located a few miles, inland. The streets that the driver took were scenic. They were lined with forestry, with an occasional nestled house. There were a few small mom and pop stores along the way. Most of the houses were set back and inclusive of large front yards. The house was near the end of a on a long and winding street. When the cab turned onto this street, she tried to catch a house number from one of the houses as they passed. The house number was thirteen and they had just passed thirty-two. She started to feel a little nervous again and opened the window to feel the cool Autumn air on her face. She felt the car slow down and looked ahead as it pulled into the driveway of the house. It was a ranch style house with a beautiful lawn and circular driveway, lined with lights. There were three lampposts in the front of the house. The house reflected an earthy, Zen feeling and she immediately felt at ease with its aura. "That'll be twenty seven dollars, miss." "Ok. I'll need a ride back as well. I'll call you when I wish to leave." Mia handed him thirty-five dollars. "Thank you. We'll be available when you're ready." "Awesome! You're welcome and thanks."

Mia took a deep breath, straightened out her skirt and rang the doorbell. A tall and dark haired man answered the door. "Hello. May I help you?" "Hi. My name is Mia. Ceridwen and Faeryn invited me." He grinned. "Good evening Mia. Welcome and please come in. They mentioned you would be attending. My name is Zephyr." "It's nice to meet you, Zephyr." His eyes were fixed, steadily on hers the entire time. There were over a dozen people there. Mia felt a little shy at first. Faeryn spotted her from across the room and walked over to her, shouting her name. "MIA!" Everyone turned to look at her. Mia's face blushed from embarrassment. "I am glad you're here. Kerry's downstairs. She'll be back, shortly. Come with me and meet everyone. Would you like a drink?" "Yes, please." Mia was edgy now. Meeting new people was not her forte. Recalling her dream and how she had interpreted it, she took a deep breath and decided to let things happen naturally. "Mia what would you like to drink? We have beer, soda and some assorted liquor." "I'll have a soda, please." Faeryn walked over to one of the coolers and opened it. "Pick what you want." Mia grabbed a can of Pepsi. "Come with me." Mia followed her to where some of the other guests were standing. "Everyone! This is Mia. Introduce yourselves." Mia's face reddened again. She felt like she was on exhibit. As the people introduced themselves, Mia reciprocated their handshakes. She was afraid that she wouldn't remember all of their names. A light haired woman and her friend approached her. They were one of the last to greet her. Mia had noticed that they waited on purpose as they both observed her from a distance. "Mia, my name is Gwen and this is Aithusa." Aithusa had dark brown eyes and shoulder length dark brown hair, tied in a ponytail. Mia extended her hand once again. "Hello." Aithusa took her cell phone out to take a picture. "Mia can I take a picture of you? Your costume is cute." Mia blushed. "Yes." "I've never seen you around here. Where are you from?" "I live a few miles

4

from here." "Kerry tells us you've never been to one of these before." "That's true. I sort of, keep to myself. This will be my first." Ceridwen returned from downstairs and Faeryn approached her. "Mia's arrived." "Perfect. I think everyone is here now. I'll go bring the food out. It should be ready." Ceridwen walked into the kitchen and picked up her cell phone to send a text. *She's here. I'm serving the food now. We'll be downstairs by eleven.*

She brought out the trays of food and placed them on the dining room table. It was a light buffet. "Faeryn, can you help with the trays? I'm going over to greet Mia." "Sure."

"Hi Mia! I'm glad that you could attend. Have you met everyone?" "I think so. I just got here. I'm a little nervous. I hope that I remember everyone's names." "Don't be nervous. I'll remind you. You can leave your pocketbook over there, in the pantry with the others, if you want." Mia tossed her bag in and shut the door. "The food is ready. Come with me. I've made some fun stuff for tonight." Mia followed her to the table and grabbed a plate. The others had already formed a line. Mia perused the food. There was an assortment of tiny food, inclusive of pigs in a blanket, tiny meatballs, sausage bites with peppers as well as a large fruit tray. Zephyr stood behind her, uncomfortably close for Mia's taste. Being the new person there, she chose to say nothing. "Mia, are you ready for tonight's festivities? I hear this is your first time socializing with other Witches." "I think so." "Solitaire or virgin?" Although she found his question to be shocking and inappropriate, she chose to keep her composure. "I'm not sure what you mean, Zephyr." "Kerry mentioned that you're the loner type. So are you Solitaire or just new to this?" She was relieved when she realized that she had misunderstood him. "Solitaire." He smiled at her. As he continued to stand uncomfortably close to her, his spectral stare caused her sixth sense kick in. She always heeded her intuition. It had never failed to warn her. She walked over to Ceridwen and he followed her again. Kerry, the food is very good." "Thanks. Is that all you're eating Mia?" "I pick. I'm not a big eater." "Please have a little more. I made a lot. You'll need a little energy for later." Mia thought that was an odd comment.

"For what, Kerry?" Ceridwen realized that she had let the words fall from her mouth before she could think. She thought of a quick fix as to not make Mia leery. "Umm, when we all go downstairs for the ritual, it can kinda drain your energy. I know this is your first time. Don't be afraid. It's beautiful." Zephyr looked at Ceridwen with an impish grin. He reached behind Mia and stroked her cattail. Mia's eyes flared and she stepped away from him. With a half smile, Ceridwen reprimanded him. Stop harassing Mia, Zephyr. Mia would you like another drink?" "Do you have coffee?" "I can make you a cup. Follow me." They walked into the kitchen and Ceridwen slid out the coffee pod tray. It was filled with assorted flavors. "Pick the one you want, Mia. Do you have a Keurig? It rocks!" "No, I don't, but I want one." Ceridwen handed her the sugar. "Do you want milk or cream?" "Cream, please." I stopped at the bakery and brought some goodies. FYI - I made the brownies. The ones without the walnuts have marijuana baked into them. Help me carry this stuff inside." Mia grabbed the boxes of pastry and followed her.

Ceridwen called everyone over. "Everyone, I have sweets. We'll be going downstairs, shortly." Aithusa approached first. "I love these evil things. She grabbed one of the plain brownies. Ceridwen pointed to the ones with the walnuts. She whispered to her. "Crap! I forget which ones have the pot. I think they are the ones without the nuts." "Then I'll try the nut one and if I feel nothing, I'll let you know. How's that?" "Deal." "I think the ones with nuts have it. I'll try and do the same." Mia grinned. "Why Mia, you like pot?" Ceridwen inquired, with a devilish grin. "Yes. It helps me feel Zen."

Gwen saw Mia with coffee and walked over to her. "Hey Mia. Coffee connoisseur?" "Yes. I love coffee. I drink a lot of it." "I'm gonna go get me a cup and join you. You wanna come with?" "Ok." Mia grabbed another brownie and followed her into the kitchen. Gwen was familiar with the kitchen, having been there many times. "I'm gonna try the chocolate one." Mia smiled. "I like medium roast and the cinnamon one." "How's the brownie?" "Very good. She said she made them herself." "Ahh I love walnuts. I could eat them plain." "Me too. I love pistachios too." "So what do you do, Mia?" "I work at a restaurant…and you?" "I own a bar restaurant. Bikers hang there." "Do you own a bike?" "Yes. A Harley. "I drove it here. Do you wanna see it? It's just outside the front window." "Ok." They walked to the front of the house and Gwen drew the blinds. "It's the one parked next to the big black truck." "Nice. It looks expensive." "It was. Have you ever ridden?" "Yes. I don't have a bike anymore though. Mine was old and needed a lot of expensive repairs. I sold it. I want to buy a car soon." "Aww that sucks." Gwen frowned.

Zephyr strolled over to Faeryn. "It's time to go downstairs. Where's our guest?" "She's in the kitchen with Gwen." "Who'll be bringing her downstairs?" "Kerry. Go lead everyone downstairs now. I'll go tell Kerry." "Don't forget to pull Gwen aside before Mia gets another drink." "Yes. Thanks for reminding me."

Zephyr signaled everyone to proceed downstairs and followed behind them as they trickled down the stairs. He walked to the back corner, room where Theron was waiting. They had originally invited him to join and lead in their celebration. Theron was in mid-conversation with another guest, when Zephyr walked in. "They're coming down now." Theron nodded.

Faeryn approached Ceridwen. "I'm going to deter Gwen's attention away from Mia so that she can stand behind the downstairs minibar before Mia is led downstairs. I've already told Gwen what Theron wants her to do. You bring Mia down afterwards." "Ok."

They walked into the kitchen and Faeryn grabbed Gwen's hand, looking wide eyed at her. "Come with me. I need your assistance." Ceridwen approached Mia. "We're going downstairs in a minute. Would you help me cover the food before we go?" "Sure." Mia was happy to help. She was starting to feel like she belonged. "So, Mia, how do you feel about everyone? Have you mingled a little?" "Everyone seems kind. So far, I've spoken to you, Faeryn, Gwen, Aithusa and Zephyr." "Great. Be honest. How do you feel about them? Can you read them?" Knowing what she meant, she wasn't going to tell her all of her feelings. Ceridwen reflected an amiable aura. She felt Faeryn was a little too veiled. Gwen felt like a bold soul. Aithusa's eyes disturbed her a little and of course Zephyr was a little scary and way too touchy for her taste. "I'm a little spooked by Zephyr. He's too touchy for me. Everyone else is cool." "I agree. He's a strange one. Come. Lets go downstairs."

Ceridwen allowed Mia to go ahead of her. As they proceeded downstairs, Mia felt a little lightheaded. Ceridwen shut the door behind them. There was a dimmed light source emanating from the back of the floating stairs. As she looked ahead, a discerned, precarious feeling filled her senses. Against her intuition, she maintained her composure and chose to forge ahead, but remained vigilant. The familiar scent of incense wafted through the air. She recognized its essence and as a result, it somewhat eased her spirit. As she approached the last step, there was an eerie silence. She felt as if she was the guest of honor and they were all waiting on her arrival. The ambiance of dimmed lighting set the stage for what she assumed to be the proper setting for a ritual. It was barely bright enough to see where you were going. Just ahead of the steps, there was a small refrigerator and a mini bar. Gwen was standing behind it. Beyond the bar, was a door and to the right of it, in the far corner, another. This door was open. As Mia turned to her right, there was a large rectangular table, which stood a foot from the wall. Above the table, hanging on the wall was a silver symbol, just like the one on the back of Mia's necklace. To the back of the room was another door. The actual color of the walls, were almost undetectable. In the dimmed lighting, they looked dark grey. The floor was marble and also a greyish color.

Mia walked over to the table. It was made of cherry wood and displayed along the sides of the table were images of the phases of the Moon. Mia caught someone staring at her, that she didn't recognize from upstairs. He was dressed in dark clothing. When she looked up he had turned around and walked away. The warmth within her body signaled the warning signs of her impending onset of anxiety, alerting her to remain perceptive of her surroundings. Her extra-sensory intuition was usually the prerequisite to this type of anxiety, the kind that cannot be diagnosed, the kind that she was born with.

"Mia. Are you ok?" Mia snapped out of her gaze and looked at Ceridwen. "Yes. I was just looking around the room. This is a beautiful table." "Thank you. I know this is all new to you. You look as white as a ghost. Let me get you a drink." Mia followed her to the mini bar. As she followed her, she looked back again to see if the man was there. Zephyr was now standing next to Faeryn. He turned to look at Mia. Mia had to force herself to turn away from the shadowed figure. His alchemistic aura kept her in an apprehensive state. Ceridwen looked at Gwen, wide eyed. "Gwen, please give me a beer. Mia? What do you want?" "I'll have another soda please." Gwen handed her the beer and glanced up at Ceridwen. She then handed Mia a glass of soda and glanced up again at Ceridwen. "Thank you Gwen." Mia smiled and turned around to see Aithusa standing right in front of her. Aithusa startled her. At first she just stared at Mia, in Silence. Mia stared into her eyes, trying to see the veiled essence of her spirit, her true self. Aithusa held an emotionless, steely stare at her, a cold, evasive gaze that chilled Mia to the bone. Aithusa held up her drink to Mia. "To many firsts, Mia." Mia clinked her glass with hers, smiled and took a sip, but remained speculative as to the true meaning behind her words. Ceridwen observed their encounter and in an attempt to get Mia to drink more, she did a toast as well. "To new friends." Mia clinked glasses with her and took another sip. Out of the corner of her eye she saw the figure in black gazing at her. She looked at him and her anxiety intensified. He was standing behind Zephyr, on the other side of the table. Mia turned around in urgency and tapped Ceridwen on the shoulder. "Kerry?" "Yes Mia?" "Who's that man next to Zephyr? He keeps staring at me and he's starting to creep me out." Knowing whom she was referring to, she played dumb. "Where?" Mia turned to point at him and he was no longer there. She looked around the room and did not see him. "I don't know where he went." "Mia you are all red in the face. Finish your drink and give me the glass. I will go get you another one." Mia gulped the rest, handed her the glass and sat down on the steps. Zephyr walked over to Mia and sat down next to her. "Are you ok Mia?" Being leery of him, she shifted over a little. "Yes, I'm fine." "Well, you looked a little spooked. That's why I came over." "There was a man behind you, staring at me. Who is he?" "I'm not sure who you're referring to. Point him out to me." I don't know where he is now." He put his hand on her knee and squeezed. "Then we will sit here until you see him. Does he frighten you?" She pulled her knee away from his hand. "A little, yes." Ceridwen returned with another soda. "Here ya go Mia. Are you ok now?" "Yes. Don't worry about me. I feel silly now." Zephyr, are you harassing Mia again?" Zephyr slid his hand around Mia's waist and pulled her close. Mia's eyes widened. "I'm protecting Mia from a big bad wolf." Trying to lighten the mood, Ceridwen mocked him. "Jackass!" Mia nervously laughed and stood up in an effort to pull his arm away from her waist. As she turned, to face the steps, she saw him again, behind the stairway. She froze and shrieked. His hands were touching the steps and his stare pierced through her. He turned around and walked away. Ceridwen pretended not to notice Theron and reacted to Mia's sound. "What's the matter Mia? You look like you saw a ghost." "He was just there, behind the steps. He must have been there behind me, when I was sitting." A tear ran down her cheek. Her face was pale. She placed her quivering hands over her mouth. "Which way did he go Mia?" She pointed to the back of the room. "He walked back that way." Zephyr stood up smiling. "I'll go look for him. Wait here."

"I'm sorry Kerry. I feel like a paranoid freak now." "Whoever he is, he's probably just curious and shy. I wouldn't worry." Mia began to feel over heated again. "Lets walk around Kerry. I need to walk off this anxiety and focus on something else. Maybe it's just the brownies making me paranoid." Ceridwen walked around the table with her. The sounds of the room and the people talking seemed to intensify. She felt over sensitive to everything around her.

Zephyr spotted Theron and approached him by the mini-bar. "You know she's paranoid and spooked by you." Theron smirked and looked at Mia across the room. "How will you know about her, for sure?" Theron looked at him and in a low toned voice, he replied. "I will know by her eyes."

Faeryn walked over to Gwen. "How much longer?" Gwen looked over at Mia. "It's already affecting her. Look at her." "I'm going over to her." Faeryn caught up with Ceridwen and Mia. Mia was standing against the table facing the steps. Her vision was blurred. As she blinked, she turned her head and saw him again, at the bar. He looked right at her, grinned and walked away again. Tears filled her eyes. With her hands behind her, Mia held onto the table. The sounds around her were beginning to muffle as if she were in a bubble. Breathing heavy, she put her hand on Ceridwen's shoulder. "Kerry, he was just at the bar and walked away again." Mia turned around to face the table, spread her arms on its edge to balance and hold herself up. As she gazed up, Theron was standing across from her, with his hands on the table and his callous eyes fixed on hers. There was less than seven feet between them. A tear rolled down her cheek. She felt both frightened and mad. Speaking in a low tone and looking at his eyes, she stuttered, barely able to get the words out of her mouth. "What the fuck is your problem?" His eyes widened, his hands slid across the table and he leaned in. He whispered to her in a sinister voice. "Hello Mia." Still facing him, she backed up, slid her hands from the table and almost lost her balance. Faeryn grabbed her arm and Ceridwen placed her hand on Mia's back to hold her steady. "That's him." She whispered to them. They were silent. He grinned while holding a steady gaze at her. She blared at him. "Who are you?" He leaned further in and whispered, piercing her eyes with his stare. "I will show you, Mia." She twinged. Theron saw a faint spark of blue light reflecting from her eyes. She felt overwhelming heat throughout her body and grabbed onto the table again. She began to hyperventilate, eased herself onto the floor and leaned against the leg of the table. Her knees were against her chest with her arms wrapped around them. Her mind felt like it was disengaging from everything. Gwen watched her sink to the floor. She stepped from behind the bar, waving her hand to everyone indicating to them to take their places around the table. Zephyr unfolded a blue blanket and draped it over the table. Mia reached for Ceridwen's leg and then Ceridwen and Faeryn knelt down beside her. Her speech was stuttered, but demanding. "I'm not feeling well. I wanna go home. Get my bag." Theron walked around towards her. He knelt down and sat in front of her. Faeryn and Ceridwen stepped away.

"Mia, I apologize if I have made you feel uncomfortable." She tightened her arms around her knees as she gazed at his face. "My name is Theron." She placed her elbows on her knee, held her forehead against her hands and muttered her feeble warning to him. "Back off." He shifted himself closer to her, encircling her with his legs. "I understand you are not feeling well." When she felt his legs touching hers, she looked up at him with dazed, glassy eyes. He moved beside her and placed his arm around her shoulder. "Mia, let me get you off of the floor." She became lethargic, surrendering herself and falling against his chest. He slid one arm around her waist, the other, under her legs, pushing himself out from under the table with his feet. He maneuvered himself onto his knees and then stood up. Her head spun from the sudden upward movement. She rested it against his chest. Her eyes were barely opened and her thoughts were erratic. She felt out of control and disconnected from her own body. He walked over to the end of the table, near the room where he was when she first came down the stairs. Zephyr stood at the opposite end of the table and the others stood along its sides. He looked into her eyes, lifted her and placed her on the table. Holding her upright, he slid beside the table and gently eased her down. He returned to the end of the table and looked across to Zephyr. Mia squinted at the ceiling and lie there, listless.

It was a few minutes past midnight. Ceridwen stood at the corner of the table, near Theron and cleared her throat before she spoke. "Theron, we are honored that you've joined us and that you will be leading in our gathering on this special night, as well." He nodded, placed his palms on the table just below Mia's feet and spoke in a prophetic tone. "I attend this evening, to celebrate with my extended family. The energy raised throughout this night will be enhanced by Mia's presence." He looked at Mia with arcane intent.

Aithusa stood near the center of the table, next to Mia. She glanced at Theron and then held Mia's hand. Mia turned her head to look at her, with one eye partially opened, and returned a faint grasp. As Mia looked on past Aithusa, through her blurred vision, she saw the silhouette of another person next to her. She looked to her right and saw Faeryn and a few others standing beside her. Zephyr placed his hands on Mia's hair. When she felt it, she lifted her head to look at him. A faint smell of incense wafted through the air. She turned to her right and saw the flames of the candles on the shelf behind Faeryn, held a steady gaze, focusing on one of the flames as it flickered. All of her senses were high. She heard obscured chatter emanating from an unknown source. She glanced down towards her feet when she felt her shoes being removed and saw Theron standing at the foot of the table, looking at her as his hands grasped her toes. The chatter seemed to grow louder. His hands slid over the top of her feet and along her calves. Her senses heightened, when she felt the warmth from his hands as they glided past her knees. She tightened her grip on Aithusa's hand. As her breathing increased, the more overheated and lightheaded she felt. She faded in and out for a few brief moments thus, releasing the tight grip she had on Aithusa's hand.

Theron slid his hands back to her ankles and continued to address everyone. "I felt her presence in the shadows of her dreams, but could not locate her. Her dreams, they are very powerful, but vague. Two of the gifts she has and is aware of are dream interpretation and strong Empathic traits. When she has these dreams, I can feel them. It's as if she knows we are present and looking for her. When I felt her dreams grow stronger, I knew she was near. I reached out to a few of you. Ceridwen and Faeryn found her." He looked in their direction and smiled. "She is the feminine of myself as well as the positive to my negative. She does not know who she is and what she is capable of. I will reveal this to her in time. Her gifts will enhance our intentions and all the pieces will always fall to our wish."

Theron took a step back with just his fingers touching the table. He then extended his hand and nodded, indicating to Zephyr and Ceridwen to begin the ritual.

A rhythmic sound of a drum began and its sounds caressed Mia's ears. Her eyes remained closed while her mind floated along with each beat. Her thoughts fused with its rhythm sending her into a deep meditation. She saw herself floating through waves of bright and soft colors. Each color's boldness was reflective of how strong each beat was. In her visions she saw a body of water, just ahead. The blue ripples in the water seemed to shimmer in synch to the drumbeats. She saw the presence of a tawny entity standing by the waters' edge. As she neared the edge of the bank, the entity became clearer. It was a lion standing alone with a frog in a jar. The lion's eyes were bright amber and were fixated on her. To her, this represented energy and the presence of a Witch. The lion represented strength, authority and shares the world of both night and day. The frog, having the ability to travel between two worlds, represents a Witch. The Amber meant protection, which transmutes negative energy into positive. The blue meant psychic energy and tranquility and the brown meant justice, sensuality and protection of animals.

With his eyes closed, aware of her meditative journey, Theron walked with her through this dream. Knowing she was a great protector of animals, he placed himself in the dream as the lion. The Lions amber eyes reflected He and Mia, the negative and positive. While he knew what her dream was showing her, he also knew it would take her some time to interpret it, and she will. He could not change her dream, however, he could distort it, thus delaying her interpretation.

As the drumming continued, Mia sat on the grass along the waters edge, next to the lion. The lion placed the jar on the grass, beside himself, where Mia could no longer see it. That was part of Theron's intercepted distortion. There was no verbal communication between them. Just the drum and the sound of the water were heard. The view of the skewed colors remained in the sky and in the distance.

Four of the Witches, inclusive of Theron, stood along the sides of the table, aligned with the direction of the corresponding Element, each carrying a basket and an item that represented the gifts given from those directions.

Zephyr:
East/Air/Yellow/Masculine
Communication, Intellect, Creativity, Sound and Beginnings
Item - Feather

Ceriwen:
West/Water/Blue/Feminine
Psychic Energy, Ebb and Flow, Death, Endings, Love, Joy, Emotion and Intuition
Item – Moon Water

Gwen:
North/Earth/Green/Feminine
Birth, Growth, Nurturing, Bounty, Healing and Beauty
Item – Sand

Theron:
South/Fire/Red/Masculine = Strength, Courage, Passion and Desire
Item – Incense and a lighter

Mia lie center with her head rested on a Silver satin pillow. Mia represented: Spirit.

Theron, Zephyr, Ceridwen and Gwen extended their baskets to those surrounding the table. Within the baskets were notes, previously written by Ceridwen and Faeryn. The notes represented additional gifts from each direction. Everyone at the table took a note or two from each of the four baskets and read them out loud.

East – Intellect, Focus and Self-control
West – Love of land, Family and Animals
North – Honor, Persistence and Courage
South – Strength, Humanity and Dignity

Mia no longer heard the drumbeat. The waves in the water were still. As she turned to look at the lion, he rose up and descended into the water. She turned to look where he had been sitting and saw the frog, now sitting beside the jar. She turned to lie on her stomach, with her elbows on the grass and her head supported by her hands. She watched the frog as she occasionally glanced at the water. The frog jumped onto her head and then lunged into the water. She sat up and placed her hands behind her back to support herself. She began to feel unsettled by the silence. She watched as the colors dissipated. They transformed into silver with grey and white hues. The drumming began again. The lion emerged from the water, with the frog in his paw. He stood in front of her, looking down into her eyes. She remained sitting, staring back at him. He knelt down with his arm extended and handed her the frog. She lay back onto the grass, placed the frog on her chest and slipped her hands behind her head. As the drum played, she closed her eyes and merged with its rhythm, once again.

Beginning with Theron and going around the table, deosil, each person took a turn, welcoming his or her departed, loved one. Holding hands to close the circle, and once again, going around the table, they then began stating their intentions and goals, projecting what each of them wanted to bring into their lives. Zepher stood between Aithusa and Gwen and continued to play the drum. Aithusa and Gwen kept the circle closed by holding onto the loops on his jeans, waist as he played. When they finished, they raised the cone of power that they had generated, by raising their hands above their heads and then released their intentions into the universe.

When the drumming ceased, Mia opened her eyes to see that the lion and frog were gone. All that remained in her sight was the night sky, the stars and the Moon. She felt alone and indifferent, but serene within herself. She sat on the grass, with her with her arms behind herself and gazed at the night sky. The water began to make splashing sounds. As she peered over at the Moonlit ripples, she felt a vague tug on her ankles, in the direction of the water. She thought that perhaps the lion and frog wanted her to follow them.

The midnight blue sky began to swirl into a vortex. Mia watched as the stars spiraled widdershins within the Moons path.

As Theron grasped her ankles, pulling her closer to him self, she awoke, inhaling loudly. Sweat dripped from her forehead. Startled, she sat up. Her pupils were blue. As she tried to collect herself, she looked at Theron and then saw the others surrounding her. Anxiety set in and overwhelmed her. Her eyes remained fixed on Theron, like a cornered cat. She sat on the table with her hands flat and her fingers spread, as if she had claws. She did not move an inch, but was ready to strike. Aware of her edginess, he stared deep into her eyes, possessing her. He moved closer to her and stood between her knees, hovering his hands just above them. He gently lowered his hands onto her thighs. Just as she felt his touch, her hands lunged onto his wrists with a tight grip and she dug her nails into his skin. His eyes squinted from the sharp pain. Glaring into her eyes and beguiling her, he continued to slide his hands up her thighs. As he moved his hands, she dug her nails deeper into his skin. Her arms trembled and tears rolled down her face, but she did not release her grip. In reaction, he moved his hands to her waist, picked her up and held her over his shoulder. The sudden upward thrust to her body jerked her equilibrium. With her head dangling behind him and her stomach pressing against his shoulder, she found it difficult to catch her breath. She dug her nails into his back, scratching it. She tried to clear her throat to scream. He walked into the back room and then kicked the door closed. He stood in front of the dresser, opened up a black box and grabbed a syringe, placing it in between his teeth. Placing one hand on the small of her back, the other on the back of her head, he lowered her onto the bed. With her knees bend over the edge and her legs taught, between his, he knelt onto the bed. He straddled onto her, leaning most of his weight on his knees. He lifted his legs, one at a time and placed her arms tightly between her own body and his legs so that she could not move them. She stared up at his face with terror and tears in her eyes. Holding a fixed stare on her eyes, he pulled the syringe from is teeth and stuck it into her arm. She wailed. He lowered himself over her chest, cradling her head in his hands. He then placed his finger over her lips and quietly whispered a gesturing sound of silence to her. "Shhh." With his face an inch from hers, he watched the gradual effects overtaking her. Her vision and thoughts slipped into a solitary, evanescent state. He lifted himself and laid himself beside her on his side. His fingers caressed her face. She stared at the ceiling with her tear filled eyes fitfully closing. He remained there until her eyes fully closed and her spirit, slipped deep within herself.

The table was set with a place for each person as well as an empty chair and place setting, representing each of their predecessors who had passed on to the Summerland. Faeryn poured the wine into each glass while Ceridwen passed the plates of food around the table. Each person was responsible for serving their ancestors food on their plate. Since this was a time when the veil between worlds was thin, the food was served as a gesture to welcome them back to this world. It would later be placed outdoors to feed animals that wandered past the house throughout the night.

Theron left from the room, locking the door behind him. "Where will I be sitting Kerry?" She pointed to his seat. "Your seat is at the head of the table." There was a name card for each person, with an additional blank card and a pen to write the names of their departed ones. To Theron's left was the blank card and to his right was a place setting for Mia. Everyone was already seated and talking amongst themselves. Theron wrote on the card to his left and then grabbed the card on his right to see who was supposed to be sitting there. He looked up at Ceridwen and placed the card back on the table. "Kerry, Mia will not be joining us." Frowning, she nodded. "I'll put her food in the fridge for later."

While everyone indulged in the feast, Gwen started a conversation. "Theron. How is everyone at home? It would have been nice if they could attend this evening." He swallowed his food, smiling. " Whom would you like to know about first?" He laughed. "Lets start with Enya." She giggled.

"They're holding their own celebration this evening. Zephyr accepted because he wanted to see Faeryn."

Faeryn blushed. Zephyr grinned at her as his teeth tore apart the roast beef. "Enya is fine and always has her hands full with her sister. As always, Mayne drives her batty. She tends to over react. Mayne is Mayne. Lucius is still a shit stirrer and Emery remains the introvert, with the exception of his occasional semi-harmless lash-outs. Sage is sweet as always and Raine is quiet until provoked." Gwen laughed out loud. "I'll have to give Enya a call tomorrow and catch up. I haven't seen Mayne at my bar in a while. What has she been up to?" "Shenanigans as always." Zephyr turned to face Ceridwen. "So, Kerry, tell us how you found her." Everyone's attention was now focused on her. "Well, as you know I saw her at the county fair. I was standing at a jewelry table with Faeryn when I felt a bizarre blast of warm air. Faeryn felt it too, so I knew that I wasn't hallucinating. The couple next to us shivered, mentioning the early chill in the air. They decided to walk back to their car for their jackets. They didn't feel it and it was then that we knew something was present. We moved to the tree next to the table, leaned against it and decided to stay put and observe. We heard a very vocal Blue Jay nearby and looked up to see it was in another tree, just above Mia. It did not move but kept up its loud jeer. We laughed when we saw her hold her finger up above her head, because she thought it would actually glide down and land on her. Well, it did! Our mouths dropped. She held it about a foot from her face and seemed to be speaking to it. She then lifted her hand to allow it to fly up and return to the tree. Faeryn and I looked at each other in astonishment. As she walked over to the table near us, she was wearing an odd blue colored fringed shirt. I've never seen this shade of blue before. I know the guys are gonna laugh at me now but it looked like the hue between blue, just before purple." Zephyr smirked and responded to her hue comment. "What the fuck is a hue?" Theron grinned and laughed out loud. She rolled her eyes and went on to tell the rest of the story.

Zephyr had disappeared with Faeryn and the others remained at the table talking. As the evening's festivities neared their end, Theron placed his hands on the table and stood up. "Please excuse me. I am going to check on Mia."

He returned to the room, locking the door behind himself. As he approached her, he saw the Moonlight from the window reflecting the soft silhouette of her face. He walked over to the small lamp on the nightstand and turned it on long enough to light a candle. He sat on the bed beside her, kicked his boots off and lay next to her, with his elbow on the pillow and his hand supporting his head. She lay on her back, facing him. His body was flush against her side. He ran his fingertips through her hair, over her eyebrow and her chin and then outlined her lips. As he gazed at her, he was intrigued by the conflict he saw before him. With all that he knew about her and all that goes on in her mind, she looked so oddly serene to him. She looked like a gentle cirrus cloud, which he knew could form into a super cell at any given moment. His fingers continued to trace her face, down to the nape of her neck and tracing her collarbone. He moved his face next to her neck and inhaled through his nose, taking in the scent of her essence. He slid his hand over her shoulder, along her arm and lifted her hand from the bed, interlocking his fingers with hers.

Deep in Mia's subconscious, she felt something touching her. She found herself at the waterside again. She opened her eyes and saw the frog upon her chest. She turned to her right and saw the lion lying beside her, mirroring the touches of Theron. She glanced up at the sky and saw the Moon glaring above. The sky was midnight blue and the stars were strangely encircled around the Moon. She turned to face the lion and looked into his bright amber eyes. His paw slid over her stomach, to her waist and he pulled her closer. Her eyes widened when his hand glided over her hips and along the side of her thighs. She turned to look at him and was enraptured by his amber eyes. His hand slid over her stomach, towards her breasts. She grabbed his hand to stop him from going any further. Although words were not spoken in this realm, she opened her mouth and was about to say: stop. He roared and the loudness horrified her, sending chills throughout her body.

Her eyes opened and when she screamed, she pulled herself out of this alternate realm. As she tried to catch her breath, she saw Theron, beside her, with his hand on her stomach. She stared at him as she gasped for air. He looked deep into her eyes, knowing all of what she had just seen and just experienced. Although she was alert and on edge, she still felt weakened and light headed. With the lion and frog still fresh in her memory, her hand trembled as she lifted it up to touch his face. With his hand still on her stomach, she remembered that his hand was touching her in the same spot that the lion had touched her. Her breathing became erratic. She realized what they represented and now thought that he was both the frog and lion. Theron knew she had just interpreted it and held a nefarious grin. His dark eyes looked right through hers, holding a heavy persuasive bind on her. Possessed by his enticement, she touched his cheek with her palm. He combed his fingers through her hair, pulling her closer to him. His kiss was fierce. She felt dominated and consumed by his will. He shifted himself above her and leaned back. With his knees on either side of her legs, reached over to the side of her skirt and unzipped it. She felt his fingers near her collarbone and gazed up at him. He slipped his fingers underneath her leotard and slid it over her shoulders and her eyes lit up as she felt the cool air against her bare skin. Tears rolled down the sides of her face, disappearing into her hair. He trailed his kisses along her neck and slid her bodysuit further downward, exposing her breasts. Mia lay there powerless and vulnerable, silently weeping. She tried to move but her muscles and will were not responding. He pulled her skirt off of her, along with the rest of her clothing. She whimpered and turned her tearing eyes to the candle and stared into the flame. The vulnerability she felt increased her anxiety, intensifying within every nerve in her body. The more she focused on the flame, the more in touch with herself she became and the more her spirit and mind re-merged with her body. She felt the warmth of the candle flame and allowed herself to be captivated by it, absorbing its feral rage. The candles flame crackled, releasing its sparks into the air.

Mia took a deep and sharp breath as she felt his hands slide along her thighs. He moved above her, overshadowing her body and eclipsing her eyes from the candlelight. She turned to face him, without a tear in her eye. As he looked into her eyes, he saw the continuum of the flame she had stared at, remaining in her eyes. Elated, he combed his fingers through her hair and stared inquisitively into her eyes. She returned his stare with hers and whispered to him. "What you take from me, without my permission, I will take back from you, times three." He smirked. "Mia." He whispered, enunciating her name. "Your threat enthralls me and I accept your challenge." He knelt back and lifted her legs. His hands slid along the sides of her thighs and his eyes pierced hers as he thrust inside her. Unaware of the strength of her own wrath, Mia felt the true untamed essence of the fire within herself. She dug her nails into Theron's chest. Her strength tested his. He pulled her hands off and struggled to hold them down. He saw the flicker of blue in her pupils grow steady and bold. Her hands pushed against his with esoteric force. His eyes seduced hers with a cold bewitching gaze that reflected images of his inner self. The images terrified her. Her hands released their grip and she surrendered herself to him. The candles violent flame flared and disappeared.

CHAPTER 2

A DARKER SHADE OF GREY

The strong scent of incense flowed throughout the room. Theron exited from the bathroom and returned to the room with Aithusa. Mia lay on the bed, wrapped in the blue satin sheet. Her mind, body and spirit were disconnected and in a suspended animation, far away from the conscious world that surrounded her. Although her eyes remained partially opened, she remained introverted in her thoughts, acknowledging nothing within her sight. She kept herself safe and hidden from reality.

Theron approached Aithusa. "I'll put her in your room. You are to keep her in there until I return for her tomorrow evening." He handed her a small box and opened it. "Every six hours, inject her. Do not forget. If she experiences rage or fright, she will be stronger than you. As of now, she is good for another four hours. If something happens that you cannot control, contact me. Understood?" "Yes. I'm going to get a few things and I'll be right back." "That's fine. If there is something you need later on, call on Ceridwen to fetch it for you. Do not leave her alone." Aithusa nodded.

Theron returned to where Mia lay, slipped his arms underneath her and lifted her up. He stared at her face, walked to Aithusa's room and placed her on the bed. He adjusted the blue satin sheet to cover her, kissed her forehead and sat on the bed next to her until Aithusa returned. Zephyr entered the room and grinned, glancing over at Mia. "Efficacious night." "Indeed." "Are we ready to take off?" "As soon as Aithusa returns."

Ceridwen stood at the entrance of the room with Faeryn behind her. Having overheard them, Ceridwen replied in a low voice. "I thought is was pretty intense." She giggled then glanced over at Mia. "Poor thing. I almost feel guilty for twisting the truth about tonight. She looks so feeble lying there." She heard Theron's wicked laughter. "She is far from helpless, Kerry. It would be in your best interest to never underestimate her." Faeryn touched Theron's arm. "Please tell me about her." He stood up. "All will be revealed in time."

Aithusa returned. "OK. I've got all I need. What time will you be picking her up?" "I will text you when I am on my way." "OK. Take your time." She grinned. Zephyr saw her facial expression. "And what's that smirking sound all about? Have you a new toy…? Anxious for us to leave?" He challenged her with a smile. Now her grin was more obvious. Theron smiled and rose from the bed. "Regardless, just don't push her too far and don't forget about the box that I've given you." Theron pulled his keys from his pocket. "Until tomorrow. Good night."

Ceridwen escorted them to the front door and held it open. "Theron, thank you again." Zephyr laughed. "The pleasure was all his." Theron looked at him with a smug expression and smacked him on his head. "Smartass. Kerry, whether you had found her or not, I would have attended. I'm eclectic. It is I, who owe you and Faeryn my gratitude for finding her." He reached for her hand and kissed it. "Kerry, until tomorrow." Zephyr kissed her on the cheek.

Ceridwen returned to Aithusa's room. The door was locked. After a few finger taps, Aithusa opened it. She was drinking a beer and had the television on. "Is there anything that you need?" "No. I'm good. I'm gonna let her rest for a half hour." She said, with a smug expression. "Ok, freak. I'm going to bed. I will have my cell on if you need me." She shut the door behind her and Aithusa re-locked it.

Aithusa's room was of average size with two windows on one side. Her full sized bed was situated against the wall and against the wall, across from the windows. Next to the bed, was a small reclining chair and a glass table beside it. Behind the chair was a closet and across the way was a flat screen TV on the wall, above her dresser. The walls were painted graphite grey with a rusty shade of orange on the woodwork. The ceiling was black with iridescent celestial stickers scattered, transversely. While most were stars, the largest were an arched display of each Moon phases. Their sharp glow added to the collective ambiance of her collection of lava lamps.

She opened another beer and sat back in her chair, glancing at the box on the table, with an occasional glance at the clock. She had another three and a half hours before she would need the contents of the box that Theron had given her. One of those late night shows were on, the one with the skeleton host. It was her favorite.

Mia was lying on the bed with one arm above her head and the other beside her waist. Aithusa was taking a swig if beer, when she heard her shifting in the bed. She turned to look at Mia, who was now lying on her side, facing her. She stared at Mia, watching her eye movement. The blanket had partially fallen off of her, exposing most the right side of her body. The glare from the TV cascaded over Mia's bare arm. She rose from the chair, placed a big pillow against the headboard and sat on the bed, next to her. Mia felt the movement on the bed and opened her eyes. Squinting from the brightness of the television, she saw someone's leg near her face. She felt disoriented and perplexed as to where she was. Her thoughts were scattered. She made a futile attempt to push herself back with her right hand. Aithusa saw her moving. She ran her fingers through Mia's hair. Mia was still experiencing hyper-sensitiveness and reacted to her touch. It felt soothing. She took a deep breath and managed to move her hand to the leg in front of her, touching it and struggling to get her words out. "Who...?" She whispered. Aithusa took another swig of her beer and put the bottle on the floor. She placed her hands under Mia's arms, shifted her over and lay next to her on her side, with her arm supporting her head. She raised her hand to Mia's forehead and swept the hair off of her face. She lifted Mia's chin and looked into her eyes. Mia squinted as she looked back into her eyes. She remembered her dark possessive eyes. They intimidated her. "Hello Mia." She whispered to her. Mia looked into her eyes and recognized her. She stuttered her words. "You...were...there..." Aithusa didn't reply. Mia recalled a hazy image of Theron and became anxious. "Where is...that man?" Aithusa chose her words wisely. "He's not here. You're safe in my room. The door is locked." Mia lifted her hand to her forehead and let it fall beside her head. Her muscles felt like jello. "Mia? Tell me how you feel." Mia gathered her thoughts and replied. "Floaty and achy." Aithusa sat up and made up a story. "I can't give you another painkiller yet. You had a lot to drink. Sit up or turn over and I'll massage your shoulders." With her help, Mia turned onto her stomach, holding the blue sheet against the lower half of her body. Her head spun a little from the movement. Aithusa sat, straddled over the base of Mia's back, with most of her weight bearing on her own knees. She proceeded to rub her neck and shoulders. "How does this feel, Mia?" Mia sighed. She edged toward the center of her back and then shifted herself further down and sat across her calves. She pushed the blue sheet up, off her legs, bunching it towards her backside. She then massaged her calves and eased upward to the back of her thighs. Aithusa heard Mia's breathing increase. She leaned in towards the side of Mia's face and then moved back onto the bed, beside her, leaning her head against her right hand. Her fingers grazed over Mia's shoulders and down her arm. Aithusa reached for her beer on the floor, finished it and put the bottle back on the floor. She then, turned back to face her. She grazed Mia's scalp with her nails. The sensation sent chills down Mia's spine. Her finger skimmed her temple and then followed the outline of her cheek. She reached for the sheet and pulled it upward, just below Mia's shoulder. Mia made a futile attempt to push herself up and turn back around onto her back. Aithusa sat up and gripped her hand, helping her turn around. Mia closed her eyes for a minute as her head spun. Aithusa lay back beside her, with her elbow supporting her head. Her fingernails gently nudged Mia's chin to face her, and then down her neck, tracing her collarbone. Mia partially opened her eyes, still feeling numb and unplugged from the reality of where she was as well as what was actually happening. Her body felt separated from her spirit, reacting in her thoughts, only to touch and sound. She took a deep breath and gazed at her. Aithusa slowly slid her hand over the sheet, across Mia's stomach. Her fingers skimmed back and forth as she watched her face. Mia's stomach twitched from the sensation. Her fingers brushed over her sternum to the top of the blue sheet. She hooked her finger under it and imperceptibly pulled it down. Mia felt the cool exposure of air over her chest. Aithusa slid her leg underneath Mia's calf and slowly parted it away from the other. She reached over to Mia's arm, glided her hand down to her hand and rubbed her thumb against Mia's palm. Stunned, Mia knew what this had meant and quickly turned to look at her. Aithusa stared back, deep into her eyes and slid her hand across Mia's stomach, down to her thigh. Mia inhaled sharply, reacting to the intense sensation of her touch. Aithusa watched intently. She slid her hand over Mia's waist and pulled her closer. Her tongue followed along her neck to her earlobe. She whispered into her ear, enticing her. "Let me take you there, Mia." Her hand slid between her legs and Mia felt an unexpected surge of elation. Aithusa's kisses were slow and deep. Her tongue matched the rhythm of her fingers as they penetrated her. Mia was bewitched with pleasure as she remained under her spell of ecstasy. Aithusa saw the faint blue light reflected in her eyes once again.

Mia rolled onto her side, with her back to Aithusa, trembling and clutching the pillow. Reality and awareness were setting in. She fought to hold back her tears. Taking advantage of Mia's enervation, she twisted around, reached over to the box and grabbed one of the syringes. Perusing her, she held it behind herself for a moment. She wrapped her leg tightly around both of Mia's legs and swiftly injected it into her thigh. Just as Mia reacted, she bear-hugged her so that she couldn't move. Mia screamed, exerting every ounce of strength she had trying to break lose. Challenged by her strength, Aithusa felt a taste of what Theron had warned her about. The haze and confusion began to set in once again. Aithusa released her grip as Mia gradually became less aggressive. Mia slowly rolled onto her back and gazed, glassy eyed, at her and seduced by the dark deception within her eyes. Her cold and arcane disposition frightened and possessed her. Aithusa watched Mia struggle to stay awake. Mia uttered to her. "Why?" She didn't respond. Aithusa rose from the bed to get another bottle of beer and change the channel on the television. Aithusa turned to face her and the sounds from the TV hummed its mumbled chatter, as Mia's attention remained fixated on her. She stood at the edge of the bed with her eyes fixed on Mia's eyes. Distracted by a flash of light from the window, Mia realized a storm was approaching. She closed her eyes and focused on the one present thing that she could draw energy from: A thunderstorm. As she heard the distant thunder, she closed her eyes and let the storm consume her spirit. She remembered when lightning crashes, it subtlety changes things around it. As the storm drew nearer, she felt its raging glory. A sudden strong wind blew the curtains. She felt a change coming in the air as the unseen forces of the storm converged its strength from the center of the earth. She knew she would be freed soon, somehow. The Universe would lead her. Her thoughts traveled deeper, within her meditative state until she fell sleep.

Aithusa sat up on the bed beside her, watching the TV and occasionally glancing over at her. Feeling drowsy herself, she shifted herself onto the bed and lay down next to her. The program was nearing its end. Aithusa shut off the TV and curled up beside her. She slid her arm around her waist and held her close. If Mia moved, she would feel it and wake up.

Mia awoke a few hours later. She felt Aithusa's arm around her waist and her leg was also wrapped around hers. She needed to use the bathroom but for the moment, was unable to move undetected. She slowly and successfully slid her legs from under hers, then turned to lay flat and attempted to slide away from under her arm. Her eyes opened. Glaring at her, she pulled her back, saying nothing. Intimidated by her dark possessive eyes, she chose her words carefully, keeping them short. "I need to use the bathroom." Mia whispered. She continued to stare at her for a few moments and then released her. Mia slowly ascended from the bed, grabbing a small blanket at the end of the bed, to wrap around herself. She closed the bathroom door behind her without looking back. Mia sat with her elbows on her legs and held her forehead. She remembered most of what happened with Aithusa but could only vaguely recall what had happened prior to this. She remembered people surrounding her as well as glimpses of Theron's face. "*What the fuck did I walk into?*" She thought to herself. She needed to call Sebastian to come get her, then switched to the last time that she had seen her clothes and bag. They had to be in the other room with the big table. She flushed the toilet and turned the sink on to wash her hands. Leaving the water running, she splashed her face with cold water and looked at herself in the mirror. Her face reflected how she felt: drained, weak and achy. Her muscles felt tight and sore. She looked up at the clock. It was 4:20 AM. She needed to assess her situation and get out, somehow. Aithusa's eyes were fixed on hers as she exited the bathroom. Not knowing where her things were, she decided to wait until Aithusa fell back asleep before she could figure out how to get away from her. Mia knew and believed that the way out would be shown to her. As she walked back to the bed, she looked around the room and saw an open box with syringes. The one that was used on her lay on the table next to the box. She lay back on the bed, slipped under the blanket and pulled it over her shoulders, holding it in her hands against her chest. She closed her eyes. She wanted her to think she was going back to sleep. A few flashes of lightning lit up the room, followed by some distant rumbles of thunder. Mia knew that storms are a powerful force of the earth and should be respected. She took this as a sign. She listened intently as the sounds caressed her ear. Not moving a muscle, she allowed her mind merge with its rhythm. She meditated on an image of Aithusa sleeping, listened to the rhythm of her breathing and synched her own breathing pattern to hers. Without realizing that she was practicing a Divination technique, Mia essentially placed herself between two realms, waking and paradoxical state. She tuned into Aithusa's frequency and projected her placid thoughts into her mind. The gentle sounds of the rain eventually lulled Aithusa back to sleep. The road came to her in her thoughts.

Keeping her breathing in pace with Aithusa's, she waited for what seemed to be fifteen minutes and tepidly slid off the bed. She slowly walked over to the other side of the bed and removed one of the syringes from the box. With her eyes fixed on Aithusa, she saw that part of her shoulder was exposed. Careful not to touch the bed with her legs, she arched over, moving her hand towards her until she was about an inch away. Her heart was pounding. She took a slow deep breath and with a swift jab, she injected her and stepped back. Aithusa jolted and abruptly sat up. She looked over at Mia and saw the syringe in her hand. Mia just watched her. The lightning flashed in a peculiar and continuous pattern, revealing the cold dark fury that filled Aithusa's eyes. Mia stepped back further, watching her as the confusion set in. Aithusa struggled to keep herself upright, using every ounce of strength she had. With a vicious voice she threatened her. "Mia…you will see me again. This isn't over." Her words intimidated her. She stood there, breathing erratically. She waited for her to become lethargic, grabbled a small blanket to wrap around herself and unlocked the door.

She looked around and realized that Aithusa's room was just outside from the room with the table. She opened the door slowly, and peeked in. No one was in there. She looked to her left and saw her clothing on the floor beside the table. She quickly put them on and searched for her shoes. As she eyeballed the table's surface, she recalled a few images of herself and cringed. She recalled the exact moment when they were pulled off of her and spotted them under the table. She remembered the kitchen pantry where everyone had stored their bags and quickly darted upstairs prowling around until she located the room. The streetlight beaming through the window lit the way around the kitchen. She opened the pantry door and felt around for her bag until she found it. Hers was one of three still in there and the only one with fringe on it. She whispered her implored thoughts to the Universe. *"Please keep leading me."* Deeply anxious, she walked out of the kitchen, listening for sounds that she hoped she would not hear. She walked across the room, trying to backtrack herself to the front door. She turned and looked around her, seeing the first few stairs that led to the second floor. She listened for sound and heard nothing. The image of Aithusa's cell phone flashed in her mind. It was on the table next to the box. If she were alert enough to reach it she would have done it already. Panicking, she carefully unlocked the door and ran out, leaving the front door wide open. She ran down the street and zigzagged down a few streets, left and right, until she ran out of breath and could run no further. With a fast paced walk, she searched for a place to hide. She spotted a brick building with a bakery on the first floor. There was an alley with a stoop set back on its far left side. It faced towards the back yard. She looked for the street sign, then back at the house for the number and ran down the alley. She grabbed onto the guardrail, sat on the bottom step and pulled out her cell phone to call Sebastian. The phone rang four times.

"Come on Sebbie...answer!!!" "Hello?" He whispered. "Sebbie! Please come get me. I'll explain later. I'll text you the address. Please hurry and don't beep. I am hiding in the alley on the side steps." "OK, OK. Are you ok Mia?" "Yes, Just hurry." I'll be right there." He hung up and waited for her text as he put his sneakers on and grabbed his car keys. She sent the text. It was a little distorted and misspelled due to the lighting conditions. She waited, in the shadows of the alley, listening for his car and hoping those people would not find her before he arrived. Waiting for him was the hardest part. Though few and far between, each time that she heard a car approaching, she jumped up to see if it was him. The wait was intensifying her anxiety. Every sound unnerved her, compounding her anxiety. When she spotted his car, she ran to it and jumped in. "GO!" She screamed.

He screeched away, driving as fast as he could, while Mia looked through the back window, hoping no one had seen them. "Mia, What the hell happened?" Her hands were shaking. She covered her face, crouched over and started cry, in an effort to release all the negativity within her. "Mia you're scaring me." She lifted her head, wiped her eyes and tried desperately to collect herself. Every time she tried to speak, she cried. "Mia, focus on my voice and take a deep breath before you speak. Did anyone hurt you?" Mia inhaled and exhaled a few times. "I'm not injured. I...don't know where to start."

Sebastian spoke calmly, asking simple questions, trying to get her to calm down and focus. "OK Mia, What I do know is that you went to a Halloween party. Is this where everything happened?" "Yes" "How many people were there?" "Maybe ten." "Male and female?" "Yes." "You had told me you met the girls who invited you, at a fair and that they said it was a Samhain celebration. Is that what it was?" "At first, yes. Then it turned into a disturbing and distorted version of it." She started crying again. Tears rolled down her cheeks. "Sebbie... this is why I don't socialize or share myself. It always turns out negative. The girls, they saw my necklace and led me to believe that they were like me. These people...none of them are like me!" Sebastian remained quiet for a few minutes. "Sebbie you're gonna freak as much as I am when I tell you what happened." She paused for a moment. "I don't even remember it all because someone drugged me... at least twice." "WHAT?" "The first time it was my drink and the second was with a needle." Sebastian's eyes flared. "Mia, did someone..." "Yes." She cut him off, crying. "Do you wanna go to the police?" "No." "How did you get out of there?" "Patience and my beliefs. I'll handle it. I just want to go home. I'll tell you everything else, then." She curled up on the seat, facing him and closed her eyes.

When Mia felt the car stop, she opened her eyes. Sebastian got out of the car and walked around to her side. She grabbed her things as he opened her door. He hooked his arm under hers and they walked to the door. "I'm gonna make some coffee. You go change and I'll meet you on the couch, baby girl." "Ok. Thank you for coming to get me." "No worries."

She went straight to her bedroom, ripped off her costume and tossed it into the garbage. She put her robe on, grabbed some clothes and hopped into the shower. She held on the wall and let the water run over her head. Reality began to set in and she started crying once again. She recalled the exact words of Aithusa's threat. And then her "what if's" began to fill her mind. *Did she look through my bag? Do they know my address?* Anxiety set in. Her thoughts became her worst enemy. She changed her focus to the shower and squirted shampoo into her hands. She proceeded to wash the night off of herself, struggling to redirect her negative thinking. *"I'm no longer there and Sebbie came to get me. I am safe now."* She reinforced positive thoughts as she rinsed off and imagined the negativity running down the drain. Sebastian knocked on the door. "Coffee's ready. I brought out your blanket and pillow." "OK. I'll be right out."

Sebastian was sitting on the couch, watching the morning news. Mia sat next to him on the couch and wrapped the blanket around herself. She grabbed her coffee and lifted her feet up, across his lap. "Are you ready to tell me what happened?" She stared at him for a few moments and lit a cigarette. "Yes." "Do you remember anyone's names?" "Only the two...the one's who invited me." She proceeded to tell him about all that she could remember and as she told him the worst of the evening, his face reflected utter horror and rage. "What was the name of the two who did this to you and what did they look like?" "Their names were never said near me. I only remember that his hair was dark, shoulder length and his eyes were dark and eerie. He had a deep voice." "What did the girl who kept you in her room, look like?" "She also had the same features only her hair was in a short pony tail." "If you saw them again, would you recognize them?" "Him, maybe. But her, yes." It was quiet for a few minutes. "I need more coffee Seb. Do you want?" "Yes." He handed her his mug, "Do you remember the address?" "I have it written down, but I don't want you going there. Promise me!" "I wont."

Mia recalled her dream from the other night and tried to make sense of it. The meaning of it and the song was a little clearer now. She brought the coffees back to the couch and grabbed the laptop to look up the lyrics. "What are you looking for?" I had a dream the night before this and there was a song in it too. "Tell me about the dream." "OK one second." She pulled up the lyrics, read them twice and took a sip of her coffee. With her jittery hand, she lit up another cigarette. She handed him the laptop. "Read this and then I'll tell you." As he read through the lyrics, Mia watched his face. Like Mia, he was very good at interpreting dreams. He knew when songs played in your mind for a period of time, that there was a message. He knew to first look for the Elements and colors, and then proceed from there by incorporating their meanings into the remainder of the details. "OK. Mia, I've got an idea but I want to hear your dream first." She reiterated the details of her dream to him and then grabbed a pencil. "I am going to write what I think it is and then you tell me." Mia grabbed a napkin and jotted her thoughts. *"These people were looking for me. I saw the people who were there and could not feel them because they hid themselves it from me. The parallel place was actually two things. How they perceive me and the house where the party was held last night."* She stared at him for a few moments. "Ok, Mia, show me what you wrote." She handed the napkin to him. He read through her words twice. "This is very close to what I see. You last sentence – I agree. Things are not as they seem."

CHAPTER 3

STOP. RESET.

It was a few days before the Full Moon. Mia stared at it as it ascended into the sky. The view of the Moon was always better on the beach. She felt closer to her there. She liked to lay sideways on the sand, close to the shore and away from other beachgoers. She watched the waves ebb and flow, listening, as she absorbed the strength of the Ocean. She was always able to go into such a deep meditative state. While she could hear the sounds surrounding her, she remained unreceptive to any of it. Music always had an unusual effect on her. There were times when a song would play in her head. If it lingered longer than a day, she knew it was a message that she needed to decipher. It sometimes gave her anxiety if it lingered. There have been some that remained in her head for longer than three days.

She didn't like to get too close to people, around too many people or negative people, for that matter. She never understood why it bothered her when she was younger. She always felt like an odd duck and never shared certain things about herself with others, particularly her views regarding her belief system. She avoided negative situations. In time, she realized that the anxiety that she felt was a result of absorbing what ever they felt. The symptoms of this Empathic trait could be easily mistaken for common sympathy. The difference is that an Empath can sense another persons true feelings, which run deeper than what is displayed on the surface. They can sense this, even from a distance, which is why public places can be somewhat challenging. When recognized, the more attuned to its symptoms, the stronger the gift becomes. She always sensed people who had strong Aura's, whether they exuded peace, anger or other qualities, as she listened to them. If it became overwhelming for her, she would somehow, politely disengage herself. Eventually she felt it was better not to get too close to people.

Approaching thunderstorms were when she felt most strong, perhaps even invincible. As they approached, the strength, darkness, lightning and wind elated her. It was their phenomenal power that had always seduced her. She welcomed them to consume her by closing her eyes and merging her spirit with them. She also enjoyed Windy days and would do the same by lifting her arms and allowing the energy of the wind to encompass her body. To her, it felt as if she were surrendering to the powerful will of dominant and veiled spirit of this Element.

She sometimes felt like a freak, but that's what made her who she is. The more she understood herself, the more at ease she was with herself and the things she felt. She had occasionally researched the entities that made her feel these things. Books, people and algorithms produced Empathy, while others reflected some sort of Psychic origins. Her circle of friends and acquaintances were small, she remained selective with those she allowed into her life. There were only five people who were aware of her veiled side. Two were female and three were male. The females were whom she confided in and shared the same beliefs and of the three males, one was her close friend Sebastian. The other two she also shared, inquired with, believed in and knew All. She decided not to label herself and to just allow what is. Her intention was to learn to fly, Solitary, on her own terms.

Following the phases of the Moon was second nature and religion to her. It kept her focused, confident, protected and positive. She always kept the yearly Moon phase calendar and the Wheel of the year, on her wall. She knew what needed to be done and when, in regard to the intent and the phase. In layman's terms, banishing a negative issue or removing a bad habit would be done during the waning phase. To begin a new project or bring in positive growth would be done during the waxing phase. The dark Moon is the time to go within ones self. This time is intended for a silent or planning period. The full Moon reveals the results of your intentions, however, on the night of the full Moon, those following the path give thanks as this night is all about her, the Goddess.

All living things were sacred to her, especially animals and trees. She considered her pets, her children and loved them fiercely. Her connection with them had always remained adamant. A Witch and their Familiar maintain a psychic bond of pure energy, communicate telepathically and enhance their collective Magick. The Familiar can enter and exit a ritual circle at will and will warn their witch of mistakes and impending danger.

Throughout most of her life, her Familiar had mostly sought her out in the form of a cat, with the exception of two dogs. Her last cat had passed away a few months ago. She was devastated and felt disconnected without him. To this day, she occasionally feels him walking on the bed just as she was about to fall asleep. She believed that when one pet was called to the Summerland, another would take its place beside her to be reborn into the role of her Familiar. She couldn't bear to be without them whether it is for an overnight stay at the veterinarian's office or worse. When each time had come to pass and they needed to go over the Rainbow Bridge/ Summer Land, she was heartbroken and remained disconnected from the Universe. She knew this was a transitory period. Her Familiar's spirit would always find her, in one form or another, whether it was to be a cat, a bird or a dog.

The Summerland reminded her of a song that she tied to her mother who had passed away when she was very young. It was called: "Theme to a Summer Place", which was also a movie. This song always seemed to play at the amusement park when her mother would take her there. After her mother passed, each time that she heard this song, she knew that it was a message from her mom, reassuring her that she was always watching over her.

She planned for and celebrated the Esbats and Sabbats, taking the time needed to plan and observe with its celebratory rituals. She enjoyed decorating for the Esbats, indulging in creating with her plethora of art supplies and crafting colorful displays that represented their meanings.

She always paid close attention to her dreams. Within them, lie the answers to unresolved, complex events going on in her waking state. They always needed to be analyzed and interpreted. Sometimes it was easy and others, difficult. There were very few people who were aware that she could do this. Those that did inquired with her to decipher them. When she did, she preferred to interpret them in person so that she could see their eyes. In dreams, the entities she looked for and paid close attention to were the Elements and colors. These were the highlights that told her the direction of the dream. She didn't need to know their whole life story or anything personal for that matter. She was always very close or on point with her interpretations. The Elements: Air, Water, Earth and Fire are very powerful and should always be respected.

Starting with Air/East – To Know - Communication and Knowledge. Water/West – To Dare – Intuition and Emotions. Earth – North – To Keep Silent - Growth and Mystery. Fire/South – To Will - Purification, Energy and Courage.

Mia rented an apartment, somewhat close to the shore. The beach was a few blocks away but she didn't mind the walk. The building was a brick, two-floor complex shaped like a horseshoe and its address was numbered thirteen, which was also her lucky number. The apartment was on the first floor and she shared it with her co-worker and friend, Sebastian. They worked at a restaurant located near the beach and occasionally had the same shift. Mia's shift was for the most part, seven am to five pm. This place served most of the usual food, with the exception of their baked goods. Everything was from scratch and it tasted so good. She had been working there for three years and she met him at this restaurant about a year and a half after she started working there, when he had applied for an available position. They were friends ever since. He was living at another residence for about five years and then the owner decided to put his house on the market and move. That's when Mia decided to ask if he wanted to be roommates with her. She put a lot of thought into it before offering. Sebastian was the most pleasant person to be around and they had many of the same things in common, particularly the things she seldom shared with others. He was always positive and considerate. He gave her a ride to work if he saw her along the way. Just his mere presence made her smile. He always looked out for her and she, he. They treated one another like twin siblings and soul mates. He had blue eyes and dark semi curly hair, which he occasionally let grow out. He was taller than her. His physique was strong but not overbearing. Mia had hazel eyes, which sometimes changed color dependent on what she was wearing. Her hair was a dark chocolate brown and mid in length. She was about seven pounds overweight and was forever exercising. He needed to eat a meatball as far as she was concerned. She was always trying to feed him because she felt he was too skinny. He wasn't. He was at the correct weight for his height. He had shared his dreams with her several times and she always did what she felt needed to be done to protect him. He was a strong man but he was also effeminate. She never questioned his sexual preference because they were not interested in each other in that way. They were just very compatible friends. Although they had their own separate lives, they took advantage when time permitted, to spend time together, whether it be a movie, a night out or their favorite dinner and a movie at home. Sometimes they would fall asleep together on the couch. They had been roomies together for four months and this arrangement worked for them.

As the week progressed, Sebastian perused his schedule and saw that he had a sudden shift change due to a co-worker's family emergency. He was needed to work the late shift the next day, so Mia decided to go to the beach. Every time she went, she traveled further down, exploring the different shores. The more she walked, the faster that annoying seven pounds would hopefully burn off. The Sun was beginning to set and there was a Full Moon approaching. She walked barefoot along the shore, occasionally putting her feet in the water. In the distance she saw a group of people on the sand playing some sort of game. She walked a little further and spotted a volleyball net. She planted herself near the shore and watched them play from a distance. There were six people playing. In the distance, at the sands edge, was another person sitting in a black truck, watching them. It was hot outside. There was a gentle breeze and a welcomed mist from the ocean. After a few minutes she turned her head to look out at the ocean. Lying back with her elbows on the sand, she stared into the sky at the floating clouds and took it all in. Eventually she just lay back with her hands crossed, supporting her head.

The ball had bounced away from them and rolled towards her. It bounced off of her and rolled into the ocean. Startled, Mia sat up. A girl with dark brown hair in a ponytail, approached. "Sorry about that." She giggled as she ran into the water to retrieve the ball. The Sun was in Mia's eyes as she looked at her. "That's ok. No worries."

"Hi, my name is Sage. I've never seen you here before." "My name is Mia. I live way back that-a-way." Mia pointed towards the direction where she lived. "What brings you to my end of the beach?" "It's a nice day and I thought I'd explore." "Cool. I'll see ya around, Mia." She waved and returned to her friends.

Mia watched her return and then realized that she was thirsty and hungry. She got up, dusted the sand off and walked towards the beachside food courts. As she approached the end of the sand and stepped onto the pavement, she noticed that person sitting in the truck. He was talking to the girl that she had just met. She noticed that he turned to look at her while Sage spoke to him. He was tall, with shoulder length dark hair. He was sitting in the back of a black Suburban truck. Stuck on his stare for a moment, she was a little freaked out because she hated when people stared at her. It always felt as if her hidden layers were vulnerable. She felt the tremored warning signs coming on and knew this feeling was emanating from him. She disengaged from the stare and walked to the food court. Her usual drink had already been decided upon before she even arrived at the counter. She ordered a blue raspberry smoothie and a hot dog. She waited for her food and then sat at one of the available picnic tables, facing the ocean. She practically inhaled the hot dog and savored her favorite smoothie while checking her phone for messages. She laughed to herself, thinking about a funny thought she had from that guy in the truck. *STRANGER! Do not get in his van for candy!"* "Curious, she glanced back over to the truck guy and saw him still there, still staring at her. He was blasting music from his truck. "The song was an eerie sounding dirge about a rooster. She lit up a cigarette and played a game on her phone. "Ugg, *I attract the strange ones all the time."*

Her phone chirped. It was Sebastian. "Whatchadoin?" She giggled and took a picture of her tongue and sent it to him. "I'm at the beach. My tongue is blue, see?" "LOL I've got four more hours kid. I'll C U at home if U R still up." "K."

She returned to her game and continued playing. After a few minutes she decided she needed coffee. She lifted her legs over the bench, rose from the table and walked right into someone who had been standing behind her. Stunned, she stepped back to see it was truck guy. *"What the fuck? Stalker! How long was he standing there?"* She looked at him. His eyes seemed to look right through hers. He extended his hand. "Hello." He said with a deep voice and an iniquitous smile. She was reluctant to shake his hand at first. "Hi." She shook it anyway. He stood there with that smile for a few moments. She was a little creeped out. "What is your name, sweet girl?" "Mia." She said in a wary voice. "My name is Hunter." *"That's not a name. It's an activity."* She mocked his name to herself. "I saw you talking to a friend of mine earlier. I thought I would introduce myself." She realized he was referring to Sage and became a little at ease. "Yes. Her soccer ball rolled by me." "Are you from around here, Mia?" "Sort of. I live back a mile or so from here." "And what brings you over to this side of the beach?" "I was walking along the shore and went a little further than I normally do." Hunter pointed behind himself. "I live in the white house behind me." He gazed into her eyes through the entire conversation, never once losing eye contact. "Am I keeping you from something?" She wanted her coffee. "I'm was just going to get coffee." "May I join you?" "OK." As they walked to the concession stand, he walked just a step behind her. He approached the attendant. "Two coffee's please. Mia, how do you take it?" "Cream and sugar." "...And the other one, black." He placed the money on the counter. *Eww. No sugar? She thought to herself.* He handed her the coffee. "Thank you Hunter." He smiled. They returned to the table. She inquired about the meaning behind his name. "I've never met anyone named Hunter before." "They call me The Hunter. My given name is Theron. I prefer Hunter." "Why do they call you that? Are you a bondsman?" He laughed. "No, Mia." She waited for him to follow up with an answer, but he didn't. *"Why doesn't he ever move his eyes away from mine? Fuck!"* She couldn't take the staring anymore. "Why do you stare at me like that?" "Does it make you uncomfortable?" "Yes. It's kinda creepy." "I think you are exquisite, Mia." She blushed, not expecting him to say that at all. She was embarrassed and turned her face towards the Moon. "Do you like the Moon, Mia?" Intrigued, she looked at him. "Did I hit a note?" He said smiling. She smiled back. "Mia, you have the Moon in your eyes." He took a deep breath and exhaled. "Mia, it was nice to meet you. " He rose up from the bench and just walked away. *"Wierdo!" She thought to herself.*

He knew who she was and he knew that she didn't remember him.

She watched him walk away, wondering why he didn't even say good-night. *"Theron?"* She thought to herself. *"I've heard that name before."* She looked at her phone, yawned and decided to head back home. She had to be in work early tomorrow.

She walked inside, changed into a T-shirt, turned the TV on and lay across the couch. Her intentions were to wait up for Sebastian, but that didn't happen. She fell asleep within a half hour.

When she woke the next morning via the alarm clock that Sebastian had set for her, she remembered a vivid dream that she had. She put the coffee maker on and hopped into the shower. Dressed for work, she made herself coffee and saw a note on the counter from Sebastian. *"I'm off today. No need to wake me. See U when U return. Have a great day sweetie. Love Seb."* He drew a heart. She smiled, flipped the note over, drew X's and O's, and left for work. As she walked, she tried to recall pieces of her dream. It was vivid and wild. She remembered seeing unclear faces and the Moon in her Full phase. She recalled seeing herself sleeping and someone watching her as she slept. She couldn't remember anything else. She let it wallow inside her mind for a while until she could figure it out.

When she returned from work, she changed her clothes and looked for Sebastian. He was in the bathroom. "Hey, do you wanna get pizza tonight?" "Sounds good, Mia. I'm meeting up with some friends later on though, ok?" "No problem." "How do I look?" "Handsome as always, sir." He grabbed his keys and opened the door for her. "Ladies first." They walked with their arms hooked together. "How was your day, Mia? Did you make alotta tips?" "I did pretty good today. It was busy though. The worst part of the day was trying to stay away from those damn chocolate chip muffins!" Sebastian smiled, wide-eyed. "I know! They're like sex!" Mia blushed and smacked him in the arm. She ordered a slice of Sicilian and a Pepsi. He ordered two regular slices and a beer. "I feel bad leaving you." "It's ok. I'm gonna go walk on the beach. I'm tired anyway."

Sebastian looked at his watch. "I've got to go baby girl. I'll see you later." He kissed her on the forehead. Mia refilled her soda and made her way to the beach. This time she was staying local. She wasn't in the mood to run into that guy again. She kicked off her sandals and hooked them onto her pinky. With her IPod in hand, she chose her playlist, put the headphones in and walked through the sand. She was still thinking about her dream. She couldn't figure it out yet. It may have to do with the people she met last night. *"It'll come to me eventually."* She thought to herself. It was dusk and a few people to her left had lit some sparklers and cracked some glow-sticks. She liked the blue glow-sticks. *"They never last very long."* She thought. She walked with her feet in the water, carrying her sandals and soda. In the distance, she saw a group of people headed towards her. As they drew nearer, she recognized one of them. It was Sage. She saw her and waved. "Mia!" *"Crap. I just wanted to listen to my music."* She thought to herself. Six people accompanied Sage. Mia smiled. "Hi Sage." They encircled Mia. This immediately made her feel leery. "Mia, these are my friends, the ones that were playing volley ball with me last night." Mia looked at her as she spoke. Sage's eyes were brown and her hair was down instead of the ponytail she wore last night. "Mia, I believe you've already met Hunter." He emerged from behind her. Sage introduced the others. "This is Raine, Emery, Lucius, Zephyr and Mayne. Everyone, this is Mia, the girl on the beach last night. Now paranoid, Mia thought to herself. *"Was I the topic of their conversation last night?"* Raine was a little taller than Mia, with long straight brown hair and eyes to match. Emery was tall and a little muscular with grey/blue eyes, long mousy blonde hair in a pony tale and a bandana. Lucius was tall and muscular, blue eyes and crew cut, blonde hair. Zephyr was tall and a little thin with semi short messy dark hair and sharp blue eyes. He had unusually long, dark eyelashes. Mayne was almost as tall as them, with dark brown eyes and dark brown hair. It was an odd hairstyle. Straight, shorter than shoulder length, cut in layers that stuck out in some spots. They all shook hands with Mia. Hunter said nothing. Mia felt awkward because they were all staring at her. Hunter placed his hands on her shoulders. Mia was a little spooked because he was touching her. "Mia it's nice to see you again." His voice spoke in a bizarre, deep tone. "What brings you to my side of town?" Mia asked, speaking in a nervous tone, with his hands still on her shoulders. "We took a walk to this side, hoping to run into you." "Me?" A little freaked out she looked at them oddly while thinking to herself. *"Why me? They just met me."* Sage smiled. "I like making new friends. We don't usually let new people into our circle but there's just something about you that captivates me." She leaned over to Mia's ear and whispered. "Also, Hunter seems to have taken a liking to you." Mia looked down and blushed, with a smirk on her face. "How do I captivate you, Sage?" Mia called her out on her comment, as she made sure to only look at her and not Hunter. "I can't put my finger on it. I'll have to get to know you better." Feeling awkward, Mia stared out at the ocean, then looked up at the Moon, taking a deep breath. Observing her, Hunter followed the direction of her eyes. Trying to break the ice, Lucius took his sneakers off, put his feet in the water and turned to look at Mia. "Hey, Mia. Come put your feet in. The water's warm." Kidding around, Sage teased Lucius. "Just Mia? Do the rest of us suck?" Lucius turned to Sage, with an evil grin and an innuendo comment. "No, Just you Sage. You suck." Sage walked up to him and punched him in the ass. The others laughed. Mia didn't get it and just shrugged it off. Mayne observed Mia as she walked into the water. Raine saw the way Mayne looked at her and nudged Sage. They both smiled at each other.

Mayne looked at Hunter and spoke in a low tone. "So that's her, huh? What's your plan?" He looked at Mayne and then back to Mia. "Tomorrow is the Full Moon. She will come to us. Then she will come to me."

It was getting dark. Mia looked at her watch. "I've got to go now. This evening was nice. It was nice meeting all of you." She walked out of the ocean and put her sandals back on. Hunter walked up to Mia and reached for her hand. "Mia, we will be having a little party on our end of the beach tomorrow evening. There will be a bonfire. I insist that you attend." He stared at her with the most enticing eyes she'd seen. She paused for a few moments. Sage chimed in. Yeah, Mia, please come." Lucius smirked and then laughed at Sage because of his nasty interpretation of the words she had just said. She felt an arm suddenly on her shoulder. It was Mayne's. "What do you drink?

I'll make sure we have it." Mayne said, smiling at her. "I don't drink. I do love coffee and blue ice drinks or smoothies." Hunter smiled. "So you'll be there?" "OK," "Still holding her hand, he kissed her forehead and looked into her eyes. "Sweet dreams... sweet dreams, Mia." She smiled at him. "See you tomorrow Mia." Sage waved as Mia walked away.

CHAPTER 4

MOON DANCE

Mia returned to her apartment and made a pit stop to get a coffee along the way. *"Sebastian will be happy that I've made new friends."* He hated that she never socialized enough, but he understood how she was, considering her last encounter. She found herself thinking about Hunter. The aura she felt from him was very bewitching. She started analyzing them in her head. *"Sage and Lucius felt very positive. Raine was a little distant. Mayne felt hospitable, and receptive but touchy. I don't like being touched. Oh here I go again, reading everyone. Cut it out Mia."* She laughed at herself and walked inside the apartment.

She was tired and decided to go to bed early, She left a note for Sebastian. *"I have to be in work at 7am. I met some new friends and I'll be meeting with them to-morrow night. See? I socialized! C U later."* She went into her room, changed and turned on the TV. She sipped her coffee thinking about tomorrow night and was thankful she was off from work the day after.

She woke the next morning, having had another dream. She couldn't re-call much except for a rising Phoenix bird with blue eyes and a part of a song, which was now stuck in her head. She couldn't remember the title, just some of the lyrics and eerie music.

♪Figure in black *which points at me*♪

She recalled the dream she had the night before and compared the two, wondering if they were connected.

When she returned home from work she jumped into shower and then looked for something to wear. Shuffling through her closet, she found her favorite fringed blue shirt and dark grey bell bottomed yoga pants. She believed that fringe, like dream catchers, distracted negative entities. She put her makeup on and blew dried her hair for a change. She was tired of the ponytail look. She also grabbed her favorite necklace that she always wore. It was a silver chain with three phases of the Moon. The Moonstone in the center, represented the Full phase and the crescent Moons on each side, representing the waxing and waning phase. On the other side of the Moonstone, was a Pentacle. To her, this represented White Magick. The points represent Earth, Air, Fire, Water, and Spirit. The circle around it symbolizes the protection, the cycle of birth, life, death and rebirth. This symbol was not to be confused with the inverted one, which to her, represented a different meaning. She slipped on socks and sneakers and walked out the door. She remembered it was quite a distance from where she was, so she picked up a coffee on the way. She put on her earplugs and walked to the beach's entrance. When she approached the sand, she removed her sneakers and socks, shoved the socks into the sneakers and rolled up her pants. She then, tied the laces into a bow, threw them over her shoulder and walked along the shore. Along the way, she kept turning around to see the beginning of the Full Moon rising. It seems larger and closer to the earth when it is just visible over the horizon.

She received a text from Sebastian. "Mia, have a great time with your new friends. Give them a chance. OK? I'll see you later and you can tell me all about tonight. Text me when you are on your way home. Love Ya!" She replied back to him. "I will and I will XOXO."

She saw the bonfire in the distance and was a little antsy. She repeated Sebastian's words. *"Give them a chance. Give them a chance."* As she drew nearer, she saw Mayne just ahead, waving to her. She walked up to her, doing the "arm over her shoulder" thing again and within her thoughts, Mia screamed. *"You're touching me!"* "Hi Mia. We've got coffee for you and your blue smoothie is in the cooler." She walked her over to the others. Sage ran up to her. "Mia! You made it! How do you like the bonfire? We just started it a little while ago. Actually, Lucius made it." "It's beautiful!" She felt Mayne's arm now around her waist instead of her shoulder and was freaking out inside her head. *"He's touching me again!"* Recalling Sebastian's words, she didn't want to be rude and pull away, so she stood there. "Lets get your coffee." Mayne grabbed her hand and pulled her towards the coolers. "Great. I need my coffee." "Mia, how much coffee do you drink?" Mia giggled. "As much as I can." "You seem so mellow." "I'm hyper within my mind." Mia took a big sip and smiled at Mayne. "Lift off, we have lift off!" "I would never be able to sleep if I drank that much." They walked back to the bonfire. Mia looked up at the Moon as she walked and Mayne watched her. "You look like you are sailing around the Moon in your mind, Mia." "I'm sorry. I always do that, you know, daydream." "It's the best night for a bonfire." Mayne stood in front of the fire, drinking beer. Lucius brought over a tray of hot dogs, with sticks to cook them. He held the tray up for everyone. Mia didn't reach for anything. "Mia, have you never roasted hot dogs like this?" Sage asked, as she put the stick through her hot dog. "No, I haven't. I'm not hungry right now." Lucius insisted. "Mia, you need to eat to keep up your strength. Eat what you can." Sage handed Mia a stick and showed her how to put the hotdog on it. "Stick only the hotdog in the fire. Try not to put the exposed part of the stick in it though." "OK."

Raine screamed out to Hunter, who was sitting in the back of his truck, talking to Enya, Mayne's sister. "Turn the music up!" He looked up and walked around the front of the truck, which was facing away from the beach and raised the volume. He and Enya then walked towards them. As they approached, Hunter noticed Mia and pointed her out to Enya. He gestured silence to the others as he approached from behind her and stood, watching her roast her hotdog. He waited for her to turn around. He didn't want to startle her while she was close to the flames. Lucius looked at Hunter as he watched Mia. "How do you know when it's done, Sage? I don't want it to burn." "Just keep pulling it out of the flame until you see it's a little browned. She pulled hers out of the flame and showed it to her. "See, like this." Mia took hers out of the flame and turned to get a bun and some mustard. As she turned, she saw Hunter and Enya, behind her. "Mia." Acknowledging her, he smiled. "I would like to introduce you to Enya. She is Mayne's sister." "Nice to meet you, Enya." Enya was about an inch taller than Mia. She had dark eyes and dark brown, neck length, feathered hair. Glancing over at Mayne, she saw the resemblance. "I met your brother. He thinks I'm over caffeinated." Hunter grinned. Enya looked at Hunter and chuckled, emphasizing her sister's gender with quoted fingers. "Yes...my *brother*...should talk. *He* drinks too much beer." Lucius fetched drinks for everyone. "Who wants a refill?" Everyone raised their hands. "OK I can't carry it all. I'm just gonna bring the coolers over here. Emery, give me a hand. Mia, do you want your blue drink?" She shook her head yes, smiling happily. Lucius looked at Hunter and he returned a cryptic nod. Mia turned to Hunter. "Do you drink too, Hunter?" "Yes, I indulge." He grinned. She touched the fringe on his shirt. When he noticed, he held his arm up to let it dangle for her. "Do you like fringe, Mia?" "Yes, it's very sixties." She dangled the fringe on her own shirt.

Dusk had begun to settle and Sage was dancing around the bonfire by herself, to the music playing from Hunters truck. Enya joined her. As she moved around, she spotted Mia. "Mia! Come dance with me!" Mia shook her head. "No way." Being the high spirit that she is, she skipped over to her and grabbed her hand gently. "Please?" she said with pouty lips. Hunter put his hand on her shoulder. "Go with her." Mia laughed and followed her. 'I don't really dance Sage. "No worries. Just flow with the music like me. Let the fire inspire!" Sage sung the lyrics to the song playing.

♪*Raven hair and ruby lips...*♪

She touched Raine's hair and then touched Mia's lips as she passed them. Emery was dragging the cooler over with Lucius as they passed. Lucius handed Mia her blue smoothie and grabbed Sage by the waist as she danced passed him. Looking him in his eyes, she continued singing, enticing him with the words.

"♪...*rock you in the night...*♪

He sung the rest of the lyrics with her as they danced together. Hunter rose and walked over to the bonfire. Mia stopped dancing and sipped her drink. Everyone gathered around the fire. He held out his hands on either side of him and everyone circled around the fire, joining hands. "Mia, come." He held his hand out to her. "What are we doing?" She asked. Tonight is the Full Moon. This is what we do." She put her drink down in front of her, grabbed his hand and Sage grabbed her other hand. Facing the Moon, they held up their arms. Starting with Enya, each person took turns saying something that they wanted to enhance or bring into their lives. Mia listened intently. Used to doing this on her own, she had never experienced it this way. When they got halfway around, she tried to think of something to say. Mia was ready by the time it was Sage's turn. After she spoke. Mia felt a little anxious. Following their lead, she spoke. "To protect animals and banish those who harm them." Everyone smiled. Sage squeezed Mia's hand. "Good one baby." Hunter then spoke. "To open road blocks that may hinder our goals." They simultaneously lifted their arms and chanted: *So Mote It Be,* releasing their intentions into the Universe.

Hunter looked at Mia. "Did you enjoy that Mia?" Mia smiled. "Yes, that was beautiful." Mia picked up her drink and followed Hunter to a nearby-beached log. He sat straddled on it and Mia sat next to him. Lucius lit up a few marijuana cigarettes and passed them around. He handed one to Hunter. Sipping her drink, she looked at him as he smoked. "I've always loved the smell of that." He offered it to her. "I don't know that I should do that. Plus it kinda diffuses my caffeine high." He laughed. "Try." She took a puff and tried to give it back to him. "One more." He pushed it back to her. "Oh the peer pressure." She took another one and handed it back to him. As she was taking the last sips of her drink, she made straw noises on purpose. "OK, now I need more coffee." "Take one more before you go." He handed it back to her. "Ok but that's it." She took another drag and handed it back to him. She got up and walked over to the coffee and began to feel a little floaty and hyper at the same time. *"Great!"* She thought to herself. *"Caffeine, Sugar rush and pot? I've just consumed three oxymorons. Lets get wild and add more coffee to the mix. "*

She walked back towards Hunter and saw Lucius adding wood to the fire. Sage stood beside him, drawing with a stick into the sand. She saw Mayne talking to Hunter. As she approached them, they stopped talking and Mayne walked over to Emery. She sat next to Hunter again. "Face me Mia." She lifted her leg over the log, took a sip of her coffee, looked over at Lucius and pointed at him. "He's quite the pyro." He grabbed her finger and pulled it down. "Never point Mia." "Why?" "Your intentions follow your finger's direction." She looked at him, puzzled, but shrugged it off. "So what's your story, Hunter, Do you have a girlfriend?" He smiled at her. "I don't date people. When you get to close things tend to go awry. Free will and do what makes you happy." She smiled. "How very sixties of you." He laughed.

Mia looked at her watch. "I should be going soon." He reached for her. "Mia, Hold on. The night is coming." He gazed into her eyes. "Mia, I see the Moon in your eyes." She blushed, remembering him saying that to her last night. "What do you see in my eyes, Mia?" Smiling, she looked into his eyes. He showed her what he wanted her to see. She looked into them, intently. Second-guessing her own eyes, she moved closer. She thought she saw a candle flame and thought it might just be the reflection of the bonfire, but then realized he was not facing it. A little spooked, she answered him. "I see fire, Hunter. Is that even possible? I think my eyes are deceiving me or maybe it's that funny cigarette we smoked. I do feel floaty right now." His eyes pierced hers and he grinned. "I like looking into your eyes Mia." He kept staring at them, making her feel uncomfortable. He moved closer to her, placed his hand on the side of her head and slowly kissed her. Feeling flush, she felt a spiritual pull from him that wouldn't let her go. He moved closer and placed his other hand on her thigh, pulling her closer to him. Her head was spinning with contradicting thoughts but she paid them no mind and just went with what she felt, because it felt good. She dropped her coffee and wrapped her arms around his shoulders. With her legs over his, she was practically sitting in his lap. With his hand on her ass, he pulled her closer, and kissed her with a fierce and deep passion. He slid his hand underneath her shirt. She stopped him and looked up. "No, there are people here." "They're not looking, Mia. They've walked to the other side of the bonfire." His hands ran slowly up the length of her thighs to her waist. She felt the heat of his hands and the familiar dominant spiritual pull again, as she stared in his eyes. He kissed her lips, trailing them down her neck and slid his hands across her back. He felt her erratic breathing. He unhooked her bra and slid his hand over her breast. She trembled, uttering sounds of pleasure. He whispered to her. "Mia, I want you." He slid his hands under her, picked her up and carried her to the sand where Sage had been drawing. Feeling a little more dizzy and floaty, she wondered what was in that cigarette. *"It should have worn off by now."*

He placed her on the sand, over Sage's symbolic drawing and stood at her feet, looking at her. When he lifted his arms to take his shirt off, she saw the fringe on his arms. It resembled the Phoenix that she had seen in her dream. His pupils were as blue as the birds were. *"Fuck! What am I doing? This happened in my dream."* He knelt down near her legs, took her hands and pulled her upright. He crawled up to her and kissed her, seductively. She felt his hands sliding over her waist and felt him unhook her bra. His enticing kisses continued as he pulled her shirt off. His kisses trickled down her neck as he nudged her onto the sand, teasing her breasts with his tongue while she squirmed in pleasure. She latched her fingers onto his hair. His lips made their way to her stomach, his tongue circling her navel while his hands slowly slid down her sides. She quivered from his every touch. He shifted himself to her feet, pulled her sneakers off then slid off her pants and lie down beside her. She felt his warm hand caressing her stomach. He nudged her chin, pulled her face to meet his and gently kissed her while his finger followed the rim of the lace on her panties. Her seductive sounds captivated him. He slid his hand between her legs and she gasped. "Mia, you are ready for me." His finger slid inside her and she moaned in his mouth as he kissed her. Her body shuddered to his rhapsody. With his eyes filled with the element of Fire, he whispered into her ear, watching her as she gasped for air. "Good girl. Ride the lightning, sweetness." He moved down and sipped her panties off. She felt his mouth on her clitoris and slipped into a whirlwind of bliss. He lifted himself up, obscuring the Moon from her view. She ached for him. He watched her panting, her hungry eyes, her desire unleashed. His eyes, wild with burning flames just as they had been with the Phoenix in her dream. He slid his hands under her knees, pulled her legs up and thrust inside her. His rhythm was merciless. Her cries of ecstasy fed into his. In the heat of their passion she felt him drawing from her and knew that her endurance was no match for his. He fed her veiled, salacious hunger and took her beyond her own limits. She lay there, trembling and feeling as if she had barely survived the wrath of a hurricane.

Lucius had slipped something into Mia's smoothie, at Hunters request and she had been feeling the effects of it, thinking that it was just the marijuana. She lay next to Hunter with her arm around his chest. Her body was still trembling against his. At times she felt like she was looking at everything through a prismatic lens, so she closed her eyes. Zephyr had begun his exodus from the beach, returning to the house. Lucius put the fire out while the girls gathered their things and headed back to the house. Hunter waited a little while longer, then stood up and put his clothes on. He lifted Mia up and carried her back to his house. Sage grabbed her things and followed him. Feeling the movement, Mia whispered to him. "Where are we going?" He intoned. "I'm bringing you home."

She woke up the next morning in the bedroom of a strange house. She looked around and saw most everyone from last night sprawled everywhere around the room, half naked. *"Holy shit! What the fuck happened?"* She panicked. Trying to recall last night's events, she remembered most of it, including Hunter, but then struggled to figure out how she ended up here. She looked around for Hunter. He was not in the room. Spotting her clothes and things on the chair, she slid out of the bed and got dressed. *"Fuck! What am I gonna tell Sebastian?"* She fished in her bag for her phone and saw four messages from him. She grabbed her things, opened the door and walked out of the room. Looking around to find her way out, she saw stairs. With her heart pounding, she crept down the stairway, searched for the front door unlocked it and left, unnoticed. As she exited the house, she quickly turned to see what the house number was. She spotted it on one of the columns. In a gothic font, the number thirteen displayed in raised pewter. She ran down the block trying to find the entrance to the beach. She had to stop for a moment to catch her breath. Thinking of a reply, she re-read Sebastian's texts and saw that he was worried. *"Hi I am sooooo sorry. It was late and I fell asleep on my new friends couch. I'm on my way home now."*

She started to have flashbacks of last night. Images of their faces and people touching others are what came to mind. She then recalled more than one person near her or sitting next to her. *"What the hell happened... an orgy?!* She recalled a movie she had seen with a song playing in the background, with the word "stranglehold" in it, while an orgy started on the dance floor. Panicking, she started to feed into her negative thinking habit. *"Unbelievable! Only me! Make new friends, he says. Be social. I'm done! I want my blankie."*

She ran most of the way home. As she entered the apartment she looked around for Sebastian, He was in his room, sleeping. *"Thank you!"* She thought to herself. She wasn't ready to explain yet. She was exhausted and decided to call out sick from work. She would switch shifts with someone if necessary. She left a note for Sebastian and went to her room.

CHAPTER 5

KARMA CAFE

Mia woke the next morning with a headache. She called out sick as she had planned on doing the night before. She crawled out of bed and went into the bathroom to get some ibuprofen. As she swallowed the pills, she stared at herself in the mirror, recapping the events of last night. She held her fist up against the mirror and whispered to herself. *"What happened last night, Mia? REMEMBER!"* She sat on the toilet holding her head. Urinating was not a very pleasant feeling this morning, to say the least. It stung. Her muscles ached as well. *"What hell did I walk into last night… again!?"* Needing a shower desperately, she went back to the room for a change of clothes. She had no intentions on leaving the apartment, so she picked out something comfy to wear. The hot water soothed her achy body. She held her neck under the showerhead to try to alleviate the tension headache. Images of last night were sporadic. She recalled the dreams, images of people's faces, the Phoenix with the red eyes and Hunter. She was also feeling a little weak in a strange way. It was like someone took a piece of her spirit and was tapping into her energy. *"I'm a freak."* She thought to herself.

Sebastian knocked on the bathroom door. "Mia? I have to pee. May I come in?" "Yes Seb." He opened the door. "OK missy, spill it now!" "Oh Seb, can you wait a little. I'm nursing a headache. I called in sick today."

Sebastian raised his eyebrow. "Did you actually drink alcohol?" "I may have. I don't know." "I can't believe it. My sweet Mia, popped her liquor cherry last night and got drunk!" "Haha very funny." "Can I flush now?" She shut the water off. "Yes, hurry and scram." He shut the door behind him.

She dried off and quickly dressed. She looked at herself in the mirror once again. *"You need to forget last night and do what's needed to remove this negativity."* She would start tonight, as the Moon wanes. She brushed her teeth then put her hair in a ponytail. *"Coffee time!"*

Sebastian was making himself some coffee. "How are you feeling now baby girl?" "A little better." She sat at the table and he made her a cup. He walked over to her and massaged her shoulders. "Oh Seb, that feels so good." "I have to be in work at noon, so I'm all yours til' then kid. Grab your coffee and get on the couch. I'll massage your feet. That always helps headaches." She picked up her coffee and he turned on the TV. He pulled her feet to his lap. Her eyes rolled back. "Ahhh. Somehow the nerves in the instep shoot anesthesia straight to your head and it tingles your head on the opposite side of the foot being massaged." "True. Every nerve in your foot is connected to the different nerves throughout your body. "I am so sorry that I didn't text you back. I fell asleep. I had a good time. We hung out on the beach and my new friend brought a few of her friends. They made a bonfire and we roasted hot dogs on a stick. I really tried Seb. I was hesitant, at first, but your words, they always haunt me. Then there were drinks that tasted good and one may have had alcohol in it…I don't know. Ahh… and there was a lot of marijuana circulating. We went back to her house and I fell asleep." Sebastian was taken aback and looked at her in amazement. "I'm astonished Mia! That makes two cherries you popped. Where is my Mia and who the hell are you?" She laughed and also sighed within her thoughts. There was no way she was going to tell him the whole story. He massaged the other foot. "Is this helping any?" Oh yes, very much." She took a sip of her coffee and grabbed the remote. "I'm gonna make breakfast for us. What do you want?" "Just toast with jelly and ice water Seb. Thanks." She stretched out on the couch and flipped through the channels. Her eyes were half closed as she watched the TV. Another image flashed in her head. It was of Mayne. Chills went through her body and she broke out in a cold sweat, refusing to accept what she thought she saw. Sebastian handed her a plate and added a handful of red grapes. "Are you ok Mia? You're sweating." He felt her forehead. "I'm ok." She sat up and took a swig of water. He sat down next to her and ate.

Deep, down inside, Mia wanted to cry.

Sebastian took her dish and brought it to the sink to wash. "I'm hoppin' in the shower. Is there anything you want before I go?" "Yes. My blankie and pillow please." "You got it."

He wrapped her like a cannoli, in her blanket and went to take a shower. Every time she felt her mind getting sucked into last night's black hole of thoughts, she whispered to herself; "*Stop. Reset.*" Simply saying, "stop" didn't work, alone. Reset; forced her redirect her mind towards another entity. It was something she picked up from an old movie. She searched for something to watch on TV. She found an old favorite already in progress, with one of her favorite actresses. It was about a guy who was given a chance to write for a famous Rock and Roll magazine. She sat upright and ate her toast.

Sebastian came out of the bathroom and made a to-go cup of coffee. "How is my blanket full of girl feeling now?" She giggled. "A little better." He grabbed his keys, walked up to her and pecked her on her cheek. "I'll text you on my break."

She took a sip of water and picked at the grapes. She lay back, curling up into a ball. The blurred sounds of the TV and its glare lulled her to light sleep. She heard the sound of glass shattering and woke up in a sweat. She realized the sound could have come from the TV, but knew that this sound must have merged with her dream. In this dream she saw a large size window, possibly a storefront window. That's all she could recall. She got up to use the bathroom and threw some cold water over her face. Her headache had alleviated somewhat, but it was still there. She opened the freezer, took out the beanbag and placed it over her forehead and then moved it to the back of her neck. She made herself another cup and sat back on the couch with the beanbag on her forehead. Sebastian sent her a text. "Mia, how are you feeling? Are you coming in tomorrow? If yes then you can take the three to close shift with me. Let me know so I can let them know." Mia replied. "A little better. I should be ok for work tomorrow. Are you going out after work?" "No baby. We'll stay in and watch a movie. What do you want to eat tonight?" She thought about it for a few minutes. She decided to make it easy on him and picked something from the restaurant where they worked. "Chocolate chip muffins and Philly cheesesteak with swiss. Get it from there. It's easier."

She scanned through the TV menu for another movie to watch. She found another old movie based on a book she had to read in high school. It was about three male siblings living together without parents and their daily lives with their friends. She hated the ending. One of the male friends was burned and died after saving a child from a fire. Her eyes were fighting to stay opened and she dozed off after a while. She woke up a few hours later and saw another text from Sebastian, "Blue smoothie, baby?" At first she was elated at the thought. Then the flashbacks started again, remembering last night. *"I bet they fucking put something in my smoothie, the fuckin' freaks."* "No thanks. I'm stickin' with water today, love." She looked at the clock and it was 4:20pm. *"Holy crap! How long was I sleeping?"* She checked her mailbox, flipped through the mail and a few assorted magazines.

"Darling I'm home!" Sebastian burst in the door, all smiles. "How are you feeling?" "Much better. I needed today. It's been a while since I took off." "Great news. I'm gonna freshen up. Did you find a good movie?" "No. I'll look now." She went to the kitchen to get napkins and placemats, returned to the couch and nestled within her blanket. She flipped through the menu on the TV. "The vampire movie with Michael is starting in ten minutes, or the Storm movie that just came out two weeks ago." He put his finger against his lips. "Hmmmm…The vampire one." "Ok. Get your blankie too." He ran back to his room and grabbed it. He tossed it onto the couch, brought the food the coffee table and went to the fridge for a drink. "You said you wanted water, right?" "Yes, please." "Ketchup?" "Definitely." He kicked off his shoes and sat on the couch, throwing the blanket over his shoulders. She rummaged through the bag of food. "What did you get?" "I got a gyro. You know how I love that sauce, but don't ask me to pronounce it." She giggled. "It's Tzatziki." "Ok smart ass." He smirked. The movie began and they started eating. "I love that song they play. What's it called; Cry little sister?" "I think so."

About halfway through the movie, the part with the fuzzy images of the characters as they jumped off of a bridge, spooked her. Her own scary images began playing in her thoughts as well. Without thinking she said her safe words out loud. "Stop. Reset." When she realized she said it, her face blushed. " Mia? Negative thinking?" She paused. "Yes but I'm ok." He was Familiar with this part of her, so he let it go.

They finished eating and she paused the movie to get some glasses of milk for the chocolate chip muffins. As she took the glasses out she had another image flash in her mind. It was the dream with the shattering glass. This time she said her words in her mind. She instead, pulled out plastic cups and filled them with milk. She put the cups on the table in front of Sebastian and sat on the couch, with her legs crossed and wrapped herself in her blanket.

The movie was near its end. Mia resituated herself, with her head on his shoulder and her legs tucked close to herself. "Pause the movie kid. I've gotta use the bathroom." Mia sat up and stretched and then refilled her glass.

When Sebastian returned, he tumble-dove onto the couch from behind it. "Seb, Do you want more milk or something while I'm here?" "No thanks." She returned back to the couch to find him sprawled across it. "Really?" She sat on top of his back, using the couch cushion as a footstool. "Mia, this isn't comfortable." Mocking him, she then laid flat across his body. "How's that?" "Very funny." He turned his body, dumped her on the couch and sat up. His face was all red. He pushed play on the movie, propped his pillow onto her lap and made himself comfortable. She put her feet upon the table and her hands on the back of her neck and leaned back against the couch. "Should we set the alarm in case we fall asleep?" "No, don't you remember that I told you that we don't have to be in until three." "Ok."

As the credits rolled, Mia looked at him and saw that he was sleeping. Remembering the Moon was now waning, she moved off the couch, trying not to wake him and went to her room to get some items that she needed to remove the negativity surrounding her. She closed her door, opened her window and looked out at her Moon. She went into her drawer and pulled out some Nag Champa incense, a blue candle in a jar and sage. "*Fuck!*" She said to herself as an image of Sage popped in her mind. "*Even more the reason to do this.*" She thought to herself. She wrote her intentions respectfully, on a piece of paper and held it over the flame of the candle. She pulled the paper back quickly, second-guessing herself. She had thought she had it backwards at first. To add a positive, the paper is placed under the candle. She lit the incense and placed it in its holder. She then, placed the piece of sage on a small dish and put them both on the windowsill. She picked up the paper and candle and placed the candle next to the other items on the windowsill. After repeating the words that she had written several times, she held the paper over the flame of the candle until it burned. When she could no longer hold it, she put it inside the candle. While waiting for the incense to finish burning, she gathered her clothes for work the next day and laid them on the chair. She lay on her bed sideway, so that she could see both the Moon and the incense. When it finished she put the things away, then closed and locked her window. She went back into the living room, turned the TV off, grabbed her blanket and pillow and shook Sebastian. "Seb. I'm going to bed. I'll see you in the morning." She kissed his cheek and went back to her room.

The milled sounds of the sanitation truck woke Mia up. She stared at the ceiling for a few minutes trying to focus her eyes from the Sunlight beaming in her window. There were a few ending words that she had forgotten to say the night before, with the incense. She was hoping it would take, anyway. She stretched herself, crawled out of bed and headed to the kitchen to turn the coffee machine on. She headed to Sebastian's room to wake him but he wasn't in there. She found him where she had left him, last night, still sleeping on the couch. "Sebby, It's noon. We have to go to work soon. I'm hopping in the shower now. The coffee is on." "Ok." He whispered. She showered, dressed and braided her hair into a ponytail. She grabbed her makeup to put it on in her bedroom so Sebastian could take a shower. "Sebbie! Get up. The showers all yours now." He rolled off the couch, onto the floor and then stood up. He popped his head into Mia's room. "Good afternoon." She laughed at him. "It's alive." "Barely." He dragged himself into the shower.

Mia watched the midday news in her room as she put on her makeup. She was waiting for the weather forecast, hoping for thunderstorms tonight so that she could re-do what she did last night because she knew that the energy from it would help. The weather finally aired and reflected an eighty percent chance, after the rush hour. *"JOY!"* She smiled. Sebastian peeked into her room. "What do you want for brunch?" "Chocolate milk toast with jelly and some grapes, please. "Ok."

He knocked on the door and brought the food into her room. "Thanks. I'm almost ready." "Ok. I'm gonna go wash the dishes. The coffee is on." "Great."

She scoffed down her food while putting her makeup and brush away, slipped her shoes on and grabbed her pocketbook. "I just have to make my coffee, Seb." "Ok. I'll meet you in the car." "Ok, deal."

They pulled up to the restaurant. Mia liked the shade of blue on the letters of the sign. "The Moonlight Restaurant." It was an unusual shade of blue. Its pigment was just before the hue of purple. This was her favorite shade of blue. The name is one reason why she had applied for the job, plus it was near the beach. The restaurant was at a light capacity when they arrived. In less than hour, the lunch crowd would begin to emerge, and then it would be nonstop until about three pm. An hour or so later, the dinner crowd would emerge. The Moonlight closes at eleven PM and re-opens at seven AM. They would both be working until closing tonight. Mia received a text but her phone was in her pocketbook so she wouldn't see it until she took a break.

The dinner crowd was finally dissipating. Mia was exhausted. There had been a party of thirteen just at the peak of dinner. She went to her pocketbook to get her cigarettes and phone. Along the way she made herself a cup of coffee and then went out back. She lit up and sipped on the coffee, savoring it. She had another hour of work remaining. She turned on her phone and saw a text from an unknown number. "Mia, This is Hunter. You wanted to know how I got my name. I am going to show you." Her eyes flared. *"Show me what? How the fuck did he get my number?"* She started typing. *"Fuck off ya freak…"* She decided not to sent it and deleted what she had typed. *"I'm not feeding into this shit."* She lit another cigarette and reread the message. *"I need to re-do my intentions the right way tonight. Obviously it didn't work."* Sebastian peaked out the back door. "Mia, come help so we can get outta here fast." She took another sip of her coffee and another drag of her cigarette. She shut off her phone and went back inside.

Mia cleaned off the tables and wiped the counters, while Sebastian was in the back doing the food prep for the following morning's shift. There were two more tables still eating and as soon as they leave, Sebastian would lock the doors. The manager had just left. As it got closer to closing time, Mia felt a little weakened from the warm sensation of the familiar spiritual pull. She walked over to her section of tables and cleaned them, collecting the tips that were left for her. As she turned around to walk back, she saw headlights glaring through the large glass windows. *"Fuck! More customers."* She thought to herself. She was cleaning the last table when she heard the door opening and paid it no mind until she heard it slam. The noise startled her. Sebastian heard the noise and came running out. She looked up and saw a few people slowly walking into the restaurant and dispersing down the isles of tables, without waiting to be seated. She couldn't see their faces because they were partially covered by the drooping hoods of their cloaks. *"Okaaaaay?" She thought to herself.* One by one, they continued to walk down the isles. The last person entered, closed door and stood there, scanning the area. He flipped off his hood. It was Hunter. Mia's eyes flared. *"He's fucking stalking me!"*

He looked directly at her with no expression on his face. Mia's jaw dropped. She ran behind the counter. The others split up, walking to either side of the counter. She ran to the back of the kitchen and slid under a counter. Sebastian yelled at them as he tried to block them from going in the kitchen. One of the taller ones punched him several times. The last punch had knocked him unconscious.

She whimpered, listening intently, holding a knife in her trembling hand. She heard footsteps approaching from different directions. One of them heard her shuffle and pointed at the cabinet where she hid. They assembled to either side of it and stood there, motionless. As Hunter walked towards the cabinet he called out her name in a low tone. "Mia." He paused. Tears ran down her cheeks. "Do you understand now?" Shivering with fear, she held the knife up higher, thinking about what he had said in the text. There was silence for a few moments and she listened intently for movement. He heard her whimpered sounds. "Mia, I don't like when you cry." Hunter saw her reflection in the glass door of a closet to her left. He stared into the glass and saw the knife in her hand. He gestured to Lucius to come to him. He whispered in his ear. Lucius put his hand in his pocket and walked over to Mayne and Emery, reiterating what Hunter had said. Emery and Mayne went to the edge of the cabinet. Mayne had an unloaded gun. They both looked at Hunter and then at the others. Mayne raised the gun, stepped in front of the cabinet and kneeled down, pointing the gun at Mia's face. Mia was just about to lunge the knife when she saw feet, but stopped when she saw the gun. Her pupils were blue. She wrapped her arms around her knees, holding the knife with both hands, pointed outward. Mayne stared at Mia's eyes, moved the gun closer to Mia's forehead and slowly edged her hand towards the knife. Mia was holding it tight and her eyes teared profusely. She let the knife go but did not come out. She whispered to Mayne. "Why?" As soon as Mayne had the knife in her possession, Emery moved in front of her, grabbed her ankles and yanked her out. The sudden jolt to her body shocked her. She screeched. Mayne held her down while Emery pinned her arm to the floor and stuck it with a syringe. Mia's screams echoed everywhere. Mayne continued to hold her down until she was no longer fighting. Mia was gasping and coughing until her cries weakened to whimpers. Hunter knelt down next to her and Mayne eased away. She lay on the floor, looking at him. She whispered again. "Why?" He wiped her tears and held her cheek in his palm.

"It was very rude of you to leave, Mia." She became dizzy. He put his hands under her arms and picked her up. Her head spun from the upward motion and she closed her eyes for a few seconds. He carried her through the kitchen as the others followed, passing Sebastian, who was still unconscious on the floor. As they passed by the tables, Zephyr threw a large heavy glass pitcher at one of the large, storefront windows. Its instantaneous, propagated cracks of the tempered glass spread and within seconds, it shattered. Mia flinched from the crash and opened her eyes. She remembered the shattered glass from her dream.

CHAPTER 6

PERCEPTION

Lucius opened the back seat door to Hunters truck. He placed her on the seat and wrapped the seatbelt around her waist. There were three rows of seats. The two back seat rows faced each other. Raine, Sage and Enya crawled in and sat opposite of Mia, with their backs facing the front of the truck.

Mia lie face down, drifting in and out. Emery, Lucius, Mayne and Zephyr drove their motorcycles back to the house. Mia felt the humming of the truck's engine. She opened her eyes and saw Enya directly across from her. As her eyes opened, her teardrops fell onto the seat. She whispered again, this time to Enya. "Why?" Enya turned away without answering. Sage felt badly for her. She felt she should at least warn her. "Mia?" Mia lifted her head to look at her. "Never make him angry." Mia closed her eyes.

About fifteen minutes later they arrived at the house, just as the others were taking their helmets off. Hunter exited the truck and walked to the back door. The girls jumped out and went inside. Mia lifted her head and watched as they exited the truck. Lucius approached him. "Do you need help?" "No. I'll be in later." He climbed in the back seat, locked the doors and knelt in front of her. Like a cornered cat, she swiftly pushed herself up and slid to the far end of the seat, away from him. Her eyes were half opened and alert from the fear of his presence. The sudden, and intense warmth that she felt caused her to realize that he had been the origin of this sensation all along. "Stop it." She whispered. It grew even stronger. "Release me." She whispered again. He remained, kneeling. "Mia, move over here." He patted the center of the seat. Trembling, she remained, holding her legs up against her chest. She felt him pulling stronger on her spirit. She cried and lowered her head down onto her knees. He reached over and pulled her by her waist to the center. She lashed out, intentionally scratching his face. He wiped his cheek and saw blood on his hand. He looked up at her and gently placed his hand around her neck. "Never...do...that...again." He enunciated. She gazed into his eyes, sobbing. He moved in closer and placed his hands on her thighs. He held her eyes captive within his cryptic stare, terrifying her with horrific images of his dark alchemy from days of yore.

An hour or so later, Hunter carried her into the house, wrapped in a blanket. Mia's puffy eyes and sweat-drenched hair disturbed those in the kitchen, rousing their disquieted curiosity. He walked into the big room and placed her on the couch, then proceeded into his bedroom. His room was the largest in the house. It contained a large cherry wood table, situated at the Northern point of the room, the focal point for their rituals. Calligraphy engraved along the edges of the table with various syllabary and rune symbols. The surface displayed an elaborate Pentacle, with its points highlighted with the colors of the respective Elements and their direction. The table was positioned below an unbreakable skylight ceiling. The Full Moon's glow against the table cast a scintillated reflection against the moonlight. Just below the Pentacle, was a sigil etched onto the table. It was created by Hunter and tattooed onto his right palm. Only he knew its meaning. The indigo blue marble floor was inclusive of a specific Italian artists spiral painting, imbedded in the same shade of grey to match the wall. No one entered this room unless Hunter was home.

He returned to her. Standing over her, he clasped handcuffs to a pipe behind the couch. "Mia. If you leave this couch, I will put those handcuffs on you. If you must use the bathroom, then now is the time." As she attempted to sit up, he grasped her arm to help her stand. She said nothing to him, wrapped the blanket wrapped around herself and allowed him to escort her to the bathroom door. Just as she pulled the door closed, he grabbed it. She looked up at him. "The door stays open." She walked in and looked at herself in the mirror. Her thoughts consumed her. *"Why?"* She blamed herself. With her negative thinking, she felt this wouldn't have happened had she done her protection ritual correctly last night, ending it with; So Mote It Be. She sat and looked to see if he was looking in. He wasn't. He was standing behind the door. She flushed, turned on the sink and splashed cold water onto her face. He pulled the door open and extended his hand. She looked up at him but didn't take his hand. She held on to the door, followed it to the wall, occasionally leaning against it. She grabbed onto the couch and sat down. "Can I have my clothes?" He didn't answer. She wrapped the blanket tightly around herself and lay down, facing the back of the couch. He stepped out of the room and locked the door.

He walked into the kitchen and saw the girls at the table. He grabbed a beer from the fridge. They looked at him in silence. He joined Mayne in the living room. She was watching TV and eating a sandwich. "Where's Mia and what kept you?" "She's in my room." Mayne looked at him, waiting for the rest of the answer. She grinned at him and turned back to the TV.

Raine reached for a snack and a drink from the fridge. "What the hell happened in the truck? He was out there for a long time." Sage looked at Enya for an answer. "Let it go. I'm going upstairs. I'll see you in tomorrow."

The lights in the room were dimmed. Mia turned and perused the room. She saw a shadow of someone pass by the door. It was Enya, going upstairs. She looked out the small window. It was set high on the wall. She saw the waning Moonlight beaming through it. She couldn't get off the couch and had nothing to work with. Within her thoughts, she repeated what she did last night in her room. It would have to be good enough. She requested the presence of her spirit guide and the North Winds to help lead the way out. She summoned the Element of Air to aid in any communication needed and the presence of Fairies to assist with the little things that she will need when she escapes. This time she ended it correctly with the correct ending: So Mote It Be. She continued to gaze at the window until she couldn't keep her eyes open any longer and fell asleep.

Mayne gathered her garbage and was heading to bed. "Later." Hunter nodded at her. He remained until the movie was over, shut the TV and grabbed his empty beer bottle. Sage and Raine were still sitting at the table. Sage had painted her nails and was waiting for them to dry. "Good night ladies." "You too." He entered his quarters and saw Mia sleeping on the couch, now facing the table. He walked up to her, knelt down and slipped his hands underneath her to pick her up. Her eyes opened partially when she felt him lifting her. He opened his bedroom door and placed her on his bed. He turned the lamp on and went into his bathroom, leaving the door open. She sat up and looked around him room. She saw a wide dresser in front of her, with some ritual items that she had been familiar with. Some she had never seen before. Hanging on the wall above the dresser, was a large encircled symbol, like the one on the back of her Moon necklace. There was a small table by the door, where his keys and other personal items were and a wall mounted TV lived above it. On the other side of the bed were two large silver knives, overlapped and imbedded into a wooden plaque. As she took this all into her mind, she noticed that the room smelled like the incense that she used at home.

The water stopped running and her attention was immediately drawn to the door. He walked out of the bathroom, and sat on the edge of the bed. He took his boots and socks off and stood up to remove his shirt. When he removed his jeans, she jumped out of the bed, panicking, then reached for the doorknob. His back was facing her as he sat on the bed. "Mia, do not leave this room." She immediately turned around. With her back against the wall, she slid down to the floor. He lay down under the sheets, with his arms behind his head, and looked at the wall in front of him. "Mia, do you see what is on the wall in front of me?" She turned her head to look at it again, but didn't answer. "What does that mean to you?" He paused for a second. "You have one on the back of your necklace." She just sat there, looking at him and thinking to herself. *"I don't know how the fuck he perceives it, but it's not the same as I do."* He turned sideways, with his elbow on the pillow and his hand holding up his head. "Mia, you had previously asked me about my name. I have now shown that answer to you. At the restaurant, you asked me, why? I am slowly exposing you to that answer, however, my question has not been answered." He looked at her, waiting for a reply. He laid his head back onto the pillow. "Mia. You have five minutes to get your little ass in this bed. It would be in your best interest to not test my patience." Three minutes had passed and she did not move. He sat up, staring at her. She jumped up, holding the blanket around herself tightly. He walked around to the other side of the bed and she jumped across the bed. She trembled, feeling her adrenaline pumping. She yelled at him. "It would be in your best interest to stay the fuck away from me!" His eyes flared. She was breathing heavily and waited defensively for his next move. Anxiety began to overrule her body. She ran into his bathroom and locked the door. Searching in the cabinets, closets and drawers, she looked for anything that she could use to protect herself. The only thing she could find was a glass on the sink. There was no sound coming from the other side of the door. She listened intently, wondering what he was doing.

He walked out of his room and went through the kitchen and into the yard in his underwear, passing Raine and Lucius sitting at the kitchen table. He returned with a sledgehammer. They looked at each other. "What the fuck is going on now?" Raine uttered.

He returned to his chambers, locking the door behind him and proceeded to his bedroom. Mia was standing at the sink. She wanted to open the door but assumed he was just standing on the other side waiting for her to do just that. The elongated silence and not knowing what was going on beyond the door, made her feel anxious. He lifted the sledgehammer over his shoulder and slammed it into the door. It protruded to the other side. Terrified, she let out a high-pitched scream. He ripped it out and slammed it into the door again. She screamed, hysterically at him. "STOP IT!" Her pupils were a piercing ice blue. In a feeble attempt to get a hold of herself, and calm her overwhelming panic, she focused her attention on one object. The closest item was the small glass on the sink. The terror she felt projected into the glass as she stared at it. The glass burst and its shattered fragments fell across the sink and onto the floor. The popping sound made her jump. She didn't understand how it broke on its own. He slammed it a third time. This time, at the doorknob, sending it flying into the tub. He kicked the door opened and found her standing in the far corner, by the closet. He saw the terrorized look on her face. His pupils were Red. He stood there, holding the sledgehammer, breathing heavily, with his eyes blazing at her. He held it up, pointed it at the direction of the doorway and whispered to her. "Now." She darted out of the bathroom, to the other side of the bed and sat on the top edge, next to the pillow. He left the room, locking the door behind him and returned the sledgehammer back to the shed in the yard, accidentally bumping shoulders with Emery, who was standing at the opened, sliding door. "What was that banging? Is everything ok?" "It is now."

He returned to the bedroom and locked the doors behind him. As he locked the door, he saw Mia was sitting in the same spot, against the headboard, with her knees against her chest. He climbed into the bed on her side and hovered in front of her. "If you challenge me again Mia, it will not end as well as I did this time."

She woke up the next morning, feeling sleep deprived. His occasional movement in the bed throughout the night continuously woke her. She needed to use the bathroom, but remained still at first, as not to wake him. She turned to look at him. He was sleeping on his stomach, facing her. She slid to the edge of the bed and felt him grasp her wrist tightly, pulling her back into the bed. "I have to go to the bathroom." He released her. She walked slowly, maneuvering around the debris. The door looked like a scene from an old horror movie. She slowly walked to the toilet. Her foot was irritated from a splinter she stepped on last night. She flushed the toilet and put the seat down so that she could look at her foot and pick it out. She got up to go to the sink and looked up at the clock on the wall. It was 11:47 am. She turned the sink on and washed her hands and face. Looking at herself in the mirror, she knew she had to bide her time until she could figure how to get out of this house. She brushed her teeth with his toothbrush and returned to the bedroom. He was sitting up in the bed waiting for her. He said nothing to her and walked into the bathroom. She leaned on the wooden footboard of the bed. Looking up at the symbol on the wall in front of her, she placed her hand on her necklace. The toilet flushed but he remained in there, cleaning up the debris off the floor. He picked up the doorknob out of the tub and turned the shower on to rinse any wood pieces into the catch screen at the drain. He placed a large towel on the floor, removed his underwear, stepped into the shower and closed the shower door. As he turned on the hot water he called out to her. "Mia, come in here." Mia cringed, but knew better than to ignore him. As she approached, she saw his blurred silhouette behind the glass. When he saw her, he slid the door opened and stuck his hand out gesturing for her to get in. She recalled what Sage had said and although she didn't want to go in there with him, she now knew what he was capable of when he was mad. She removed her blanket and stepped in. He slid the door shut. She stood under the showerhead, looking down, as the water ran through her hair. He lathered himself and handed her the bar of soap as he rinsed himself. She stood there, with her hands covering her breasts, as he washed his hair. When he finished he looked at her. "Mia, use the soap." She looked up at him. He took the bottle of shampoo, squirted it into her hair. He took the soap from her hand, and turned her around, facing the wall. He slid it over her neck, shoulders and arms, lathering it as he moved down her back, continuing down to her legs. He stood up, moved her arms out of the way and lathered her from top to bottom. She tried to hold back her tears. He moved her under the showerhead, allowing the water to cascade over her body. He grabbed her hands and held them against the wall above her head with a steely expression. She looked up at his face and saw the steady, emotionless expression in his eyes.

"You constantly defy me, Mia." She looked away from him, choosing not to fight him. She needed to gain his trust so that he would let down his guard and she could get out of this house. He kissed her fiercely, seizing her like a wolf consuming its prey.

He handed her a towel, dried himself off and went into the bedroom to get dressed. She combed her hair and sat on the bed, wrapped in the towel. He sat on the bed next to her and put on his boots. "We will go into the kitchen to get something to eat. After that I will be going to get a new door. You will stay in here until I return. Do you understand me, Mia?" She didn't answer him. "He repeated himself. "YES?" "Yes." She whispered. She put on the clothes that she had previously worn. She followed him to the kitchen.

Zephyr was sitting at the table, talking to Enya when they walked in. Mia sat next to him. Enya looked at Mia. "Do you want some coffee Mia?" She nodded. "Hunter?" Yes, Thank you." There's Kaiser rolls, butter, cream cheese and jelly on the table, thanks to Zephyr." "Yeah I made breakfast for everyone." Zephyr smirked. Hunter made his coffee and turned to Mia. "Eat." She picked up a roll and put jelly and cream cheese on it. He whispered into Enya's ear. "Get her a change of clothes." He sat at the table, across from Mia and took one of the rolls and buttered it. "Zephyr, I need your help to take the old door down and bring it to the store. They can measure the shit there." "No problem." "Thanks for the food." "You're welcome."

Enya returned with the clothes and discreetly handed them to Mia. "Go in the little bathroom over there and put them on." At the very east, Mia had expected a t-shirt and a pair of sweatpants, but instead she was given a two-piece set of PJ's and a pair of underwear. Hunter saw her look at Enya with a distraught expression on her face and raised his voice. "What's the problem, Mia?" "Nothing." She changed and returned to her seat.

"Thank you for making coffee, Enya. You are too good to me." Hunter said, grinning. He kissed her on the cheek. "I am, aren't I?" Mia ate half of her roll and was full. She sipped her coffee and looked out through the sliding glass doors, which led to the yard. She remembered where the front door was from the last time she was there, but was unfamiliar with the yard. "Are you ready Zephyr?" "Yeah. I'll go get my tools. I'll be right back." "I'll meet you in there." "Mia, are you finished?" "Yes." "Come with me." She rose from the table and followed him through to his chambers, to his bedroom. He pointed to the bed. "Sit." Zephyr returned with the tools and entered the bedroom. "What the fuck happened? I thought the door just cracked and split?" Hunter didn't answer. Zephyr got his tools out and helped him take the door down off the hinges. "Lets, carry this to the entrance of the big room first. I have to do something first, before we take it out to my truck." They picked the door up and placed it against the wall near the outer door. Hunter returned to his bedroom. "Do you need to use the bathroom?" "No." He walked to his dresser, went into the top drawer and returned with handcuffs. Mia saw them and looked up at him as he approached her. Tears filled her eyes. "Give me your right hand." He cuffed her to the bed and exited the room, locking the door behind him. Zephyr stood, waiting for him. "Where's Mia?" "She is in my room." They picked up the door and walked through the front door, to the truck.

Mia lay down on the edge of the bed, with her hand dangling off the side. Thoughts were racing through her mind. All of which result in leaving this house. The New Moon has passed and the Full Moon is approaching. She hoped to be out of there, well before then. She knew what she needed to do. She focusing on the four key words of the Pyramid and would plan her next course of action based on its foundation. She dozed off, letting her mind settle.

Zephyr shuffled around the radio stations while Hunter drove. "So, do share how this door was destroyed." Hunter grinned. "I told her to get in the bed. She did not. I gave her a five-minute warning. She ignored it. I walked towards her. She locked herself in the bathroom. I used the sledgehammer to open the door." Zephyr looked at him with a bizarre expression. "A little extreme?" "I made my point."

Hunter and Zephyr returned with the new door. When Hunter unlocked the door, he found Mia sleeping on the bed. They proceeded to the bathroom, carrying the new door and latched it onto the hinges. The hammering woke Mia, startling her. She sat up in the bed, watching them. As they began to clean up, Zephyr needed a hand vac. He looked at Mia. "Mia, can you go ask Enya for a hand vac?" Hunter answered for her. "She can't get up. She is cuffed to the bed." "You're one deranged motherfucker. I'll be right back." Hunter put the tools in Zephyr's tool bag and went in the bathroom to wash his hands. Zephyr returned with Mayne.

Mayne walked in sipping coffee. "I heard about the door." He turned to look at her with his eyebrow up. "And what did you hear?" Mayne sat on the bed, next to Mia. "Mia was a bad girl." The vacuum was turned on. Mayne turned the TV on and sat back on the bed against the pillows, flipping through the channels. Mia lay on her side, her back facing Mayne. In a mischievous mood, Mayne slowly moved her foot towards Mia and pushed her off the bed. Flustered, Mia stood up, holding back the urge to knock her teeth out. Mayne saw the handcuffs on her wrist. "Kinky, Hunter! Are you leaving anytime soon? No reason." She looked at Mia with a sadistic expression. Hunter walked up to Mia as she rubbed her sore wrist. He picked up her hand and looked at it. Mia implored, "Please make him leave." He laughed. "Make HIM leave?" He looked at Mayne, then Zephyr, smiling. Mayne turned onto her stomach, facing her. "Mia, Mia, Mia."

Mayne heard Enya calling out to her from the kitchen. She crawled off the bed, leering at Mia as she walked out of the room.

"What's up, Enya?" I need you to take my car and go get some groceries for me. I have a headache. Do you mind?" "No. Make a list cause I'll forget."

Sage came downstairs and greeted everyone as she went straight for the coffee. "Good morning, peeps" Enya smiled. "Sage, there's rolls on the table courtesy of Zephyr." "Great!" She sat at the table and took one. Emery came strolling in. Mayne was standing in the way of the coffee. He smacked her on her head. "Shift it." Enya handed her the list. "Where are you going?" "I have a top secret assignment for Enya." Enya smirked. "You're an asshat. It's a grocery list, Zephyr."

Zephyr walked past the kitchen to go downstairs and put his tools away. He briefly greeted them as he passed. "People." "Wait. What's with the tools?" Sage inquired. "A door needed to be replaced." He kept walking down the stairs. She looked at Mayne. "What door?" "Hunters bathroom one." "What happened to the old one?" "Go ask him."

Zephyr returned and was waiting for Lucius. Sage asked him what happened and he reiterated what Hunter had said to him, word for word. Sage's face turned white as a ghost. "Are they still in there?" Without waiting for the answer, she left the table and ran in there. She saw his door was opened and entered. "Greetings." She uttered as she stood at the entrance. Hunter looked up at her. "How can I help you?" He lay sideways on the bed, at Mia's feet watching TV. She looked at Mia and sat on the bed next to her. "Whatcha watchin'?" She glanced at Mia, then Hunter. He was watching the movie, intently. "One of the Titan movies." She leaned over to Mia's ear. "Never anger him. I told you that." Mia looked at him. "I need to go to the bathroom." He lifted himself off the bed and unlocked the cuffs. She walked into the bathroom, only closing the door, halfway, to appease him. He sat in her spot, next to Sage and inquired about her day. "What are your plans for today?" "I'm going to go to an outdoor concert later, with Raine...and You?" He grinned. I will be spending the day with Mia." Mia cringed.

When Mia returned, she saw them on the bed. Hunter looked up at her and stood up. She walked over to her spot and sat down, holding her wrist up. He put the cuffs on her and crawled back onto the bed. Sage stayed to watch the end of the movie. As the credits began to roll, Hunter went into the kitchen to get beer. Mia watched him leave the room then turned to look at Sage. Sage looked at her and took a deep breath. "Mia, never challenge him in any way. His rage goes from zero straight to ten and he is merciless. He will always find you and will do it in the most deranged way." Listening to her words, Mia felt anxiety setting in and she looked away from her, hiding her tears. Hunter returned and stood at the entrance of the door, holding a beer and a soda, gesturing for Sage to leave. Sage stood up and walked out of the room. "Enjoy your concert." He shut the door, took a swig of beer and locked it. Sage looked back when she heard the lock turn and then returned to the kitchen. Mia was leery of him as she stared into his eyes. He stared back as he sat himself on the bed, next to her. He handed her the soda. "We will be watching movies together the entire day, Mia." With her hand trembling, she took a sip of soda. She spoke to him in a timid voice. "What will it take to keep these cuffs off of me?" He paused for a few seconds, and then answered her. "They will be removed at the end of each movie." She had a puzzled expression on her face. He reached into his pocket, unlocked the cuffs and removed it from her wrist. She sat up, shook her hand and massaged it. "Sit on the edge of the bed, with your feet on the floor." He placed his beer on the nightstand and knelt directly in front of her. Placing his hands on her knees, he slowly slid them to the top of her thighs. "Take your shirt off for me Mia." She looked at him and now realized what he had meant. He watched her as she pulled it over her head. "Stand up." As he removed the rest of her clothing, she clenched her jaws and tried to restrain from crying.

Mayne returned from the store with bags of groceries. "I brought some beer, too." Enya started unpacking them. "Thanks for going." "Where is everyone?" "Zephyr is in the living room waiting for Lucius. They're going to the movies. Sage and Raine are upstairs getting ready to go to a concert. I however, will unpack these groceries and go back to sleep. My headache is still throbbing." "You should smoke. It makes your headache fade. You know where I keep it. Help yourself."

Mayne went to the living room and sat on the recliner. "What movie are you going to see?" "I can't pronounce the name of it. It starts with an M. You wanna go with us?" "No thanks, I'm takin' a ride on my bike. I'm meeting some friends at Gwen's bar." Sage walked into the room and threw herself across Mayne's lap. "How do I look?" "Where ya goin?" Raine and I are going to the outdoor concert. Answer the question." Mayne answered her, smiling with gritted teeth. "The answer is, you should get off my lap or we're both going nowhere." Sage pursed her lips. "Perv!" Zephyr laughed and politely complimented her. "You look wonderful." "Thank you." She got up and walked to the back yard to wait for Raine. As she passed through she peeked through the glass door of the big room and saw Hunters bedroom door closed.

Hunter flipped through the TV channels while he waited for the sequel to begin. Mia was in the bathroom trying to collect herself. She had told him she needed to use the toilet. She once again, left the bathroom door ajar. When she returned, she sat on his side of the bed and lay down sideways, facing him. She was hoping he wouldn't put her in the handcuffs. When the movie began, he grabbed her wrist and slid her over to cuff her again. He lay aside her with his head on the pillow facing her. She felt his hand slide around her waist and pulled her against his chest. He reached for the remote and pressed play. She watched the movie while thinking of how to gain his trust. She glanced at the clock. It was 4:20 pm. She knew she had about an hour and a half until he uncuffed her again.

He paused the movie halfway through, put his jeans on and stepped of the room. She sat up and took a sip of her soda and then stood up to stretch. An idea had dawned on her as she started to put her clothes back on. Much like swimming out of a rip tide, she needed to go with the flow, rather than against the grain. If she began to show him what he wanted to see: subtle signs of her acceptance, then her way out would be dependent on his trust. She knew that she needed to appear convincing. She crawled back into the bed, covered herself with the sheet. Hunter returned with the drinks, handed her another soda and restarted the movie. She lay sideways with the pillow under her head and swiped one of his elongated pillows to hold against her stomach and between her knees, knowing he would notice. He leaned against the backboard and drank his beer. The movie played on for twenty minutes and then he paused it to use the bathroom. When he returned, he gazed across at the silhouette of her body. The sheet wrapped tightly, allowing the light from the TV screen to trace every curve of her body. She knew he was looking at her when she heard him suck his teeth. He slid onto the bed and pulled her against himself. The movie was near its end. The road was revealing itself to her. It was time.

CHAPTER 7

QUID PRO QUO

She felt his hand move away from her. He reached into his pocket to get the key to the cuffs. She stopped his train of thought when she grasped his hand, pulling it back over her waist. She slid her hand slowly over his forearm, down to his hand. She gently pushed back, enticing him as she pressed herself against him. He seemed to feed right into it. His leg wrapped around hers and his arm tightly clutched her waist. Her body responded to his every touch. She kept her hand on his, following it as it slowly drifted past her stomach to her thigh, grinding her body against his. He pushed his leg under hers and thrust inside her with carnal force. She moaned loudly. Feeling her body tremble, she felt as if he was depleting every ounce of energy she had. Her nails dug into the sheets as he unceasingly thrust into her. Mia gasped trying to catch her breath. The sheets were soaked from the sweat exuding from their bodies. He collapsed beside her, breathing heavily. He depleted her of all of her strength.

She pulled the sheet over herself, curled up on her side, trying to collect herself physically and mentally. She was hoping he would uncuff her, but she didn't think he would just yet. He said nothing to her as he put his jeans back on and left the room. She wondered why he had suddenly left. Her speculated curiosity left her teetering on the two results: Did he fall for it or did he realize what she was doing.

He knew.

He went to the kitchen for another beer and something to eat. Enya ran downstairs to find Hunter. She had just received a phone call from Mayne. She was in jail. "Hunter, I need your help. Mayne was in a fight and she's been arrested. She's ok, just a broken finger. Can you go get her at the precinct?" "Yes. What happened?" "I don't know. It never fucking ends with her." He handed his beer to her. "Finish this for me." He got up and returned to his bedroom. Mia heard the door unlock and was on edge. He didn't look at her. He put a shirt on and sat on the edge of the bed and put his boots on. Mia turned onto her back, to look at him. He took his keys and wallet and locked the door behind himself.

She had just given herself to him, Willingly, so to speak and was perplexed by his avoidance. She needed his reaction in order to go forward. She lay down closing her eyes, recalling her ritual from last night and went through the thought process once again. She got up and put her clothing back on, including the shirt, to an extent. She crawled back onto the bed and managed to wrap herself in the blanket.

Hunter walked into the kitchen and grabbed two bottles of water from the fridge. Enya was taking more ibuprofen, Her headache returned from the stress of her sister. He reassured her. "Don't worry. This is what she does." Enya looked at him with a disgusted face. "We'll be back. Go back to sleep." He attached the bike-trailer to his truck and took off.

Hunter arrived at the precinct and approached the front desk. The bail was $400. He paid it and waited for her in the waiting area. After about twenty minutes she was released. She collected her things and walked towards Hunter. "Thanks. I'll pay you back when we get home." He paused to ensure that she saw his simpered expression. They walked out of the building. "I need to get my bike. It's at Gwen's bar." No problem. We will just put it in the trailer and I'll drive us back. I can smell your breath." "Great." They jumped into the truck and he handed her a water bottle. "What happened?" "I don't wanna talk about it." "If you say that to Enya she will think you were wrong." "Is your finger broken?" "No, just sprained badly. I'll get over it." "Whose face received that punch?" She sneered and shook her head. "The loser, obviously." "Well you'd better think of a good story for Enya."

They arrived at the bar and Hunter hitched the bike onto the trailer. Hunter had been contemplating about Mia and her little game. He had an impish notion and his demeanor roused Mayne's curiosity. "What are you smiling about? Me again?" He paused for a second. I would like you to do something for me." "What?" "This will be something that you will want to do. When we get back home, I want you to follow me into the big room and wait for me to call you in. I am going to blindfold Mia and let her think it's me. Does that cheer you up?" Mayne's avid smile was evident. "I'm in. What happened that led to this?" "If your not telling, then neither am I."

They pulled up to the house and Hunter walked around the back of the truck, to unhinge the bike "Leave the bike there. I'll get it off the truck later." They walked in the front door and Mayne went upstairs. "I'll be right back." "Be quiet. Don't wake up Enya." "Good thinking."

Hunter unlocked the door to find Mia sleeping. He sat on the edge of the bed and removed his boots. He then, went to his dresser to get a blindfold and another set of cuffs. Spooked, Mia felt the bed move and sat up. "Do you need to use the bathroom?" He asked in a low voice. "Yes." He walked over to her, unlocked the cuffs and she ran into the bathroom. She really had to go badly. When she returned he was sitting on her side of the bed waiting for her. Her relief turned back to anguish. She walked back to the bed and sat.

He placed the blindfold over her eyes. "Move to the center, Mia" He held the cuffs in one hand and reached for her wrists. He put them above her head, re-cuffing her wrists, separately. Her anxiety reflected in her breathing. "Why are you blindfolding me? I don't like this. I'm afraid." "I enjoyed what you did earlier, Mia. I wanted to repay you with the same kind of pleasure that you gave me." He left the room, closing the door behind him. Mayne had just entered his chambers. "I'm getting some beer. Do you want one?" "Two. Thanks." "Wait here."

When he returned, he unlocked the door, gestured to Mayne to remain silent and locked the door behind them. He bit the cap off of the bottle, drank half of it and placed it on the table. Mayne stood at the foot of the bed, looking at her. He crawled onto the bed, kneeling over her and grasped her head, deeply kissing her. "Are you ready, Mia?" He crawled off the bed, reached for his beer and pulled up a chair. Mayne crawled onto the bed, and hovered over her. She kissed her stomach and slowly moved upward. Her teeth grazed her breasts and Mia's body twitched as she continued to taunt her. She slid her hands over her thighs, stopping just before her panties. Mia felt her tongue on her naval. Mayne grasped the lace of her panties with her teeth and pulled them off of her. Mia panted. Mayne's tongue followed along her inner thigh, stopping just before Mia's groin and then she looked up at her, watching her moan and tremble with anticipation. Her fingers clenched tightly when Mayne's tongue grazed her. Her relentless teasing made her manic. When she felt the warmth of her mouth, she moaned loudly, her back arching from the unbridled sensations of pleasure. Mayne's versed talents and attention to detail was something that Mia had never experienced before and Mayne also knew that this was her first time. When Mia felt her fingers invade her she moaned in bliss. Hunter watched, grinning perversely as he waited for the right moment to remove the blindfold. He rose slowly from the chair, quietly walked over and hovered over her. He looked up at Mayne, then back at Mia and pulled the blindfold over her forehead. Mia's eyes opened and saw Mayne above her. Her high-pitched scream could have shattered glass. She became physically violent, trying to kick her. Her pupils were blue. With a callous expression, Hunter moved directly in her face. His gritted teeth, exposed like a rabid dog. The malice within his eyes glared its wicked and feral intent, sending chills right through her soul.

"Don't fuck with me, Mia. I fuck back!"

He walked over to the dresser, returning with a syringe. When Mia saw him with it she hyperventilated. He jabbed it into her arm and she screamed violently. He left the room, leaving her there with Mayne and slammed the door behind him.

Hunter went to the kitchen, fetched a few more beers and walked out to the yard. Not being a fan of the Sun, he preferred the serenity of the night-time. He dragged one of the lawn chairs into the shade, sat and lit a cigarette. Raine and Sage returned from the concert. They changed into their bathing suits, grabbed beer and went into the yard. "How was the concert, girls?" Raine replied in a high-strung voice. "Oh Hunter it rocked! There were fire-works too!" "Yeah and some girls were throwing bras on the stage!" Sage added, still riled up from the show. He smiled. "How did you get home?" "We hitched." Hunter frowned. "I told you not to do that." Sage defended and justified their choice. "No, it was ok. We passed on a few until we saw some girls who we had met at the concert. They pulled over and offered us a ride." They put their beers down and jumped in the pool. "Hey, we heard Mayne was arrested. What happened?" "A Fight." Raine shouted in jest and raised her fist. "The bitch needs anger management!" Sage chimed in. "Ya think? Hey, where's Mia?" She's in my bedroom." "How long until she can come hang with us?" "It's up to her."

Mayne joined them. "Ahhh the person of the hour. Who won?" "Who the hell do ya think, won, Raine!?" "Oh yeah? Well what happened to your pinky finger?" "It's sprained." Mayne walked over to Hunter with a sublime smirk and sat next to him. Hunter laughed. "Well?" Mayne replied in a low voice. "That was epic." "Did she give you any grief after I left?" Yeah. Her threats were entertaining. But, then she mellowed out." Hunter rose from the chair and went inside. "Good night all."

He returned to his room and locked the door behind himself. Mia turned her head away from him. He reached over her, unlocking the cuffs. She rolled onto her stomach and pulled the sheet over herself, weeping silently. He sat on the chair, removed his boots and went into the bathroom.

Although she had faith in what she believed in, she was feeling as if what she did was not strong enough. She waited for the road to pave itself for her once again and knowing this, gave her hope, Love and Light.

He returned from the bathroom realizing that he had forgotten his cigarettes and keys in the yard. He walked out of the room to go get them, locking the door behind him.

Lucius and Emery were sitting at the bar with Mayne. Hunter grabbed his keys and cigarettes and approached the bar. Mayne was showing off her sprained finger to them. He shook his head and walked back into the house. He stopped in the kitchen, grabbed a donut and another beer and walked back to his bedroom.

In Hunter's absence, Mia darted into the bathroom, before he returned. She returned, spying his half filled beer on the table. She walked over to his dresser, opened the top drawer and reached for one of his syringes. Listening for him, she emptied the syringe into the bottle, ran to the bathroom, wrapped the syringe in tissue paper and threw it in the garbage. *"OK Road. Keep leading me."* She thought to herself. She took her clothing from the floor, and hid it under her pillow. Feeling confident, she climbed back into the bed. *"I'm gonna fuck you back even harder!"* She whispered.

She closed her eyes when she heard the door unlock. He walked in and removed his socks and jeans. He sat on the bed, flipped through the channels and lit a cigarette. He glanced over at her, then stood up to get the ashtray and remembered his beer. She heard the bottle scrape on the table. He drank a couple of swigs while watching a late night talk shows. He took another drag of his cigarette, put it out and finished most of the beer. He climbed into the bed, under the sheets. He decided to leave her alone for the rest of the night and turned on his side to watch the show. Mia was facing him in the bed. She waited about ten minutes before she peeked at him.

She felt him shift in the bed, and listened to the TV, waiting for a few sets of commercials to air. She peaked through her right eye, the one closest to the mattress, so he wouldn't see it. He was sleeping. She waited another ten minutes just to make sure he was in a deep sleep. She tested it by slowly sitting up. If he woke, she would just say she was going to the bathroom. He didn't. She quickly put her clothing on. With her eyes on him, she slowly walked over to the door. Her nerves were on high anxiety at this point because if he woke, there would be no way out of this. She unlocked the door, turned the knob gently and walked out. She ran to the outer door of the big room and stopped to listen for voices. She heard them in the yard. She peeked to see if anyone was in the kitchen and darted to the front door. Her heart was pounding. She saw a pair of slip on sneakers and a jacket and put them on. Then unlocked the front door and ran for her life. Thankful that no one had been on the street to see her, she quickly turned up a side street. She ran to the main street and flagged an approaching cab. She gave the driver directions to her apartment.

When she arrived, she instructed the driver to wait for her because she needed to get a few things and be driven to another location. Mia realized that she did not have her keys, so she knocked on the landlord's door. When he answered, he was a little annoyed because it was late. She apologized and asked him to unlock the door. He went to get the key. When he returned she told him to give her two minutes so he could lock it again. She ran in, put a pair of shorts on and grabbed a duffle bag, shoving a weeks worth of cloth-ing and other essentials into it. She took her ATM, credit card and some cash from her drawer and left.

She tossed her duffle bag onto the back seat and climbed into the cab. "Can you take me to the nearest, decent motel?" "Yes." They drove for about fifteen minutes, passing a few up because she didn't like the looks of them. They were kind of seedy looking. They finally parked in front of a well-known Inn and she paid the driver, respectfully tipping her for waiting, grabbed her things and walked inside. The desk clerk was on the phone. He gestured that he wouldn't be a minute, so she placed her things on the floor and waited.

"How can I help you?" I'll be staying for a week or so. Can you give please me a good rate? "Certainly. I can give you a weekly rate for three hundred and eighty dollars." "Can you lower the price please? I don't know when my cousin is getting out of the hospital and we are far from home." She made up the story. "I'll see what I can do." He stepped away to speak to his manager. She looked around seeing that the place was clean and not too shabby. "If you pay now, I can do two-hundred-ninety. That's the best I can do for you. "OK." She handed him the credit card. "Just one week for now. If he gets out sooner, will the price be lower?" "Yes. We wont charge your card until you check out. We just need it on file." "Thanks. I really appreciate this." He handed her the key. "It's room four-twenty." "Thank you."

She grabbed her things and walked down the hall, observing and inspect-ing the general ambiance of the place. She entered her room, turned on the lights and locked the door behind herself. Looking around the room, she placed her stuff on the table, peeking under the bedspread and in the bath-room to ensure that it was clean. She turned on the TV and threw herself onto the bed. She was exhausted and hungry. Thankfully, the place she chose had a bar-restaurant. Although the food was limited, considering the time of night, she was able to get some bar menu food and a soda. She returned back to her room and watched TV while she ate. After a sip of soda, she grabbed a change of clothes and took a long needed shower. She stood in the shower, with her hands against the tile wall and let the hot water run over her achy shoulders. After an extended shower, she put her clothes on, almost crawling into the bed, when she remembered to reiterate what she had been doing, nightly, with her ritual items at this time. She opened the window, lit her blue candle, incense and sage, thanking the powers that be for guiding her and asking for further protection, going forward. She doused out the items and closed the window. She was about to climb back into bed, when she realized that she had forgotten to say the proper closing words. She ran back to the window and added the proper respectful ending to her words. She climbed back into bed. She would try Sebastian in the morning.

CHAPTER 8

CARA MIA

M ia walked along the beach near her motel, quite a distance from that house where she had been at week ago. She had no intentions of returning anywhere near the apartment for a while, for fear that Hunter would return. She needed to get in touch with Sebastian. She walked around looking for a store to by a pre paid cell phone. She found a local electronics store and purchased the cheapest one. As she exited the store, she took a deep breath, inhaling the fresh air as she gazed at the sky. It was an eye-catching Sunset. As dusk slowly took over the sky, Mia watched as the beachgoers gathered their things to leave. Facing the Sunset, she felt its remaining rays spread warmth over her body. She gazed at the rays as they slowly faded into black. In the far distance the silhouette of someone was approaching in her direction. The Sun's remaining glare distorted her vision. As this person neared, she was able to make out some features. Her radar was up. He had shoulder length, dark hair and a strong physique. As he walked, it became apparent that he was headed towards her. Feeling apprehensive, she sat up and looked at him. His eyes were a striking shade of Green and his expression was serene.

"I hope that I have not disturbed your Zen." He smiled as he looked at her. "My name is Mason." He knelt down and extended his hand to hers. When she lifted her hand to him, he kissed it. She blushed. No one had ever done this to her. It left her feeling fluttery. "My name is Mia." "Ahh, Cara Mia". He flirted. She giggled. "I saw you on the beach, alone. You should be careful of predators. Do you have mace or something to deter them if one should surface?" At first, she laughed out loud, thinking about the madness that she had been through. Then she apologized and responded. "Why? Are you a predator?" He grinned. "No, but you need not fear me. I'm here visiting my family. I just arrived his morning and I thought I would take a walk on the beach. Since I don't live near one, I thought I'd step away and take advantage. "Where are you from?" "A few places, but I'm currently living West of here. Nevada." She watched his eyes as he spoke to her, trying to feel his aura. His eyes and words seemed to fuse into a soft symphony of solitude. He seemed very charming. "What leads you to the beach on this fine evening, Mia? Do you live here?" She paused to think. She didn't want to tell him why she was here, about the house and all the drama that went with it. "I like to come here at dusk to relax." "I was just about to get a coffee from the refreshment stand. Would you like to join me, M'Lady?" "Yes, thank you." He extended his hand and pulled her up. They walked over to the stand. There were picnic tables there. "You sit and make yourself comfortable. How do you take your coffee?" "Cream and sugar, please." He returned moments later. They chatted for a while, comparing their likes and dislikes. He reached into his pocket to pull out a pack of cigarettes. "Do you mind?" "No. Not at all." He offered her one and she accepted.

He pointed to the Full Moon. "Beautiful, isn't she?" "Yes. Do you follow the Moon_Mason?" "Religiously. It affects everything Mia." "Yes." She smiled. She looked at her watch and had realized she wanted to try to call Sebastian. "I've got to go now. Thank you for the coffee, Mason." "You're welcome. I'll be here for at least a few weeks. Perhaps we'll run into each other again. Good night Mia." He gently reached for her hand and kissed it once again. She giggled and blushed once more. "Goodnight Mason."

He watched her as she walked away, waited a few minutes and resumed his beach stroll. Mia was a little enchanted by his presence. He seemed to have an inviting, positive aura about him. She felt safe in his presence.

As she approached her motel, she pulled out her cell phone and tried calling Sebastian again. He didn't answer. She called a close associate from work and they said he had called out sick today. She briefly filled the person in on what had happened and then asked for the number that he had called from and they reiterated the same cell number that she already had. She then asked if he called again, to please call her immediately. She tried his cell again but it went to voicemail, so she left him a message. "Sebby please call me. I'm ok. I'm at a motel. I'm really worried about you. The restaurant said that you had called them, so please call me or text me." Frustrated and confused, she put the TV on and watched it with the phone right next to her. She eventually fell asleep.

She woke up the next morning, recalling a glimpse of an image from her dream. It was of a wolf, standing on an incline, perusing the acreage before him. She also remembered there was a West wind. The next things that came to mind was The Full Moon tomorrow night and the word; "predator." She thought of the wolf for a few moments and was distracted by a text from Sebastian.

"Mia, I'm ok. I was in the hospital. I had a concussion but I'm fine. Are you ok? Where are you and what happened? I don't think it's safe to return to the apartment or work and you should do the same. I'm staying with a friend. Please delete our texts, just in case. I'll keep in touch." She was relieved. She replied, letting him know where she was and that she was staying put until she heard from him and then deleted it. She hopped in the shower and headed out to get a roll and coffee. She was thinking about Mason's alluring charisma while sipping her coffee. She decided to walk around and maybe go see a movie later.

The evening was approaching. She headed back to the beach, hoping to see Mason again. She passed by the beach café, where they were last night but didn't see him. She gazed across the ocean. There were a few thick clouds floating by, infused with a little grey. She walked onto the sand, took her sneakers off and let the ocean soothe her feet, while she connected with the Element, Earth in order to ground herself. She closed her eyes and focused on its cool and gentle embrace while taking in the salty ocean air and thinking about its potential raging glory. From its gentle waves at low tide, she thought of how they now felt upon her feet. Her simulated thoughts of apocalyptic clouds approaching in the distance brought forth her beloved memories of thunderstorms. Imagining the characteristics of the rising tides, the gusts of wind, the ebb and flow, deviating from its now serene extant, to its feral and unmerciful fury, were a means to how she could tune into the true essence of the Elements and become one with them.

There were less people on the beach, because it had become cloudy and cool. She looked in the sky for her Moon and saw its glow, peeking through the clouds. Tomorrow night it should be full. She loved how close it seemed as it first ascends above the horizon. She could almost touch her. Her favorite Full Moon was the Harvest Moon. Thinking about Sebastian and work, they may let them go for the sudden absence. They probably would have to get new jobs and move elsewhere.

As the Sun set, Mason appeared in the distance. "Mia" He called out to her and she smiled. She walked towards him and they sat at a table that he had already claimed. As she approached him, he was smiling at her. He was wearing denim jeans, a white collared shirt, unbuttoned midway and sandals. She noticed that he was also carrying a blazer. On the lapel, was a symbol, one she did not recognize. She stole a glance at his chest and hoped that he didn't notice. He extended his hand to her, took her hand in his kissed it. "Good evening Mia Amore." She giggled. He escorted her to the table, where their coffee's awaited them. "Cream and sugar, correct?" He said smiling. "Yes."

"So how was your day Mia?" "It was very relaxing. I saw a movie earlier and walked around for a while. How was yours?" "It was very positive and productive. I helped my brother set up his yard for an outdoor family function tomorrow." "Sounds like you worked hard today." "It does, but not with him. There's always some kind of mischief going on there." He chuckled. "What was your movie about, Mia?" "It was an animated movie about a fish named Nemo. This theatre shows older movies. "I think I remember that one." "You've seen it? " "No I didn't, but I did see the previews on TV." "How did you know I would be here?" "I took a chance and when I saw you walking over, so I went ahead and fetched our coffee's." "That was very thoughtful of you." "It was my pleasure." He placed his blazer on the table and Mia reached to touch the pin on the lapel. "What does this symbol mean, Mason?" "I belong to a men's club. We host charity events. This is our symbol." He showed her his matching ring. "That's nice. It looks expensive too. What do you do for a living?" "Construction. Ironically so, I'm a stone Mason." "I've looked up my name. It means "mine" and "goddess", but I doubt there's any open positions for this." Mia giggled. "What is your occupation, Mia?" "Oh, it's nothing special. I'm just a waitress at a restaurant." "That's nothing to frown upon, M'Lady. It's honest days work. It's a hard job and you're on your feet all day." "Yeah. The tips are good and I get to meet a lot of nice people. What kinds of things to you build at your job?" "I cut stone that's used for many different purposes.

"Mason, I may only be here for another day or so. Would you like to keep in touch?" "I would like that very much. Mia." They exchanged phone numbers and then chatted for a while. "Mia, I need to return to my brothers house. Will I see you tomorrow evening?" Smiling and entranced by his green eyes, "Yes, Mason. You will." He stood up, looking for her hand. She giggled and lifted it. "Until tomorrow Mia."

She watched him as he walk into the distance. He slipped his hands into his pockets. She noticed the Moonlight outlining his body, his walk, his swagger, sweetly intriguing her. He made her feel like she was in an old-fashioned love movie. The way he kisses only her hand, not expecting more and the way he addressed her, made her feel that he was honored to be in her presence. She finished her coffee and brought another one with some snacks to bring back to the motel. She decided to look for a new apartment and jobs for her and Sebastian. When she returned, she sent him a text. "I'm looking for a new apartment and jobs for us. Delete this text." She searched through the Internet, on her phone, found a few leads and jotted them down. She would call them tomorrow, after he texted her back.

She woke the next morning and immediately checked her cell phone. There were no messages. She hopped into the shower and got coffee and a roll. She went ahead and made some phone calls to the leads she had found. The jobs were filled already. She left a message for a potential apartment and went about her day, wherever the Universe decided to take her.

She made her way back to the beach just before dusk and walked along the shore with her feet in the ocean, picking up a few seashells along the way. She felt a few gusts of wind and lifted her arms up to let it encircle her. A few people were playing Frisbee with their dog. She watched them for a few minutes. As the Sun set she wondered where Mason was. The Frisbee people eventually left. She walked a little further into the ocean, allowing the surf to tickle her feet. Another gust of wind came and she lifted her arms to embrace it once more, then suddenly felt two hands slide over her waist. It was Mason. She gasped. "Mia, you must pay attention to everything around you. I could have been a predator." She nodded and laughed nervously. "Hi Mason. You sir, are very stealthy." In one hand he had a small blanket and the other was a cup holder with two drinks. He handed her the drinks and placed the blanket on the sand. "What's this about Mason?" "I decided to make this evening a little different. I brought two blue raspberry fruit smoothies instead of coffee. I also brought a blanket so that we could sit under the Full Moon together." Her face lit up. "Mason, that was so incredibly thoughtful of you." He placed the cup holder onto the sand, then took her hand in his, kissed it and helped her to sit. He sat next to her and handed her one of the drinks. "Why blue raspberry Mason? Is that your favorite?" "Yes. I was hoping that it was yours, as well." "It is. I also like that it leaves my tongue blue. I like sticking my tongue at people and freaking them out." They laughed. "How was your party?" "It's still going on and will for the whole night. I snuck out to see you, Mia." He gazed into her eyes and smiled. His eyes and old-fashioned charm captivated her. His sincerity felt genuine. He was sweeping her off her feet and she was letting him. She took a few sips and stuck out her tongue. "It's Not blue yet Mia. Take a few more sips." She smiled took another sip, swashed it around her mouth for a few seconds and flashed her tongue at him again. "Yes, Mia, it's blue now." She giggled like a child.

Twilight eclipsed the blue skies, revealing the true brilliance of the Full Moon. "Mia? Look at her?" He pointed to the Full Moon." "Mason, you referred to the Moon in the feminine gender. So do I." He smiled. "Perhaps we have things in common." Mia smiled, curiously wondering if he followed the phases as she did. "She's extra large and bright tonight." "That's because tonight is the Super Full Moon." She was impressed, but remained reticent, preferring to listen for now. He proceeded to tell her about his views of the Moon phases. She listened intently, sensing the fervency in his eloquence, his words, conjuring unimagined images of the Moon's glory within her mind and his seductive eyes, bewitching her with no mercy.

When he finished speaking, he noticed that she was still staring at him as if he hadn't stopped. He gazed at her, affectionately. "Mia, may I kiss you?" Mia was taken by surprise with his question. Her heart fluttered with delight. "Yes, Mason." He gently ran his fingers through her hair, his bedroom eyes hypnotizing her. She felt the increased rhythm of her pulsing heartbeats. He kissed her so slowly and passionately. Chills traveled throughout her body. As she put her hands on his shoulders, he swiftly embraced her, kissing her ferociously. She was deeply entranced by him. He stopped just to look at her face, the blood rushing through their bodies like two wild animals in heat, aching, panting and eager to consume each other. He held her face in his palms, the sweat on his face, his steely eyes, his salacious breath, steady, his lust for her, so adamant, it frightened her. "Mia, I want you to think about what I am going to ask of you." Puzzled, she questioned him. "What is it, Mason?" Mia, I want you. I want you now, under this Full Moon. I realize that we have only just recently met. If this is not the direction that you wish to pursue with me...if you're not ready, then I will stop." Mia was astonished by his words. She broke into a cold sweat, opened her mouth but was speechless, suspended in time, trying to think of the right words to say. "Think Mia. Make the right decision for you. I don't want you to have regrets." She gazed into his warm eyes, searching for the answer.

She felt a little lightheaded, saw her hands shaking and chalked it up to nerves. Her eyes followed the outline of his shoulders. She traced her finger along his strong arms and placed her hands against in his, interlocking her fingers with his and stared into his eyes. "Yes, Mason." He slid his hands around her, never losing eye contact and slowly laid her onto the blanket. He kissed her so sensually, so deeply, at times she thought he was trying to reach her heart with his tongue. His seductive scent, enticing her, peaking her senses and adding to their collective madness. She ached for him, his every touch tingled her skin, as if Fairy dust had touched her. He stopped and gazed into her eyes before he went further. "Mia?" He whispered. I ask again. Are you sure?" "Her steely eyes burned through his. "Yes, Mason. I'm sure."

The ambiance of the Moonlight enhanced the plankton's glow along the shore, casting glistening highlights across the oceans surface. Even the grains of sand seemed to shimmer in synch to the queue to the plankton and the gentle ocean waves. She laid her head upon his chest, tuning into the frequency of his heartbeat. It too, seemed to be in synch with the oceans waves. He felt her shivering. He covered her with his shirt and pulled her closer. "Mia, you will catch cold if I don't warm you up." She sat up with the shirt wrapped around her. It was big enough for her to wear as a dress. "Would you like to get dressed and drive over to my family's place?" "How far away is it?" He pointed in the direction of that house. "It's a few miles down the road." "She felt compelled to tell him a seriously edited version of why she didn't want to go near that area. "Mason, I need to tell you something. I don't want to go near that area because about a week ago, some people were stalking me. I am afraid of them." With a stern expression, he sat up and looked at her. "Mia,

I am glad that you shared this with me. You have nothing to be afraid of. I can tell you that they will not lay an eye or hand on you without my knowing about it. If they do, I will be there within minutes. You have my cell phone number. I promise this to you. You have my word. Who are these people and at what house are they residing?" She felt comfortable enough to tell him at least that. Mia. Put your clothes on. I don't want you to get sick." They got dressed. She still had his shirt on but it was unbuttoned. He buttoned it. "But this is your shirt, Mason." "Mia, you are more important to me. Finish your drink. Lets just lie down under the Moon and the stars for a while. I will walk you home later." She finished her drink and once again flashed her tongue at him. He smiled. "Come closer. I can't see." He really just wanted to kiss her again. She snuggled with him. "It's blue Mia." She giggled and then he kissed her.

The day had caught up with her. She laid her head on his chest, closed her eyes and allowed his heartbeat to lull her to sleep. He lay there staring at the stars for a little while longer and then turned to look at her. She was sound asleep. He whispered to her. "Mia?" She was silent. "Mia?" He whispered her name a little louder. She didn't budge. He nudged her and there was still no response. He shifted his body, as not to wake her, and gently picked her up. When she felt movement, she opened her eyes. When she realized that she was in his arms and being carried, she placed her arm around his neck. She didn't even ask where or why he was carrying her. She was safe, in the comfort of his arms and that was enough for her.

He walked off the beach and placed her on the back seat of his truck. He was bringing her home to his family's house, as he had secretly intended.

His brother is Hunter.

CHAPTER 9

BEWITCH ME ONCE

Hunter remained inside his room waiting for Mason to return with Mia, while the others waited in the yard, indulging on a few liquid spirits at the bar and singing along to the music playing. ♪*...You fly so high...*♪

Mason arrived at the back yard's entrance, carrying Mia. Enya rushed over to unlock the gate. Those at the bar stood up. Mason gestured with his lips for their collective Silence. He carried her into the house, through the kitchen. He walked into Hunters room, placed her on the couch and covered her with a blanket. He approached his brother's room, knocked lightly before he opened the door and peeked in to let him know he had arrived with Mia. Hunter walked out of his bedroom and approached her. She was still in a deep sleep. They quietly stepped away from her. "She should awake shortly. She's small, so I did not need to put that much in her drink." Mason assured him. "I'm going upstairs to change. I'll be back before she wakes."

The others began to enter the house to get ready. Hunter walked to the back of the big room and sat in the large chair. Zephyr walked into the room and stood next to him. Mayne entered and sat in the floor next to Mia. If she tried to leave, she would stop her. Lucius walked into the room. He saw Mia lying on the couch and walked quietly to the back of the room. Mia shifted and moved her arm over her forehead. Seeing this, Mayne waved her hand to get their attention. Mia sensed a change around her. It didn't smell like the beach anymore. She smelled an unfamiliar scent, of something burning. She opened her eyes and at first saw the dimmed light above. Blinking her eyes into focus, she saw a familiar skylight. She no longer sensed Mason. Startled, she turned to see Mayne sitting on the floor before her. Enya and Raine walked into the room and shut the door. Mia felt like a trapped cat. As she looked around the room she recognized Emery, Lucius, and Zephyr. They moved aside, simultaneously revealing Hunter, sitting in the chair and looking directly at her. Her pupils were blue. She felt overwhelmed with anxiety and was prepared to fight. The rage was generating within her like she had never felt before. *"FUCK! Where is Mason."* She thought to herself as she searched in her pocket for her cell phone. Of course it was not there. The first thing that she had assumed was that they had attacked him as they did, Sebastian.

Hunter greeted her with a sadistic grin. "Hello Mia. Have you seen the Full Moon this evening?" She stared at him as he spoke to her. She became enraged but chose to reply in an even tone. "What the fuck do you want from me?" No one answered. Mia kept looking at the door hoping Mason would arrive. She kept scanning around the room, to ensure that no one moved. Her fingers were spread apart, digging into the cushion of the couch. No one moved or spoke. They waited on Mason.

Mason peeked over the bannister as he walked down the stairs and saw that the door to Hunters room was closed. He knew Mia had awoken. He slowly opened the door and walked in. "MASON!" Mia screamed his name and ran to him. Tears ran down her cheeks as she jumped into his arms. He wrapped her within his robe to give her the feeling of security. "My sweet Mia. I kept my promise. I told you that I would know if they as much as set eyes on you and that I would be here within minutes." He put his hand on her chin and lifted it up so he could see her face. "Mia, you belong to me." He kissed her vehemently. He opened his robe and turned her around to face them. "Mia, you belong to us." She looked at them in horror and then spotted

Hunter, callously leering at her. He rose from his chair and approached her. Her face reflected nothing short of terror. She backed herself against Mason.

"Mia, this is my brother." Hunter stood inches from her. With tears of distress, she spun herself around, grabbing Mason by his arms. "Mason, what the fuck are you saying to me?" He placed his arms on her shoulders. "Mia, don't use that language. I told you my family was preparing for a celebration. I never once lied to you."

In a defensive, panicked state, she stepped away from Mason. Her animosity was evident and written all over her face. Hunter inched closer to her and Mason moved beside her whilst the others scattered themselves around the room. Her pupils were blue, once again. She felt like something inside her was about to detonate. Hunter kept his eyes locked on hers. Her body was trembling as she slowly continued to walk backwards without losing eye contact. His eyes were dark and lethiferous. He slowly reiterated Mason's words. "Mia, you belong with us." His voice went through her like an icicle. Her eyes reflected the rage and fear that she felt. She shouted at him. "FUCK YOU! DO NOT TOUCH ME!" Her rage caused the lights in the room to flicker. Everyone witnessed this and knew that it was her energy that was causing this. Hunter saw her eyes and was prepared to subdue her if she were to become out of control. No one moved and the silence in the room seemed like an endless void. Mason reached for her shoulder and she jerked away, looking at him with vengeful hatred. As she pulled herself away from him she noticed a sword on the wall, next to the couch. With the exception of Mayne, no one was nearby. Pumped up with panic stricken adrenaline, she darted towards the sword, yanked it off the wall and held it up, near her head. The sword was heavier than she had anticipated. She struggled with the weight of it and almost lost her balance. With her back against the wall, she could clearly see anyone who would attempt to approach her. Hunter's pupils were Red. He would not risk anyone's safety. He turned and walked back to his bedroom. Mia watched as he walked away and then quickly turned her attention back to everyone else. Her heart was racing and she was breathing erratically. There was intense Silence as Hunter walked back into the room. Mia turned to watch him as he approached her. He stopped midway. His eyes were piercing hers and her eyes remained steady on his. She refused to show him fear. He pulled a small rifle out, from behind himself, pointed it at her and pulled the trigger. A dart flew out of the barrel, stabbing her just below her shoulder blade. As she reached to pull it out, her muscles quickly became weakened. She dropped the sword and looked up at him with tears in her eyes. She grabbed onto the couch and Mason ran over to catch her before she fell. He lifted her, carried her over to the table and placed her onto the table. She was aware of her surroundings. The sounds, smells and sights were distorted and blurred. Mason remained beside her. She watched him pull the hood of his cloak over his head and then gazed at his face. He placed his palm on her cheek and noticed the tears running down her cheek. The others walked towards her, all donning similar robes. As she looked around, she saw that these people were now surrounding her. She lay on the table unable to move. She was still wearing Mason's white shirt and her denim shorts. Hunter sat in his chair, summoned for Sage and whispered into her ear. Sage returned to the table. She removed Mia's shoes and began to unbutton her shirt. Mia looked up at her. Sage consciously avoided looking at her. Mia turned and looked up at the ceiling, silently crying.

Hunter rose from the chair and walked over to the table. The only light in the room was the Full Moon, beaming through the skylight. He stood beside her and she looked steadily into his eyes, noticing the Moon's reflection in them. She had seen this look when she first met Hunter. It was almost the same look in his eyes when they had returned from the restaurant and were alone in his truck. This time it was fiery.

As Mason held her hand loosely, he felt it trembling. Zephyr stood on the opposite side of the table and held her other hand. Hunter leaned closer to her, with his face an inch from hers. He placed his hands on her cheeks and looked into her eyes. She couldn't turn her face away from him. As she continued to gaze into his eyes, they became more and more esoteric. Her Sprit became spellbound. Her hands stopped trembling and went limp. Mia heard whispers that seemed to be in synch with each other. She couldn't interpret what was being said. He placed his hand on her stomach and then walked to the table's far end, below her feet. Feeling listless and hazy, she disengaged from everything and stared at the Moon through the skylight. The chatter continued for several minutes, eventually becoming white noise to her. She felt hands grasping her feet. As she continued to look up at the Moon, a dark shadow slowly crept up over her, eclipsing her view of the Moon. She gazed to either side of herself and saw them encircled around her but they were not looking at her. They were looking up as they chanted. When she looked above herself, she saw Hunter staring down at her. She was consumed by the glare of blue in his pupils. He spoke to her, in his deep, eerie voice. "My eyes reflect to you, what I see in your eyes, Mia."

The chanting slowly dissipated as the others exited the room. The blue light from his eyes blurred her vision, as if she were staring into the Sun and she was surrounded by a sensation of overwhelming warmth. The Moonlight was once again in her vision. She felt his hands sliding slowly away from her feet and up along her calves. His shadow shifted over her again, like a veil blocking the Moon. As he hovered above her, he slid his hands into hers and held them down above her head. She felt his fury and strength rush in and through her like the wind and static of a ferocious storm. He seized her body, mind and spirit. Her screams of ecstasy fed his stamina. She pulled her hands free and she banefully dug her nails into his arms. From a defiant state to complete submission, her body was responding to his every move, rising to meet him. The heated and unforeseen strength within her, escalated. She grasped his shoulders, her nails painfully digging into his skin. He felt and saw the uncontrolled Element of Fire blazing within her and reflecting in her eyes. He grasped her wrists, holding her down with one arm and felt the unusual strength of her hands as she pushed up against his. His adrenaline fed off of her fervid sounds. He became merciless. At the height of their un-harnessed energy, he struggled to hold her still. Her strength challenged his. He embraced her tightly as she cried out.

He felt her trembling in his arms as he carried her to his bedroom. He placed her onto the bed and lay beside her. She quickly pulled the blanket over herself, without taking her eyes off of him. Not a word she said to him while she lay there, quivering and holding the blanket tightly near her chin. He reached over to her and placed his hand on the side of her face, whispering his spine-chilling words to her. "I will always find you." He grinned, maliciously. He rose from the bed and stepped into the bathroom, leaving her to fester in his alchemistic words. She did just that. Her anxiety layered itself within her, growing in its intensity. She focused on his words, how she so foolishly fell for Mason's sleight of hand and succumbed to Hunters will. What perplexed her most was Hunters peculiar alchemy. He made her feel, see and experience things that were not of the scope of her realm. She knew the anxiety was not irrational and was, in fact, justified. The sound of water running caused her to clench her teeth and sent her into a panic. She grasped the blanket and slid herself upright, against the bed's backboard. The sound of the bathroom's turning doorknob had the same effect on her as a scratched chalkboard. As he exited the bathroom, he wiped his mouth with his sleeve and stood at the foot of the bed. He leaned in, placed his hands on the bed and peered at her for a moment. Gaping at him like an eagle, she clenched the blanket at her neck. Her seething adrenaline enabled her to strike him if he so much as touched her. She watched him closely while he walked to the opposite side of the bed. He sat on the bed against the headboard and inhaled sharply before he spoke. "What did you see Mia?" The pitch of his voice was deep and spectral. He waited for her reply. She continued to stare back without answering. His patience grew short. "Answer the question." He smiled, banefully. "No." His eyes flared, reacting to her defiant answer. Leery of his next move, she shifted to the edge of the bed and he lunged toward her, tightly grasping her upper arm. Her feeble attempt to swing at him was intercepted. He gripped her wrists and pulled her in against himself, piercing her eyes with his and she squealed and writhed to no avail. He grasped her jaw and berated her in a rigid tone. "Let me be clear on what I expect from you. If I ask you a question, you will answer. If I tell you to do something, you will comply. If there is something that you need, you will ask me first. I will dictate everything that you do. Heed my words. There will be repercussions if you challenge me." His words spiraled her into a fiery rage. With tears in her eyes, she held her furious stare at him and struggled to free her wrists. His grip was so painfully tight that her fingers tingled. She wanted to spit in his face, but refrained. Instead, she replied to him in in a sharp voice. "Do you want your answer?" "Yes." With a snide expression, she arrogantly whispered her enunciated answer to him. "Fuck...you!" He remained silent for a few moments. With his teeth gritted, he made a sucking sound through them and smiled maliciously. "Fuck me? I believe we have already covered that." He released her wrists and backhanded her across the face. She fell hard, onto the bed. The sudden blow to her face left her head and vision spinning. The wind was knocked out of her and she struggled to catch her breath. Her face was flush and the mark he left on her cheek was as red as her rage. She coughed and wept as she lifted herself up. She sat against her legs and wiped her face. Her hand came away from her face streaked with blood. When she had realized her lip bled, she gazed up at him with a hell bent stare. He knelt inward, grasping her chin tightly and giving her another command. "The way that you speak to me will change as well." He slid off of the bed and walked over to the dresser. She looked around the room and saw lamps on both nightstands. She jumped off of the bed, grabbed one and pulled the cover off of it. She cracked the bulb against the nightstand, brandishing it at him. He charged at her like a wolf claiming his next meal. He slammed his hand around her neck and dragged her over to the armoire, thrusting her against it. She held onto his wrists, trying to peal them off but his fingers would not budge. Her face was red and she gagged, gasping for air. He reached into the top drawer and jabbed her arm with a syringe. He released his grip on her neck and she fell against him, holding onto his shirt. She wailed against his chest. As her body began to weaken, he lifted her up and placed her back onto the bed. He pulled the blanket over her, placed his hands on either side of her and hovered over her face. He smiled. "Goodnight Mia."

He climbed into the bed beside her and wrapped his arm around her waist. Her body was listless. She stared at the ceiling, sobbing silently, thinking about this man who lay next to her and of her careless answer to his question. Immersed in these thoughts and the labyrinth of madness she was traveling through, her mind began to drift into a spiraling esoteric trance. He ran his fingers through her hair, watching her intently until her eyes finally closed and she was in a paradoxical sleep.

Within the dimensions of her dream, she floated pendulously, through brilliant waves of color and sound. Feeling the delicate plushness of that which carried her, she peered beneath herself to see its consistency. While cascading down this tendrillar blue wave, a blur of Green began to reveal itself, indicating the end of her sliding vortex ride. The transition from the wave to the Green entity was seamless. When she perused the area she realized that she had landed on a verdant grass field and noticed a pond to her right. She stood up and walked over to the body of water, watching its aberrant shimmering ripples. Standing at the waters edge, was the origin of the moving water. The ponds surface was strewed with frogs, floating on lily pads. A bizarre and sudden surge pushed them closer to her. The first thing that she had noticed was their peculiar eyes. Each frog's set of eyes depicted a different color. Scrutinizing each one, she became spooked by the one thing that they seemed to be doing in synch. They held a collective, uncanny gaze at her. As each lily pad touched the water's bank, the frog it carried, leaped onto the grass and sat before her. As she stepped back, they, in turn, leaped forward, holding their fixed and glassy gaze. She sprinted a few yards away and stopped to look back at them. Their collective leaps continued, as the gathered and fell in line at her feet. Unnerved by their ludicrous behavior, she ran away from them as fast as she could. A sudden brisk gust of wind blew about, causing leaves and other debris to hinder her sight. Unaware of what stood ahead of her, she slammed into a brawny entity. The sudden collision dazed her for a few moments. Feeling herself being embraced by this piliferous being, she opened her eyes to see what it was that held her, but it spun her around and held her tight, without giving her a chance to see itself. There, in an obverse and barrier-like stances, stood the Frogs. Their eyes reflected an increased effulgent hue, casting their continuous fixed stare upon her. Her futile struggle to break free left her wailing in its grip. As she focused on their gaze and the tight grip restraining her, the anxiety shifted to raw panic. Her voice erupted into an ear-piercing scream, emitting visual and vibrating sound waves and causing the leaves on the trees to flutter. The air and sky seemed to warp in view, as if she were looking through a kaleidoscope. Her scream echoed through time, carrying into the world that she slept in, inevitably waking Hunter. Her scream did not startle him in the least. He had been watching her from within her dream. He shifted himself to his side, observing her. Her hair and skin were soaked with sweat. Holding an orphic stare, he placed his hand on her stomach, feeling and listening to her oscillated breathing. His touch pulled her back into the reality surrounding her, shifting her attention to him. "What did you see Mia?" His haunting voice and peculiar question left her at a loss for words. She lay there, unsure of how to answer him, knowing that if she did not answer, he would become angered. He inhaled sharply, smiling and she took that as a sign and replied with a half-lie. "I'm not sure." He gently picked her hand up, held it to his lips and kissed it. "I think you're sure. I know what you've seen. I want you to tell me." He moved her hair off of her forehead. "The events within your intense dream caused you to wake up screaming. You're sweating." "Why do you want to know about my dream?" "I know about your dream. What I want to Know is how you have interpreted what you have seen." She had yet to decipher this, however, when she did, she would not tell him. "I saw Frogs. Each frog had a different colored set of eyes. They followed me and I ran from them. Then something large and furry grabbed me and forced me look at them. That's when I screamed." She paused for a few moments. "I don't know what it means." She pulled her hand away from him. "How do you know about my dream and why do you want to Know how I've perceive it?" She stared at him while wrapping the blanket around herself and then proceeded towards the bathroom. He stood up, cut her off at the foot of the bed and tightly embraced her from behind. She struggled to break free from his tenacious grip. He turned to face the wall, where the dresser stood and whispered into her ear. "Look up." He held her chin upward, to look at the symbol on the wall, above the dresser. "The answers you seek are always in front of you, Mia." She held her necklace in her palm, comparing its quinary symbol to the one on his wall. He reached into her palm and picked up her necklace by the chain, sliding the Moon pendant to his fingertips. He turned it around to show her the back of it. "This is the same symbol that is on the wall in front of you, Mia." As she glanced up at the wall, she recalled having this one sided conversation with him before. He had pointed out that her necklace was the same and had asked what the symbol meant to her. She stared at the symbol on the wall, noticing several pewter Frogs, arched, just beneath it. Frozen in a moment of déjà vu, she thought of the dream she had just experienced and was aware that a frog can walk through both worlds. She recognized the symbols in front of her. Focusing on the feel of his embrace, the comparison of the two realms now felt surreal to her. She shivered. The thought of him walking through her dream chilled her to the bone. He had noticed that she was as still and immersed in thought. He released her and turned her to face him. Her face was pale and emotionless. He placed one hand on her shoulder and the other on her cheek, possessing her eyes with his. "I am sentinel." His words reaffirmed her perception. His stone-cold eyes remained fixed on hers. She felt him looking within her spirit and sensed that every feeling and thought that she had, was visible to him. His invasiveness frightened her. She wanted to pull her eyes away from his, but couldn't. His eyes were steely and bewitching. "Lets go back to bed." His words broke the silence and the release of his spiritual hold on her as well. She looked down at the floor, trying to collect herself as he slid back into the bed. Without looking at him, she walked into the bathroom, closing the door behind her. She sat on the chair, silently crying. His commanding words continued to repeat themselves within her thoughts. She wiped the tears from her face and felt a stinging pain. When she looked into the mirror she saw the welted reminder of his feral temper on her cheek. She splashed cold water on her face and searched around for something to apply to her wound. There were no first aid supplies of any kind. Toilet paper and other general toiletries were stored under the sinks cabinet and the closet contained only towels. She dreaded the return to the bedroom. Further delaying the inevitable would only result in his inquiring presence. She took a deep breath and opened the door. His eyes were fixed on hers. He smiled at her. "What kept you?" "I was looking for something to put on this cut." She pointed to her cheek. He grinned. "It will heal." She climbed into the bed, slid under the blanket and lay on her back. He un-crossed his arms from the back of his head and turned to face her. She could feel him staring and resisted the compulsion to look back at him.

The Moonlight cascaded through the window, casting silhouettes of light over her face. He saw her staring at this light and watched her intently. She stared at the Moonbeam and allowed her light to encompass her. A few tears ran down her cheek while she spoke the Goddess, within her thoughts. *"Why have you abandoned me?"* Her tears turned into a reticent weep. She knew that on the night of the Full Moon, it was all about respecting and thanking her, the Moon. It was not a night for Moon ritual requests.

"Goddess, I know that this is your night. I'm terrified. Please lead me out of here."

As she closed her eyes, the tears fell down the side of her face. She pulled the blanket up to her neck and crossed her arms tightly around herself. He slid his hand over her waist, pulling her closer. She twinged from his touch. He turned her around to face him and placed his palm on her cheek. She felt peculiar warmth exuding from his hand and was tempted to look at him. His eyes frightened her, so she resisted the urge. Then she heard him take a deep breath. "Goodnight Mia." He clasped his hand around her wrist. She didn't move a muscle and now wouldn't be able to move without waking him. She lay there wide-awake, looking around through the Moonlit darkness of the room and listened to the distant sounds from the other rooms.

A breeze ruffled the curtains, swaying their silky fabric like the flow of the ocean's waves in a storm. Although the window was facing the foot of the bed, the breeze seemed to have sought her out. The smell of the sweet night air flowed towards her, descending over her like fog encompassing the ground. Mia inhaled, taking in the scent as it flowed over her face. To her, air was a strong Element of communication. She believed this was the beginning of a message from the Goddess. She closed her eyes and immersed her mind with its gentle gusts, picturing herself rising up from the bed, unnoticed and merging with it. She slipped into a deep meditative state, not allowing a muscle in her body to so much as twitch. The air continued to stream over her face, eventually lulling her to sleep.

A strong gust of wind blew against her as her eyes opened within her dream realm. Within this trance, she found herself driving fast on a motorcycle, alone on a highway. A pertinent song played on the radio. ♪Bat outta hell♪ The dashing white lines and lights on the highway became streaked blurs. There were no other vehicles on the highway and the enticing scent of sweet freedom in the wind fed her need for speed. The highway was hers and hers alone. The brilliance of Full Moon lit her way and no one could stop her now. There was a large red sign up ahead and its words slowly came into her focus. It read: *"DON'T STOP"* in large white letters. Every few miles, the same sign re-appeared, burning its baleful image within her mind. Although she had no intention on stopping, the repeated message seemed more than aberrant to her. The sign remained in the back of her mind, only to be trumped by the exhilarating feeling of freedom taking its precedence. The scattered stars displaying across the enchanted midnight blue sky were as endless as the highway. The end of the song played its baneful lyrics and its spectral ending melody compelled her to slow down. She stopped and stood on this eternal highway. Her feet barely reached the ground. She hopped off of the bike, parked it and walked a few feet ahead of it. A cold, brisk breeze blew against her face, sending chills down her spine. The cold body of air lingered, causing her to shiver. The sound of rustling leaves emanated from the wooded area to her right. When she glanced over to look, the eyes of an animal peered out at her. She ran back to the bike, jumped on and kicked back its kickstand. A wolf emerged, stopping just a few feet away from her. Its pearly blue eyes were fixed on her. As she reached in her pocket for the keys, it snarled, revealing its vicious, saber-like fangs. Her hand remained steady in her pocked, watching the wolf for any change in expression or twitch of its body. When it stopped growling, she slowly pulled the key out of her pocket while maintaining her arm at her side. The weight of the bike was beginning to take its toll on her muscles and her leg spasmed. The involuntary reflex from the pain moved her leg and spooked the wolf. It lunged at her, knocking her and the bike to the ground. The wolf stood with its front paws upon her chest, growling malevolently and intimidating her with its fangs. Its vicious eyes subdued her, piercing through her soul and making its feral alpha status clear to her. Nose to the wind, the frigid wind fluttered the wolf's fur, distracting its scent driven attention, redirecting it to the Full Moon. Its blaring howl echoed through the night sky, summoning the collective howls of wolves hiding in the shadows. She wept. The visceral sound of their chimed voices reached an unearthly pitch, waking her from the dream.

She woke, wild eyed and gasping for air. Hunter opened his eyes to see her shivering in a cold sweat. She glanced at him. His sinister laugh and wicked stare petrified her. He took a deep breath and with malicious intent, he howled. She panicked, realizing that he had been in her dream once again. With a hell bent rage, she jumped onto his chest, grasping his hair, tightly. "WERE YOU THE WOLF?" Her rage was so intense that she cried tears of anger. His steely expression and silence frightened and frustrated her. He grasped her shoulders, tossing her onto her back and then pinned her to the bed. "No." He held her there for a few moments, staring into her eyes. His harshness startled her. She didn't dare question him any further on this.

She watched him walk into the bathroom and then curled up under the blankets, staring at the window as the radiance of the rising Sun began to peek through the curtains. She heard the shower water running and realized that she needed to use the bathroom. She wrapped the blanket around herself and she snuck in, undetected. In a subversive mood and a facial expression to match it, she flushed the toilet and ran out. Standing just outside the door, she listened for a few minutes. He said nothing. She lay back on the bed, listening from there. When the shower stopped running, she looked towards the door and listened in anticipation. After a few minutes had passed, he came out of the bathroom and walked passed her with a towel wrapped around himself. He didn't look at her. He dressed himself and then stepped out of the bedroom, locking the door behind him. When he returned, he had a change of clothes for her, in his hand. "Come into the bathroom." She looked up at him, but didn't move. "Why?" She whispered. He raised his arm and pointed to the bathroom. "NOW!" His loud voice went right through her, causing her to jerk. She slid out of the bed and ran in. He tossed the clothes on the sink and pulled the chair in front of it. "Get in the shower. Do not use the hot water." She looked at him as if he were certifiably mad. "No! It's too cold. "Then it will suck to be you." "Why are you doing this... just because I flushed the toilet?" "This is not a debate. Get in." She stepped into the shower and grabbed the sliding door to shut it. He caught the door before it closed. "This stays open. You are not to turn on the hot water. Do you understand me?" He stared at her, waiting for her reply. She knew better than to avoid his question. She replied with another defiant remark. "I understand. If you think I'm gonna take a cold shower, then you must be fucking high." He laughed. "Wrong answer." He reached in and turned the shower on, aiming the showerhead directly at her and she stepped away from its cold aim. He stepped back and sat on the chair. "Do as I've asked or I will do it for you. Choose now." His impassive expression showed her that he was not going to continue to entertain this game with her. She cringed, glancing up at the showerhead and darted into its cold streams, squealing. She stepped away and lathered herself from head to toe. With a deep breath, she moved into the stream again, squealing louder. He laughed again. "Suck it up, cupcake." Irked from his comment, she was about to tell him to fuck off, but decided to keep her mouth shut this time. She turned the shower off and covered her private parts with her hands. Shivering, her teeth chattered when she extended her hand and spoke to him. "Towel, please." He stood up and handed her one. She winced at him. "Are you happy now?" "Has my point been made clear?" "This isn't over." He raised his eyebrow and grinned. "I'm always ready for your feeble challenges." He handed her a change of clothes. I will be in the bedroom. Get dressed and comb your hair. The blue toothbrush is yours."

She looked in the mirror. The wound on her cheek was no longer visible. She knew that this cut could not have just disappeared overnight. Then she remembered the bizarre warmth that she had felt from his hand last night, when he touched her cheek. She put her clothes on, brushed her hair and teeth and returned to the bedroom. He was sitting on the bed, against the headboard, watching the television. "The cut on my cheek is gone." With an accusatorial stare, she waited for him to reply. He smiled and then made that annoying teeth-sucking sound that always made her feel uneasy. He shut the television off. "Come over here." He gestured for her to sit. Leery of him, she sat at the far end of the bed. "Mason, Zephyr and I will be away for a day or two. Each person in this house will be watching you. In my absence, you will answer to Mayne, who will be made aware of the rules that we've discussed." He stood up and put his boots on, then arched over the bed with his face an inch from hers, and put his hands on her knees. He squeezed her knees tightly, ensuring her undivided attention. "I expect you to heed these rules, Mia." He grabbed his cigarettes and cell phone from the dresser. "Lets go. We're having breakfast now."

She followed him into the kitchen and stood against the refrigerator, watching him. He grabbed two mugs from the cabinet, turned the coffee machine on and raided through the assortment of coffee pods. "Which flavor do you want?" She stepped over and pointed to one of them. "Sit at the table." She sat against the wall on the bench side. The blinds on the glass door, which led to the yard, were not completely closed. The Sun peeked through, in between the slats. The smell and sound of the coffee brewing wafted throughout the kitchen. He placed the sugar and milk on the table and handed her the coffee. "What do you want; Eggs or cereal?" "Eggs." He opened the refrigerator and grabbed the eggs and bacon. He tossed some bread into the toaster and proceeded to cook. The essence of the bacon drifted through the house. He placed the plates, forks and butter on the table and turned on the kitchen TV. She crossed her arms on the table and lay her head down. She was scared and wanted Sebastian. She was worried about him. The last time she saw him he was on the floor at the restaurant, unconscious. She knew there was no way he would be able to find her, even if he was ok. She was alone and being held hostage by these people. She thought about the last two dreams and tried to interpret them. She recalled the entity that held her and the Frogs that surrounded her. She then remembered the recent dream with the wolf on the dark and cold highway. She shivered with the thought of those images. She only had vague ideas of their meanings. Her attention was distracted when she heard someone walking down the stairs. She lifted her head to see who it was. Mayne walked in, peered over at Mia and stepped over to the stove. She inhaled, taking in a whiff of the bacon. "You're makin' me breakfast?" He smiled. "I will." She made a cup of coffee and turned to look at Mia as she took a sip, then walked over to the table. She sat next to her and slid into her, rudely pushing her over with her hip. Mayne stared callously into Mia's eyes as Hunter reiterated to Mayne, the rules that he had previously dictated to Mia. Mia returned the stare, challenging her to show her that she was not afraid of her, even thought she was, in fact intimidated. He served the food and sat at the table, looking at Mia. "Mayne is as feral as I am. The difference between her and I is that she lacks the ability to think, prior to acting on her rage. She is relentless. If you challenge her, you will not heal as quickly." Hunter looked directly at Mia's lips and cheek, grinning. Her suspicion of him was now confirmed. She kept her eyes only on her food, refraining from looking at Mayne or Hunter, for that matter. She felt that the words that he had used to describe Mayne's demeanor, were meant to frighten and constrain her. She took them with a grain of salt. When he leaves, she would intently look for a way out of this house. She knew that there was always a weak link.

Mayne's elbow accidently touched her and Mia concurrently slid herself over an inch. Mayne stared at her for a few moments, then pulled her back next to her and wrapped her leg over her lap. "Please move your leg off of me." Mayne smirked. "No." Mia made a futile attempt to push her leg off, but Mayne tightened her leg muscles. Hunter looked at Mia and then questioned her in a sharp tone. "Is there a problem?" Mia looked at him. "Yes! He won't take his leg off of me." Hunter glanced at Mayne and laughed. "He..."

He couldn't hold back his laugh. "He likes to harass people." Irritated, Mia huffed. "Please move your fucking leg off of me now! I'm not asking again." Mayne gave her an icy look and then dismissed her idle threat. "What time are you guys leaving?" "Midday. Mason and Zephyr are still sleeping." Mayne's antagonistic attitude towards her, made her irate. She slapped her hands onto Mayne's thigh and dug her nails into them. Mayne squinted and hissed from the sharp pain. She dropped her fork and grabbed Mia by the neck. Mia let go but Mayne did not. Gasping for air, she struggled to pull her hands off but she couldn't budge them. Tears flowed from her eyes. When she stopped struggling, Mayne let go. She lay on the bench, coughing and crying, trying to catch her breath. Mayne slid off the bench to refill her coffee, saying nothing to her. When Mia calmed down, she sat up and took a sip of her coffee. Her face was reddened and her eyes were filled with tears. She didn't look at either of them at first. Hunter stared at her, tapping his fork. Mia watched his fork and then slowly shifted her eyes to meet his. Saying that he warned her would have been inane at this point. His frigid look was sufficient.

Mayne leaned against the counter perusing the mess that Hunter created whilst cooking breakfast. "Ya know, Enya's gonna be pissed about the bacon grease all over the stove." Hunter leaned over the back of his chair. "I cooked. You clean." "Oh so that's how it works. You're erroneously singular in that statement." "How so?" "Mia ate too." "True. You can clean the stove and Mia will clean the dishes. Fair enough?" He turned to look at Mia and smiled. "The two of you can bond." Mayne took another sip of her coffee, smiling nefariously at her. Hunter lit a cigarette and tapped Mia's plate. "Finish your breakfast, then you can help Mayne clean up the kitchen. Understood?" Mia pushed the food around on her plate. "Yes." She looked up at Mayne and made a snide comment to her. "Keep your paws to yourself! Understood?" Mayne grinned. "Well maybe if we bond, like Hunter said, I'll be touching you in a different way." Mia pursed her lips. "Not a chance, ya freak! Try it and I'll knock your teeth out." Hunter laughed out loud. Mayne walked over to the table with her eyes flared and leaned into her. "If I had feelings that might have hurt them. I have only one feeling and it's only used for fighting and fucking." Hunter smiled and finished his coffee. "I'm going to make some phone calls. I'll be back shortly. Play nice." He left the room. Mia finished her food and brought the dishes to the sink. She turned the faucet on, watching the water run as the thoughts ran through her mind. *"I can't believe I'm washing dishes in this fucking house."* She bode her time, waiting for Hunter to leave. Once he leaves, she'd simply wait patiently for the first link in this chain to break and set her free.

Mia searched for the sponge and saw that Mayne was using it to clean the stove. "Do you have another sponge?" "They're under the sink." Not a word was spoken between them while they cleaned. Mia placed the last dish in the rack. She turned the faucet off, glanced over at Mayne and walked over to the sliding doors that led to the back yard. She parted the blinds and gazed at the pool. The gentle ripples in the water reflected the Suns bright rays. She placed her hands flat against the glass and closed her eyes, feeling its warmth emanating through it. She wished that she could just transpose herself to the other side of it. The distinct sound of a Blue Jay made its presence known. She opened her eyes and saw it perched on the edge of the pool's ladder. It fluttered over towards her, landing on a crate just outside the door and looked directly at her. Mia slid down onto her knees, touching the glass with her palm. The blue jays demeanor changed rapidly, chirping in an excited manner and vigorously fluttering its wings. It then took off, soaring over to the fence on the other side of the pool. She knew it was trying to tell her something but couldn't figure out its message. Frustrated, she wept, fogging up the glass in front of her. She wiped it with her shirt and stood back up. She continued to watch it as it sat on the fence looking back at her.

Mia's enigma fascinated Mayne. She knew Mia was unaware of her own full potential because she had never been in an environment that nurtured and enhanced her gifts. Her pristine, untapped energy was like untouched snow. The temptation to challenge her was irresistible. She lit a cigarette and leaned against the stove, observing her. Poised like an animal of prey, she perversely scanned her from head to toe. She ground out her cigarette and calmly approached her. Her eyes followed down the length of Mia's hair. She leaned into her and rudely sniffed, taking in her scent. Mia felt the sensation of her breath against her neck, flinched and took a step back. "What the hell are you doing, freak?" Mayne stared at her in silence, riveting her with her dark, impish eyes. As Mia moved away from her, Mayne reached out to grab her shoulder. Mia caught her hand, squeezing it with forcible strength. "Did I stutter, freak? Hands off!" "I didn't touch you."

Hunter returned. "Enya's awake. I came to check on the progress of you're teamwork." He looked at them, grinning. "I see the Kitchen's clean and your holding hands." Mia swiftly released Mayne's hand and sat at the far end of the table. Mayne glanced at Hunter and then back at Mia. "See? She and I can achieve something together without fighting." Hunter sat at the table beside Mia and put his hand on her shoulder. "Why do you look flustered, Mia?" She gazed up at Mayne in utter disgust. "I'm fine." Mayne stepped over to the blinds and peeked through them and swiped the keys to her bike. "I'm makin' a beer run. I'll be right back. Do you need anything?" "No. Thank you. Why are you taking the keys to your bike? Take the truck." "Oh yeah, Thanks. Hey, There's a scratch on my bike. Do you know anything about it?" "No. Where is the scratch?" It's on the front fender, across the blue paint." "It can be fixed. Don't sweat it." Mia waited for the sound of the closing door. With tears in her eyes, she mustered up courage to plead with him "I want to go home." He smiled, and touched her cheek. "This is your home." "No it's not. Why are you keeping me here?" "We've addressed this. What was my answer to you?" "I don't belong here. I am nothing like you." She held up her necklace. "You and I have two different perspectives regarding this symbol. Either way, that doesn't give you the right to hold me hostage here." He paused for a moment. "Ask me the right questions and you will get the answers that you seek. Until then, you will have to settle for learning the answers as I show them to you." He held her chin up with his finger. "Keep in mind, that if you try to leave, I will find you." Tears rolled down her cheeks. She turned to gaze out at the yard through the partially opened blinds.

Zephyr strolled into the kitchen. "Hey." "Good morning. Where is Mason?" "He should be here in a few. What time are we leaving?" "We're waiting on him." He grabbed a mug and made himself some coffee. "Are there any donuts?" "Check the fridge." He sat at the table, across from Mia and ate the donut while gaping at her. She paid him no mind until he slammed his hand on the table making her jump and squeal. "Good morning Mia." He smiled at her with his teeth gritted. "I didn't mean to scare you." Hunter laughed at him. "Yes you did." Mason laughed. "I did."

Mason was overheard in the hallway, pleading with Enya to make him breakfast. She walked in with Mason hanging off of her shoulders and continuously kissing her cheek. "Mason, ask me nothing until I've had my coffee." "Sit, I'll make it for you." As he pulled out the chair for her, he saw Mia. "Cara Mia!" His affectionate smile lit up his face. "Would you like some coffee too?" Her expression reflected the bitterness she still harbored for him. She looked directly at him, scratching her forehead with her middle finger. Her rude gesture was not well received. The others laughed. He slid her over, sitting next to her. She was now sandwiched, uncomfortably, between he and his brother. He combed his hand through her hair and grasped it tight, forcing her to look at him. "Mia. I try to set the precedence for the day in a positive manner, however, if you would rather start the day with me on a negative tone, I can certainly oblige." Those at the table stared at her. He was silent for a moment, staring into her eyes austerely. He then slid off the bench and fetched Enya's coffee. Mia faced Hunter and whispered to him. "I need to use the bathroom." He pointed to his right side. "You know where it is."

Mason placed Enya's coffee on the table. "Thank you Mason." Enya sipped her coffee. "Is it to your liking, M'Lady?" "Perfect. Thanks! When will you three be returning?" "We should be back in a day or two." Hunter reiterated to Enya, the rules that he had discussed with Mia, pointing out that if in the event, an issue arose with Mia, that Mayne would handle it. "Mia is aware that she is to abide by these rules. If there is something she needs,

she is to ask you or Mayne for it. She is not to be left alone at any time."
"Understood. Where's Mayne?" "Beer run." She smirked. "Naturally."

Zephyr slowly slid out his chair and stood whilst eyeing Mia. "Have a nice day, Mia." He paused and grinned at her in the vilest manner. "I'll be right back. I gotta get a few things. Who's driving, M'Lord?" Hunter shook his keys. "I am. We'll take my truck. It's a long drive. Bring some movies." Mia opened the door to see Mason standing before her. The chill between them was evident. He strolled towards her, forcing her to walk backwards until her back was against the wall. He stood an inch from her and leaned in to her ear. "The next time that you make a gesture like that to me, I'll follow through with its meaning." She cringed. He moved away from her ear, stopping only inches from her face. His malefic eyes subdued her. Hunter slid off the bench and put his mug in the sink. "I will be in the living room. Summon me when you and Zephyr are ready to leave. Hunter looked at Mia and gestured with his finger, for her to follow him. "Come with me." When they entered the living room, he pointed to the large couch. "Sit" He knelt down in front of her, placing his hands on the couch, on either side of her thighs. "The rules that we've discussed are not to be broken and as you have experienced, they're not theories to be tested." His hands slid to her knees. "Is there anything that you require from me before I leave?" She closed her eyes and lay across the couch, opposite of him. "A blanket." He stood up, pulled the small blanket off of the recliner and covered her. He sat beside her, at the other end of the couch and turned the television on. Mayne returned, carrying a case of beer on her shoulder. "Hey. Were you waiting on me?" "You're on time. The guys should be ready, momentarily." She glanced over at Mia. "What's her deal?" "She's just resting. Mason traumatized her." Mayne smirked. "I'm gonna put this in the big cooler, in the yard. I'll be right back."

Mason entered the room. "Ready?" "Yes. I'm waiting for Zephyr." "He's coming. I'll meet you in the truck." Hunter stepped over to the window and remotely unlocked and started the truck just as Mayne and Zephyr walked into the room. Hunter opened the front door and looked at Mayne. "I will check in with you later." She nodded. Mia overheard everything that was said, but pretended to be asleep, to deter them from bothering her. The sound of the door closing gave Mia a feeling of relief. This meant three less roadblocks. The chain was weakening and the path to her freedom was slowly revealing itself to her.

CHAPTER 10

OF WOLF AND MAYNE

Mia was exhausted and emotionally drained. She was aware that Mayne was the only the only one in the room with her at this point and was in no mood to interact with her. Memories of Sebastian came to mind. She thought of him often, worrying about how he was and if and how he would ever find her. Her thoughts spiraled into her usual habit of negative thinking. She quickly snapped out of those thoughts when she realized that it would be easier for her to find him. The Moon was beginning to wane. With that in her mind, she turned to lie flat on her back. She focused on her own complete stillness and let the sounds of the TV lull her into a meditative and placid state. She aligned thoughts of the waning Moon with enervative visions of her imprisonment. With the help of the waning Moon, her intentions were to banish their strength over her and to harm none in the process.

Mayne cracked open her second beer just as Enya entered the room. Enya sat on the recliner and spoke in a low tone. "Are you ok in here?" "Yes." "What's with the case of beer?" "I'm hangin' in the yard tonight, with her attached to my hip." She pointed to Mia. "The venue is me, with music, beer and food. Care to join me?" "Maybe I'll make something if I'm in the mood." Enya glanced over at Mia. "Have you spoken to Mia yet?" "About what?" "The rules in Hunters absence." "I did." "And?" "...And what,

Enya?" "Could you be a little less vague, jackass?" Although some of the words were inaudible, Mia listened intently to their conversation. "What? Hunter made breakfast, the three of us ate together, I harassed her a little and then her and I cleaned." Mia clearly overheard that part of the conversation, sat up and addressed Enya. Enya's eyes were as dark as Mayne's eyes, but instead, they reflected a sense of composure. She knew that Mayne was feral, but was unsure about Enya's disposition. "That's only partially true." Mia had festered up the courage to speak and now had their undivided attention. Enya sat next to her. "What do you mean, Mia?" Mayne's eyes pierced hers in an intimidating manner. "He wasn't very pleasant towards me and neither was Mason for that matter." "He?" Mia pointed at Mayne. "What did Mayne do?" "He choked me." Mayne lost it. "You dug your fucking nails into my leg!" "And why did I do that?" "All I did was put my leg over your fucking lap!" "No. You touched me with your arm, so I moved away from you. Then you pulled me back and pinned me to the bench with your leg, so that I couldn't move. I asked you to move your leg off of me twice and you wouldn't." Enya scowled at Mayne. "Was Hunter present while this happened?" "Yes. He laughed, but did nothing." Enya sighed. "Then after we cleaned, I stood by the glass door and he snuck up behind me and smelled me, like the freak that he is." Enya couldn't hold in her laugh. "Mia, I'm going to give you a friendly tip. Never challenge Mayne." Smiling, she emphasized the gender title. "HE... has anger issues and goes from zero to ten in a split second. Choose your battles wisely." Mayne gave Mia a wicked look, while picking her teeth with a toothpick. "Mayne, please keep in mind that she is justifiably on edge. I want the two of you to let this one go. Fair enough?" Enya looked at Mia, first, waiting for her reply. "Yes." Then Enya faced Mayne. "And you?" "Sure." Mia looked at Mayne. "Just know that I'm not afraid of you. If you bully me, I'll fight back." "I'll keep that in mind." Mayne grinned.

"Why does he obey you, Enya?" Enya grinned. "Because he knows better." Mia began to speculate Enya's true colors. She lifted her legs onto the couch and nestled them against her stomach with her arms wrapped around them. "Enya?" "Yes." "Why am I being kept here?" "I'm going to ask that you try to figure that one out on your own and that you save your questions for Hunter." Enya rose up from the couch. "I need more coffee." She went back to the kitchen, leaving them to themselves.

Mia shifted to the end of the couch and lay her head on the arm, facing the television. She noticed that Mayne was still looking at her. Mia tried to make peace with her, for her own sake. She knew she needed to gain her trust. A movie was just about to start. "This is a good flick Mayne. Sit next to me so I can put my legs over YOUR LAP." Mia emphasized her last words. "You got jokes now, smart ass?" "Kind of. You can sit next to me if you want." "What movie is this?" Mayne stood up and planted herself on the couch. "Lost Boys." Mia threw her feet onto Mayne's lap. "Please massage my feet?" Mayne looked at her cockeyed. "Are you fucking kidding me?" Mia pouted and retracted her legs. "Ya know, the less you say the F word, the more of an impact it will have, when you really need to say it." "Yeah?...and you should cut back on that fucking coffee." Mia shook her head. "Hey Enya? Can you bring me another beer?" She shouted back. "Anything else, your highness?" "No, that'll be all, thank you." She finished her beer and glanced at Mia. "Give me your fuckin' feet." Mia shifted herself put a pillow underneath her head and shifted herself closer.

"Is this your peace offering?" "Don't push it, fuck nuts." Mia laughed. *"Trust earned."* She thought to herself. Enya returned with two bottles of beer. "Thanks." "Well isn't this nice." Mayne smirked. "She's quiet this way."

Raine ran down the stairs and was headed for the kitchen when she had heard people talking in the living room. She saw Enya at the entrance and made a pit stop. "Well isn't this special. Hey, can I be next in line for a foot massage?" She walked in and sat on the coffee table, directly in Mia's line of sight. Mayne snickered. "Be careful. She bites." She looked at Mayne, pursing her lips. "Hi Mia. Please don't bite me ok?" "Hi." Mia remembered her but was leery of her at first. She remembered her from the few times she had saw her at the beach. Though she did no harm to her, she was still a part of their collective circle.

"Hunter left already?" "Yes, about a half hour ago with Mason and Zephyr. Where is Sage?" "Let me check." Raine looked down her shirt and then in her pocket. "I don't know." "Funny." "I'm kidding. I think she's in the shower. Is Lucius or Emery up yet? I need one of them to drive me to get cigarettes." Mayne grinned. "Let me check." She peeked down her shirt. "Nope, not there." "Touché." Enya laughed. "I am surrounded by jackasses. Later people." She walked out of the room. Raine swiped one of Mayne's cigarettes. "What's your plans for today?" "Here, then the yard with beer later. You're welcome to join me." "Sounds good. Sage could use some hair of the dog. She's nursing a hangover." "I've got something for that. Tell her to see me later." "Will do."

Mia switched her foot. "Do this one now." "You realize you're the only one I've ever done this shit for." "I'm honored, your highness. What do you take for hangovers?" "Pot. You should smoke it." "Me? You're the one who needs to Zen yourself." "We'll both have some later."

Sage made her presence known as she dramatically pranced into the kitchen. "I'm dying Enya. Please give me coffee and ibuprofen." "You'll live. Make yourself coffee. The ibuprofen is in the top drawer, in the bathroom behind you." "Oh, please just pamper me?" She threw herself on the table's bench. "I'll get it for you. Mayne said to see her for your hangover." "Thanks Raine. You love me. Where is she?" "She's in the living room with massaging Mia's feet." "You're kidding me." "I kid you not." "Hunter left?" "Yes. About a half hour ago."

Lucius slid across the floor and pushed Sage over. "Good morning ladies. What are you making, Enya?" "What are you cooking?" "Me? You want me to cook? I'll cook. I can make waffles." "Go to town. They're in the freezer."

"Here ya go Sage." She handed her the pills and a mug of coffee." "Thanks. I'm going inside to witness and possibly take advantage of this bizarre phenomenon. Maybe she'll massage my shoulders."

When she entered the room, she saw Mayne watching the television. Mia had nodded off. "Hi there." Mayne gestured silence and pointed at Mia. "I hear you're showing your unseen soft side today?" "Huh?" "You were massaging Mia's feet. Can you please do my shoulders?" She sat on the floor between her feet, with her back facing her. Mayne huffed, but did it anyway. Sage moaned. "Uggg. That's helping. What do you have for my hangover?" "My pot, but you'll hafta go get it. I can't leave her alone and I don't wanna drag her upstairs with me right now. She's quiet and I wanna keep her that way as long as I can." "Give her some too, then." "I will, later, even if I hafta put it in a brownie to get it in her." Mayne slowly moved her hands down her spine, sending chills through Sage's body. "Ugg. How did you learn how to do this so well?" Mayne grinned. "I can do many things like this." "Very funny." "I'm just sayin'." "So how is she?" "We got off to a rough start. All is good and she's quiet." "You make her sound like a fire cracker." "She's more like an M80, but I can snuff out her fuse." Sage laughed. "Yeah, you are one wicked mother fucker. I hear you're having a small party in the yard. What can I bring?" "Yourself. Get Enya to make something good." "Ok. I'm going upstairs to your room. Do you want me to bring you some?" "No. I'll get it later."

"Waffle, Sage?" "Yes, please. Lucius popped two waffles into the toaster. "More coffee?" "Why yes. Thank you. "Enya, what are you making for this afternoon?" "Something simple. I'm making barbeque wings. They're already in the oven." "Cool. Mayne wants you to make some brownies, but you have to see her first." "Why?" "She wants you to make the special ones. It's mostly for Mia, but everyone likes them. I can help." "Ok. After you've finish eating, will you go get it from her? That would help. I'll start mixing." "Ok."

Lucius was enjoying playing the role of a butler. "Put your dishes in the sink, when you're done, people. I'll wash them." Enya grinned. "Why thank you, Lucius." "You're welcome. I am in charge of this task and I shall succeed. I have spoken. For now, I shall go harass Mayne." Enya chuckled. "Mayne?" "Yes. She likes it." "Where is Emery?" "He's out jogging." He slid across the floor and dashed off dramatically, into the living room. He pranced into the room, tripped and fell on the floor. The loud thud startled and woke Mia. Mayne laughed. "Are you ok, idiot?" "Yes. I meant to do that." Mia sat up. "Enya's making wings and brownies." "Cool. Thanks for wakin' Mia." "I'm sorry, Mia." Mia stared at him and then tapped Mayne on the shoulder. "I need to use the bathroom." She paused the television. "Follow me. You can use the one in my room. I need to get something in there, anyway." Mia walked in front of her. Mayne shouted to Enya as they passed the kitchen. "I'm going upstairs. I'll bring it down in a few minutes." "Great."

Mayne unlocked the door and let Mia into her room, first. The bathroom is across from the bed." She went into her closet and pulled out a few buds. She sat on the bed and rolled a few, saving some for Enya. She waited for her and then lit one up. "Sit." She took a toke and handed it to her. "Does this have anything funny in it?" "No, but mine is strong." Mia took a toke and handed it back. "You got it all soggy." She ripped the soggy part off, took a toke and put it in her mouth, backwards. "Come closer." She blew the smoke into Mia's mouth. Mia coughed. She waited for her to stop and did it three more times. "Ok that's enough." "Just one more." Mayne ground it out and lay back on the bed for a few minutes. "How do you feel?" "Ok. I don't feel anything." "Give it a few minutes. Lay down next to me." "Ok, but if you try anything, I'll slug you." Mayne laughed at her. "Is that so?" "Yes. Did I really hurt your legs?" "Yes. The next time you do that, I'll declaw you, like a cat." Mia turned sideways to face her, with her hand supporting her head. "You're too extreme." "So, I'm told."

"Why and are you always so aggressive?" "I'm a lone and vicious wolf. It's in my instinct to behave as such. Why do you ask?" "Have you ever really hurt someone?" "If I feel threatened, which doesn't happen often. If necessary, I'll rip someone's throat out with my teeth." Mia cringed and then reached over to her mouth. "Open." "Why?" "I wanna feel how sharp they are." "You're definitely high." She stuck her finger inside and felt the edges. Mayne nipped her finger. "Ouch!" She paused for a moment to look at her finger. "Did I threaten you?" "You couldn't threaten me if you tried." Mia felt a sudden rush of oblivion and fell onto her back. Her eyes felt like cumulus clouds. For the first time in a long while, she felt as if her anxiety ceased to exist. She lay there as if she had no muscles. Mayne watched her with devious grin. "Ya feelin' it, huh?" "Yes." "Ride it for a few minutes, then we'll go back downstairs. Enya's makin' some food. We're all gonna hang in the yard. I've got beer too." Emery knocked on the door. "Who?" "It's me." "Come in." "Hi there." "What's up?" "Hunter sent me a text. He said you had a scratch on your bike. I'll fix it tomorrow." "Thanks." "What's this about?" He pointed at Mia. "She's high." Mia stared at him. She knew she had seen him before, but couldn't remember his name. "Do you have one rolled?" "There's some on the stand. Take one." "Thanks. I'll see you downstairs." Mia whispered to Mayne. "Who was that?" "Emery." "Oh." His name didn't trigger a memory.

While slow in thought, Mia could see yet another path beginning to clear its way for her. She would be outside soon. The links to the chain that binded her, were weakening. She remembered the wolf from her dream, recalling Mayne's words as well as her sharp teeth. She suspected that Mayne might have been the wolf. She also knew that wolves were easily distracted.

CHAPTER 11

STEAL AWAY

M ia sat on the lounge chair near the pool, while the others lingered at the bar. Her mind was fixated on getting out of there and finding Sebastian. As the minutes passed, Mia continued to observe their habits, peeking through her partially closed eyes while pretending to be sleeping. Mayne reached into her pocket, removed a set of keys to her bike and tossed them on the bar. Mia heard the sound and opened her eyes. *"KEYS! There's my ride!"* She thought to herself. How she would get them became her next hurdle. She thought intently about her next steps. The timing must be on point. Her thoughts ran rapid. She knew that one does not steal a Harley and survive, however, this would be the sweetest revenge for choking her.

Observing, as they wandered in and out of the house, she paid close attention to how often they glimpsed over at her, to ensure that she remained in sight. She looked up at the sky and saw that the Sun was beginning to set. Tonight is a New Moon and she knew this was ideal for planning. Her path was leading her.

Within her mind, Mia mapped the layout of the yard, estimating the timing of each move and the location of the bike. Mayne and the others needed to be at an unnoticeable and soundless distance. The yard was elevated from the beach, encompassed by a high, wrought iron fence. The outside of the fence was covered with additional fencing of black PVC. There was a wrought iron gate, to her right and it was locked. The bike was parked on the other side of it. The only way to the beach was back through the house. She needed to get to the bar, take the keys, go in the house and exit through the beachside door without being noticed. The current entities on her side are the loud music, beach people, dusk and hopefully their eventual drunken ignorance. Cash and a cell phone will be needed as well. She began to monitor all possible roadblocks and everyone's changing attention spans. Once she was on the bike there would be no turning back. Mia had not forgotten what Mayne did to her with Hunter. She is worried about Sebastian. Fear is now just distant thunder. She was going to text Sebastian to let him know, but decided against it. *"If you want a plan to work smoothly, work Solitarily."* She continued observing the habits of this coven of people. She needed Mayne's attention to be away from the keys and for no one to be in view of the front door at the same time. With the exception of a few bathroom trips, everyone was involved in their conversations at the bar or in the pool. The voices and movement among them seemed to fuse in synch with the usual beach noise and became white noise.

When she opened her eyes, she knew it was go time. She took a deep breath, arose from the chair and walked towards the bar. On her right was the pool leading up to the bar and at her left was the house leading up to the sliding doors. As she neared the bar, she saw Sage in the pool. Sage looked up at her as she held onto the side. Noticing this, Mia knew there would be an inquiry coming on. "Where ya goin'?" Mia froze in her steps, paused and answered calmly. "To get a cigarette from someone and go to the bathroom." Sage shrugged her shoulders and dismissed it. Mayne was at the center of the bar facing Raine and Emery stood behind the bar quickly grabbing beers and in a rush to return back to the pool. Mia asked Emery for a can of soda and he tossed her one. She looked over to Mayne and waited a few moments before she tapped her shoulder. Mayne turned her head to look at her. "Can I have a cigarette?" Mayne pushed the pack towards her and continued her conversation. With her eyes on the keys, she took one from the pack, lit it and placed the box back on the bar. She cracked open the can, grabbing the keys at the same time. The sounds cancelled each other out, so no one had paid it any mind. She glanced at the pool, saw no one looking and darted inside the house. To her right was the bathroom. She heard a flush, followed by the sound of someone washing up. Mia waited a moment. The bathroom door opened and Lucius emerged. Mia quickly went in as if she had to go and Lucius commented. "You might wanna hold your breath." She cringed. Lucius returned back to the bar. Someone had left their cell phone in the bathroom. It may have been Lucius's. She pocketed it. Mia waited about 20 seconds, slowly opened the door and peered out. No one else was inside the house or looking in from the yard. Across from the bathroom was Hunters room and to the left was the hall leading to the beach door. On the table near the door was a credit card and some folded cash. She grabbed it and glanced back to ensure that no one was there. Then she opened the door, closing it gently and walked out towards the beach. She broke into a cold sweat and took several deep breaths. She counted the money and stuffed it in her pocket. It was only twenty-three dollars. To her left was Mayne's bike. She peered through the fence gate to see if anyone in the yard was looking and quietly approached the front of the bike. The back half of the bike was the only part that was visible through the gate. Glancing around, she looked for any beachgoers who may be looking her way. She had on dark grey yoga pants that were flared at the bottom. She rolled them up tightly above her knees so they wouldn't touch any moving parts on the bike, then untied the helmet from the seat and put it on. She pulled the keys from her pocket, placed them into the ignition and grasped the handlebars while slowly retracting the kickstand. Ahead of her was the cement walkway. The trees on the right side of the house blocked the view to that side. She rolled the bike a few yards away from the house before she started it. She knew that Harleys were loud, especially Mayne's.

Mia paused, hopped on the bike and started the engine. The powerful and vibrating sound echoed everywhere, disturbing the serenity of the sunbathers nearby. She balanced herself on the bike, took a deep breath and looked back at the house. Someone's head peeked over the gate to look. They seemed to be waving and pointing to the others in the yard. A few other heads peered over the gate as well. Mia held up her right arm, flashed her middle finger at them and sped off loudly. The sound was like the freight train sound of a tornado. She felt the vibration of the bike on her thighs and it pulsed throughout her body. Tears ran down her cheeks. As she reflected on the slow moving minutes it took to get from the lounge chair to the road, she could feel the overwhelming fear and tension releasing from her muscles and jaw. She was finally free. She sped down a road that led to the highway, glanced at the speedometer and slowed down a bit. The last thing she needed was to be pulled over. At the highway entrance she sped back up to a little over fifty miles per hour.

If the rage on Mayne's face could start a fire, the house would be leveled to ash. "She stole my fucking bike!" She paused for a moment and looked all around. "How the fuck did she get past all of us?" She had attempted to jump over the gate but realized it would be pointless. Everyone was standing around waiting for direction. Enya grabbed Mayne's arm tightly to get her attention focused. "Listen to me and everyone shut the fuck up now! No one calls the police. Emery, Raine and Lucius; you take Mason's truck and follow. Sage, stay here and make calls. Let others know the bike was stolen. Tell them not to approach her. If she is seen, call us. No one forget your cell phones." She looked at her sister; "You and I will get in my car and drive in the direction that she was headed towards. Along the way we'll ask if any one saw her. I'm certain that people saw and heard that bike."

Everyone scrambled for their keys and phones. Since Raine had only one beer an hour prior, she volunteered to drive the truck. Mayne couldn't remember where she left her phone. She grabbed a studded belt and a rope, and threw it on the floor of Enya's car as she got in. Every one drove off. Enya glanced at Mayne. "It's amazing how fast people become sober and focused when there's a crisis." Mayne didn't reply. Her pupils were flaring, red and the silence in Enya's car was eerie. They drove towards the far end of the beach where they had last saw her and slowed down to inquire with people as they drove by them. In between stops, Mayne called some of her friends to alert them and ask them to help search. While Raine drove, Emery and Lucius did the same. Within a half hour all their contacts were aware of the situation. Enya asked Mayne to contact Hunter. "I don't wanna do that. He asked me to watch her and I failed." Enya replied: "He's not gonna be mad. He expected this from her. If you don't tell him, he will be mad. From where he is, he can at least tell you her general location. Then you can call the people you know nearby there and hopefully pinpoint her.

It had already been a half hour since they had last seen Mia. She decided to contact Hunter. When he answered, she explained what happened to an extent. She felt that he didn't need to know all the details now. He laughed, entertained by her tenacity and replied: "I didn't think she had the balls to try to leave again. I wish I were there. Oh, the fun I would have with this." Mayne thought about how he thinks and laughed. Then there was a pause. "As of right now, she's a few miles North, near the restaurant where she worked with Sebastian. Enjoy the hunt. That's how I got my name." He hung up.

Mayne looked up the fastest way to get there and reiterated the directions to Enya. She called Emery and the others to meet her there. Then proceeded to call some people she knew in the area. Emery and the others followed suit.

Out of nowhere, Emery started laughing. Raine was curious as to what was so funny. "What?" "This will be a fun cat and mouse chase. Don't stress. Enjoy it." Emery laughed and texted Mayne and the others. "MEOW! CAT AND MOUSE HUNT IS ON BITCHES" Riling everyone up, the text resulted in replies of competition and various painful end outcomes for Mia.

Mia had been riding for a half an hour when she finally reached her apartment. She realized she didn't have the key so she rang the doorbell and knocked several times but no one answered. She called his cell phone and he did not answer. Panicking, she asked around to see if anyone had seen him. No one had. She called the restaurant and they said he was taken to the hospital and has not been heard from since then. They also asked what happened to her as well as inquiries about the incident at the restaurant. "I was kidnapped and he was knocked out by one of the people who broke in. I can't find him. I'll call back and explain further, as soon as I can." She hung up.

Her frustration was evident. She needed to gas up, use the facilities and eat something. She returned to the bike and drove, while trying to think of people that he may be staying with. She spotted a small bar/restaurant along the highway and pulled up around the back entrance because she didn't want anyone to see the bike. There were a few people outside smoking. She walked in the back door and saw there were only a few people inside, most of whom were sitting at the bar. There were three people sitting at the booth on the right, by the kitchen door. She approached the bar. "Can I please have a soda and a menu?" "Sure." "I'm just going to use the ladies room and I'll be right back."

After using the facilities, she approached the sink. As she washed her hands, she glanced up at herself in the mirror. *"Holy crap! The bartender must think I'm a freak."* She splashed her face and made a feeble attempt to fix her hair. As she walked back towards a booth, the woman approached her carrying her drink and dropped the menu onto the table. She picked it up and took a sip of the soda. Some mellow sixties music was playing on the jukebox.

♪*Incense and Peppermints*♪

There were a few people sitting at the bar. The three people at the table were paying their bill and then left a few minutes later. Mia picked something cheap and fast, from the menu. The waitress returned. Hi. I'm Gwen. "Are you ready to order?" "Yes. I'll have a hot dog and fries, please." "Do you want anything on the hot dog?" "Just mustard. Thanks and another soda please?" Gwen watched her as she chugged the first one. "Sure." She looked at her for a moment and walked back to the bar. After trying to place her face, she remembered her and knew that Mia did not recognize her.

Someone walked over to the jukebox and fed it a few dollars. The genre of the music changed. An eerie song played.

♪Where you goin' for tomorrow♪

She decided to attempt to contact Sebastian again. She sent him a text. *"Seb, it's Mia. I stole this phone. Please, please call me asap."* A few seconds after she hit send, the phone rang. The phone reflected an unfamiliar number and she thought it might be Sebastian. She pressed the answer button on the screen. "Hello?" There was silence. Mayne recognized Mia's voice and clenched her teeth. "Pay close attention. I will find you." Mia froze for a few seconds and thought to her self; *"FUCK!"* Her fear turned brazen. "Hey Mayne? No! You listen now! Do you remember what you did to me? Fuck you! I got your bike! Fuck off!" She slammed the phone down. She realized the people in the bar heard her. They were staring. "I'm sorry about that." She said to them. Gwen replied, laughing: "Hey, no worries. We hear that all the time." Gwen reached for her phone and walked in the kitchen to peek out of the back window. She saw the bike, took a picture of it and sent a text to Enya and Emery.

"Was that Mia?" Enya inquired. Mayne turned to look at Enya. "I called my cell just now. She just told me to fuck off and hung up on me." She logged on to an app on her sisters phone to locate her cell.

Emery and Enya's phone's chirped in synch. Emery read the message from Gwen. "Mia's here eating. I'm lookin' right at Mayne's bike. It's in the back lot." Emery shouted: "Found her!" Raine shouted. "Where is she?" Emery replied: "That's Gwen. She's at her bar." Emery returned the text. "We're on our way" "Raine sped up and Emery called Enya's phone.

Just as Mayne attempted to track her phone on Enya's phone, it rang. "She's at Gwen's bar!" Emery was so loud that Enya heard him. Mayne replied. I know. I saw Gwen's text. The little bitch has my fuckin' phone too! I called it a few seconds ago." Mayne texted Gwen and told her to make sure no one lets on that they were on their way. Gwen was just about to fetch Mia's food from the kitchen when saw the text from Mayne. She called her back. "What do you want me to do to stall her? I don't want her to get suspicious and leave." Mayne replied; "Do you have anything that'll make her feel loopy, fast? She's small. It'll affect her quick." Gwen laughed. "Do I have any…Have you forgotten who you're talking to? I'll empty something in her soda. How long until you get here?" "About a half hour I guess." "OK".

Gwen emptied a capsule from her stash, emptied the contents into the soda and stirred it. She placed the items on a tray and proceeded to Mia's table. "Here ya go, miss. Enjoy." "Thanks" Mia checked the time on her cell while she drowned her fries in ketchup.

Mayne called Emery and told him to tell the others to meet her in the back of the bar, drive up quietly and park at the furthest end of the lot. When Mayne and Enya arrived, Mayne jumped out of the car when she saw her bike. She took the belt and rope from the floor of the front seat. As she shut the door, she told Enya to wait for the others while she pushed her bike to the front entrance.

Raine drove up and parked beside Enya's car. "She said to wait here. She's pushing the bike to the front." When Mayne returned, she had a cigarette in her mouth. She pointed to Lucius, Raine and Emery. "You enter in the back door quietly. Enya will go with me through the front. When you get inside, stay there til' you see us get inside. Emery texted Gwen to let her know they were there. Gwen looked at the others at the bar wide eyed, motioned her face towards the front door and gestured for their silence.

Mia felt lightheaded. She stopped eating and took a sip of her drink. She chalked it up to anxiety. When she started to sweat, she darted into the restroom and throw cold water on her face. She held onto the edge of the sink, waiting for the dizziness and palpitations to subside. She returned to the booth and sat down. She placed her elbows on her lap, held her forehead and thought to herself. *"This is the last thing I need. Really? Food poisoning from a fuckin' hot dog."* She pulled her feet onto the bench and sat with her legs crossed. Gwen returned to her table and saw her fidgeting. "You ok, kid?" "I'll be fine."

The back door opened and closed, undetected. Lucius pointed to Mia and the others stood nearby and waited. Gwen saw them and quickly looked at the front door. The people sitting at the bar were curious and looked around. Gwen gestured to them to remain silent. Mayne slammed open the front door, let Enya in and slammed it shut. Startled, Mia looked up and felt her head spin. Her eyes opened wide. She couldn't believe that she had found her. While feeling floaty from the soda, she also felt fear and reacted with nervous laughter. *"Un-fucking believable!"* She thought to herself. Mayne stared directly at Mia, her red pupils, piercing through her like the angel of death.

Mia stood and sat on the edge of the table. The movement made her dizzy and unfocused for a few seconds. Staring back with a smartass smile, Mia laughed, then reached in her pocket and dangled the key to her bike. Those at the bar were speechless and in disbelief. Mayne's eyes flared. She darted towards Mia and Mia's smile quickly changed to fear. Mayne lifted her arm and back handed her in the face so hard that Mia fell onto the floor. Enya screamed. "Mayne!" Emery laughed out loud. "Bitch slap! Damn!" The others there were dumb founded. Still in shock, she tried to pick herself up and Mayne jumped on her, pinning her on the floor. Mayne tied the rope around her wrists and dragged her into the bathroom. She searched around the room looking for something to tie her to. She dropped the belt on the floor, picked Mia up by the arms and then grabbed her by the neck. She pushed her over to the pipes running horizontal, beside the sink. She shoved her face against the wall and tied the rope to the pipes. Feeling severely dazed, Mia tried to yell and fight her but was not strong enough. Every time she tried to speak she coughed and whimpered. Mayne recalling the last phone conversation with Mia and repeated Mia's words back to her.

"FUCK ME, HUH…? YOU GOT MY BIKE… FUCK OFF?" Then she heard nothing but silence for a few moments. Mayne picked up the studded belt, yanked the back of her pants downward and repeatedly lashed Mia across her backside. Mia's shrieks were heard throughout the bar. Some were unnerved while others laughed. Enya struggled to hold herself back from going in there to stop Mayne. She has seen her sister's anger before. She looked over at Gwen who had the same look on her face. No one moved.

Mayne dropped the belt on the floor and like a sadist she took pleasure in watching Mia writhe in pain. She pulled a switchblade from her back pocket, sliced the rope and let her fall to the floor. Mia howled from the pain when she landed. She curled up on her side, trying to collect herself. Mayne picked up the belt and rope. "We leave in fifteen minutes. Be out there." Mayne walked out.

Everyone's attention collectively deviated to the bathroom door as it swung open, to see who would emerge first. Mayne stood at the door, holding a cold and steely stare. She panned across the room at everyone and then approached the bar. "We leave in fifteen minutes." She gestured to Gwen for a beer, spun the barstool around and sat, gazing at the bathroom door. Everyone was silent. All that could be heard was the sound of glasses and beer bottles tapping on the bar and the music playing.

♪…*Play us a tune*…♪

Mayne's cell phone rang at Mia's table and Mayne found it on the booth's seat. She walked over to answer it. "Who?" "Hello is Mia there?" She laughed at the caller. "She can't come to the phone right now. Can I take a message?" The caller hung up. She looked at the number and turned her phone off. She saw her keys on the floor, picked them up and returned to the barstool.

Mia lay on the bathroom floor faced down. She had to use the toilet and now faced the task of getting up to get to the stall. She lifted herself with her elbows, and then pushed herself onto her knees. The pain shot through her backside and legs. Twinging and gasping from the pain, she pushed herself over to the sink to lift herself up. The pain was excruciating. She sobbed and cursed Mayne. Now standing, she pulled her legs as she walked towards the toilet. When she finally made it to the seat, she realized it would be too painful to sit. Instead, she hovered.

Enya bolted into the restroom to check on Mia and to see if she could hurry her up as well. She opened the door and didn't see her at first. "Mia? It's Enya. We're leaving. Do you need help?" Mia's attitude turned to bitterness. "Really? Now you wanna help me?" Enya walked over to the stall. "Look, you brought this on yourself. I just came in here to get you because we're leaving now." "So leave!" Mia shouted. "Not without you sweetheart." She flushed and then opened the door. Enya placed her arm under Mia's and helped her walk to the sink. Mia's face was reddened from crying. Mia looked furiously at Enya. "DON'T TOUCH ME!" Mia's hair was a stringy mop. She slowly walked to the sink, stopping when it hurt too much. She dried her hands on her pants and with Enya's help, turned around to walk to the door. She placed her arm over Enya's shoulders. Every time she moved, she cringed from the pain. Enya held the door open and they looked out at everyone as they starred. Mia wept and just looked down at the floor as she walked.

Raine slid off of the bar stool and took a few steps toward them to get a closer look at Mia. Stunned, she shouted; "Holy shit! I hafta say you have the biggest balls I've ever seen, Mia" Enya laughed. "OK enough with the jokes." Mayne spoke loudly, looking directly at Mia. "I'm not done yet, Mia!" Mia looked up at her, let go of Enya, and put her hands on the table. "Fuck you Mayne! I'm not afraid of you!" Enya gave her a minute, then grabbed her arm and started walking again.

When they neared the bar, Mia let go of Enya. Mayne focused solely on Mia as she approached. Music played in the background.

♪…hard lovin' woman, *got me feelin' mean*…♪

Mia grabbed onto the bar and looked at Gwen. In a raspy voice, she spoke to her. "Can I have scotch?" Gwen poured a shot glass and Mia guzzled it. Everyone stared at her as if she were a freak show. She glanced at each of them. "What the fuck are you all looking at? You wanna see what she did to me? Is that it?" She slowly and painfully reached to her pants, slid them over her waist until they dropped to her ankles. She slid the backside of her panties, half-way down. Everyone saw the red and raised welts across her ass and legs. Mia looked at Mayne with seething hatred. She sat there with no expression on her face. "Mayne tied my hands to a pole, like the coward that she is and beat me with a belt!" Mia pulled up her pants, twinging from the pain as she bent down.

Emery approached her. "Mia, lemme' ask you somethin'. Was it worth it?" Mia turned to look at Mayne her replied. "Yes!" Mayne's eyes widened. Emery was in disbelief. He looked at Mayne and then back to Mia, shaking his head. "You got a death wish, girly"

Mia recalled that she had left Mayne's phone at the booth and slowly walked over towards it, hissing from the pain with each step. Lucius laughed at her and commented out loud. "Hurtin' Mia?" Mia didn't respond. When she finally made it there she couldn't find it. She panicked and thought to herself. *"Fuck, she found it."* Then recalled the text to Sebastian. She turned her head to look at Mayne, who held the phone up, purposely waving it.

She faced the bench and placed her hands on it. Slowly lowering herself to the seat, she pulled herself across it and lay there, sobbing. She felt dazed, sick and weak.

Mayne finished her beer and stood up. "Lets go. Who's taking her back?" Enya replied. "I will, I just need someone to pick her up and carry her to my car." I'll do it." Emery volunteered. Emery walked over to Mia. "Mia, Do you wanna try to stand up on your own? Then I'll carry you to the car. Mia pushed herself up slowly and Emery grabbed underneath her arms to pull her upright.

Before Emery picked her up, Mayne moved close to Mia's face. Mia became frightened. "Take my bike again." She said with steely eyes and a vicious tone.

Everyone said their goodbyes to Gwen. "It's been an entertaining day." Gwen nervously laughed. Emery lifted Mia carefully, trying not to put pressure on her legs, and carried her over his shoulders. Mia cringed. Enya ran ahead to open the rear door to her car. Emery placed Mia upright and she crawled in slowly, lying across the back seat. He then reached in, fastened the seatbelt and closed the door. Enya turned on the ignition and glanced at Mia. Mayne peered into the back seat window and then looked at Enya. "I'll be following right behind you." She then turned to look at Mia. "Touch my sister and I'll tie you to my bike and drag you." Mia cried, silently.

Mia fell in and out of sleep, waking from the jolts of sudden stops. They said nothing to each other for the entire ride back. Mayne followed closely behind, occasionally speeding up to look in the car to ensure that Enya was ok. Emery called Sage to let her know that they found Mia and that they were on their way back.

One by one, they arrived at the house. Mayne sped up in front of Enya and parked. Enya pulled up next to Mayne's bike and the others in the truck, followed behind. Enya called Emery over to help her get Mia out of her car. Sage opened the front door and stood on the top of the stoop. Emery opened the car door, crawled in and shook her. "Hey. Wake up, Mia. I'm gonna slide you out by your ankles." Mia lifted her head, slid to the end of the seat and Emery helped her to stand. Mia held on the car roof for a moment, trying to balance herself. Her eyes were barely open. When she stood up, the pain shot up and down her legs. She gasped and cringed. Mayne stood in front of Mia, holding a steely expression. She grabbed Mia by her neck and dragged her over to her bike. "Move!" She shouted. When they stood beside the bike, she pushed her down onto the ground, next to the hot chrome exhaust pipes. Holding her face just inches from the hot pipes, she loudly repeated her threat

with gritted teeth. "Take my bike again!" The others gasped, watching in horror. Mia shrieked. Mayne had no intention of burning her face, but had clearly
made her point. She let go of Mia and walked into the house, leaving her on
the ground. Raine and Lucius followed. As she passed Enya, Enya smacked
her in the head. "What the fuck is wrong with you?" Mayne laughed. Emery
picked Mia up and carried her into the house. Mia was shaking and crying,
hysterically. "Where should I put her, Enya?" She pointed to the yard.

He placed her on one of the lawn chairs, near the sliding doors to the
house. Mia turned onto her stomach to prevent any painful pressure on her
backside. Raine and Sage emerged out of the house, grabbed some beer and
cigarettes and sat on the side of the pool, dangling their feet in the water.
"Raine! I can't believe what Mayne just did to Mia. I felt my heart pounding!"
"I know! Mayne freaked me the fuck out!" Raine shook her head.

Sage glanced over at Mia. "Ya know; she has a serious limp. How bad are
her wounds? Did you see them?" "Yes, I did. They're pretty damn bad. Go over
and look if you want." Sage walked over to her and sat beside her. "Mia, can I
get you anything?" Mia lifted her head, " A cigarette and a shot of something
strong." OK. She gave her one of hers and lit it. Then went to the bar, poured
some whiskey and returned. "Mia, do you want me to get some ice or something
for your legs?" "No. I'm gonna go in the pool. Just let me finish my cigarette.
Will you help me over there?" "OK." Raine lit up another cigarette. Looking at
Mia's face, she reached to her face to move her hair away from her eyes. "Mia,
why did ya do it?" I needed to find Sebastian." "Did you find him?" "No." Mia
took another drag and put it out. She kicked her sneakers and socks off and
slowly rolled off the chair. Kneeling, she grabbed Sage's hand and pulled herself
up. Pain and stiffness ran through her backside. She started to pull her pants
down and gestured to Sage to help with the lower half so that she didn't have
to bend. Sage looked at her wounds. "Holy shit, Mia. Have you looked at your
legs?" Mia slowly lifted her foot as she pulled them off of her feet. "My ass too."
She flashed her for a second. "Fuck!" Sage turned around to look at Mayne and
yelled. "Mayne! Really?" Mayne flashed her middle finger. Mia put her arm over

Sage's shoulder, walked slowly to the pools edge, turned around and threw herself in pool, backwards. The cold water eased some of the pain. She waded to the far corner, placed her arms on the side and rested her head on her hands. Sage held a nasty look at Mayne as she walked back over to Raine. Sage turned around and repeated herself again to Mayne. "Really?" Mayne responded in a sarcastic tone. "Are ya sayin' that I went to far, Sage?" "Ya think?" "I don't think so. I'm not done." "You're fuckin' certified." Mayne looked at Emery and he laughed. Mia heard her, turned around and shouted back at her. "Hey Mayne, Fuck you! Shut up!" Emery and Mayne looked at each other and laughed. Lucius opened another beer. "Everyone's got secret jokes tonight. Where did Enya go?" Sage replied; "She's inside. I think she's in the shower." Mayne sent a text to Hunter. "I found her and we're back at the house."

Enya returned, carrying a large bowl of popcorn and some other various munchies. She went behind the bar for a drink. Lucius dug in. Chuckling, Lucius said; "Oh yes, this goes perfect with beer!" Lucius looked over at Raine and Sage. He threw a few popcorn kernels at them, one at a time. The bar was about four feet from where they were sitting. They didn't notice because he kept missing them. Frustrated, he got up and moved a little closer. "Two points!" He uttered, chuckling. It bounced off Raine's head. Raine was involved in her conversation with Sage and became distracted and annoyed. "Cut it out, fuck nuts!" Lucius, who had already had several beers since his return, grabbed a handful, threw it at them and ran behind the bar. Some of which met its demise in the pool. Sage scooped most of it all up, quickly walked over to him with handfuls of soggy, dripping popcorn and put it down the back of his shirt. Lucius yelled and laughed at the same time. Sage laughed. "HA! Don't start nothin', won't be nothin'."

Mayne's phone chirped from an incoming text. It was Hunter. "We return tomorrow night."

Sage and Raine changed into their bathing suits and returned to the pool. When they returned, Sage lured Lucius closer to the pool. "Hey Lucius, help us clean up this fuckin' popcorn before it gets in the filter." He walked over to them and they jumped in cannonball style, purposely splashing him. He was soaked. Lucius did the same and the girls screamed.

Immersed in thought, Mia recalled her last dream of the "Don't stop" signs and the presence of the wolf. She easily deciphered this dream and knew that the wolf was Mayne, however, she was utterly disgusted at the fact that she didn't recognize the significance of the signs. Their collective meaning was now, obvious. She should never have stopped at the bar.

Raine and Sage waded over to Mia and latched their arms to the sides of the pool and whispered her name. Mia opened her eyes but didn't lift her head or answer. Music was playing.

♪*...soothing light at the end of your tunnel...*♪

Mia heard the haunting words and felt as if she were living them. She wanted to cry, to scream, to scream so loud that her Goddess's ears would bleed from the frequency of her pitch. She felt it would be futile to even try. Her plea for mercy would only fall on deaf ears. Nothing mattered to her.

Mayne finished her beer and told Emery to give her twenty minutes. Emery nodded. Mayne picked up one of the beach towels and walked over to Mia. Extending her hand, Mayne knelt down and grasped Mia's wrist, pulling her to the ladder. Mia looked up at her as she floated over. Holding on to her, she pulled herself out of the pool. Mia stood there in her underwear and soaked shirt, shivering. Mayne handed her the towel and Mia wrapped it around herself. Mayne picked her up and carried her into the house. She was drunk and in so much pain that she didn't even fight her. She just figured she was taking her inside so she could change and go to sleep.

Emery stepped behind the bar, opened another beer, poured two shots and handed one to Enya. "I'm not askin'" Emery replied; "Don't" and smiled.

Sage and Raine looked at each other. "What the hell was that all about?" Raine whispered.

Mayne proceeded upstairs to her room, stood Mia on her feet and closed the door. Mia's eyes were wide opened. She had a bad feeling, recalling what was said before about "not being done". As Mayne reached for her, Mia, became startled, backed up and held her hand up to block her. "I'm just taking the wet towel from you." "I'm ok. I just need a change of clothes." Leery of her now, she tried to think of something to say so that she would not harm her again. "Look, I'm sorry that I took your bike. I needed to find Sebastian and I knew that no one would have let me go. This won't happen again." Emotionless, Mayne watched Mia as she spoke. She walked over to the dresser and pulled something out of it. It was a blindfold. Mia thought that she was giving her a change of clothing, so she let her guard down. Mayne walked behind Mia to look at her wounds at first. She touched one on her leg and Mia twitched. As Mayne placed the blindfold over her eyes, Mia stopped her. "Stop! What the hell is that?" "You took my bike when I couldn't see you. Now it's your turn." As Mayne went to put it in her again, Mia swatted at her arms and scratched her. Mayne looked at her arm and saw blood. She took the blindfold, wrapped it tightly around Mia's neck and pulled her over to the dresser. Choking, Mia tried to pry away Mayne's hands. "I'm putting this on you, one way or another. You choose." With no intention of using it, she pulled a syringe out of the drawer. Mia froze. Mayne released the blindfold from her neck, put it over her eyes and tied it tightly. There was a short silence, then the sound of a switchblade opening and closing. She did this on purpose to spook her. Without sight, all of her other senses were heightened. She felt the slightest air movement. She stepped around to face her. Mia wrapped her arms around herself. Mayne gently pulled away the towel and Mia stood, shivering and trembling, with her arms near her sides and her fingers spread apart. She heard the sound of the knife again and then felt the cold blade on her neck. "Am I still a coward, Mia?" She didn't answer. "Don't move." Mayne commanded. She sliced her shirt at the shoulders and let it fall to the floor. Her bra met the same fate.

She hooked her finger underneath the side of her panties and sliced. Mia screamed. "Stop." Mayne stood up directly in front of her and whispered into her ear. "How does this feel?" "Just stop." She whimpered. Mayne replied; "Stop? I didn't have that choice." Mia heard the sound of something dropping on the dresser. Mayne had thrown the knife there. Then she felt Mayne's hands slide around her waist and over her backside. She slowly pushed her to the bed and edged her to sit. She whispered into her ear, taunting her. "Do you want me to stop?" "Yes." she whimpered. Her hand slid in between her breasts and then slowly over her stomach. "That's how I felt when you were on my bike." She pushed her down onto the bed. Lying beside her, she ran her finger over her lips and cheeks. "So... Fuck me, huh?" Mia didn't dare respond. She ran her fingers down her neck, along her collarbone and over her breasts. Mia gasped. Her hand moved past her stomach, to her waist. Mia felt her hand on her thigh and grasped her arm to stop her from going further. Mayne shouted. "No!" Mayne watched her face, and then slid her hand between Mia's legs. Mia clutched the sheets tightly in her hands and shrieked.

The door opened and closed silently. Emery was now in the room and stood in front of Mia, watching. Mayne glanced up at Emery, slowly hovered above Mia and moved down, between her thighs. She felt Mayne's breath there. Her body shuddered as she cried out. The fear and pleasure that she felt at the same time were overwhelming. Emery watched as her body quivered. Mayne purposely grasped her thighs tightly on her wounds and Mia cried out from the pain. Her eyes teared and her pupils turned blue. Mayne stopped and stood up. The room was silent. Mayne quietly walked over to the side of the bed and knelt down slowly, near her face. Emery crawled between her legs and hovered over her. Mia thought it was Mayne. Emery unzipped his pants. When Mia heard the sound of the zipper and realized what was to follow. Emery waited for Mayne to remove the blindfold. Mayne looked at Emery and hovered next to Mia's face. She reached over to the blindfold and pulled it off of her. At first, Mia saw Mayne's face next to hers and then looked down to see Emery between her legs. Emery lifted her legs up and thrust inside her. Mia felt fear, rage and ecstasy at once and her screams were heard throughout the house. She scratched and punched him. She tried to get up but Emery's weight was like an anvil upon her. Mayne whispered slowly in Mia's ear. "Now you feel as violated as I did."

Emery smiled at her sadistically and then went into to the bathroom, while Mayne sat on the bed. Mia curled up under the sheets and cried. When Emery returned, he walked over to Mayne and whispered in her ear. "She has no fucking clue about you."

CHAPTER 12

HEAL ME

Emery lay beside Mia, twirling her hair and whispering her name into her ear. She lay there, traumatized and unresponsive to him and existing only within her mind, disconnected from everything surrounding her. Mayne touched her face with her beer and she jerked from the cold feeling. Mayne covered her with the blanket and crawled on top of her, face to face. "Was your ride as good as mine?" Mia turned her head away from her. Emery snidely commented. "So was it still worth it, Mia?" She didn't respond. Emery grinned. "Ahh, so the answer changes now." Mayne smiled and looked at her empty beer bottle. "I'm outta beer. Peace-out, Mia." They left to go downstairs, leaving her there to wallow in the aftermath of their actions. Mia curled up into a ball and wept.

They returned to the yard and saw the others gaping at them. Mayne sat behind the bar, snatched two beers, handing one to Emery. They looked at each other with smartass grins. Enya stared at Mayne. "What?!" Mayne snapped at her. Lucius was laying on one of the lawn chairs and was three sheets to the wind. Sage and Raine eavesdropped while observing them from a distance. She asked what the others wanted to know. "What did you do with her and where is she now?" Emery grinned. "She's probably sleeping now. She's very tired." Emery and Mayne looked at each other with brazen expressions and Raine shook her head in disgust. "That's not what I asked. Did I stutter?" She shouted, sarcastically. Enya waited for the answer but wasn't sure if she really wanted to know. "I thought you were just bringing her inside to bed. Why did it take so long?" Emery replied with a brassy answer. "She did. I helped." "Oh you helped huh? Cut the shit and talk!" Mayne laughed. "OK. I started and Emery finished. That's all you want to know." Both Enya and Sage held a speculative expression.

Sage stormed inside and found her in Mayne's room. She opened the door slowly and walked over to find her half asleep and wrapped in the blanket. "Mia?" she whispered. Mia clutched the sheets tightly in her hands but did not answer. She sat on the bed beside her, lightly touching her shoulder. "Mia?" she whispered again. Mia opened her eyes and looked at her without answering. "Tell me what happened? What I do know is that Mayne carried you upstairs. I had thought that she was bringing you upstairs to let you sleep. Then, Emery disappeared and they both returned over an hour later. I asked them and all that they gave me were smart ass answers." Mia's eye's reflected her broken spirit, causing Sage's eyes to widen with anger. She lay down beside her, touching her hair. Mia answered her in a raspy voice. "I thought so too. That's not what happened." Sage waited for her to collect herself. "Mayne started to pull the towel off me. I stopped him. He said he was just taking it off of me because it was wet. I said all that I needed was a change of clothes." Sage's eyes widened when she realized that Mia referred to Mayne as male. "Then he went over to the dresser but didn't return with clothes. Instead, it was a blindfold. He tried to put it on me and I stepped back. He wrapped it around my throat and threatened me with a syringe." She started sobbing again. "Take your time, Mia." There was a momentary silence. "Did Mayne..." Mia cut her off. "Yes." She cried again. "When he stopped, he must have stepped away for some reason. I didn't know where he went at first. Then I felt his presence again. His hands were on my knees. The blindfold was removed by him, however, it was actually Emery's hands that were on my knees." Mia became hysterical and pleaded with her. "Please don't let them near me. Don't leave me alone." "OK I won't. Just let me get you some clothes. I'll be quick. My room is across from this one."

Sage was speechless and filled with rage. She ran to get them and helped her get up to put them on, then curled up under the covers with her until she fell back asleep.

Sage couldn't sleep. She kept recalling Mia's words and recalled the moment when she had heard her screams. She sent a text to Enya. "I'm up here in bed with Mia. She's sleeping and I'm not leaving her alone. Your sister and Emery are fucked up! They forced her to have sex with them. She is terrified of them now, especially your sister. She also does not know about Mayne. She thinks she is male."

Enya's phone chirped. She read Sage's text and looked directly at Mayne, then at Emery, in utter disgust. Emery returned the stare with a grin. Mayne laughed. "What's your malfunction, Enya?" "That text was Sage and I know what you both did." Emery replied; "Oh do you now?" Enya lit up a cigarette and pointed at them. "You went to far this time. You've traumatized her and now she's terrified of the both of you, especially you Mayne." "Good." Enya smacked her in the head. "Don't talk back to me, Mayne!" Raine was listening to them. "What the fuck did you do?" Enya showed her the text. Raine's reaction was venomous. "If I knew that you were doing that, I would have took a fucking bat to your knees!" "Hey, Raine. Don't tease me. You know how violence excites me." "Fuck off, Mayne!" Enya stood up and slammed her hand on the bar. "Sage is sleeping with her tonight in your room, Mayne. You are both not to go near her. My door will be open. If I see either of you go in that room, I'll knock your teeth out. Try me!"

Mia awoke just before ten am. She felt a body beside her and glanced over to see that Sage was still there, sleeping beside her. She got up and went into the bathroom to take a shower. Each step was painful. She looked at herself in the large mirror on the back of the door. Her eyes were still puffy. Then she looked at her backside. The marks were horrific. She turned on the water and carefully stepped into the bathtub and tried to wash yesterday off of herself. Sage woke up when she heard sounds from the bathroom. She knocked on the door. "Mia? Are you ok?" "Yes, I'm just taking a shower." "Ok. I'm right out here if you need me."

Sage turned on the TV and glanced out the window to see if anyone was in the yard or on the beach, then lay back down on the bed. Someone knocked on the bedroom door. "Who?" Sage asked. "It's Raine." She opened up the door and quickly locked it. "How is she?" Sage pointed to the bathroom. "I just woke up. She's in the shower. She wanted me to stay with her. She's terrified." "Where is everyone now?" "Except for Enya, they all slept in the basement rooms. They were pretty smashed last night. Enya told them to stay away from this room." "Good. I'm gonna go get some clothes for her. Stay here with the door locked. When she gets up will you stay with her while I hop in the shower?" "OK" Sage opened the door, peeked out and ran to her room. She knocked on the door and threw a change of clothes on the bathroom floor. "Mia, it's just me. There's a change of cloths on the floor for you. Raine is here too." She shut the door. They sat on the bed and quietly chatted about what happened. "Enya was so livid, that she left her bedroom door open to make sure no one came in here. They are so fucked up. Mayne is fuckin' certified when she's mad. She's almost like Hunter is." "Raine, wait till' you see her. She was a hot mess last night. She was wrapped in the blankets half asleep when I walked in."

Mia exited the bathroom, wrapped in a towel and walked slowly to the bed with a hairbrush in her hand. She saw Raine and sat down next to them. Raine didn't know what to say to her. She took the brush from her, sat behind her and brushed her hair. Mia sat there quietly with her eyes closed.

"Mia, I'm gonna take a quick shower, then we'll go downstairs to get something to eat. Raine said that they're sleeping in the basement rooms. They were drunk and won't be getting up anytime soon. Enya told them to stay away from you so don't be afraid, ok?" She didn't answer. She kept reliving what had happened, as well as everything that Mayne had said. Mia moved away from Raine and lay back down on the bed.

Raine grabbed a piece of paper and jotted a quick note to Enya to slip under her door. *"Sage and I are downstairs in the kitchen with Mia."* She scribbled her
initial. She looked at Mia, lay on her stomach beside her and watched the TV.

Sage came out of the bathroom and saw her lying down again. "Is she
ok?" Raine shrugged her shoulders. "Mia, lets go get some coffee. Can you
get up on your own?" Mia slowly sat up and spoke in a raspy voice. "Keep
them away from me." "We will. Wait a few seconds, while I put this note
under Enya's door." Sage hooked her arm under hers and was about to help
her get up when she heard Raine inhale sharply upon opening the door. A
hand grasped the seam of the door and pushed it open. Mia looked up when
she heard the sound of a deep voice. "Ladies." It was Hunter. Sage was confused by his early return. "What happened? I thought you were returning
tomorrow." "My plans have changed. Where were you going?" "We're going
downstairs for coffee." "Mia Will be delayed. She will join you downstairs,
later." He stepped aside, holding the door open, gesturing for their departure.
Mia painfully shifted herself to the far side of the bed, holding Sage's hand
and pulling her. "Please don't leave me." Sage felt her quivering from fear.
"Hunter, she's afraid. I can't leave her." She saw his callous expression. "This
is not a debate." She remained on edge about his intentions with Mia, but she
chose not question him further. Raine stood at the entrance, waiting for Sage.
As Sage attempted to slide off of the bed, Mia grasped her hand tighter, pulling her back. "Mia let go of her hand."

She flinched from the sound of his sharp tone and let her go. Sage and
Raine left just as Mayne walked in, noticing Mayne's sly smile as she walked
in. She stood at the foot of the bed, looking directly at Mia with a dispas-
sionate stare. Mia panicked when she saw a syringe protruding from her
hand. Mayne placed it on the table and leaned against the armoire next to
it, watching her weeping with a delighted, cold expression on her face. Mia
slid to the far corner of the bed, wrapping the blanket around herself and
kneeling to avoid putting pressure on the back of her legs. Hunter closed
the blinds and stood at the edge of the bed, observing her terror-stricken

state. He knew she was on the verge of rage and chose not to make any sudden movements towards her for the moment. She watched him diligently while keeping Mayne within her peripheral view. Unaware of their intentions, she assumed this was about the events from yesterday and had a feeling this was not going to end well. He flared his eyes at her and pointed to the edge of the bed in front of him, indicating for her to move herself before him. Her fear prevented her from approaching him and her erratic breathing indicated her peaked anxiety to him as well. Enrapt of her current state, he spoke to her in a calm and steady pitch. "Which rules did you disregard yesterday?" His disposition reflected his ever-consistent state of restraint. Mia chose to keep her silence. She glanced at Mayne and noticed that her continuous fixed stare had remained on her. She heard him inhale sharply; reflecting his impatience towards her and it became evident to her that the standoff was about to end. He shifted and his slight movement triggered her defenses, her posture reflecting that of a cat, about to strike. The lights flickered. Hunter looked at Mayne and nodded. Mayne reached behind herself, knowing that she was watching her every move. Mia saw her pick up the syringe. "NO!" Mia shouted. The lights once again, flickered. "Mia, I want you to lay down, on your stomach. I am not going to hurt you." She heard and understood his words, however, the sound of his voice chilled her to the bone. She trembled as the tears flowed down her cheeks. Hoping to appease him to some extent, she moved herself only halfway towards him, kneeling and balancing herself at the center of the bed. Mayne slowly walked to the side of the bed, opposite of him. When Mia's focused her attention on Mayne, Hunter swiftly grabbed her ankles and pulled her onto her stomach. Mayne simultaneously jumped onto the bed, pulling her arms from under her. Before Mia could scream. Mayne grasped the back of her neck and held the syringe to her face. "If you move, I'll stick this in you." Mia's fear turned to rage. The lights flickered violently, followed by the sound of electrical current. The lights shut off. Mayne was about to inject her. "Wait." He placed his hand flat, on the small of her back and spoke in a calming tone. "Mia. I just want to look at your wounds. Calm yourself now." Mayne lay beside her with her hand on the back of Mia's neck. Mia stared into her eyes, whimpering. For the first time, she saw a rare reflection of tranquility within Mayne's eyes. The trembling began to decrease in its intensity. Mayne wiped the tears from her eyes and then placed her hand on Mia's cheek to maintain Mia's focus on her. Mayne began chanting, holding Mia's vision captive while keeping her spellbound with her voice.

She felt Hunter hands on the waist of her pants. He removed them and inspected the wounds on the back of her thighs. She hissed when she felt his palms touching them. He placed his hands flat, on the bend of her knees. The feeling of the unusual warmth from his hands had peaked her curiosity. She battled her fevered desire to know what was happening but was seduced by the lure of Mayne's chanting. She felt the nerves in her thighs pulsating from his touch as he eased his hands over her wounds with tenacious focus. The whispered words ceased. She looked at Mayne and saw an unheard of, serene smile on her face. Mayne grasped her shoulder and nudged Mia to turn onto her back. Mia inhaled sharply and flinched, expecting pain. There was none. She sat upright, sliding her feet to raise her knees and felt the skin on the back of her thighs. There was no pain. The wounds were gone. "What did you do to me?" She stared at him as he sat down beside her. He took a deep breath. "Your blatant disregard of my rules is unacceptable, however, the result of your actions was deserving, to some extent." He smiled and paused for a moment, staring at her in silence. He then waved his hand in an upward gesture. "Sit up." She shifted herself on the bed, sitting with her legs crisscrossed. She was not happy with his words and did not feel she deserved any of it. Just as she was about to speak, he placed his index finger over her lips. "I warned you about Mayne. While she and I are quite the same, rage and restraint are where we differ. Think about my rules. Choose wisely." He placed his hand on her shoulder. "Stand in front of me." He pulled her close and slowly slid his hands from her back, down to her thighs. "The next time you challenge us, the end result will not be the same as it is now." She grasped his shoulders. "Wait. Tell me what you both did to me?" "Like I said, your pain was deserving to some extent.

Your answer shouldn't be difficult to decipher." Once again, his answers frustrated her. He rose up from the bed and she pulled him back down. "Fine. I'm going to decipher it now, with you both here." Mayne smirked and crossed her arms behind her head, lying flat on the bed. "I remember your hands on my legs and they were really warm. It felt like tiny vibrating waves on my skin." She glanced over at Mayne. "...and you were whispering things. What were you saying?" Mayne grinned. "I said what needed to be said." Mia huffed and frowned. "The pain is gone. The wounds are gone. Somehow, you both healed me. I want to know how." "How can I tell you this if you chose not to follow rules? Your answer is in the Pyramid." Hunter stood up. "I'm going to the basement to reset the breakers. I know that you saw the lights flicker. Are you aware of why and how they went out, Mia?" "No." "What caused the lights to flicker?" Mia recalled the buzzing sound prior to the lights going out. "That is also your answer to how." He pulled her in close and placed his hands on her cheeks to focus her attention, enunciating certain words to see if she would recognize the entity that he would refer to. "Mia, listen to my words. See, feel, listen and become one with all that surrounds you. To understand the potential of your true self, seek, experience and practice what you wish to embrace, all on your own. Know that it takes belief, endurance and respect to achieve your goals. In doing this, your intentions will have a solid foundation to support that which you believe in and all that you dare to do will be achieved. This is why I remain silent about your answers." He glanced down to her necklace and encircled her pendant with his fingers in the shape of a triangle. She gazed up at him. "I understand. It's the Pyramid that you speak of. I know that I'm somehow responsible for the behavior of the lights. I don't understand how you both healed me. I'll figure this out on my own."

"I'm going to he basement and then, to sleep. Keep the noise level at a minimum. Like Enya, I do not like to be woken up."

Mayne slid her hands around her waist. Resting her chin on her shoulder, she whispered into her ear. "Coffee time." As they walked down the staircase, the lights turned on. Mayne walked into the kitchen with her hands on Mia's shoulders. "I've returned her, as promised." Mia sat at the kitchen table next to Raine while Mayne made the coffee. Sage watched her slide onto the bench. "You're sitting...on your ass. No pain? What gives?" Hesitant to answer at first, Mia looked up at Mayne. She was getting two mugs from the cabinet. She turned around to look at Mia, dangling one of the mugs from her pinky finger and holding her index finger to her mouth, gesturing for Mia to be silent. "It doesn't hurt anymore." Sage held a suspicious look on her face and then smiled. After speculating what had actually happened, she was relieved that it wasn't negative. She respected her silence.

Mayne and Mia joined Sage and Raine in the kitchen. "What do you wanna eat, Mia?" "Cereal." Mayne placed the two mugs of coffee on the table and slid Mia's over, in front of her. She sat at the end of the table, with her foot on the chair, across from Mia. Raine rudely tapped her spoon against her mug, while staring at Mayne with a suspicious expression on her face. Mayne stared back at her. "WHAT?" Raine just shook her head.

Sage observed that Mia was seemingly pain free and remarked. "You're sitting on your ass. No pain? What gives?" Mia glanced at Mayne, who was pressing her index finger across her lips. Mia responded. "It doesn't hurt anymore." Sage was suspicious but smiled. Speculating what had happened, she was relieved that it wasn't negative. Raine rudely tapped her spoon against her mug, while staring at Mayne with a suspicious expression on her face. Mayne stared back at her. "WHAT?" Raine shook her head. "It must be nice to be you, huh?" Mayne grinned. "Yeah. Why? Do you wanna be just like me when you grow up?"

Lucius heard voices coming from the kitchen as he approached the top of the landing. As he walked in, he stopped in his tracks when he saw Mia sitting there. Mia saw Lucius but then quickly looked the other way. Sage immediately addressed him. "Listen, before you say anything, just shut the fuck up! Understand?" Lucius smirked. "And good morning to you too?" Lucius grabbed a mug of coffee and sat at the other end of the table, by Raine. When Lucius looked at Mia, smiling, Sage felt he wasn't taking her seriously. "If you say anything I'm gonna punch you." Lucius laughed again. "What? I can't talk?" Looking at Lucius, she banged her mug down on the table. "That's not what I meant. You know what I meant." Lucius turned on the TV and took some food out of the fridge. Sage shut the TV off. "Leave it off. Hunter's sleeping, jackass!" Lucius had a smart-ass thought. He saw someone's key chain on the counter and swiped them. He chugged down the coffee. "I'm gonna go take my bike out of the garage, park it out front, take a shower and go for a ride." He placed the keys on the kitchen table in front of Mia, staring at her and laughing. Mayne covered her mouth to hide her laughter. Mia pursed her lips at him. Raine replied to him. "Oh you got jokes today?" Sage slugged Lucius in the arm and shooed him away. Raine whispered some advice to Mia. "Never show someone you're afraid. It gives them power over you. Instead, just plot your revenge."

Lucius returned downstairs to get his cigarettes. Mia put her arms on the table, closed her eyes and rested her head. Raine tapped Mia's shoulder. "When Lucius returns, would ya like me to stick my foot out or throw a banana peel on the floor?" Mia lifted her head and smiled at Raine. "Banana peel!" "Consider it done. This is the perfect example of what I've said." She got up, grabbed a banana, cut it up and put it in her cereal. She swung the peel, in front of Mia to make her laugh. "This is gonna be funny. I can't wait." Mia chuckled. Mayne stood up and peaked in the refrigerator for something to eat. "That ain't right. If anyone does that shit to me, they better run." "How's that not right? Compared to the shit you do, I'd say its kinda mild." "Fuck off Raine."

Sage pulled chocolate chip muffins out of the oven, took one for herself and placed the rest on the table. She read Mayne's shirt. "Nice shirt Mayne. Are you trying to say something to Mia?" She was wearing her favorite white shirt, on purpose. *Gas, grass or ass. No one rides for free.* Mia read her shirt. "Did you wear that because of me?" "Why? You wanna go for another bike ride?" Mia's jaw dropped. "WHAT?" Mayne shut the refrigerator and leaned up against it, eating a donut and grinning at her. Mia stood up and pointed at her. "How dare you say that to me!" Mayne put her donut down on the table and grabbed her finger. "Don't point your fuckin' finger at me! Do it again and I'll break it!" Mia pushed her hand away. "Don't touch me!" Mia slid back onto the bench. Raine shouted at her. "You're an asshole Mayne." Mayne flashed her middle finger.

Mia nudged Raine underneath the table with her foot and looked at the banana peel. Raine grinned and tossed it over the table, onto the floor. Mia put her hands over her mouth to cover her evil grin. As Mayne passed Sage, she immediately saw it there. She stood for a moment staring at Sage. Sage struggled to hold in the laugh. She picked it up off of the floor and tossed it into the garbage. "Funny, Sage." "Me? I didn't do it, but I would have." Raine laughed hysterical. Mayne looked at Raine then grabbed some coffee, purposely sat down across from Mia, staring into her eyes. Mayne saw Mia looking down, covering her face. "Did you think that was funny, Mia"? Mia said nothing, unsuccessfully holding back her giggling. Mayne continued to stare at her "That's ok. I thought your face was funny last night when you saw Emery between your legs, instead of me." Mia looked steadfast, at her. Sage smacked Mayne in the head. "Say something again to her and I'll go wake up Enya." Startled, Mayne glanced at her and then back at Mia. "I'm hungry." Mayne uttered to Sage. "There's cereal and muffins on the table, ya filthy animal! If you want something else, make it yourself." With a fixed stare on Mia, Mayne stuck her finger into Mia's half eaten chocolate chip muffin. "That's not what I meant." Raine looked at her. "Fuckin' sociopath!" Sage kicked Mayne in the shin. Mayne jerked, but maintained her perverse eye contact with Mia.

Mia jumped from the table, poured more coffee into her mug and went outside to the yard. She lay on the lawn chair with her knees up, sipping her coffee. She saw a bag of water balloons and a toy beside them used to fill them with water. She decided to fill them with some ice water from the cooler nearby. Inside the cooler was an opened bottle of ice-cold red wine. She thought about what Raine said earlier and realized that the wine will stain. She filled up some balloons with the wine, placed them in a cooler and slid it under her chair."

Sage watched at Mayne while she peered through the back yard doors. "If you follow her, I'm gonna go get Enya." Mayne smirked. "Are you threatening me or challenging me"? She rose from her seat and slid the door open. Mia spotted her, grabbed two balloons and hid them. She stepped outside and walked slowly towards her. Mia grabbed two balloons, one in each hand and held them beneath the chair. When she was within a few feet of her, she held the balloons behind her back, stood up and threw them. The impact was epic. Her precise aim landed the balloons onto her chest, bursting at impact and the shocking, icy liquid caused her to scream. She ran to the other side of the pool and screamed for Sage and Raine. Startled, they ran outside thinking Mayne was attacking her. They saw Mayne, soaking wet with red wine all over her white shirt. "Mia ran over to them. Raine howled. "Oh this is way better than the banana peel!" Sage shouted in a sarcastic voice. "Ohhh, your favorite shirt is ruined, AWWW!"

Furious and shell shocked from the cold wine; Mayne looked directly at Mia and threatened her. "So you wanna play again? Watch your back." She walked back into the house. Raine gave Mia a high five. "Don't be afraid of her threats. She's just pissed that you got her. So plot your next attack before she does."

Mia was proud of herself but still leery of what Mayne said. "Is he bipolar? How does he go from nice to vicious in a split second?" Raine smirked at Mia's gender title for her. "Yeah, I know. He's special like that." She filled a few more balloons while trying to think of a few other shenanigans.

Mayne's cell phone rang. It was Hunter. "There's noise." "Sorry about that. I took care of it." "Where are you?" "I'm in my room changing my shirt." "Keep Mia with you. She stays with you tonight. You are the only one in the house other than myself, who can control her. Use other means if you deem it necessary. "Fetch Enya I want to talk to her." Mayne went to Enya's room and woke her up. She knew that she didn't like to be woken up, but didn't care because she was still perturbed about being kicked out of her own room by her last night. She banged on the door. "WHAT!?" "It's Hunter." She opened the door, swiped the phone from her and then slammed it shut. Hunter recapped what he had told Mayne. "Mia is afraid of her. She won't stay in there." "Mayne will handle it." He hung up. Enya tossed the phone on the floor and tried to go back to sleep.

Mayne put on another shirt and returned downstairs. She walked up to Sage and in a malicious tone, repeating what Hunter had said. "Hunter just called me from his room. He said to keep the noise down and that Mia stays in MY room tonight. Don't tell her. I'll take care of it." Mayne made a sandwich and went to the living room to watch TV. Raine and Sage looked at each other. Raine threw her hands up. "Really? Noise? She's the shit stirrer." "I'm not telling Mia. She'll flip out."

Lucius returned with a cigarette hanging from his mouth and reached for a beer from the refrigerator. "Where's Mia?" Remembering that she had the water balloons, Raine pointed to the yard. Lucius walked outside and spotted her. Raine laughed. "Next target." Raine watched through the sliding glass doors. Mia spotted him, grabbed two balloons and waited for him to approach. As Lucius drew closer, she emerged from her seat with the balloons behind her and threw them. One landed on his stomach and one on the front of his pants. She yelled; "Bulls eye!" She wasn't afraid of Lucius so she just stood there laughing. Raine ran outside. Lucius howled loudly from the cold feeling, looked at his clothes and then at Mia. He didn't run after her at first. He wanted her to feel at ease before he ambushed her. The moment she looked away, he charged at her, picked her up and threw her into the pool. She screeched. Sage heard her and ran out. "What the fuck?" Lucius was laughing so hard that his face had turned red.

Mayne heard her high-pitched scream, paused the movie and went outside to see what happened. She saw Lucius with red all over his clothing and assumed that Lucius threw her in, as payback. "She did the same thing to me when you were in the shower, only I haven't paid her back yet. I'm saving this for tonight." Mia looked at her as she spoke. "ARE YOU THREATENNG ME AGAIN, MAYNE?" She pulled herself out of the pool and walked right up to her face. Raine watched avidity. "I'm not gonna let you bully me. You wanna start something then I'm gonna finish it, NOW!" "Don't challenge me Mia. You'll always be sadly mistaken." Mayne walked back into the house to get a cigarette. Mia ran to get another balloon and returned. No one said a word. They were watching Mia in amazement. "MAYNE! Get the fuck out here now!" Mayne's eyes flared. She walked back outside, looking steely eyed at Mia. Mia threw the balloon at her, but missed. Mia didn't run this time. She stood her ground. Mayne dropped her cigarette and sprinted to her. She grasped her shirt and slammed her against the house.

"Guess what, sweetheart? Hunter called. He said that you'll be staying in MY room with me, tonight. If you have a problem with that, then I'll find a way to convince you!" Everyone was silent and Mia's face changed from fearless to restraint. Mayne grasped the back of her neck, pushed her indoors and upstairs, to her room. Mayne shuffled through her dresser and pulled out a change of cloths for Mia and herself. "Put these on and make it quick." Mia went into the bathroom to change. When she returned, Mayne grabbed her hand and dragged her back downstairs and into the living room. "Sit and shut the fuck up." Hunter called Mayne's cell. "Put Mia on the phone." She handed it to her. "It's Hunter." "Yes." "Mia. I am trying to sleep. If you yell again, you will be spending the day in my room. Understood?" "But…" He cut her off. "Understood?" "Yes." He hung up.

Emery woke from the yelling and went upstairs. "Who's yelling?" Lucius filled him in. "It's been an entertaining morning." "I can see that from your clothes." "Are they still out there?" Emery poured a mug of coffee, saw chocolate chip muffins and took two. "Just Sage and Raine. Mayne and Mia are in the living room." Enya was also woken from the yelling. Livid and cranky from the noise, she was unable to go back to sleep. She hopped into the shower and went downstairs. Upon entering the kitchen she saw Lucius and Emery at the kitchen table. She poured some coffee and went to the living room. She saw Mayne and Mia, oddly watching TV together. She noticed Mia's flustered face and leered at them both. Mayne was sitting at the end of the couch with one arm over the back and one foot on the floor. Mia was siting on the opposite side, with her legs crossed against herself, watching TV with an obvious attitude. "Was it necessary to bang on my door, asshat?" "Yes it was. Did you sleep well?" "Don't be a smartass. What the hell was all the screaming in the yard about, before?" "Water balloon fights." "Nice." "What's this about? Did you make up? "We're watching a movie." Mayne was short with her and also didn't like to be questioned. "That's not what I asked." Feeling less intimidated because of Enya's presence, Mia looked up at Enya and spoke. "I threw a water balloon at him and then he threatened me. When I fought back, he got mad, threatened me again and dragged me here." Mayne kicked her leg, in the middle of her sentence. Knowing there was more to it that that, she let that one go. "And last night?" Mayne became agitated. "Let it go, Enya." Mayne threatened Mia with a hell-bent glare. Mia answered sarcastically. "Oh you wanna know what happened last...?" Mayne cut her off. "Did I not say sit there and shut up? Enya, go inside." Enya stood up and in a stern voice, Enya responded. "You and I will talk later."

Mayne glared at her and then turned back to the TV. Her eyes always seemed to pierce Mia's soul. Mia had wished that she didn't say anything. She thought to herself; "Blood is thicker than water and a*t the end of the day, Enya is his sister."* Mia resituated herself on the couch, resting her head on the arm of the couch. She glanced at Mayne through the corner of her eye and saw that Mayne was immersed in the movie. Mia tried to understand the enigma behind her silence and rage. She thought to herself. *He doesn't speak much and keeps his opinions to himself. He never tells anyone anything until its necessary. Why do I allow him to intimidate me? Yet here I sit, just because he told me to sit.*

Mia imagined beating her senseless with a bat for what had happened last night. Her feelings confused her. She thought about the earlier occurrence with Hunter and Mayne and tried to conceive how she was healed, comparing it to the affect that she had on the lights. Joy, rage and fear are three different entities. When she was enraged, she could not control herself. When she was elated, afraid or angry, it innervated her. With this in mind, she thought of this feeling of innervation and it's meaning. The intensity if her feelings seemed to exude from her in an extant form, animating through random entities, such as light fixtures. It seemed unrealistic much like her anxiety. She analyzed and comparing thoughts of conscious and subconscious intentions, direct and indirect energy, in an attempt to decipher the gray area of reason for the healed wounds and the flickering lights. Yesterday, inclusive of stealing the bike, there were times when she was highly elated and times when she feared for her life. She stared at Mayne, torn by her feelings of both like and hate. She wanted to stab him and be embraced by him. She hated his stare and loved it at the same time. She could not escape his bizarre hold on her. She tasted blood and wanted more. Mayne mystified her and challenged her at the same time, whereas Hunter intimidated, possessed and overpowered her. Although unresolved, she felt her thought process was going in the right direction, but was tired of trying to figure it out for the moment. Feeling frustrated and fiendish, Mia forcefully kicked Mayne's foot just to antagonize her. The unexpected blow startled her, knocking her foot off of the couch. Mayne flared her eyes. "What the fuck?" Mia stared back, clearly looking for a fight. She wanted her to react. Mayne turned her attention back to the movie.

Enya refilled her coffee and saw the chocolate chip muffins. They were her favorite. "Who made these?" Sage replied, proudly. "I did! Have some." "Thanks." She sat and indulged. "I found it very peculiar when I walked inside to see them sitting on the couch, watching TV together. What gives?" Sage filled her in on the morning drama and last night as well. Listening intensively, Enya's mouth dropped. "That explains the fucking noise this morning. My sister is fuckin' deranged." Sage chuckled. "This morning I had to threaten her with you, to diffuse it." "Meanwhile they're sitting in there, together and on top of that, Mia thinks my sister is male." Sage shook her head. Enya walked over to the microwave. "I think I'll go make them some popcorn for shits and giggles." Sage recalled the popcorn shenanigans last night and giggled. "What's so funny, Sage?" "Just know I'm not cleaning up anymore popcorn." She smirked. "Why? What happened?" "Popcorn fight in the pool last night." "Nice!"

The sounds from the TV were slowly becoming white noise. Mia started to fall in and out of twilight. Enya walked in with a smart-ass grin and loudly placed the bowl of popcorn on the table. "Play nice." She looked at them with a mischievous expression and walked out of the room. Mia sat up, stuck her hand in the bowl and grabbed a handful. Mayne grabbed the bowl, put it on her stomach and picked at it while watching the movie. Still feeling bored and antsy, Mia threw a kernel at Mayne and it hit her in the face. She shrugged it off. Mia threw another, trying to provoke her. "Stop!" *Ha!* Mia thought to herself. She threw another. Mayne looked at her. "I said stop." "No." Mia paused, repeating words from the night before. "I said stop last night and did you?" "Touché!" Mayne held a Mona-Lisa grin. She threw another. Mayne put the bowl on the table, paused the movie and sat up. "You're really annoying me." "Good." Mia ascended from the couch, picked up the bowl and dumped it over her head. She fell back onto the couch, laughing mischievously. Fed up, Mayne huffed and stood up. She brushed the popcorn off of herself and held the stance of a raging bull about to charge. "RUN!" Mia did just that. "SHIT!" Mia screamed. She ran out of the room like a bat out of hell, through the kitchen, almost knocking Raine over. She made it to the yard and spotted the cooler. With an evil grin, she grabbed the balloons and quickly ran to the other side of the pool.

Feeling victorious, she waited for Mayne to get outside and threw the balloons at her and shouted. "It's so fuckin' on!" One missed her and the other hit her in the leg.

Emery was sitting on one of the barstools with Sage, witnessing the lunacy. "Oh, there's a hole in that bucket!" Sage rolled her eyes. "I'm not even asking."

"FUCK!" Mayne roared, chasing her with heated vengeance. Mia's high-pitched screams pierced everyone's ears. She ran in the opposite direction, around the pool and back inside the house, stopping to look for the banana peel in the garbage. She tossed it onto the floor and paused for a second to witness Mayne fall. Enya was sitting at the table, observing the circus. She yelled. "BANANA PEEL!" Mayne stopped short and saw it on the floor just in time. She gave Mia a fiery death stare. "YOU'RE FUCKIN DEAD!"

Sage shouted the blame at Enya. "You hadda make popcorn!"

Mayne sprinted over the banana peel and nearly caught her. Mia screamed, ran inside and up the stairway. She stopped at several doors, only to find that they were locked. At the end of the hall, was the bathroom. Just as Mia grasped the doorknob, Mayne caught her. Her screams were nearly glass shattering. They heard her downstairs and in the yard. Emery laughed. "I think the suspect has been apprehended!" Lucius looked at Emery. "I think Mia likes this." They laughed. Being the shit stirrer that Lucius is, he ran to the base of the stairs and sung some inciting lyrics, to add to the drama.

♪*I like to teach you all the rules...*♪

He laughed hysterically. "I crack myself up!"

Mia knew exactly why he had sung those words. Mayne was amused. She lifted Mia over her shoulder and carried her to her door. She unlocked her door and slid Mia onto the bed, re-locked the door and looked at Mia impishly. Mia couldn't stop laughing. Mayne inched towards her. "Do ya think you're funny, Mia?" Mia nodded and laughed walking backward. Mayne backed her against the wall, pinning her hands above her head. Mayne's vicious and hungry eyes reminded her of the wolf from her dream. Mayne kissed her forcefully. Her hand slowly slid down her back, pulling Mia's body closer. Mia's heart palpitated with elation. Mayne pushed her onto the bed, licking her teeth like a hungry wolf. Mia panted in anticipation from Mayne's dominant allure and stood up in front of her in a challenging, alpha stance. She felt captivated by the touch of Mayne's hands on her skin. She reached under Mia's shirt and unhooked her bra. Mia gasped as she caressed her breasts. She pushed her back onto the bed, kissing her aggressively. Mia knew that Mayne had an appetite and she wanted to feed it. She consumed her with no mercy. Mayne touched every sensitive spot, her hands caressing her, sliding over her waist, her ass and her thighs, focusing on all the right places. The sensation of her fingers slowly penetrating her, every stroke, leading Mia to a slow climax and experiencing the full affects of Mayne's salacious appetite. Mia's body shuddered and her moans fed Mayne's appetite. She felt her mouth slowly moving down her neck, kissing and licking every inch of her along the way. Mia panted, trembling in anticipation when she felt her kisses on her belly. She felt spellbound and torn within her own opposing notions about how she felt about Mayne: hate, love, the lines between seemed to blur. Mayne slid herself upward to face her. Her piercing eyes captivated Mia. She slid her hands through Mia's hair and held her head tight. Mayne whispered. "Are you ready for me?" Mia clutched Mayne's arms, looked deep within her eyes and saw the chilling and wicked darkness inside of her. Mia watched her as she moved away from her face. She felt her breath on her sex and her eyes rolled back, paralyzed by her rapture. Mayne's erotic madness, animalistic and relentless, never once allowing Mia to regain control until she brought Mia to full orgasm. Mia's cries of ecstasy, her body, quivering from new sensations, were a level of elation she had never felt before until now. Mayne crawled above her, licking her lips and whispered to her. "Taste yourself." Mayne's kisses, sensual, soft, arousing Mia once again. Mia tasted blood and wanted more. She slid her fingers through Mayne's hair and kissed her aggressively. She wrapped her leg around Mayne's and pushed her over, onto her back. "My turn. Now you dance with me."

Mayne slid off of the bed and went into the bathroom. Mia sat up, wrapped the sheets around herself and turned on the TV. When she returned, she was carrying a hairbrush for her. "You might want to fix your hair." Mia attempted to stand up, and lost her balance. Mayne caught her in time and helped her stand. "That was your fault." "How?" "My weak legs." Locked within her arms, Mia gazed up at her searching in her haunted eyes and once again, bewitched by her eyes. She put her clothes on and brushed her hair and tied it into a ponytail. Mayne took her by the hand and led her back downstairs.

CHAPTER 13

A Feast of Friends

The Full Moon was approaching tomorrow night. Sage and Enya were preoccupied with making the house presentable while Raine hustled to get the yard ready for the weekend festivities. The guests whom had just arrived, were Gwen, accompanied by three people from her circle, Ceridwen, Faeryn and Aithusa. They were invited to stay for the weekend in celebration for the upcoming Esbat.

Emery and Lucius had just returned from picking up the groceries for tomorrow as well as for the barbecue this evening. They dropped off the bags and ran out to help with the guest's luggage.

Mayne and Mia entered the kitchen to find Gwen and Enya preparing some of the food for this evening. Mia recognized her and cowered behind Mayne. Smiling mischievously, Gwen greeted her. "Well, look who it is. Hello, Mia." Mayne reached around and pulled Mia out from behind her. Mia's face turned several shades of crimson. "Hi Mayne. What's the matter Mia? Cat got your tongue?" Mia was silent. Mayne grinned, slid her hands around Mia's waist and replied with a sarcastic pun. "She's a little tired." Enya looked at her. "Yeah, I'll bet." Gwen took a step back, looking at them. "So how did we get from near death by your hands, to where your hands are, now?" Mia slipped back, behind her. Mayne sucked her teeth, smiling arrogantly and proceeded into the yard with Mia close behind her. Gwen looked at Enya, puzzled. Enya pointed up. "Full Moon…"

Mayne brought Mia over to a lawn chair, closest to the bar. "Stay here." Mia sat obediently. She reached for a beer and sat on the bartender chair, across from Ceridwen. Mia saw them glancing at her as they chatted amongst themselves. She didn't recognize Gwen's friends, at first. One of them had been sizing her up. It was Aithusa. Mia hated being stared at, so she crawled on the lawn chair and sat, sideways, as to not face her.

Lucius fetched the meat for the grill. He rewarded himself with a beer and turned on the ignition and flames spewed upward. He had stepped back just in time. "Who the fuck used the grill last and didn't clean it?" Enya and Gwen and Sage brought out the food that they had made earlier and placed it on the table next to the bar. Enya replied to him. "I believe it was you, sir-jackass!"

Everyone picked at the food and caught up with one another. It was dusk and the Moon was 98 percent full. Mia gazed at it as it began to rise above the fence. Sage walked over to Mia with a plate full of wings. "Come eat." "Mayne said to stay here, plus those people keep staring at me and I don't want to stand next to them." "Fuck them. If they do, I'll tell them to kiss my ass." Mia giggled. When she grabbed her hand, Mia pulled back. Sage rolled her eyes, sighed and walked over to Mayne. "Mia won't get out of the chair and come with me to eat, because of you." With her mouth full, Mayne looked at Mia, pointed and waved her finger, gesturing for her to come to her. Mia sprung from her seat and stood before her. "Eat something." She walked over to the table, avoiding all eye contact, took a plate and perused the food spread. There were three kinds of salad, chili and assorted barbecued items. She scooped a little of each salad, grabbed a soda and quickly returned to her chair. Sage glanced at Mia's plate and watched her as she returned to her chair without saying a word. Sage looked at Mayne. "Really?" Gwen also watched Mia return to her seat. "She's very submissive to you, Mayne. What gives?" "I'm alpha." Aithusa grinned. Mayne continued her conversation with Aithusa. "I heard what happened with you and Mia. Fuck, if I woulda let her get away with that shit." "Has she seen you?" Aithusa glanced over at Mia and then looked back at Mayne. "No. I don't think she remembers me. I haven't forgotten our encounter." "Yeah, I heard. She does have balls. I'll give her that." "Hunter did warn me." Aithusa went behind the bar to get another beer. "Do you want one?" "Yeah." "I heard what happened at Gwen's bar. I wish I had been there." Gwen chimed in. "It was an edge of your seat nightmare." Mayne looked at Gwen. "It won't happen again." Emery laughed. "It didn't end there." Aithusa listened intently to Mayne, wanting to know more. "Yeah? Reveal." Mayne laughed, shaking her head and drank her beer. Emery stood up. "When we got back here, we parked our bikes. Raine parked the truck and I pulled Mia out of the truck. Mayne grabbed her and pushed her face near the hot chrome pipes on her bike" Aithusa and Gwen's eyes widened and Aithusa roared. "Malicious!" "Yeah, Mia's face was fuckin' epic. It didn't end there either." Mayne held her hand up. "Ok! T.M.I. Enough!"

Enya went inside to get her cigarettes and returned toting a huge bowl of fruit salad. Some threw pieces of fruit in their drinks. Gwen pulled up a barstool next to Enya and helped herself to some fruit. "Enya, what's the story with your sister and Mia?" "What do you mean?" "She was pretty messed up when you guys left my bar and had to be carried out. She went from a little rebel to obeying her every command." Enya was silent for a few moments and thought intently, prior to answering her. "Mayne is dominant...of few words...and has a wicked side. You've witnessed that before. In conflict, you either learn to see things her way, or you've inevitably chosen your own demise. If it were anyone else but Mia, it wouldn't have ended as well as it did." Gwen chose to let it go.

Sage overheard and waited for Gwen to walk away. "Enya, I think she's trying to find out what's so special about Mia." "I know. She's just curious."

Sage approached Mayne to inform her that she was going to bring Mia over to get some fruit. "Your highness, I request your permission to bring Mia over here for fruit." She spun her seat around to look at Mia and summoned her, once again. "MIA!" Startled, Mia jerked from her blared voice and walked up to her. "There's fruit over there." Sage shook her head in disgust. Mia walked over to the table and made herself a plate. Emery was weaving from the shots he had consumed earlier. He leered at Mia, up and down. Mia sensed him gazing at her and against her own best judgment she looked up at him, his sly smile giving away his nasty thoughts. Emery put his fingers on the button of her denim shorts, beneath the waistband and tugged. "What do ya got in there, Mia?" Mayne listened, in anticipation for her response. Lucius answered for her. "She's got a lion in there!" Mia smacked Emery's arm and scratched it in the process. "DON'T TOUCH ME!" Lucius stepped in front of her and put his finger under her chin, teasing her further. "Ooooh! Tough little lamb!" Emery smiled and stood, knocking Lucius out of the way and put his hands on her shoulders. "Why Mia, why didn't you show me this side of you last night. It would have made things interesting." Furious, she shook herself free from his hands, threw her fruit in his face and turned to run back to her chair. Barely holding back her laughter, Mayne caught her by the arm as she passed and abruptly pulled her close. Mia whimpered. "Go sit. I'll bring you another bowl." She wiped her eyes with her sleeve and returned to the chair. Enya rose up from her seat and quickly walked over to the other side of the bar. "Listen closely jackasses, cause I'm only gonna say this once." She looked at Lucius, Emery and lastly, Mayne, with a forewarning fury, jabbing each one of them with her fingernail. "Stop harassing her. Stop pushing her. Stop touching her. If it happens again, I'll wake up Hunter. Enough! Understood?" Mayne looked at Emery and Lucius, holding her hand up to simmer their collective chaos. "Listen guys, we don't wanna to wake him, so back off of Mia."

Mayne handed Mia another bowl of fruit and returned to the bar. Mia swung herself around, to face the house.

Back at the bar, some festivities were taking place. Zephyr pulled out a mirror and Raine grabbed her cannabis stash, rolled a few and passed them around. Mayne indulged in both, avidly.

Mia picked on the fruit while trying to calm herself. Raine walked over to her. "Mia, good job! You're learning. Just don't cry. You shoulda punched Emery in the teeth!" She patted her on the shoulder, walked to the pool ladder and sat on its edge.

Aithusa brought her own special blend and lit one up. She grabbed two beers and snuck away. She sat on the chair beside Mia, facing the opposite direction. Mia turned to see who had sat on her chair but was only able to see the back of her head at first. She put the other beer down, cracked open the other one with her teeth and offered it to her. Mia froze. "Hello Mia. Do you remember me?" Apprehensive, Mia just watched her in silence. Aithusa took a deep toke, moved herself closer and tried to blow it into her mouth. Mia backed up. "Awww come on Mia. Consider it a peace offering. I'll be insulted if you don't." Mia felt uneasy. "No. Mayne will be mad." "No she won't." "How are you not mad at me?" Aithusa kept eye contact, deliberately intimidating her. "Ahh... You remember me now. I didn't say that I wasn't." She took another toke, put her hand on the back of Mia's neck and pulled Mia's face to hers. Aithusa pressed her lips against hers and blew the smoke into her mouth. Mia coughed, inhaling some of it. "Breath it out of your nose this time." She took another toke and as she blew it into her mouth, she kissed her. Mia tried to push her back but she wouldn't release her. She grabbed her neck and pulled her down onto her lap. "Don't move." She took another toke and forced the smoke into Mia's mouth once again. Mia pushed herself away and rolled off of the chair onto the ground. Her eyes teared from coughing. She sat up with her hands on the cement. Furious, she looked at her, raising her voice. "Don't touch me and get the hell off of my chair!" Aithusa ignored her request and lie back, onto the chair, smiling.

Feeling lively, Mayne was now in the mood to harass people for her own entertainment purposes. She stood up, finished her beer and went to get another. She casually walked over to Raine and pushed her into the pool. "Fuck! Mayne! You're an ass!" she yelled. When Sage saw her looking at her she jumped into the pool before she could push her in. Both Raine and Sage splashed her violently until she stepped away. Mayne spotted Mia sitting on the ground. She sucked her teeth and with impish swagger, she made her way over to her. She placed her hands on Mia's shoulders and squeezed. With angst, Mia turned to see her there. Aithusa stood up, slid her hand around Mia's waist and blew smoke in her face. "We'll catch up later, Mia."

Mayne slid her arm around Mia's waist, pulled her close and brushed the hair away from Mia's face. She eased Mia back onto the lawn chair and forcibly kissed her. When Mia felt Maybe's hand underneath her shirt, she grasped her hand to stop her. "Please stop. They'll see." Mayne replied in a cold and ireful tone. "No." She opened the button on Mia's shorts and unzipped them. Enya ran up to them and smacked Mayne in the head. "We have guests! Cut it out!" "What the fuck, Enya!" She sat up and looked at Mia in frustration. "Never say no to me!" Flustered, Mia sat up and zippered her shorts. Mayne callously left her there and returned to the bar.

Emery and Lucius had been watching and snickered at Mayne as she reclaimed her seat at the bar. Lucius taunted her. "Ya left poor Mia all frustrated. That ain't right. You should go take her upstairs and finish what you started. "When I want to, I will." "Oh really? You're feelin' mighty confident. She may turn you down." "She does what I want." Mia overheard Mayne and was mortified by her blatant statement. Without Mayne's explicit permission, she defiantly marched over to her, her thoughts filled with malicious intent. Mayne watched as she approached and spoke in a harsh tone. "Did I say, get up?" Mia's eyes widened. She shouted at Mayne. "I DO WHAT YOU WANT? FUCK THAT! I DO WHAT I WANT AND GIVE YOU

NOTHING... AND NO, YOU DIDN'T GIVE ME YOUR FUCKING PERMISSION TO GET UP! YET HERE I AM!"

A cold, spectral silence followed. Everyone remained silent in anticipation of the imminent danger that was about to befall on Mia. The slow, eerie scraping sound of Mayne's bar stool sent chills through Mia's body. Their eyes locked. Although Mia firmly held her ground, deep inside she felt her courage slowly diminishing. Mayne's aura seemed to morph into an eclipsed version of itself and casting its shadow over its next target. Clenching her fists, Mayne sucked her teeth and eyed her down and up. "Mia, would you like to test your theory right now?" Mayne rose from her chair, slowly and stood in her face. Mia knew not to challenge her with an answer. Although Mia was now intimidated, she held her ground and didn't show her fear.

Enya returned from the bathroom and immediately sensed the tension in the air. "What? Another fucking standoff?" Raine climbed out of the pool and stood a short distance, behind Mia. Mayne didn't budge or release her cold fixed stare on her. She raised her arm and pointed into the house, gesturing for Mia to go inside. Mia flared her fingers, in anticipation of a fight and shouted defiantly, feeding into Mayne's furor. "NO! Did you not comprehend the words that just came out of my mouth? Do you need me to break it down for you? You disrespected me...took me for granted! Fuck what you want!" The stringed lights, encompassing the yard noticeably flickered. Seeing this, Enya ran into the house to wake Hunter. Mayne slammed her beer down loudly, stepped behind the bar. She reached underneath and took the dart gun that she had placed there earlier. She walked back towards Mia, with the gun pointed at her. Shrieks and whispers of disbelief were heard in the background. Mia's jaw dropped. Frozen with fear, she panicked and began to hyperventilate. Within seconds, her eyes rolled back and she fainted. Raine partially broke her fall and sat on the ground holding Mia's head on her lap. She patted her cheeks repeatedly and then slid an ice cube from her drink, over her forehead, but she didn't respond. In a panicked state, she emptied her drink onto the ground, scooped water from the pool and poured it over

Mia's head and neck, trying to wake her. "Can someone help me?!" Raine shouted. Faeryn and Ceridwen ran over to them. Sage pointed to the chaise. "Slide that chair over here. I wanna lift her up and put her on it."

The girls quickly dragged the chaise over to Mia. Sage hooked her arms underneath Mia's arm. "Faeryn, you lift her by the back of her knees and Kerry, you lift from the small of her back." The girls took their places. "Ready? On the count of three…" Mayne jumped out of her chair and shouted at them. "Step away from her now! When she wakes up, I want her to see only me!" They looked at Mayne as if she were insane. Duly acknowledging her psychotic expression, they did as she asked. Enya and Hunter stood at the door, observing. Raine gently slipped her legs out from under her and gently placed her head on the ground. Gwen was speechless. She whispered to Aithusa. "Too many lines?"

Mayne held her focus on Mia, waiting for her to regain consciousness. The intensity grew, seconds turning into minutes. When she opened her eyes, the first thing that she recognized was the nearly Full Moon. She then, looked forward to see Mayne standing before her. "GET UP!" Mia gazed at her, still feeling dazed and unfocused. Mia ignored her, turning her attention back to the Moon while remaining still and not moving so much as a finger. Mayne went into the house, passing Hunter and Enya, without acknowledging their presence. She returned and stood over Mia, dangling a belt from her hand. Enya grabbed Hunters wrist. "You need to stop her." "I will, if I deem it necessary." Enya clenched her fists in frustration. When she saw Mayne swing the belt, she screamed and clutched Hunters arm. "MAYNE!" Just as she swung it towards her thigh, Mia sat up, holding her arms over her head. Mayne's piercing stare terrified her and she became hysterical. "UP, NOW!" Mia rose, unsteadily, and stood before her, looking down at the ground and weeping. With her teeth gritted, Mayne grabbed Mia's jaw tight and pulled her face to hers. "Keep fucking challenging me and you'll lose every fucking time." Mia squealed from the pain. She wrapped her arms around herself, recalling the bathroom incident at the bar and trembled just as she did then.

Enya was livid. "She's out of control, Hunter!" She slammed her hand on the counter and looked at Him. "Why didn't you stop her?!" "My intervention was unnecessary." "And what would have happened if…" He cut her off. "Mayne knows what it takes to control her."

"Go sit on the fuckin' chair, now." Mayne commanded, pointing to it. Mia lay down on the lawn chair and curled up into a ball. She eventually stopped crying and just gazed at her surroundings. Hunter approached Mayne and pulled her aside. "As she becomes versed and gains confidence, she will continue to test her limits with us. Always be prepared for the inevitable. The feral side of her is to be suppressed until she respectfully understands All."

Hunter peered over at Mia and then walked over to her. He knelt beside her, running his fingers through her hair. His touch startled her and she turned her head to see him smiling at her. "I observed your altercation with Mayne." She didn't know where he was going with this, so she chose not to speak. "The lights flickered again, Mia." He smiled, waiting for her to reply. Remembering their earlier discussion, she knew that he was trying to make her understand the Element of its cause. "What were you feeling when you were fighting with Mayne. Do you recall the exact moment?" She looked away from him for a few moments, trying to recall the whole incident within her mind, from start to end. She remembered the lights flickering, however the exact moment escaped her. "I remember the lights, but not the moment." "It was when you summoned your courage to challenge her. She ordered you to go inside. What did you say to her?" "I said no." He placed his hand on her cheek and smiled. "Now make the connection."

He rose from he chair and walked over to the bar. Gwen and the girls ogled him as he approached. With Hunter being highly regarded in many circles, they felt star struck in his presence. He perused those surrounding the bar and greeted the guests. "Gwen, Kerry and Faeryn, I am pleased that you have chosen to join us this weekend. How was the trip here?" "It's our pleasure. The traffic was a little slow in some spots. Where is Mason?" "He'll be joining us soon."

"Care for a drink, Hunter?" "Yes, Lucius and no ice. Thanks." Zephyr mocked Lucius, making kissing sounds and then sneezed while speaking. "Kiss up." "Do you see how he treats me Kerry? He's a disrespectful bastard." Ceridwen smiled, interlocking her arm with Zephyr's. "Yeah, but he's a sexy bastard." Zephyr smiled and flexed his biceps. He kissed her, passionately and then whispered into her ear. His words caused her to grin and blush in embarrassment. Lucius smiled at them. "Hey! Get a room!" Lucius looked at Enya, smiling. "They're so disrespectful, right Enya?" Gwen laughed. "Lucius, you know this happens every time they're together. They're like magnets." She held out her shot glass. "Fill us up, Lucius." He lined up the glasses up and poured. Gwen held her glass up. "To fevered lust!" Everyone raised their glasses and laughed.

As the night progressed Mia became more and more withdrawn, allowing the sounds that surrounded her to become imperceptible. She hid herself within her placid state of mind, pondering the subject of the flickering lights and incorporating all things said by Hunter. She began speculating all the possible common denominators surrounding these light flickering events. She ran through these points in time, within her thoughts. The most recent being earlier with Mayne and prior to that was with both Mayne and Hunter on the morning after she had stolen her bike. At first she thought the denominator was Mayne. She recalled the Samhain party. She realized that the common denominator was herself, however, this still did not explain the flickering lights. She glanced over at the bar and stared at Mayne, Hunter and Aithusa. As she looked at each one of them, the first vibe that she felt consisted of rage and fear. It was within these incidences, that she felt as if she were not in control of herself. With Aithusa, she was both in and out of control. She realized that she was a part of the cause of the flickering lights and the candle flame's flaring rage. It was now becoming clear to her.

"Good evening everyone! I am now going to passionately kiss each female guest. Prepare to be seduced!" Hunter rolled his eyes and shook his head, then faced Enya. She laughed out loud. "He's your brother!" "That, he is." Mason leered at Gwen. "Are you excited Gwen?" She covered her face from embarrassment. She was, in fact, excited, however, she also secretly wanted Hunter but would never admit to it. Mason locked eyes on his first prey. He set his sights on Gwen, smiling seductively as he approached her. Enticing her with his piercing green eyes, he combed his hands through her hair and fervently kissed her. Enya looked at Hunter and rolled her eyes. He pulled away from her, licking his lips in an obscene manner. "Delicious." He turned around and spotted Faeryn at the other end of the bar. Their eyes locked. Hunter laughed out loud and smacked him in the head as he passed by. With his teeth gritted, he slowly walked behind the bar and then rushed up on her. He pushed her against the fence, with his body pressed against hers. He held her hands against the fence and kissed her with heated intensity. He released her, bowing to her as she panted and looked her in the eyes and licked his lips. "Pure decadence, Gwen." He turned to Ceridwen. Her eyes widened and she hid within Zephyr's chest. "Oh Kerry, your breaking my heart." He displayed his irresistible puppy eyes and drooped his lip. "Oh Mason! You can have a hug and cheek kisses, only." He smiled and played along. They lovingly embraced and then looked at each other. When she moved in to kiss his cheek, he shifted his mouth to her lips and she stopped him with her hand. "Mason!" He laughed and stole a check kiss. "Well I seem to have a dilemma now." He looked at everyone at the bar with a distraught expression. Lucius responded. "Poor Mason. What prey tell, is wrong?" "I have an unassigned kiss remaining and it must be released." Sage chimed in. "Or you'll turn into a pumpkin?" He smiled. "Much worse." He glanced over his shoulder and saw Mia, lying on the chaise. His eyes squinted. He glanced at Mayne, wide-eyed and Mayne snickered. "You're gonna open Pandora's box, Mason!" Feeling mischievous, he quietly made his way over to Mia, knelt beside her and whispered to her. "Cara Mia." She turned around to see him smiling before her and quickly sat up. Leery of his intentions, she sat still and silent, preparing for what may come. "I saw you lying here all alone and decided to join you. Have you seen the Moon? She's almost full." He serenaded her with some of the lyrics from the song: "Amore". As he sang the word amore, he moved closer, sliding his hands through her hair. She froze. Just before his lips touched hers, she planted her palms on his chest and pushed him with every ounce of strength that she had. He fell backwards onto the cement. Emery and Lucius howled. He frowned and pushed himself back in front of her. "That wasn't very polite Mia." His green eyes seemed to darken. He sat down next to her with his hands folded and fingers clenched. "It is said that you get what you give. Once again, I come to you in peace, only to receive negativity from you." Her anxiety increased. Observing her tense state, he realized that he had made his point. He placed his hand on her shoulder, lightly massaging it. "Lets reset this." She looked at him with a strained expression on her face. She had seen his cunning, seductive smile and had no intention of feeding into it, this time. He gently took her hand in his, pulled it slowly to his lips and kissed it. She remained reticent, watching his body language in anticipation of the inevitable. He observed her, waiting until he felt that she was at ease with his presence. She watched as his eyes wandered across her face to her lips and then slowly wandered downward. He inhaled sharply and pushed her down into the chair, forcefully kissing her. She struggled relentlessly, digging her nails into his arms. She tried to push him off but his strength and weight overpowered her. She was able to wriggle her leg beneath him. She swiftly jerked her knee near his pelvis, sending him upward, in avoidance. The expression on his face indicated that he was not going to let this one go. His anger fed into her rage, however, she remained motionless, leading him to believe her feigned, surrendering state. Drawing from the adrenaline rush induced by her anxiety, with a swift motion, she pushed, hurling him onto the cement, once more. Hunters resonated laugh was heard. "Do you need some help, little brother?" He shrugged his shoulders and laughed, holding a sinister grin. "This is just foreplay and you know how I love a challenge." As he rose up, she jolted from her chair and ran to the other side, against the house. He picked the chair up and placed it to the side. He slowly walked towards her, enunciating his words. "Mia, my love. That was very, very naughty. You could have hurt me." He slammed his hands against the house, on either side of her head. Just as she ducked to try and run under them, he slammed his body against hers, pinning her to the house. With a tight grip, he placed his hand around her neck. "We've had this discussion before. You have once again, taken my polite disposition for granted." He slowly released his grip and backhanded her across her face. She fell onto the ground and remained on her hands and knees. She held back her tears, refusing to show weakness. Her rage ignited. She gritted her teeth and stood up. Her piercing eyes were fixed on him, depictive of her virulent and malicious intent. The lights flickered violently, once again showing the guests a taste of her potential. Aithusa smiled mischievously, having already witnessed this behavior by challenging her with a candle, against Hunters advice. Mason pointed to the lights. She saw them through the corner of her eye and realized that she had unintentionally tested and proved her theory on Mason. Hunter and Mayne slowly approached them. Mason kept his focus on Mia while holding his hand up to Mayne and Hunter. "STOP." He approached her calmly and spoke to her in a soothing voice. "Mia, Focus! Listen to me. Do you see what you are doing?" Hunter stood behind Mason. "You've pushed her to far. She doesn't understand." Hearing what he said, Mia glanced at Hunter and them looked at Mason with tear filled eyes. "I see. I understand." She paused for a moment. "Did you attack me for this purpose?" He smiled. "No, Mia. Not at first. I wanted to kiss you. I was determined to convince you to give me that kiss. When I held you against the wall, I saw your fire coming alive. That's when I pushed you further." Mia watched the lights return to their steady glow. "Is this part of the reason you hold me here against my will?" Mason frowned. "Mia, You belong here with us." "Why?" She whispered, wiping the tears from her eyes. Hunter sat on the chaise. "Sit, Mia." She stepped over, holding on to his shoulder and sat. "I've told you why." She shouted in frustration. "I am nothing like any of you! I would never put a negative into the Universe. I would never harm anyone or take away their free will. I would never change the course of someone's life without their explicit consent! I am well versed in the Rede. I follow the rules of the Pyramid and respect the Elements. I am well aware of when to do what, dependent on each phase of the Moon. I will not allow my views to be distorted with your organized deceit!"

The silence that followed seemed endless. Hunter continued to stare at her with a steely expression on his face. Mayne and Mason watched Hunter, knowing he would soon explode with rage. The others at the bar were in disbelief of how she had spoken to him. He grabbed her arm with a taut grasp and pulled her in close. The spectral deep pitch of his voice resonated through everyone. "With whom do you think you are speaking to in that disrespectful manner?" As he spoke, his flaring eyes depicted the infernal eruption within him. Terrified, she cowered before him. His grip on her arm was painful. "Your insolence has gone to far this time." He stood up, still holding her arm tightly and dragged her inside. She screamed and dropped herself onto the floor to slow him down with her dead weight. He continued to drag her across the cement until they were at the door. "GET UP!" She stood up, trembling and crying profusely. He yanked her inside. She tripped over the track of the sliding door and fell. He dragged her across the floor, disappearing into the big room.

Gwen's hands were visibly shaking, having been unnerved by what she had just witnessed. She stepped behind the bar and poured herself a glass of wine, waiting anxiously for Enya to return. She listened as Enya spoke with Mason and Mayne. Having never witnessed Hunters rage, Faeryn, Ceridwen and Aithusa were anxious and stunned as well. Faeryn kept glancing into the house while the girls chatted amongst themselves. "What is he doing with her in there?" Gwen replied. "I have no idea." She looked to Sage and Raine for an answer and Sage, in turn looked at Lucius. Recalling the last time this had happened, he chose his words wisely. He turned to Sage. "If memory serves me right, this had happened once before in my presence, Sage. It was when we returned from the restaurant where she worked. There's nothing to worry about ladies. He's simply... resetting her."

Emery brought out the jello shots that he had made earlier. They were an evil concoction of Jack Daniels, Sambuca and Bustelo. Enya immediately indulged in few. Raine grabbed her cigarettes, a few shots and brought them to the pool, where Sage was hanging off the side of the pool, floating herself. Raine sat down, beside her and handed her a shot. "What fuckin' hell the last two days have been." "I'm tired of the drama." "The yard is a mess. I'm not cleanin' tonight. Let them do it. Fuck it." Raine lifted her shot glass. "To a drama free tomorrow."

Enya stepped behind the bar and made herself a drink. "Gwen, would you like another drink?" "Certainly. Will they be coming back out here tonight?" "Lets hope so." Enya sighed. "I've never seen him like that before. As for your sister, I can't even begin to count how many times she's snapped at my bar." Enya laughed. "Yeah, well we both know there's a few screws lose with her." Faeryn approached Enya. "Hey, Enya, I need to use the bathroom, but I'm a little leery of going inside right now." "You can go inside. There's one just past the kitchen. They're in Hunters bedroom. You won't even see them." "Ok. Thanks." She walked inside and lightly knocked on the door. No one answered so she entered. As she turned to shut the door behind her, she listened for any sound coming from his room. There was no sound. When she came back out of the bathroom, she looked around to see if anyone was looking and then tip toed over to the entrance of Hunters room. The door was opened, however, Hunters bedroom door was closed. There was no sound. Although she was tempted to walk in further, she didn't dare. She returned to the yard. Just as she stepped to the door, Enya stopped her. "Faeryn, would you please do me a favor? Go in the fridge and get me a few limes?" "Sure." She shuffled some of the apples to the side and found them. Just as she closed the refrigerator door, she heard the sound of a door closing, followed by footsteps. She stepped over to peek and saw Hunter approaching, with Mia behind him. He stopped short and reached behind himself to catch Mia. With her hands full of limes, Faeryn looked up at him, stuttering her words. "I... I was just getting limes...for Enya." He smiled at her. "Please feel at home when you are here. He reached behind himself and pulled Mia out from behind and placed his hands on her shoulders. Faeryn noticed the aberrant expression on her face. "Mia has something to say to everyone. Please join us outside." "Sure." She followed behind them and brought the limes over to Enya. As they walked out of the door, the talking ceased and everyone's attention was now focused on them. Mia hated being stared at. Their gaping eyes seemed to bore right through her, invading her mind and soul. "Mia has something to say to everyone." He stood behind her, squeezing her shoulders. She sobbed nervously from the stage fright and whispered. "I can't." He whispered back. "The alternative is to return to my room. You choose." She whimpered. The look on everyone's face was that of anticipation and impatience. He squeezed tighter and she cringed. She opened her mouth and the words wouldn't come out at first. She wiped her eyes, composed herself and mustered up the courage to speak. "I'm sorry for everything that I've said." As she searched each persons face for their acceptance, Ceridwen grabbed her drink from the bar and walked over to her. As she approached, Mia stepped back, against Hunter and he slid his hands down her arms, holding them against himself. "Mia, you're forgiven. We didn't take it personal." Mia gazed at her face, recalling the Samhain evening and the fair where she had first met her. "You're the reason that I'm here, Ceridwen." Ceridwen looked up at Hunter, unsure of how to respond. Mia stared, impassively at her. Hunter took a deep breath, grasping her neck. "What is your point?" "I remember the fair. I remember the Samhain party and I remember all who were there." Ceridwen walked away, choosing not to further partake in the conversation. Hunter turned Mia around to face him. "What else do you choose to remember?" Tears filled her eyes. She knew that his question was arcane and that his point was paradigm. She didn't respond. "Your perception of these occurrences is misconstrued. Decipher that." As he released her, she spoke up. "I remember your presence that night. I also remember seeing the candle that I was focusing on, flaring." He tugged on her pendant. "Do you recognize the pattern?" He gently placed his hands on the sides of her face. "Do not disrespect me again. Sit in the chair, behind you."

He returned to the bar, pushed Lucius off of the bartender stool and fixed himself a drink. Gwen smiled. "Top me off." "This is whiskey." "That's fine." She held her glass up to the Moon and then to him. "To her." The glasses clinked. "What happened in there?" He smiled and put his glass down.

"She needed an attitude adjustment." Mayne smirked and chimed in with a snide remark. "Yeah. I'll give her the next one."

Mia lay on the chair facing the pool. She quietly called out to Sage. After the third time, she heard her and swam over. "What baby?" "Please call Mayne over here." Sage was baffled. "Are you serious?" "Yes." Hesitant at first, she slowly swam backwards, then turned to Mayne's direction and swam to the bar end of the pool. The thought of talking to Mayne utterly disgusted her. "She wants you over there." Mayne walked towards her with her beer in her hand and cigarette in her mouth. She stood next to her. Still lying sideways, she continued to look forward. She took the cigarette out of her mouth and sat, with her legs crossed, on the ground directly in front of Mia's view. With the beer in her hand, she leaned back, swigging the beer. There were no words at first. Mayne saw tears falling down her cheek. She placed the bottle down. "What do you want?" Mia sniffled and looked up at her. "Stay."

Raine kept a steady eye on them for a while, but eventually zoned out from the effects of the liquor. Enya was tired. "I'm abandoning you people. Tomorrows will be a long day and I need my sleep. Everyone should know where they're sleeping. If not, figure it out. Peace out." She grabbed her things and escaped to the sanctuary of her bedroom.

Sage climbed out of the pool to get another beer. Lucius saw her approaching. Opportunity knocked in his head when a provocative song began to play.

♪ *Hot as a fever...*♪

He grabbed her in his arms, singing the lyrics. She played into it and danced with him. Gwen laughed. "And with that, I'm going to sleep." Faeryn and Ceridwen followed. Emery looked at his watch. It was about midnight. He took another beer, balanced the leftovers in his arms and made his way inside as well.

Raine was still in the pool. Feeling tipsy, she emerged from the pool, reached for a towel and went to the bar. She watched Sage and Lucius dancing around and giggled at them. When things moved to one of the lawn chairs, she decided to go to inside. Mayne heard a noise and looked to see where it came from. Lucius and Sage fooling around. She turned to look at Mia, who was asleep on the chair. She stood up, stretched and searched around to see where everyone else was. She then glanced back at Mia, picked her up and carried her inside. Emery was in the kitchen putting leftovers in the fridge. As Mayne passed him, he saw Mia in her arms. "Goodnight little lamb."

Mayne walked upstairs, unlocked her door and closed it shut with her foot. She put Mia on the bed and grabbed a change of clothes and went into the bathroom. When she returned, Mia was sitting up, half awake. She was waiting for Mayne to finish so that she could use the facilities. She washed her face and used Mayne's toothbrush. When she returned, Mayne handed her a change of cloths and threw herself face down, onto the bed. She was shot and drunk from the evening's festivities. Mia went back into the bathroom to change. She was hoping Mayne would be out by the time she came back out. When she returned, she saw her lying in the same position. She walked quietly over to the bed, pulled the corner of the blanket over and slowly climbed in. She lay on her side with her back facing her, trying to stay as close to the edge as possible, without touching her. Mayne was not asleep yet. She felt her get into the bed. Mia waited until she thought Mayne was in a deep sleep before she made herself more comfortable. Her arm kept going numb no matter which way she had placed it. As the time passed, she turned to look at her. She was sleeping on her stomach. She then, turned to lay flat on the bed and eventually dozed off. As she slept, her dreams began to haunt her. She tossed and turned, pulling the blanket away from Mayne and wrapping it around herself like a cocoon. Eventually she settled and fell into a deep sleep.

Mayne woke and glanced at the clock. It was after four am. She was thirsty and wanted a snack. She glanced at Mia, grabbed the jeans she wore last night and went downstairs. She peaked towards the living room's direction and saw someone's feet hanging off the couch, proceeded to the kitchen and opened the fridge. Hanging off the door, she gazed at the contents and spotted iced tea and donuts. She poured herself a glass, grabbed a donut and sat at the table. The silence of the house gave her some much-needed solace. She put the glass in the sink and walked back upstairs. In her absence, Mia had overtaken most of the bed. She maneuvered her way back into the bed, wrapped her leg over Mia's legs and slid her arm around her waist.

CHAPTER 14

THE ROOSTER

Mia woke just before dawn, thinking of Sebastian. She slowly slid out of the bed, trying not to wake Mayne. She took her phone and went into the bathroom, hoping he would answer this time. First she texted him to say she was actually the one calling and not Mayne. The phone rang almost four times. She thought it was going to voicemail again, when he finally answered. Mia whispered. "Sebastian!?" "Mia!" "I've been trying to call and text you. Why didn't you answer?" "I'm sorry. Where are you? I've been so fucking worried. Those people, they threatened me again. They found out about the last time that we had texted each other and found me. I was in the hospital again and I couldn't talk because I had a fractured jaw. They gave me a final warning. They said that if I contact you again, that they would hurt you!" "WHAT!?" "Fuck! Who hit you?" "The big guy with the crew cut. Please tell me where you are. I'll come get you." "I don't think it's a good idea for you to come here. They're everywhere, all the time. When I get out, I'll call you, somehow. OK, no texting for now. Only calls. When I call, I'll text you, first. The code, text word will be the date we met." "OK." "Are you ok?" "My jaw is sore and other than not being able to chew, I'm fine. How are you and what the hell is going on? Why did they take you?" She heard a noise coming from the bedroom. "I don't know. I gotta go." She flushed the toilet and turned the sink on for a few seconds for normalcy purposes. She then deleted the texts, placed the phone on the on top of the folded towel and walked out. Trying to hide her inner rage she walked out yawning as if she were going back to sleep. Mayne was sitting up, waiting for her to finish. Mia was worried that that Mayne may have heard her. She climbed back into bed, thinking about all that he said. Knowing now that it was Lucius who beat up Sebastian, she was hell bent on revenge. When Mayne went into the bathroom, she grabbed some clothes from her drawer and threw it under the bed with the clothes that she had worn last night. She crawled back into the bed and lay on her side facing the edge. Mayne walked out and went back to sleep. Mia waited for almost an hour and slid out of the bed, watching Mayne as she quickly dressed. She slipped out the door looked around and swiftly and quietly walked down the hall to listen for anyone downstairs. She walked down the second flight to the basement floor, peaked around and didn't see him anywhere. As she crept back up the stairs, she heard the sound of an engine. She shuffled to the living room and looked out of the window. He was out front, putting his helmet on. With no time to lose, she ran to the kitchen and stole Enya's car keys to chase him. She was going after him with a fiery vengeance. By the time she had made her way outside, he had taken off. She ran to the car, started it and screeched the tires as she recklessly sped off. Enya had been upstairs sleeping, when she heard the noise. She sprung out of bed and ran to her window. When she peered outside, she saw tire marks and then noticed her car was missing and shouted. "FUUUCK!"

Hunter and Mason were sleeping in their rooms and Emery was sound asleep, in the basement. Enya ran downstairs and saw Aithusa standing at the front door. "Did you see who stole my car?" "No, but I heard a loud screeching sound. When I looked out of the window I saw it driving off." Panicking, Enya ran back upstairs to Mayne's room and banged on her door. Startled by the banging, Mayne fell off of her bed and ran to her door. "WHAT?!" "My car was just stolen. Whoever took it left skid marks in the street." Mayne turned around to see that Mia was not in the bed. "Where is she?" "How the fuck should I know, Mayne!" Mayne slid on her jeans, and ran downstairs calling for her. "MIA?" She ran out to the yard and didn't see her there.

She went downstairs to see if she was there. Lucius was in his bedroom and Emery was in the shower. "MIA!" she yelled again. Emery yelled from the bathroom. "She's not down here. What's up?" "Enya's car was just stolen and I can't find Mia." "Do you think she stole it?" "Yep!"

Mia floored the gas, trying to catch up to Lucius. He drove to the highway entrance and merged. He then turned off the highway to get onto another that was mostly lined with trees. She was about a quarter mile behind him when he noticed a car speeding up in his side view mirror. He glanced over; saw that it was Enya's car and immediately pulled over to the side, assuming that there had been an emergency. Mia skidded to a stop, a few feet from him. She turned the ignition off and left the keys in it. She popped the trunk, got out of the car and went into the trunk looking for something to use as a weapon. Lucius took a picture of Enya's car with Mia standing at the trunk, typed his location and sent it to Enya, Mayne and Hunter.

He shouted. "Mia, what's going on?" Rummaging through the trunk, she found a pocketknife, slipped it in her back pocket then found a metal bar underneath some old newspapers. She grabbed the bar, left the trunk open and slowly inched towards him. "Sebastian's jaw was broken, Lucius. Any idea how that happened?" Perplexed, Lucius looked at her, wondering how she had found out. "That night at the restaurant, that same someone knocked him out. He had a concussion." She clenched her teeth, took a deep breath and swung the bat at his head. He ducked just in time. "Are you fucking kidding me, Mia? I'm not gonna fight you. Put the fucking bat down, NOW!" Just as he finished speaking, she swung at his head again, nearly hitting him. "You're really pissing me off girl!" She quickly retracted and swung at his legs, making contact with his thigh. Livid, he leaped towards her and she swung again, catching him in the arm. As he grabbed his arm she swung at him again. He kicked the bat out of her hands and then pushed her to the ground. She fell hard. Just as she hit the ground, Hunter arrived with Enya, Mayne and Emery. They jumped out of the truck, assessing the situation. Lucius shouted to them. "She found out about Sebastian, swung a bat at me a few times and got me twice!" Mia was lying on the ground and was about to lift herself up when she saw them standing there. She paid them no mind. Leery eyed, with malicious intent, she slowly raised herself up onto her hands and knees. Looking directly at him, she stood up. She spit dirt and blood from her mouth and reached into her pocket to get the knife. She opened it, and stood next to his bike. "Which hurts more Lucius, stabbing you… or your tires?" She saw his viciousness in his eyes and knew she had certainly hit the wrong nerve with him: his bike. He stood with his fists clenched, his face, red with fury. He lost control. He tore the ground, running to her. With quick reflex, she instinctively stepped to the side and nicking him on his forearm, with the knife. As Mia ran to retrieve the bat, he dove for her ankles and she fell. He grasped her ankles and dragged her in. With the knife in her hand, she turned her body around and lunged it at his arm. He caught her wrist in time and clutched it tightly, until she was forced to let it go, from the pain. He was still hovering over her when she attempted to knee him in the groin. Her aim was close enough to hurt and distract him for a second. She slid out from under him and then leaped on top of him, grabbing his shirt and knocking him over. She dug her nails into his face, just missing his eyes. The adrenaline from her anxiety fed her endurance. He grabbed her, tearing her shirt and threw her to the side. He rolled over and as he tried to get up she punched him in the jaw. The punch had hurt her hand more than it did, him. He stood up, lifted her up by her arms and slammed her against the tree behind her. He backhanded her across the face and she fell to the ground. She tried to stand, but only managed to hold herself steadily, on all fours. Dazed and in pain she remained there, spitting and panting. He wiped the sweat off of his forehead while she struggled to stand again. Her pupils were blue. She raised her arm and with her eyes fixed on his, she pointed directly at him. "I will make you feel what Sebastian felt. I'm gonna hit you where it hurts, most." She staggered over to his bike to knock it over. Just as she stepped up to it, she lost her balance and fell onto it, almost knocking it over. Lucius had run to the side of the bike and caught it, mid fall. Mia was hunched over the bike between the seat and the tank. He wrapped his hand around her neck and grabbed her arm, lifting her up. She dug her nails into his harm to try to force him to release her. He shoved her backward and she fell backwards on the ground. He stood above her. "When we get home, your ass is mine. Watch your back sweetheart."

With her physical energy expelled, she was forced to tap into her own resources. She pushed herself a few feet away from the bike and sat on the ground, with her legs and palms touching the ground. Looking at Lucius and perusing his immediate surroundings she saw that he was standing next to his bike, just below a tree. With intense focus, she stared at the tree, flattening her hands on the ground to connect with the earth that fed its the life force. Beginning at its trunk, her eyes slowly followed upward along its majestic branches, watching the leaves intently as they individually swayed with each passing breeze. She closed her eyes and respectfully tuned into its life force, inhaling slowly and deeply, taking in its unique essence. She allowed her thoughts to blend with the wind as it swept over her face. Knowing what she was about to do, she would need to accept the karma that it may return to her. She knew that karma returns itself, without help and should NEVER be intervened by anyone. She knew the Universe already had its own plans for him, but she didn't want to wait. Her anger distracted and distorted her from the Rede that she followed. Although she did not want to kill him, she did want him hurt, like he had hurt Sebastian. She Knew that if she Willed this to happen and Dared to follow it through, she would Keep Silent, indefinitely.

With the tree above Lucius fixed within her mind, she requested the presence and assistance of its Spirit. She summoned the Elements: Air and Earth. She then requested the presence of the North wind as well. As to do no harm, she requested for only the sacrifice of the tree's dead branch above him. She directed the combined symphony of these Elements, to assist the tree so it could release this branch above Lucius and fall onto him. When she felt the wind begin to increase, she opened her eyes. Raising her arm, she pointed her finger above the tree and then slowly traced its core downward, stopping when her finger reached him. She whispered to herself. *"The spell has begun. So Mote It Be."*

A Northerly wind began to stream, carving its path towards them, gradually increasing in its urgency in order to assist the Air to communicate her intentions. Her eyes widened in elation with each fluctuating blast, further empowering her tenacity. With unceasing focus, she watched the leaves flutter, increasing their sways with the momentum of each gust.

Hunter had been intently observing her and was now well aware that there was Magick afoot, by her hand. She raised her finger and pointing it to a specific branch. He looked to the direction that her finger and eyes were fixed upon and slowly approached to this destination. There was a cracking sound. Hunter looked up into the tree and saw the loose branch, dangling just above Lucius. It was about to break lose. Just as it broke loose, he quickly raised his arm and pointed, causing it to sway away from Lucius' head. Lucius saw this and diverted it with his hand. It slammed onto the ground, shattering into fragments of its former extant. The branch caused his finger to bend back. At first he thought it was broken, but was only sprained.

Distracted from her focus, Mia saw the branch hit the ground and realized what he had done. She saw Hunter walking towards her with his eyes blazing and stumbled as she stood. She glanced at his face. His face held an icy expression and his eyes sent chills through her body. He clutched her head in his hands. With his face a few inches from hers, his eyes penetrated hers. She saw in his eyes what she was unable to see before. Revealing more of himself within them, she saw images of him, what he is, what he had done and what he was capable of as well. Her body trembled. She was frozen with terror. He released her. Stunned, she stood there, still looking at him with tears in her eyes. He moved away from her and she remained, staring into the distance with obscured vision. She didn't move. The images continued to flash in her mind, mentally and physically paralyzing her. She tried desperately to snap herself back into reality. She took a step towards the direction where all were parked, and stopped. She slowly walked past Lucius without acknowledging his presence. She felt the strange spiritual pull as she took each step. She was fighting her own will to move away from the entity that had a hold on her. She knew this was Hunter. She saw the dark silhouette of the truck. Taking slow steps, she reached for the side view mirror to hold herself up. She held on to it, steadied herself for a moment and rested head against its metal frame.

The images continued to flash within her mind. She silently whimpered, gasping from the pain. Hunter walked over to her, picked her up and put her in the front, passenger seat of the truck. He placed the seatbelt around her waist and shut the door. Mayne and Emery climbed into the truck. Enya started her car and left. He walked over to Lucius, whispered a few words and returned to the truck, swinging his keys. He opened the door, put the keys in the ignition and turned to look at Mia. No one spoke. Mia faced the side window, holding her knees against her chest, silently crying. He started the truck and drove. She gazed out the window and watched the highway lines as they passed. It made her dizzy after a while so she shut her eyes. The images started to flash in her mind again so she tried to keep them open. As they stopped at the red light, Hunter lit up a cigarette and offered one to Mayne. She took a drag of her cigarette and eyed Mia's seat. She pushed the reclining lever down with her foot so that Mia's face would be in her view. The sudden drop of the seat stunned her. As she looked up at her, Mayne slammed her legs on top of the seat, surrounding both sides of Mia's head and then stared at her. Startled, Mia glanced back at her and then laid her head back down, facing the door. Mayne enclosed her calves on her head and Mia reacted by punching her calf. Mayne grabbed her hair and wrapped her legs around Mia's neck. "Punch me again, Mia!" Mia managed to pop open her seat belt. She maneuvered out of her leg lock, jumped onto Mayne's lap and wrapped her fingers in her hair, digging her nails in her scalp. Mayne clasped Mia's neck, nearly chocking her. Hunter slammed on the brakes, skidding the truck to stop. Mia fell to the floor, below Mayne. He rose from his seat and yanked Mia back into her seat. Holding her arm tightly, he raised his voice. "Put your seatbelt on, Mia." He started the truck up and drove.

The traffic had slowed to a stop. Hunter had caught up to Lucius and was positioned, side by side with him, on Mia's side of the truck. He peered through the window to see her and she returned his stare. As the traffic let up, she watched him as he slowly began to drive ahead of them. Looking out of her window, she raised her index finger and was just about to point it at Lucius, when Hunter slammed on the breaks once again and pulled over, startling everyone in the truck. He unbuckled his seat belt, grabbed Mia's hand and raised his voice at her. "Mia, I know what you were doing! I know that you understand that your intentions follow where you point. Do you realize that you could have killed him?" He squeezed her finger tightly. She was frozen with fear and did not respond to him. "Answer the question now!" His fiery eyes and raucous voice petrified her. He bent her finger backward and broke it. Mia howled. He moved back into his seat and proceeded to drive. Astounded and silent, Emery and Mayne looked at each other.

Cradling her finger, Mia crossed her legs on the seat, put her head down and cried out loud. Her finger began to swell and she felt the pain traveling through her forearm. She pushed the seat back, turned to lay sideways on the seat, facing Hunter and silently wept.

CHAPTER 15

THE FEMALE OF THE SPECIES

The traffic slowed once again. Mia's sobbing had begun to irk Hunter. "Mayne, Do you have any rolled?" "Yup." What kind?" "My kind." "Light up." Mayne took a toke and passed it to Hunter. He took a toke, then placed his hand on Mia's neck and pulled her closer to him. "Open your mouth." He put the lit end of the cigarette between his teeth, took a deep toke and blew it into her mouth. "Inhale!" She coughed. Inhaling deeply, he repeated it four more times. He took a few more hits for himself and handed it back to Mayne. Mia released her legs from her arms and stretched them out onto the floor. Gazing through the windshield she allowed herself to become comfortably numb. Her crying had become minimal and her eyes felt like cirrus clouds. The fear or anxiety released its hold on her, minimizing the pain in the interim. She placed her wounded hand on her lap and sunk into her seat. Hunter turned to look at her. He glanced into the rear view mirror, at Mayne and smirked at her. Emery finished the last of it. Feeling numb herself, Mayne stretched out and lay back in the seat. The traffic started inching. Hunter turned the radio on. Ironically, a two-fer was in play and was near the end of a song, which related to their current mood. Hunter laughed. He stopped at the red light, sang along with the next song and touched Mia's hair.

♪...learning to fly...♪

Mia slowly turned to look at him. She thought about the lyrics, realizing that they strongly related to her on more than one level. She had practiced learning to fly, solitarily with her beliefs, for half her life. This particular and peculiar flight that she was now experiencing, differed from the others. She looked at his hand, watching him shift gears. When she saw his leg move to press on the brakes, she looked down to his feet, then back up at his face. He placed his hand on her cheek. She turned to face Emery and Mayne. She felt bad for hitting her. Mayne stared back at her with no expression. Mia slowly turned back and looked at her waist. She unbuckled her seat belt, climbed into the back seat and sat between them. Turning sideways, she lay back, placing her head on Mayne's lap and her feet on Emery's lap. Baffled, Mayne lifted her arm as Mia laid her head down. Mia turned her head and stared at her. Mayne's dark eyes did not intimidate her now. She once again, felt that unusual bond to her. Mayne gazed at her and ran her fingers through Mia's hair. Mia closed her eyes and enjoyed the tingling sensation.

The truck pulled up to the house. Enya had already returned and Lucius was sitting on his bike, waiting for them. Emery jumped out of the truck and walked over to him. "He broke her finger." "Why?" "When you were driving beside us, she pointed it at you when you took off." "Good. I wanna watch her as she passes me. She needs to live in fear for a while." Emery shook his head. "I'm going inside. I'm hungry." Mayne sat up and shook Mia. "Mia, sit up." Mia lifted her head to look at her. As she sat up, she felt her head and vision spiral. She looked through the windows and saw that she was back at the house. The door opened and Hunter held his hand out to her. "Take my hand." Holding her injured finger close to her chest, she grasped his hand, slid out of the truck and Mayne slid out behind her. Mia proceeded to walk to the house ahead of them. When she saw Lucius, she stopped in her tracks. "Come over here Mia." She didn't move. "I'm not gonna say it twice." As he slid off of his bike, she watched him, leery eyed and took only one step closer to him. He reached out, grabbed her forearm and pulled her closer. Mayne walked over and stood next to him, looking at her and smiling. He grabbed her by the wrist and looked at her broken finger. "That looks painful Mia." She started sobbing, frightened that he was going to further injure her finger. Hunter stood behind her. Lucius loosened his grip on her wrist, placed his arm around her shoulder and spoke calmly to her. "I know what your intentions were. You could have killed me, twice." He tightened his arm around her, pulling her face closer to his. He held up her wrist to her face and clenched it tighter. "I should break your wrist Mia." She looked at him diffidently and wept. He turned to Hunter and whispered. "Which room?" "Mine." He winked at him. "Have you seen my room, Mia?" She looked at him in horror and panicked. She had not seen it and was now panicking from his words, wondering what he had meant. He grabbed her arm to lead her into the house. She screamed, pulling herself back. Grinning and taking pleasure in terrorizing her, he lifted her up, holding her tightly and walked into the house. He held her tightly as she writhed in his arms. Mayne grinned at her and opened the door for him. He walked through the kitchen, past Hunters room to the steps that led downstairs to his room and stopped. Her screams penetrated through the house. He laughed in her face, placed her down on the floor and whispered in her ear. "Psych!" Grinning, Hunter put his hand on her shoulder, turning her around. "This way, Mia." Wide-eyed and panting, she looked back at Lucius. He looked her in the eyes and spoke in a steely voice with a facial expression to match. "Live in fear."

Cradling her injured finger, she walked just ahead of Hunter, through the big room, to his bedroom and shut the door behind him. He led her into the bathroom and filled the bathtub with warm water. He pulled a chair over to the tub and sat. "Remove your clothes and get in the tub." Distraught at first, she didn't move and looked away from him. He held a blank stare at her. She turned around to face the tub, removed her clothes and sat, holding her knees against her chest. "Dunk your head into the water." She covered herself with her hands, dunked her head and sat back up. He poured shampoo on her hair and lathered it up. "Mia do you understand why I broke your finger?" She listened to him, but didn't answer. Waiting for her to reply, he washed her back and handed her the washcloth and soap. He left the room to speak to Enya and to get a beer and his cigarettes. When he returned, Mia was still sitting in the same position. The bar of soap was floating in the water and the washcloth was hanging on the side of the tub, dripping onto the floor. "Mia do you remember when my brother brought you back here?" The silence continued. "When you became frightened, did you see the lights flicker?" The shampoo was irritating her scalp. She held her nose and dunked herself, returning to the same position. She didn't look at him. She just stared at the faucet. "Do you remember when I showed up at your job?" Recalling that night, she clenched her arms around knees, tighter. "Do you recall the Samhain party that you attended?" She thought about it as she listened to his questions. "Mia, I know that you pay close attention to your dreams. I can see them. I am sometimes in them with you." When he saw her lift her head, he knew that he had her full attention. She looked up, but didn't look at him. Fixated on her dreams, she began to recall them in her mind, trying to understand what he had meant. His questions now led to more questions, but she didn't want to talk anymore. She had chosen not to interact with anyone. She became introverted and shut down from everything. He ground out his cigarette and gazed at her. He reached over to her and gently pulled her chin to face him. "These questions lead to your answers." She looked down as he turned her face. She would not look at his eyes. He reached for her hand to look at her broken finger. He held her hand in his palm and covered it with his other hand. Her hand felt oddly warm. She felt him pulling on her spirit again and did not fight it this time. "Pay attention." He paused for a moment. "Do not point with negative intentions." She closed her eyes, recalling when Mason also told her not to do this. "Get up and dry yourself." He held up a towel. "There are clothes hanging on the back of the door." She wrapped the towel around herself and stepped out of the tub. She stood there while he opened the drain. He stepped out of the room for a few minutes to get himself a change of clothes. She dried herself off, reached for the clothes and put them on. While brushing her hair, she looked in the mirror at herself.

With her hand on the mirror, she moved closer to it, looking deeply into her own eyes. Hunter returned and stood behind her. He stared back at her, holding her attention within the reflection in the mirror. She couldn't release her eyes from his. Looking at her in the mirror, he slid his arms around her shoulders, took a deep breath and spoke to her. "Mia. I know that you are hiding deep inside yourself. I will pull you out." He reached for the brush and ran it through her hair. She took the brush from him, put it on the sink and used the comb. She felt paranoid because she didn't want him to have strands of her hair. "Go sit on the bed and wait for me. I'm taking a shower. Mayne is there, waiting for you." She finished combing her hair and left the room.

Mayne was sitting against the headboard watching the television, with the remote in one hand and a beer in the other. She turned to look at Mia. Mia crawled onto the bed and slid under the blanket. She propped up the pillows so that she could see the TV over Mayne's legs whilst lying sideways, next to her. Mayne threw the remote onto the bed, slid down next to her and wrapped her arm around her shoulder. Mia put her injured hand on Mayne's stomach and stared at the TV. The swelling seemed to be going down but the symptoms were still there. A Commercial was airing. Mayne turned her side and faced Mia. Mia stared deeply into her eyes, looking past the darkness she had always seen in them. Mia held Mayne's eyes captive within her own, pulling her into the essence of her own mind. Without words, she thought of only the things she wanted Mayne to see. *"What is my connection with you? Why am I drawn to you?"* Mayne brushed a lock of hair away from Mia's eyes. Mia closed her eyes and let her mind wander. She recalled most of what Hunter and Mason had said to her about pointing, why she belonged to them and how he could see and be in her dreams. *"Does he know what I am thinking now? Has he always known? Is this how he always found me?"* She felt Mayne shift herself and then wondered if she could see what she was thinking. With her in mind, she thought of Mayne's bike. She thought of that day and how it felt, riding it. She recalled the wind in her face and feeling of how powerful and fast it was. Her old bike was elementary compared to Mayne's bike. The fear that she had felt when she first took off, the release of that fear and the vibration of the motor between her thighs were so euphoric and empowering. Mia was so deep in the thought of reliving this particular memory that she was unaware that her hand had grasped Mayne's shirt and that she inadvertently wrapped her own leg over Mayne's. She felt Mayne move again, snapped out of her thought and quickly turned to look at her face. She was staring back and grinning at her. Mayne had been focusing on her the entire time. "Would you like to go for another ride, Mia?" Mia's eyes widened and she quickly sat up. *"FUCK, she can!"* She thought to herself. Mayne smirked at her. "I can." She grabbed Mia's arm and pulled her closer. "So, you like how my bike feels between your thighs?" Hunter walked out of the bathroom and glanced at them. "Am I interrupting?" "Mia was just thinking about how she likes the way my bike feels on her thighs." Hunter laughed. "Oh does she now?" "We were just about to go for another ride." He smiled and sat down next to her. She moved herself away from him. "I'm sorry to delay your plans, but we need to go join the others in the big room. Full Moon tonight, Mia." He looked at Mayne and smiled. "You can go for your ride later." He looked back at Mia and saw that she was anxious. "Light up and give her some." Mia watched him like a hawk as he walked away. Mayne reached in her pocket and turned to face her. "Look at me." She put the cigarette between her teeth and blew it into her mouth. She took a toke, put it back in her teeth and reached over to Mia, repeating it three more times. She took a long toke and reached for Mia again. She blew the smoke in her mouth and then kissed her. Mia pulled away and sat against the headboard. Relieved in a way that Hunter had appeared when he did, but at the same side of the token she was relieved that he had also walked away. She felt the numbness beginning to set in and turned to look at Mayne. She had just taken a toke and was grounding it out. The room was filled with smoke and Mia watched it as it floated gracefully through the air. She closed her eyes and allowed her thoughts to flow freely. *"The answers to my questions were within the questions that he had asked me."* She vaguely thought about Hunters questions, closed her eyes and drifted off. As she closed her eyes, the smoke and sounds merged with the scenery within her mind, forming a strong vortex of wind. Mia rode the swift and spiraling waves, looking downward into its depths. When the smoke cleared, she found herself back at the lake. She looked around for the lion and frog but did not see them. Mia saw something in the distance on a bench. As she approached it, she saw that it was a frog. It was a little larger and thinner than the other one. She stood in front of the bench, paying close attention to its unusual colors. This frog was an iridescent shade of Green. Mia knelt down in front of it. The frog looked up at her and they locked eyes. She placed her hand on the bench next to it, with her palm facing up. The frog placed its front leg on her palm. The leaves on the ground began to flutter around, following the path of a warm breeze. It encircled them and then ceased, leaving only the warmth in their presence. Mia felt a little hazy and overheated. It was the same feeling that she felt when Hunter was near. She nervously looked around for him but did not see him. Her attention returned back to the frog. She picked up the frog and sat on the bench with her ankles crossed. Cradling it in both hands, she held it closer to her chest. The frog faced her and placed its front legs against her stomach. She thought this was adorable and lay down on the bench, placing the frog on her chest.

There was a bizarre, vibrating noise surrounding them. The ground began to pulsate. She looked behind the bench and saw what seemed to be crystal columns, slowly rising from the ground. She watched as each column emerged, surrounding the circumference of the lake and ending where it had begun. Mia stood up and walked behind the bench. Holding the frog in one hand, she reached out to touch one of the columns. It was cool to the touch and unmovable. She looked down on the ground, picked up a twig and threw it through this bizarre ring of columns. The twig passed through and fell to the ground. Taking a panoramic view of the barrier surrounding her, she found herself feeling sad and peculiarly subdued. With a tear in her eye, she turned to look at the frog. It looked up at her and leaped out of her hand to the other side of the columns, landing on the ground. It sat there for a moment, looking back at her. Mia grasped the columns with both hands as she looked back at it. Hearing footsteps approaching from behind her, she turned her head and saw the lion and the frog. She waved and pointed, directing their attention to the new frog. They glanced at the other frog and returned their attention back to Mia. She held onto the columns and watched as it quickly leaped away into the distance. Mia turned back around to look at them. The lion stood in front of her, staring into her eyes. He took her hand and led her back to the bench. She sat down, expecting the lion to sit beside her, but instead he walked away with the frog in his paw. The sound of the wind from a vortex in the distance was growing louder. She looked up at the sky and saw a swirl of Purple and Black clouds. The leaves began to flutter along with the wind and quickly followed its coiling, tempest path. Mia stared into its vertiginous depths, feeling its strength begin to pull her. With all of her might, she held tightly onto the bench as her body floated within its gale strength. Its tempest roar frightened her. Within its mistral rotation she saw the purple and black clouds forming into two elongated arms. As they drew closer, it's eerie hands formed and her eyes widened as she watched it reaching out, toward her. She felt them grasp her ankles and could no longer hold on to the bench. Fear engulfed her as she flew backwards into its abyss.

She felt someone pulling on her legs and opened her eyes. In a swift motion, Mayne pulled her to the edge of the bed. "Mia, Get up." Flustered, she sat up and looked at her in angst. "Tell me about your dream." Mia didn't respond. Thinking about the dream and what it's meaning could be, the image of the crystal columns and the other frog, flashed in her mind. Mayne yelled. "Lets go!" Mia jumped up and followed her into the big room. She sat on the couch and watched as everyone gathered around the table. Mason was slipping his arm into his cloak when he saw her. He sat down next to her, looking at her with his captivating eyes and placed his hand on her knee. "Cara Mia. I hear you've been causing a lot of mayhem lately." He nudged her chin with his finger, to face him. Your wicked behavior enthralls me, but why so naughty?" She didn't reply to him. He kissed her lips and then joined the others. They stood around the table and began their ritual. Still feeling numb, Mia slowly rose up and walked around them, outside of the circle. She listened and watched as they chanted. She stood behind Sage for a few moments and then nudged in, fitting herself between Sage and Raine. She weaved in and out of their circle, following the edge of the table and looking at them as she passed. Feeling a sense of déjà vu, she recalled images of past events like this one. She remembered the first time at the Samhain party and then again with Mason. She climbed upon the table and sat with her legs crossed, perusing them and feeling as if she were transparent. Mia heard the sounds of a slow rhythmic drumbeat playing behind her. She spun around and saw Lucius with the drum. The chanting began with Emery and the others merged, joining with his words. They glanced at her occasionally as they chanted. Mia looked through the skylight and saw the incandescent glow from the Full Moon. She stretched out her legs and placed her hands behind herself. Leaning back, she stared at the Moon, watching as a few stray clouds floated in front of it.

The rhythm of the drumbeat increased. Her heightened perception from the marijuana allowed her mind to drift with the stray clouds that passed in front of the Moon. She slid backwards and lay on the table, watching and listening. Her thoughts were interrupted by the strong scent of incense. A candle was lit and its glow flickered on the ceiling next to the glass above her. She turned her head to her right and saw that Enya was looking directly at her. Enya's dark eyes seemed to channel through her. Her eyes did not reflect what Mayne's eyes did. Mia saw the reflection of the candle in her eyes and gazed at the flame. As she raised her hand to Enya's face, she could feel the heat from it as if her finger was in the fire. The drumming stopped. Mia lay there entranced within Enya's glare. Enya placed her hand on Mia's head and followed her locks to their ends. Zephyr stepped closer to Mia and touched the lock of hair that lay against her cheek and walked away. Mason, Raine, Lucius, Emery, Sage, Aithusa, Gwen and Faeryn followed suit, each touching her face and hair. Hunter approached her and lowered his face to hers, blocking Enya's view. She saw the symbol of the frog in his eyes. Mia took a deep breath and felt a cold sensation throughout her body. She realized what the lion and the frog represented. In this instance, they were Hunter and were one. The lion meant superior strength and the frog was a symbol for Witch. Enya was the iridescent green frog. She recalled the night they had entered the restaurant and the way they were dressed. The night she was with Mason also came to mind as she also recalled waking up in this very room and when he entered the room shortly thereafter. He was dressed the same. Hunter slid his palms on either side of her face. "Are your answers revealing themselves to you?" He kissed her lips, stood back up and left the room. Mayne slid her hands underneath Mia and picked her up and Mia gazed up at her. "Where are we going?" "Upstairs." Mayne's answer didn't seem to faze her in the least. Mayne watched Enya dousing the candle and incense. Enya poured herself a glass of wine and led them to her room. "Come." Weary, Mia rested her head against Mayne's chest as they ascended up the stairs. Enya unlocked her door and let them inside first, closing the door behind herself. Mayne lowered Mia onto the reclining chair, next to the bed. "I'll be right back." Enya questioned her. "Where are you going?" "To get one of my joints." Enya stepped over to her and whispered. "Why do we do this now, instead of the shot?" "That's only for when she's out of control. This is easier and she doesn't fight me. I think she likes it" "Is it strong enough?" Mayne grinned. "Mine is."

Enya closed the door. She took a few sips of her wine and placed the glass down on her dresser. She walked over to the closet and reached into a large oak box. She withdrew a few items and placed them on the round table, next to the window. She walked over to the armoire, slid open the top drawer and pulled out a few more items. Crouched in the chair, Mia watched as she went back and forth. Enya pulled a fold-up chair over to the table and sat with her back facing her. Mia listened to the sounds of her shuffling items. Curious, she stood up and approached her. Enya looked up at her. "How is your finger feeling?" Mia lifted her hand up, wiggled it and made a sour face. "Hunter partially healed your finger. I am going finish what he started. Didn't you feel the warmth? That's what he and Mayne were doing." Mia wanted to ask her how they had done this but she chose to continue to refrain from speaking. Mia perused the items on the table. There was some black cord and a tiny round mirror. Next to that was a stick of burning incense, a black candle, a jar of honey and a few other things. As Mia reached to touch the jar, Enya raised her hand to cover it. "Don't touch anything." She turned her head and spoke in a stern tone. "Go sit back in the chair."

Mayne returned and closed the door behind herself. Looking directly at Mia, she gently took her arm and led her back to the chair. She grabbed an ashtray, knelt in front of Mia and lit it up. She moved in front of Mia's face and placed her hands on the sides of the chair. She put it between her teeth and moved in, towards her. Mia turned her head to the side and giggled. She grabbed her jaw and blew into her mouth. She waited for her to exhale the smoke and did it again. Mia started to cough. Mayne gave her a sip of her beer and then repeated it again, three more times. On the third time, Mia put her hand on Mayne's collarbone, pushing her back. Mayne swiped her hand to the side and spoke with a rigid tone. "Open your mouth." Intimidated by her, Mia inhaled it and looked at her with a sour face. Mayne stared back and then stood up. She lay back on the bed, against the headboard and finished smoking it. Enya lit the candle and continued with her preparation. Mia watched the flame. It's flickering light slowly hypnotizing her along with the help of the marijuana's gradual effects. With the candle's intermittent highs and lows, the flame flared, bowing to Enya's respective Magick. Mia knew that the high flame had meant that Enya's intentions were working. She watched its random sparks and also knew that this reflected strong bursts of energy. Enya dropped something on the floor. Mia looked to see what it was and saw black cords, partially braided. Enya looked directly at her as she picked it up. Her stare was steady, spectral and cold. Mia watched her as she finished braiding it. She heard her uttering words as she counted each braided level. When she finished, she stepped over to Mia and knelt down, before her. "Give me your left wrist." She wrapped the braided bracelet around her wrist and tied its ends together. She returned to the table and wrote something on a brown piece of paper. She opened the jar of honey, placed it inside and closed it. She picked up the tiny mirror, placed a small piece of paper on it and tied it with a piece of cord. There was something printed on the paper but Mia could not see it clearly, from where she sat. Mia looked back over at the candle. As she stared into the flame she thought of the Amber eyes of the lion. Although she felt the lion represented Hunters strength, its eyes no longer intimidated her. She wondered why the lion was almost always holding the frog. It was as if he was trying to show her something. The lion's behavior towards her had always been kind and composed and sometimes he reminded her of Sebastian. Mia stopped within her thoughts and opened her eyes. She thought about the mannerisms of the lion, each time that she had seen him. She wondered if Sebastian was also a witch. She also realized that the lion was sometimes Sebastian. He was gently trying to show her that they were all very strong Witches. She glanced over at Mayne and then at Enya. Then she thought about Hunter. Then she recalled his questions to her and the incident with Lucius, Hunter and the branch. She attempted to resituate herself from the slouching position that she had sunken into. Her head spiraled as she moved forward. She rested her head on the arm of the chair and curled up on the chair. There was a knock at the door. Hunter walked into the room. As he walked towards Enya, she recalled a peculiar set of words that Hunter and Mayne had said. They said that they could see her dreams and are within them as well. She glanced at him for a few moments. Enya had just finished what she was doing and stood. She watched as they whispered and then he turned to Mia. "Give me a hand before you go." Enya walked over to the bed and pulled it a few feet away from the wall, with their help. He and Mayne then left the room. Mia heard all the noise but paid it no mind. Her thoughts were becoming cloudy. Just as she closed her eyes, Enya approached her with her hand extended. "Stand up." Enya led her to the bed. "Lie down on the bed and make yourself comfortable. I'm almost done." Mia crawled onto the bed. "Lift your head." Enya pulled the pillow over placed it under Mia's head. She stepped over to the door, dimmed the lights and returned to the table. Mia struggled to keep her eyes open. She saw Enya return but couldn't see what was in her hands. Mia's eyes closed and opened like a projector in slow motion. She saw glimpses of Enya slowly walking around the bed holding a silver, pointed object. Mia gave in to her heavy eyes, allowing her mind to sink into the abyss of the high.

CHAPTER 16

The Alchemistical Dragon

She woke within her dream realm to the sounds of drumming. She found herself lying sideways on the bench. Knowing where she was, the first thought that popped into her mind was Sebastian. She sat up and immediately looked around for the lion. The Full Moon had sunk into the horizon, allowing the Sun to emerge. Its light glistened, revealing the crystal columns. They were now encircled around her, much closer than before. The columns ran from behind the bench, edging as far as the lake's bank and back. She stood up and approached it, looking beyond its barrier and following its new path, her hand touching each column. With the exception of one, they were collectively cool to the touch. She stopped in her tracks and held onto it with both hands. The color of this peculiar column was the same as the others. The longer she held on to the column, the further its warmth increased, releasing it when it became too hot. She felt a tap on her shoulder and turned to see the lion, standing before her, however, the frog that had always accompanied him, was nowhere in sight. He placed his paw on her shoulder and pointed at the Sun. She saw the dawn in one eye and the stars that appear before the Sunrise in the other. The lion placed its paw on the side of her head and held her left wrist up to her face. He stared at her with a wild-eyed gaze, holding up his clenched paws and standing in a defensive-like stance. She knew that he didn't want to fight her, but sensed that he wanted to fight something else.

Puzzled as to what, she placed her hands on his paws, saw the fire within his eyes and searched within them for the reason. Within the flames, there were dark spots in the center of his eyes. The symbols slowly emerged and formed into frog symbols. He opened his mouth to roar. There had never been sound in this realm, within her dreams. The sound was loud and distorted. The energy from it launched the wind, projecting it in spiral waves of red and scarlet. She held on to him with her eyes tightly closed. The wind abruptly stopped and Mia opened her eyes to find that the lion was gone and she was now hugging a tree.

A cryptic sound woke Mia. When she opened her eyes she saw Enya sleeping soundly, next to her. The light from the Moon was shimmering through the window. She slipped quietly out of the bed and walked over to the window to look at the night sky. It was a clear night and the stars wee aligned in brilliant splendor. She wanted to request guidance from her Moon but was still groggy and unable to focus. The sound caressed her ears once again. It was coming from outside of the bedroom door. Mia peered at the door and then walked slowly towards it. She placed her ear against the door and held onto the doorknob, noticing that it was unusually warm to the touch. As she grasped it, she had noticed that her finger was healed. There was a warm draft flowing from underneath the door. She listened intently, grasping the doorknob once more. There was no sound. As she cracked the door opened, a low-pitched, purring sound pulsated through the hall. Wary, she peaked out of the crack to ensure that it was safe to exit the room. As she stepped into the hall, the sound increased. It was coming from one of the unoccupied rooms and now sounded like the purr of a large cat. At first, she thought it may be the lion, but she knew that she was not dreaming. As she approached the door to last room on the left, she saw light cascading from underneath the door. The light radiated warmth on her bare feet. She grasped the doorknob and the sound increased. It sounded like a large cat gnawing on food. With heed, she turned the doorknob and opened the door. The light and the warmth flowed over her. There on the floor stood a white kitten. It looked up at her and meowed. Mia walked inside and scooped it up.

She cradled it in her arms. It purred and climbed her shirt, nuzzled its face against her neck and chin. Its paws kneaded into her. Infatuated by its charm, she lifted it to her face and gave it butterfly kisses. The door slammed closed, stunning her. Fear reflected in her eyes and she quickly turned to see who was there. She saw no one. She placed the kitten on the bed and faced the door. Anxiety began to overwhelm her. She wrapped her arms around herself. The incandescent light, blanketing the room seemed to brighten as if the Sun were rising within it. The closet door creaked. She glanced over at it; saw that it was open and peeked inside. Nothing was in there. The kitten began to purr unusually loud and she turned to look at it. It was no longer there. Sitting on the bed, in the same spot that she had placed the kitten, was a frog. She stood still. She knew that it was now evident that there was a Witch in the room. As she stared at this frog, she noticed it was different from the other two. Although it was not much bigger than the others, its difference was the color of its eyes. They were white with an orphic pearly sheen. A cryptic whisper came from behind her. Frozen with fear, she raised her eyes up in hopes to see a reflection in the window in front of her. It reflected the silhouette of an enigmatic entity behind her. Its dark and misty shape shifting form swayed in synch to the air that blew through the curtains. The light within the room dimmed. As the light dimmed, a candle on the nightstand in between Mia and the bed lit itself. Mia gazed at the flame as it burned. Its oracular flame slowly grew higher, jumping sporadically to entice her. She lifted her hand and slowly moved her finger to the flame. Her finger was less than an inch from the flame when she felt the entity's presence behind her. It whispered slowly into her ear. *"Am I what I seem?"* Mia froze. The voice whispered to her again. *"I have not forgotten what you did to me, Mia."* The hand moved to her throat, grasping it gently. The other hand slid around her waist. Its touch was cold. Mia looked back up at the reflection on the window and now saw a dark-haired entity behind her but could not make out its face. Its eyes were reflective of the light from the candle and were looking directly at Mia's reflection. She felt it near her shoulder and heard its breathing. A spectral sound echoed throughout the room, whirring like a decrepit organ, with pitches of ghastly notes. The entity's hands slipped away from her and she no longer felt its presence behind her. Mia swiftly turned around and saw that it had vanished. She looked around the room. There was nothing. The candle was still burning but its flame was low and steady. She felt somewhat safe now because this meant it was gone, along with its Magick. She darted to the door and just as she turned the knob, she heard the clicking sound of its lock. She felt warm air encircling her ankles, traveling upward to her face. She was too afraid to look at first. The flame from the candle flared and crackled loudly. She knew it was present again but did not dare look to see where it was. The sound of air flowing through a seashell cascaded throughout the room. She wrapped her arms around herself once again. The kitten returned and was rubbing against her ankles and weaving between her feet. She looked down to look at it and it sat down in front of her, staring up at her. When she reached down to pick it up, it backed away and darted behind her. Lured by it, she turned around to chase it and stopped abruptly. Aithusa was sitting on the edge of the bed with her hands clasped together and grinning. "Meow." Her elvish eyes penetrated Mia's. "Come here, Mia" Mia stepped backwards until her back was against the door. Fear pervaded her mind as she cowered against the door. As Aithusa's eyes burned through her, Mia's fear grew stronger, causing the flame on the candle to rise. When Mia turned to see the flame, it crackled, drawing from the strength of her fear.

Drawn to the candle, Mia slowly approached it. Her eyes remained fixed on the flame, purposely feeding her fear into its persuasive and enigmatic energy. She remembered the flame in the Lions eyes and now knew why he held up his paws. Aithusa glanced over at the candle and then back to Mia. She stood up and walked over to it, standing on the opposite side of Mia, facing her. Aithusa looked into the flame, holding an arcane gaze within its fiery, seething rage and without taking her eyes off of it, she spoke to her, slowly enunciating her words. "Look into the candlelight, Mia." The flame flared. "Now look at me." Mia raised her head and faced her, looking into her arcane eyes. Holding Mia's eyes within hers, she raised her hand, placing her finger in the flame. Aithusa watched as Mia raised her hand and did the same. She again, slowly enunciated her words. "My spell is alive." Aware of what she was doing to her, Mia allowed the fire to possess her. Her eyes widened, mirroring its feral energy. She focused on only one phrase, repeating it until the flame became fully charged with her fear and burned within her spirit. Mia whispered. *"I am the flame."* She took a deep breath and closed her eyes, reclaiming the untamed energy within its blaze. The candle fluttered violently, imploding on itself and was doused, leaving a faint wave of smoke wafting above it. Within her mind, she pictured the floor below her and envisioned a circle around her feet. The circle surrounding her became visible to Aithusa, glowing into a scarlet hue. Using this feral pyre of Element, the circle ascended over Mia's body, surrounding her in a transparent cone shaped veil. Mia opened her eyes, slowly panning her focus from the floor, upward. Her eyes remained locked on Aithusa, who had been watching her intently, exhibiting a sinister expression. Aithusa approached Mia and stood in front of her. She lifted her arm, raising it above her head. Mia watched as she extended her finger outward and traced a line, which descended to the floor. Her eyes returned to Mia, staring at her with malicious intent. She raised her arms above Mia's head and with her fingers extended, she grasped the protective cone that Mia had built and tore it open. Mia watched as it fell to the floor and vanished. She could not understand why her Magick had failed. She stared at Aithusa's expressionless face. Aithusa moved in closer, reached out to her and whispered into her ear. "Meow." Mia now realized how she was able to tear down the cone. She remembered that cats could enter all types of sacred circles. Mia pushed her hands away, scratching her in the process. She grasped Mia's wrists tightly and pushed her against the door. Mia squirmed, trying to free herself but Aithusa pushed against her. She released Mia's hands and held her head tightly, forcing Mia to look at her. The anger within Aithusa's eyes paralyzed her. Mia looked into her eyes with a grim expression and began to weep. She saw what was to come. Mia raised her hands, placing them loosely onto Aithusa's wrists. Aithusa's hands slid down to Mia's cheeks. "This will not end as it did the last time. Pleasure and pain will be one." She wiped Mia's tears away with her finger and slid her hand to the back of her neck, combing her fingers through Mia's hair. She kissed her lips, and trailed kisses down her neck. She stepped back and took her by the hand. "Come." Aithusa walked to the bed and sat at its edge with Mia between her knees. "Undress." She placed her arms on the bed, leaning back, with an ominous smirk. Spellbound and immersed in Aithusa's eyes, Mia abandoned her own will, surrendering to her command. Aithusa watched her as she disrobed. Mia stood in front of her, hypnotized by the strong persuasion of her spell. Aithusa glanced over at the candle and as she slowly turned back to look at Mia, the wick had sparked once again, relighting itself. As the flame shimmered, Aithusa watched as it reflected its luminescence over the silhouette of Mia's body. Mia saw the candle relight itself and knew Magick was still alive within the room. Aithusa rose from the bed and ran her fingers over Mia's shoulders, tracing her arms with her fingertips. Mia trembled, unable to find the will within herself to fight the savage aura of her enchantment. She slid her hands over Mia's waist, tautly embracing her. She grasped her hair tightly and painfully, kissing her with hostile fury. Aithusa steering her onto the bed, staring into Mia's eyes with a lustful vengeance. She placed her hands on the sides of her thighs, slowly sliding them up to her waist. Her kisses grazed her neck, and trailed over her collarbone. Her teeth grazed her nipple and Mia writhed from the pain and pleasure. She slid her hand over her waist, pulling her thigh inward. When Mia felt her hand between her legs, she panted from the anticipation. Her fingers slid inside of her and Mia moaned. Aithusa whispered into her ear. "I know, baby." She crawled above her and consumed her mouth with her deep kisses. Mia responded, returning her kiss. Aithusa pushed herself up and hovered over her, staring at her with malicious intent. Aithusa's words sent Mia over the edge. "...Time for the pleasure with pain."

CHAPTER 17

INCENSE AND RAINBOWS

The most horrific screaming awakened Enya, causing her to nearly fall off of her bed. Her heart was pounding like a jackhammer. She turned to see Mia sitting upright, beside her in a tempestuous state. Enya moved in front of her and grabbed her shoulders. Mia was in such a panic-stricken state that she had become unhinged from reality. Enya sat over her legs, trying to shake her back to the here and now. 'MIA! LOOK AT ME! FOCUS ONLY ON MY VOICE!" She kept screaming. Her face was Red from coughing and crying and her hair and face were soaked from sweat. Her fear driven dismay reflected in her blue pupils. Enya saw her eyes and screamed for her sister. "MAYNE GET THE FUCK IN HERE NOW!" She embraced Mia tightly, wrapping her arms and legs around her as she tried to calm her. She lowered her tone to a soothing level. "Mia. Focus on my voice. I need you to calm down. I am here. Nothing is going to happen to you. Did you have a bad dream?" Mia's screaming curtailed to coughing and wheezing. Her eyes were swollen and her body trembled uncontrollably.

Mayne slammed the door open, in the assumption that something had happened to Enya, "WHAT THE FUCK HAPPENED?" She saw Enya holding Mia. "Just come over here, dammit!" Mayne crawled onto the bed and Enya whispered into her ear. "Look at her eyes. I think she's had a bad dream."

Enya slowly released her. Mia stretched her legs out and as she wiped her eyes she noticed that her own hands were trembling. Mayne crawled up to her and sat straddled, over her legs. "What the fuck is going on with you?" Mia didn't answer her. She just gazed at her as if she were looking right through her.

Aithusa entered the room and Mia snapped out of her panic driven trance, wide eyed at first glance and she silently cried. The sight of her sent a burning sensation of fear, deep within her stomach. She hyperventilated and coughed, causing herself to dry heave. Enya's eyes flared. She raised her voice to Mayne. "Go get Hunter." Aithusa placed her hands on the bed and leaned in. grinning at her. "Yeah, tell us about your dream, Mia." Mia shivered, looking her straight in the eyes. Enya immediately shifted her focus directly at Aithusa. "How do you know she had a dream?" Aithusa turned back to look at Mia. "Yes, Mia. How do I know? Tell Enya." Mayne ran to fetch Hunter. As she approached the foot of the staircase, she saw Hunter, already on his way up. He did not have a pleasant expression. She filled him in on what happened as they walked toward the room. Mia wrapped her arms around herself and zoned out. She realized Aithusa was in her dream, just as Hunter and Mayne had been, before. As her anger grew, her fear began to dissipate. Her feebleness was quickly replaced with malicious intent, which mirrored within her eyes and seared through her veins. She took a sharp, deep breath and leaped on top of Aithusa, grasping her throat and slamming her head onto the bed. Mia clutched her throat again. Aithusa clenched her teeth and jerked her body, flipping her off of the bed. Mia fell onto the floor. She jumped back up before Aithusa could get to her. Enya screamed to Mayne and Hunter. "GET IN HERE NOW!" Aithusa laughed deviously, further inciting Mia's fury. "Bring it Mia. Show me what you got." Mia lunged into her, knocking her against the side of the bed. She hooked her arm around Aithusa's neck, pulled her up and rammed her knee into her stomach. Aithusa laughed at her again and swiftly grabbed Mia's legs, pushing her weight into her. Just as they fell onto the floor, Hunter and Mayne rushed into the room. Mia jumped onto her and dug her nails into her shoulders and Aithusa felt the sharp pain and hissed. Aithusa tilted her body to the side, wrapped her legs tightly around Mia and pinned her to the floor. Hunter grabbed Aithusa's arms and as he lifted her up, Mia reached out and caught her hair. She was just about to punch her in the stomach when Mayne grabbed her arm and jumped in between them. She pried Mia's hand out of Aithusa's hair, pushed Mia onto the bed and held her down. She pinned her hands above her head. Mia fought futilely to get out from under her. With her face an inch from hers, Mayne looked her directly in the eyes and shouted. "MIA! ENOUGH! YOU NEED TO CALM THE FUCK DOWN NOW! YOU'RE NOT GETTING UP!" Mia's face was flush with rage. She panted, trying to catch her breath. Aithusa leered at her with a brassy grin and left the room.

"What happened?" He inquired in a sharp tone. "She woke up screaming from a dream." Enya paused for a moment. "I think Aithusa was intentionally in it." He stood before Mia. "Is that so, Mia?" Pursing her lips, she slowly turned, suspiciously eying him and he snapped at her. "No, I was not present in your dream." Mayne shifted herself off of her and sat beside her. He sat in front of her, looked into her eyes and grasped her jaws. "Show me." He demanded. Her eyes teared. She forced herself to recall and relive the imagery from her dream. As she remembered the last of them, her breathing became erratic. She pushed herself to the far end of the bed and wrapped the blanket around herself. Hunter looked at Enya and Mayne, as he fought the urge to laugh. He stood up, stepped a few feet away from Mia and gestured for Mayne and Enya to do the same. He knew what Aithusa had done, what she was planning on doing as well and reiterated that to them, adding a few words. "Aithusa is bitter about what Mia did to her. She needs to stop challenging her. I've previously addressed this to her. Apparently I will need to address this again. If she choses to disregard me, then it may result in her own demise." Mayne smirked. "Laugh if you will. You and I can control her, but Aithusa cannot." Enya walked back to her bed and sat next to Mia. "Well they are leaving tomorrow night. I think Gwen said she needed to get back to her bar." Mayne stepped over to the bed and threw herself on it. She lay next to Mia, with her hand over her eyes. "I'm really fucking tired. What are we doing people?" Hunter walked over to Mia and pushed her hair away from her face.

"I'm going to speak to her now. Mayne, bring her back to you're room to sleep. I will stop in before I go back downstairs." "Fine." She nudged Mia with her elbow. "Get up." Mia sat up and looked at her, then glanced at Enya and stood. Enya crawled back into her bed. "Shut the light and door on your way out please." Hunter left the room. Mayne grabbed Mia's hand and led her back to her room. Mia paused and stood by the door for a moment and then locked it. Mayne rolled her eyes. "She won't come in my room." Mia looked up at her with an apprehensive expression, then climbed into the bed and slipped under the blanket. Mayne held an irascible expression. "You're on my side." Mayne sighed and went into the bathroom. Mia lay on the bed staring at the ceiling, trying not to think about what happened. Every time she heard a noise she looked at the door, thinking that it was her, trying to open it. She heard a door shut, out in the hall, followed by footsteps. There was a knock at the door and Mia jumped out of the bed and ran into the bathroom. "What the fuck? Can I brush my damn teeth in peace?" Mia said nothing. The knocking became louder. Mayne stepped out and opened the door. It was Hunter. Mia heard their voices but couldn't make out what they were saying. "I spoke to her. I am correct. She is in fact, bitter over what happened between them when we first found Mia and she also wanted to challenge her out of curiosity. Where's Mia?" "She's in the bathroom hiding. She thought it was her at the door and ran in while I was in there." He smiled. "She fears and challenges you, yet she feels safe with you. It must be that alpha image that you exhibit." Mayne flexed her arm muscles and he snickered. "Did all go well with Enya?" "Yes." Hunter entered the room, closed the door behind himself and spoke in a low tone. "Aithusa made one mistake. Within Mia's dream, she cast a spell on her, however, in essence, she also broke the Pyramid, by telling her that her spell is alive. I need to ensure that Mia does not remember and realize this. If she does, she will know what Enya did and may now be versed in breaking it." "Crap." She paused for a moment and then held a mischievous grin. "I can keep her fuzzy and occupied." "Do what you need. I'm going to have a word with her." He smiled and called out to her. "Mia?" She panicked and locked the door. Annoyed, he raised his voice. "Are we doing this again?" At first she didn't understand what he meant. There was silence for a few seconds. She remembered the sledgehammer incident, quickly opened the door and looked up at him with a feeble expression on her face. "Mia, I have spoken with Aithusa. You need not be frightened." Her face cringed. "Do you have a question?" She looked away and said nothing. He placed both hands on the top of the door. "Mia when I ask you a question, I expect a reply." She looked up at him and shook her head. He focused on her for a few moments to feel her aura. "The next time that I ask you a question, you will answer me, verbally." As he left the room he gestured to Mayne to follow. She grabbed her keys and walked over to the entrance of the bathroom. "Mia. I'll be right back. I'm just getting a beer. I'll lock the door." Mayne walked down the stairs with him. "Ya know she's still not talking to anyone. "I am aware." "I'm surprised that no one else heard her scream." As they entered into the kitchen they saw Faeryn sitting at the table, eating a bowl of cereal. "Did something wake you?" Hunter inquired. "I heard the screaming, but I heard your voices and didn't want to go interfere." "Sorry about that. Mia had a bad dream. All is well." "Great. I couldn't go back to sleep, so I came in here for a snack." Mayne took a beer and left without saying anything. "Is she ok?" "If you mean Mayne? Yes. She's just tired and cranky from being woken up."

Mia quickly darted over to the nightstand. She was looking through the drawer for marijuana because she needed to calm herself. There was none there. She slid over to the dresser and rustled through the drawers. Mayne unlocked the door, walked in and saw her. She froze. "What are you looking for?" She slowly walked up to her. "My bike keys?" Mia shook her head nervously. "Then what?" Mayne's dark eyes flared. She whispered. "I wanted to smoke." "That's not where I keep it." She walked over to the closet and knelt down, opening up a wooden box. She grabbed an ashtray and sat on the bed. "Come over here." Mia slid onto the bed in front of her, with her legs crossed and watched as she crushed the leaves and rolled it into a cigarette. Mayne lay across the bed, reaching for the nightstand and fumbled through the drawer for matches. When she struck the match on the box, its spark caused Mia to jerk. She purposely held the flame up in front of her for a few moments. The flame captured her attention as Mayne had intended. Mia gazed at it, recalling Aithusa and the candle. Mayne smirked and then pulled it away to light the cigarette. She took a toke and handed it to her. "Do you know how or do you want me to do it for you?" She nodded and took it from her hand. She took a deep drag and coughed as she exhaled. "Take smaller tokes." Mayne watched her as she took two more drags and handed it back to her. Mayne took a few drags and then slid herself in front of her, wrapping her legs around her. She put the cigarette in her mouth backwards, clenched her teeth then placed her hand on her shoulder, pulled her closer and blew the smoke into Mia's mouth. She waited for her to exhale and did it once again. She lay back on the bed, took another toke and pointed to her. "If there is something of mine that you want, you ask me for it. Understood?" Mia nodded. "Do you want more?" She nodded again. "Come over here." Mia crawled upon her and hovered above her face. She put it back in her teeth and placed her hand onto Mia's shoulder. Mia inhaled the smoke from her mouth, remaining above her. Mayne's eyes were fixed on hers as she took another toke and put the remains of it in the ashtray. Mia shifted back, straddling herself upon Mayne's legs. She gazed at her as she began to feel the effects of the pot. Mayne placed her arms behind her head. "Feel better?" Smiling, Mia nodded. With a skeptical expression, Mayne raised her eyebrows at her. "Have you never smoked pot... other than with me?" Mia whispered her reply. "Not very often. Yours is different." "I know. Its stronger." Mayne grinned. Mia closed her eyes for a few moments, floating along with her thoughts. She felt so relaxed and no longer felt even the slightest ounce of residual fear. She felt safe. She slid her hands onto the bed and hovered over her. Then took a deep breath and looked deeply into Mayne's eyes. "I always see and feel things in your eyes." "What do you see?" "I see the depth of your darkness." Mia paused for a moment. "I see and feel the volatile fire within you. I've experienced this a few times." Mayne lay there with an intense stare, listening to her. "I feel bewitched." She paused for a second. "You have a frightening and irresistible seize on my soul." Mia took a deep breath again. "I am afraid of who you are. I feel protected by you, as well." Mayne placed her hands on Mia's cheeks. "You only see what I choose show you." Mayne paused and pushed the hair away from

Mia's eyes. "You're the only one who has ever had the balls to challenge me when I am mad. You're also the only one who can endure my wrath." Mia was in awe from her words. She did not realize that she had viewed her in this way. "You're much stronger than you realize and when you understand yourself, you'll be like me." Mia reflected a look of doubt. "I've always been leery of people when they looked in my eyes for too long." She paused for a moment. "What do you see in my eyes?" Mayne inhaled sharply, sucking her teeth. "I see everything, just as Hunter does." Mia held an apprehensive gaze. "So… you go in my dreams?" "Yes." Mia wondered if she saw the lion and frog. "What do you see in them?" Mayne put her palms on Mia's cheeks and pulled her closer. "I see your fire." Mia stared into her eyes and saw a flame reflected in each of them. "Mia. When I see you, I see a wild-eyed girl with a distant blue surge of energy hiding within your soul. That's how I knew it was you." These answers generated additional questions within Mia's thought process. "I don't understand. Is this why you keep me here?" "Mason answered you. You belong with us because you are one of us." Mia recalled the day that he had betrayed her, looked away and pouted. "I have a lot of questions." "I see. Hasn't Hunter answered any?" "Some… but in riddles, though." "You can ask me one more." Mia looked up at the ceiling, considering which one to ask. "How do I only show you what I want you to see?" Mayne chuckled. "Good one." She paused and grasped Mia's shoulders. "What do you want to hide from me?" "If I tell you that or think about it, you will know." "Correct. That's your answer." Mia smiled. "I think I understand." "So, what do you want me to see?" "What I try to hide from you." Her enigmatic expression held Mayne's attention. Mia glanced over at the ashtray. "Can we finish the rest of that?" "Yes." Mayne smiled at her, reached over to the ashtray and lit it up. She took a hit and handed it to her. She gazed at Mayne in a peculiar way. She looked over at the nightstand and saw her keys and then turned to look back at her, holding a pixyish expression on her face. She then put the joint in her teeth, placed her hands on the bed and slid herself over, up to her face. Mayne laughed at her. "Oh you want to try this on me now?" Mia smiled and blew the smoke into her mouth. "Do you know what that's called?" Mia shook her head, watching her exhale. "Shotgun." Mayne paused for a moment. "Mia, there are some things you don't have to ask me for." She pierced Mayne's eyes with an inviting expression. "Yeah?" She then slid off the bed and stood in front of the nightstand and eyed her keys. She glanced over at Mayne and then back to the keys. Entertained by Mia's mischievous behavior, she watched her intently. Mia reached for the keys, hooking the loop onto her pinky. She swayed her hand over in Mayne's direct view, dangling the keys in her face with a come hither smile. She recalled the last time she dangled them at her. She was sitting on the table at Gwen's bar. It was then, that she saw Mayne's fiery rage. With that in her mind, Mia slowly walked over to the dresser and hoisted herself up. She extended her hand and dangled them once again. With an insidious grin, Mayne slowly pulled her hands from behind her head and sat up. She rose from the bed and strolled towards her. "It's dangerous to taunt me. You know this." As she approached her, Mia lifted her hand up and dangled the keys in front of her face. Mayne stood inches from her, keeping her arms at her side. Her eyes remained locked on hers, possessing Mia's eyes and watching the keys within her peripheral view. Her stare held Mia static, inducing hypnotic, provocative thoughts. Within a flash, her teeth were clenched tightly on Mia's finger. Mia was caught off guard and let out a faint squeal. Mayne grasped her wrist, wrapped her lips around her finger and slowly sucked on it, sending shivers through Mia's body. Her hands slid through Mia's hair, tightly grasping the locks between her fingers. She heard the increasing rhythm of her breath and whispered into her ear. "You wanna play with my fire?" She held her head steady, forcing Mia's focus on her piercing stare. Mia's hands trembled, seduced by the fiery annihilation within them. Mayne gently kissed her lips, slowly tracing them with her tongue. She hooked her finger over the button of Mia's shirt, pushing down until the thread gave way and sent the button flying. One by one, the remaining buttons fell victim to the same fate. She parted her shirt, slid her hands over her bare shoulders and swiped the shirt off of her. The keys fell from Mia's hand, crashing onto the floor. Her hands glided down Mia's arms to her hand, grinding into her palms with her thumbs. Her fingers entwined with Mia's, pinned her hands against the wall behind her and kissed her coercively, sending shivering pulses throughout her body. Mia struggled trying to break her hands free from her grip. The more she tried, the tighter she held. With her mind bewitched within Mayne's feral stamina, Mia bit down on Mayne's lip. The sharp pain caused her to release Mia's hands. She clutched Mayne's hair, pulling her close to her. Mayne purposely licked her injured lip and Mia's eyes burned with enticement. As Mia wrapped her legs around Mayne's waist and pulled her closer. In response to her last question she provoked her in a wanton tone. "I don't play with fire. I control it." Mayne's eyes flared at her wildly and she laughed at her in the most unnerving way. "Oh Yeah?... I'm gonna lay your fuckin' ass to the sheets." Mia now knew she had opened Pandora's box. Fear and thrill became one. She swiftly lifted her off of the dresser and threw her onto the bed. Mia's head spun from the sudden jolt. When she refocused, she saw her standing in front of her, panting with a wolf-like gaze. As Mia slid backwards, Mayne grabbed her ankles and pulled her back to the edge. She grasped the legs of her pants and yanked them off of her. Mia quickly knelt upright and almost lost her balance. Mayne caught her and wrapped her arms around her waist, holding her body tightly against her own. She nudged Mia's chin to meet her lips and kissed her with sublime intensity, sucking on her tongue and biting her lip. Mia felt her hand ease along her ribs, caressing her breasts with lustful ardency. Her hand grazed down to her thigh, pulling her in closer. Mia moaned, tilting her head from the intense sensation of her touch. Her thighs quivered in echoed elation to the rhythm of her fingers. Mayne eased her onto the bed, devouring her mouth with kisses, trailing them over her neck to her breasts. She felt Mayne's teeth grazing and biting her nipple and she squeal from the pain. The touch of her callous hands fed into Mia's elated state, causing the sweat on Mia's body to sting. Mayne hovered above her with an icy gaze. She kneeled between her ankles and slowly licked her calf, her hungry lips roaming, trailing her tongue along her inner thigh. Mia squealed when she felt her teeth tightly clenching her thigh. She sat up, desperately tugging on Mayne's hair. Panting from the sharp pain, she begged her. "Please stop... it hurts!" Her feeble plea fed Mayne's fiery. Mayne unclenched her teeth, switching the pain to pleasure and seized her body like a starved wolf, bewitching Mia with her erotic madness. The rollercoaster of elation was more than she could endure. Mia tried to back away, only to be pulled back. Mayne growled as if Mia were stealing a meal from her. Her tongue, ethereal, her lips, sublime, her arms wrapped tightly around Mia's thighs, pulling her back each time Mia tried to slide away. Mayne owned her like a wolf owned its kill, feeding from her, never letting up until her hunger was satiated and her thirst, quenched. Mia fell backwards, crying out in ecstasy. Covered in sweat, she lay there in a state of annihilation, scorched from the fire she had innately claimed she'd control. Her head spun from her erratic breathing. Mayne slowly edged herself up as she kissed her stomach, trailing up to Mia's neck. With a baleful expression, she hovered above Mia's face, grinning. "No one can control fire, Mia." She gently kissed her lips. "I know…but it can be guided." Mia smiled mischievously.

CHAPTER 18

BREAK THE CHAIN

"Reach over and shut off the lamp." Mayne pointed at it as she pulled the blanket over Mia and herself. Mia held a cranky expression. "But I'm not tired now." Mia reached over for the remote and turned on the television. "Are you kidding me? You should be spent. I know I am." Mayne sat up, sighing loudly. "I'm hyper now." Mayne rolled her eyes. "Great!" Mia lay facing her, curled up under the blanket. "Mayne?" She covered her eyes with her arms and answered. "Yes." "Why hasn't Sebastian tried to contact me?" "Is this gonna be question night?" "Tell me the truth. Is he ok?" "I don't know and he's fine." "I want to call him." Mayne sighed, slid off the bed and walked over to the closet, returning with another joint. She lit it up, and handed it to her. "Sit up and smoke this so that the both of us can go to sleep." "Only if you take me on your bike tomorrow, to go find him." Mayne's eyes widened. She thought about what Enya had done earlier and knew this was not possible. "We'll see." Mia smiled, satisfied about her possible small victory and decided not to push it any further. She took a few puffs and handed it back to Mayne. "I need to use the bathroom. I'll be quick." Mayne grabbed the remote off of the bed and switched the channels until she found something mellow. She put the ashtray on her stomach and lay back, watching the program. Mia returned, slipped under the blanket and leaned over next to her face. She stared at her while she smoked. "What?" "Do the backwards thingy. Put it in your teeth."

Mayne laughed at her. "Thingy?" She put it between her teeth and blew the smoke into Mia's mouth. Mia inhaled, smiling. "Yes. Thingy." "One more time, then lights out." Mia moved in closer this time and kissed her as she blew the smoke into her mouth. She laid back and pulled the covers over herself. Mayne ground out the joint, placed the ashtray on the nightstand and turned the lamp off. She rested her head on the pillow and placed her hands above her head. Mia turned sideways and curled up beside her, with her arm around her waist. "Mayne?" "Crap!" She paused for a second. "What?" What is my connection to you?" "Cut it out with the questions and go to sleep or I'll bite you again." Mia huffed and closed her eyes.

The light from the flickering TV screen danced shadows of light on her eyelids, casting endless hues within her mind. While she listened to the television, she began to feel the floating feeling that she liked so much. The yawns commenced and she gradually began to soar softly into a deep sleep. Mayne lowered the volume on the television and set the timer for thirty minutes. She turned onto her side to watch Mia as she slept. She brushed the bangs off of her eyes and saw the movement in her eyelids. She knew she was already dreaming. She shifted her pillow closer, wrapped her arm around her and shut her eyes. Mia felt her touch and it gave her a sense of security. With her head nuzzled under Mayne's chin, she grasped her shirt, tightly. The television shut itself off, leaving the humming sound of white noise strumming in Mia's ear. The sound woke her up and she found herself at the banks edge, facing the water. The strumming sound mirrored itself in the waves of the water. She lifted her head and gazed into its harmonized ripples. She pushed herself up and sat on her calves, absorbing the panoramic view of the water and watched as the waves slowly dissipated. The lake was placid. There was no sound. Not a leaf fluttered. The air surrounding her was neither, cold or hot. It was daylight and although the Sun was not visible, it cast back an unusual hue of blue across the sky. It was a bright bold blue, blended with a slight touch of Purple. She had only seen this unusual color in acrylic paint. She loved this shade so much that she had purchased a case of the two-ounce bottles. It was called Rhythm "N" Blues. The surroundings left her feeling wistful. She thought about home and how much she'd missed painting, which led her to thoughts of Sebastian. She missed him so much. Her heart was dispirited by his lack of contact with her. She faced the water, laid on her stomach with her hands underneath her chin. She gazed intensely at her reflection, wondering how deep the water was and thinking of and relating to an old proverb she recalled. *"Still waters run deep."* The depth of the water was as mysterious as the entities about herself that she sought so desperately to fathom. She extended her hand and held her palm flat, hovering it just above the water. With her eyes closed, she channeled its verve, feeling its magnetic surge against her palm and within her mind. She felt a splash on her hand and opened her eyes. The water was rising to meet her. Gazing into its depths, she saw an ascending blue shimmer of light, emanating its beams towards the surface. She balanced herself, carefully kneeling inward, over the water. The blue entity drew closer to the surface, revealing its essence. It seemed to be gliding directly toward her. Drawn to its color, she sunk her hand into the water to reach for it and the water immediately stopped rising. The blue entity accelerated to the surface. Mia nearly fell in, trying to grasp it. As she pulled her hand out of the water, it darted to the left and then propelled itself onto the top of her hand. It was another frog and peculiar one at that. She knelt backward, onto the grass, cupping it with her other hand. Its blue color was bold and bright. The light from the sky did not reflect from them, just like the onyx stone. What she found peculiar about this one was its onyx eyes. She ran her finger over its back. Resting her arms on top of her knees, she curiously stared at this new frog, knowing what it represented. Thinking of the other Frogs and whom they had represented, she felt leery of this one because of its familiar ethereal gaze. Looking away from it for a few moments, she perused the area, wondering where the lion was. She carefully stood up and turned around to see him standing behind her, a few feet away. He was standing with his paws behind his back, peering at her with a Cheshire cat-like grin. He made his way over to her and glanced at the frog. Still smiling, he placed his paw around her shoulder leading her to walk with him towards the bench. When they approached the bench, he released his paw from her shoulder and continued walking slowly, past the bench. He glanced back at her and gestured for her to walk further. Just as she took another step, she felt a sharp pinch on her palm, forcing her, out of reflex, to drop the frog. It had bitten her. It jumped onto the bench and looked up at her. The lion extended his paw and it hopped onto it. He waved his other paw abruptly, to coax her to approach him and she followed. By the third step, she bunked into something unseen to only her and was startled. With her hands raised, she slowly inching forward, feeling around for what she had bumped into. She felt something solid and cold to the touch and as she grasped both hands onto it, it began to reveal itself to her. It was a crystal bar. The other columns slowly appeared, surrounding her in its crystalized imprisonment. With both hands on the columns, she looked up at the lion, still retaining his unearthly smile. She could not understand why he would lead her there, knowing these columns would block her from following him. Disheartened by this and his distorted grin, she gazed at him teary eyed. She turned around, with her back against the columns, slid herself down to the ground and cried. She felt his paw on her shoulder and shifted around to face him. His amber eyes were blazing at her. She noticed that the blue frog was nowhere in sight. He raised his paw and punched through the center of one of the columns, splitting it. He knelt down, pointed one of his claws directly in her face and then made a fist as he pierced her eyes with his boldly. He extended one of his claws and drew a picture of three of the phases of the Moon in the dirt. Holding onto the columns, she watched as he scratched into the dirt. When he finished the drawing, it reflected a Waxing, a Full Moon and Waning Moon. He then poked a hole into the center of the Full Moon and imbedded a stick into it. The lion nudged her chin to look up at the Sun and then pointed back at the stick. The shadow from the Sun cast its glow and shade over it. Realizing that he had made a Sundial, she nodded her head and then with a baffled expression, she pointed at the Moon drawing. He pointed at the center of it, touching the Full Moon with his claw. Looking from the moon to the dial, she struggled to understand what the two of them had in common with her. When she looked back, the lion was gone. The impassiveness set in as Mia sat sunk back onto the ground. She looked to her left and eyed the endless row of crystal columns that imprisoned her. She knew the Lions fist meant that he wanted her to fight, but who and for what? A few tears fell from her eyes as she stood up. She walked around aimlessly for a few minutes until she came upon a young tree that stood about six or seven feet above her. She stopped in her tracks when she saw a young Blue Jay on the ground. Its mother was just above, perched on the branch above it. The mother dove down and stood next to it, watching as it made a few feeble attempts to fly on its own. Mia smiled, watching intently. This was her favorite bird. The mother flew back onto the lowest branch. The baby bird looked up as she soared and then made a few more unsuccessful attempts. The mother descended to the ground, next to the baby, fed it and returned back to the branch. The mother's stern, eloquent caw thrilled Mia. She wiped away the tears from her eyes, startling the baby. The baby took off, soaring towards the mother and successfully landed onto the branch next to her. Mia was so elated to be present for its very first flight. She looked past the tree and saw the Crystal columns behind it. Looking as far above them as she could see, she thought to herself. *"I need to learn how to fly solo, too."*

She felt a few drops of rain on her head and ran underneath the tree, where the Blue Jays were perched. The tree sheltered her from most of the raindrops. She watched as they gracefully fell onto the leaves and eventually cascading onto the grass. A few drops had fallen into her hair. The rain became steady. She noticed that it seemed to be slowly changing its angle of direction. It was behaving as if gusts of wind were present and assisting its oddly directed stream. There was not even as much as a breeze present. She placed her hands over her head and looked out over the grassy field. The rain was now streaming sideways, aiming directly at her from all four directions. Squinting her eyes, she looked overhead and was saddened to see that the Blue Jays were gone. Surrounded by these columns, with nowhere to go for shelter, she kneeled down and leaned against the tree. Soaked and shivering, she lowered her head onto her knees. Her tears merged with the raindrops on her face. She felt something overshadowing her and was startled by its sudden presence. She felt comforted by its warm and fuzzy embrace as it sheltered her from the rain. She knew it was the lion and wrapped her arms around his neck. He lifted her up, cradling her in his arms and she rested her head on his chest. He carried her across the field of grass, stood at the waters bank and kissed her forehead. She felt a sudden and swift movement and opened her eyes just as he swung her into the water. Airborne for a split second, she barely caught a glimpse of the lion before her body hit the water. Every nerve ending jolted from the chill of the cold water as she sunk deeper into its depths. The tiniest glimmer of light reflected from the surface. She desperately tried to swim towards it, relentlessly paddling her arms and kicking her legs until her muscles painfully locked up. With her eyes opened she held onto her breath and drifted aimlessly within its depths. As she slowly spiraled around, a school of frogs encircled her. The blue frog positioned itself directly in front of her face. Mia's eyes opened wide. She now faced the inevitable. She could no longer hold her breath.

Mia sat up, abruptly, gasping for air and drenched in her own sweat. She had felt as if she had almost drowned in her dream. Mayne was sound asleep. When she collected herself, she slid off of the bed and went into the bathroom. Gazing at herself in the mirror, she turned the sink on and splashed her face with cold water. She pealed off her sweaty clothes and stood in front of the full- length mirror on the bathroom door. She spotted a bruise mark on her inner thigh. When she remembered where it came from, thoughts of the blue frog biting her in her dream, led her to realize that this the frog in her dream, was Mayne. She turned the shower on and stepped in. The streamed warm water felt so soothing as it ran over her hair and down her back. Envisioning this dream as well as the others, she placed her hands on the shower wall, just below the showerhead and attempted to decipher their meanings. She switched the stream of water to a pulsated flow to sooth her aching shoulders. The sensation of the water mirrored patterns of the pelting rain in her dream. The feeling of the lion's body sheltering and embracing her recaptured the sense of security that she had felt with him. This inevitably led to the simmering feeling of despair and betrayal, when he had tossed her into the water. Images of the Crystal columns, the Blue Jays, the Frogs, the Moon phases and Sundial, drawn in the dirt by the lion flashed in her mind as well. She remembered the Frogs swirling around her within the depths of the water. *"Still waters run deep."* Came to mind again and her focus returned back to the wading Frogs in the waters dark abyss. She knew that they had intentionally surrounded her for a reason. Her own detailed cogitation of events surrounding her semi-pseudo encounter with Aithusa held its own bold influx of powerful and mysterious, layered messages. What had intrigued her most was the kitten that lured her and the enthralling control that both she and Aithusa held over the candle's flame. Mia was perplexed by how Aithusa enchanted her, recalling when she held her finger in the flame, enticing her into doing the same. Glancing at her finger, what had puzzled her most about this particular memory was why its flame did not burn her. She wondered why she would show her this. As she slathered the shampoo into her hair, Aithusa's words burned in her mind. She whispered them several times, to herself. *"My spell is alive."* Of all of the subliminal messages that her dream reflected, these words had stood out the most to her. The Crystal prison, the pummeling rain, Aithusa's words and being tossed into the water, seemed to be interpreting into the same meaning. The message was slowly becoming clearer to her. As she rinsed the shampoo from her hair, a clue had dawned for her. The lion wanted her to wake up and fight. As she lathered her body and rinsed, she repeated Aithusa's words again, thinking what part these words had played in all of this chaos.

The knock on the door started her, causing her to jolt. Mia had been so deeply entwined in her thoughts when she heard Mayne walk in. "It's me. I need to use the facilities." "Ok." Mia quickly rinsed the soap off and slid the shower door opened to grab the towel on the floor. Waiting for her to flush, she dried herself and wrapped the towel snugly around her body. Mayne turned the sink water on and washed her hands and face. Mia stepped out of the shower just as she had proceeded to brush her teeth. She sat on the chair, staring at her and waited for her to finish. Mayne grabbed a paper cup to rinse her mouth and as she tossed it into the trash, she caught Mia staring at her. She placed her hands on the sink and returned the stare. For a few moments she couldn't speak. Mia's thoughts were in disarray, hypnotized by her lingering and mysterious stare. Even upon waking, Mayne's eyes remained dark and oracular to her. Knowing what effect she had on her, Mayne cracked an evil smile, breaking the silence.

Mia whispered to her as she composed herself. "I need some clothes." Without saying a word, she left the room and returned with two sets of clothing, one for herself and one for Mia. She handed them to her and stepped into the shower. As she took them from her hand, a painful reminder of last night had resurfaced. She hissed as she looked at the bite mark on her finger and then looked at the one on her thigh as well. Mia purposely mentioned both bite wounds to feel for her reaction. "The bite on my thigh is still sore and I seem to have woken up with an additional bite mark on my finger." Mayne slid the shower door open a few inches and grinned. "Would you like me to kiss them?" Mia's face turned several shades of crimson. She put her undergarments on and sat on the chair, re-inspecting her thigh. "You were in my dream and I know that it was you because you bit me. You were a blue frog." She paused for a moment, waiting to hear what she may say. Mayne slid the shower door opened and wrapped the towel around herself. Mia grew impatient. "What were you and the other Frogs doing?" Without a response, Mayne slid on her jeans and stood at the sink, combing her hair. Annoyed by her silence, Mia rose from the chair and slid in between her and the sink, insistent on her attention. Mayne raised her voice. "What?" Mia pursed her lips. "Please answer." Mayne placed her hands on the sink and leaned closer, pinning Mia against it. "Yes, I was there. Figure it out." Mia sternly snapped another question at her. "Who is the lion?" "Question time again?" "Would you rather I revert back to my silence?" Mayne's sigh was intentionally rude. She paused for a moment and then flared her eyes at Mia. "You're quieter in my bed." With her eyes partially closed, Mia looked at her with an insidious glare. "Oh, so you've got jokes now, Smartass." Mia swiftly dropped down; clenching Mayne's legs with both arms and bit her thigh. Mayne howled loudly. "FUUUUCK!" She sucked her teeth. Mia hated and feared this because it always meant she was about to do something wicked. She knelt down, causing

Mia to lose her balance. She slid her hands underneath her back and legs, lifted her up and carried her out of the bathroom. She threw her onto the bed and sat on the small of Mia's back, facing her legs. She pinned her faced down. Just as Mia caught her breath she felt Mayne's teeth sink into her derriere. Mia shrieked. Her face to flushed, bright red and her eyes teared from the pain. Just as she felt her unclenching her teeth, she felt the sting of her slap on the other cheek. Mayne spun around and lay beside her. "So, are we done, or do you want to keep challenging me?" Mia pushed herself up, sitting on her calves and wiped her eyes. For a moment, Mia's anger took over and she jumped on top of her, pinning her arms against the pillow. Mayne laughed sarcastically. "Really?" Mia stared at her for a few seconds, jumped off and stormed into the bathroom. She partially closed the door to look in its mirror at her fresh bite mark. There was an emerging bruise but the skin wasn't broken. Mayne slowly opened the door and peeked in. Mia shifted over and looked up at her with a disgusted expression. "Look what you did! Now I have another bruise!" "Touché." Mayne grinned proudly. "Touché? You bit me three times, so if it's touché, then I owe you two more!" Mia pointed her finger at her and then quickly retracted it out of fear, when Mayne stared her down. "Do you like to provoke me?" Mayne paused for a moment, waiting to see if she would answer. She looked at Mia's hair, grabbed the comb and pulled the chair over. "Your hair's a fucking mess. Sit down." Mia looked at Mayne with a crazed expression. "I can't! My ass hurts, remember?" "Then sit on one cheek." She pushed her down into the chair and combed her hair. Mia re-situated herself, recalling a promise made to her. "Are we going on your bike today?" Recalling Enya's spell, Mayne smiled. "After we eat breakfast. I need coffee." Mia smiled. "Where are we going?" "Why? Are you planning on wandering away?" Mia turned to look at her, answering softly. "No." She slipped the comb in her back pocket. "Come on. Lets go downstairs."

Mia slipped on her shoes and rushed to catch up to her. She approached the top of the stairwell, glanced at the mid sized chandelier above and proceeded to descend down the stairs. She stopped when she saw Lucius, sitting midway and talking on the phone. He looked up at Mia, with a mischievous smile. "Well, look who it is?" He stood up, placing his arm against the wall, blocking her path. "Hey, can I call you back?" He tossed the phone on the step behind him. "Where ya going, little lamb?" She shifted over, trying to pass him and he extended his other arm to the bannister. "Why the rush, baby girl?" He stared at her, trying to catch her attention, but she kept looking the other way, saying nothing to him. He stepped up to the stair that she stood upon and she, in turn stepped up to the one above. He grasped her upper arms tightly, so that she could not move. Holding her chin gently, He whispered to her. "I haven't forgotten Mia." His face was uncomfortably close to hers. Intimidated by him, her fear overcame her courage and she once again, became introverted. Rather than cry and reveal her fear to him, she closed her eyes, recalling what she had done the last time he had threatened her. The gentle sounds of chiming glass were heard. She intently focused on the chandelier. He looked up and saw it shaking. Enraged, he immediately returned his focus back to her. As her fear increased, the chiming sounds of its crystals grew louder, intimidating him and feeding into his anger. He tightened his grip on her, holding her against himself. Exposing his teeth, his seething expression reminded her of the fangs of a wolf. "Go ahead Mia. It will fall on the both of us." "LEAVE HER ALONE LUCIUS!" Sage yelled as she ran up the stairs. "Back away now, Sage!" She glanced up and saw the quivering crystals. "Mia! Look at me now!" She demanded as she stepped up to her. A tear ran down Mia's face but she did not respond. Sage approached her slowly and touched her cheek in an attempt to get her to refocus. She pulled Lucius' hand off of Mia's arm. "Just fucking go downstairs Lucius! I'm sure that somehow you asked for this anyway, ya jerk!" He released her and stepped down a few steps. Hunter and Mayne stood at the bottom of the stairs, looking up at the chandelier. Hunter was annoyed by her behavior. As he ascended, the crystals stilled themselves. Sage placed her other hand on Mia's shoulder and whispered into her ear. "Hunter is coming now and he doesn't look happy. Please stop. If it falls, it will hurt us both." Mia realized that she was no longer controlling the crystals and when she saw Hunter's face, she looked at him. She knew he had stopped her. Hunter grabbed Mia's hand and led her downstairs to the kitchen. As she passed Mayne, she flared her eyes at her, whispering in her own defense. "He provoked me. Why didn't you stop him?"

Hunter sat beside the table and pulled another chair directly in front of himself. "SIT!" She watched Mayne as she passed, taking a seat at the far end of the table. He pulled in close to her and placed his hands on her knees. "We've been here before." He paused, with his eyes locked on hers, holding her attention. "We've discussed the meaning of intentions, yet you walk in circles, disregarding what I've told you." Mia took a deep breath, but did not respond. She knew that he was angrier than his voice had led on to be and his eyes had reflected that. She stared at the floor, holding back her tears. "If the light had fallen, the three of you could have been hurt, electrocuted and a fire could have ignited as well. That is why I stopped you." Just as he admitted to this, with an accusive look, she slowly raised her head to face him. Her feeble attempt to pull her wrists free from him, causing him to tighten his grip, thus further agitating him. "Your intentions towards Lucius were unjustified. He was not a real threat, nor was he the last time this had happened." Sage chimed in to defend Mia. "Hunter, he was harassing her. Mia? Why don't you speak up?" Hunter looked at Sage and then back to Mia. He moved his face an inch from hers, knowing his eyes intimidated her. "Your lack of communication with me will end soon. If this happens again, you'll be once again, spending your days and nights locked in my room." Lucius was standing at the entrance listening to them. "…and if Hunter isn't home, it'll be my room." Mia could no longer hold back her tears. She looked at Hunter and silently cried. Hunter made a mug of coffee and retreated to the living room. Mayne refilled her coffee and made a cup for Mia. She wiped her eyes and pulled herself to the table. Mayne questioned her inactions. "Why didn't you say something?" She hovered over her coffee, sipping it and then looked up at her. "I didn't want to." "What happened?" "He waited until you were out of sight, cornered me on the steps and harassed me. He's still mad at me." "Well you should have called out for me. Anyway can you blame him? You could have killed him." "I can't help it. When I get scared or angry, it just happens." "You need to control your anger and think before you direct it." Mia looked at her in disbelief. "Oh, not you, though!" Mayne smirked, proudly at her. "Smart ass! I'm not using Magick, you are. My anger is just that. You know this." "I do and you remind me of it, often. You always tell me not to challenge you because I'll always fail. Someday you may scare me and make me just as angry. So maybe it's you who shouldn't challenge me." She felt a little tenacious, having said that, to her. Mia looked up at her, holding an arrogant expression on her face. Mayne returned an icy stare, on purpose and held it long enough to make her feel uneasy, thus decreasing her confidence. Her smile quickly dissipated. With her mouth half full from the donut that she held in her hand, she pointed the other half at her. "It seems as if you are challenging me with what you just said." Mia got up to refill her coffee, thinking before she answered her. "I'm not challenging you. I'm just reiterating what I said before. I can't control what happens. What would you have done if it were you on the stairs instead of Hunter?" "The same thing, but with less patience. You wouldn't be sitting because your ass would be sore." Mia was furious by her reply. "Why the physical threat?" "Because at this point, you should have known better." Mia was silent. She knew she was right. "If it happens again, I'll scream for you." Mia recalled what she had said earlier, regarding her doing the same as Hunter. Mayne refilled her coffee and then sat back down. "Are we done with the fucking questions?" Mia looked up at her. "No." She rose from the chair, walked over to her and straddled herself on her lap. "One more." "What did you mean when you said you would have done the same as Hunter did?" Mayne paused for a moment. "Because he and I are the same."

Raine entered the kitchen. "Oh how cute! Hiya...I need coffee, now!" She sat at the table and helped herself to a donut. "Enya's coming. She's inside with Hunter. What's new?" Mayne laughed. "Mia's harassing me." Raine smiled. "I heard about Lucius harassing you, Mia. Good job!" Mayne frowned. Enya walked in with Hunter. "Of course I come in here to find a mess." She made herself a cup off coffee and sat next to Mayne, looking at the two of them. "What's this about?" "Mia's harassing me." "Good." Hunter walked over to the counter and leaned against it. "So what's every ones plans for today?" Raine saw Mia smiling at Mayne and leaned in. "Hmm, What's with the smiling Mia?" Mia said nothing. In a low tone, Hunter questioned Mia's secretiveness. "What your secret?" Mia flared her eyes and looked at Mayne. He stepped over and leaned in. "Come on. Tell me Mia." She cringed and turned away. "I'm taking her for a ride on my bike." With an unsettling expression, Mia looked at him, expecting him to say that she could not go. "How nice for you, Mia. Why do you look distressed right now?" She whispered the answer to Mayne. "I thought he was going to say no." She laughed and repeated it back to him. "She thought you were gonna say she couldn't go." He smiled. "Mia, of course you can go with her." Mia looked at him, perplexed by his response. Mayne pushed her off of her lap. "Go put on jeans and a jacket. You can't ride with exposed skin." "Ok!" She ran upstairs to change, passing Lucius as if he were not there.

Enya grinned at Mayne. "So, she speaks only to you." Mayne tugged at her imaginary collar. "Yep." Enya sat at the table, sipping her coffee, knowing what was going to happen when Mia returned. Raine observed her expression and glanced over at Mayne and Hunter who held the same expression. "Is this a Pyramid moment?" Enya placed her finger over her own mouth, as a gesture to keep silent. "Ok. Enough said." Sage was looking over the contents of the refrigerator for something appealing to eat. Calculating its contents, she peeked into the freezer and took a bag of frozen peppers. "I'm making omelets. Anyone want?" Raine stood up and walked over to her. "Yes, please. What are you adding?" "Peppers, cheese and sausage." Enya turned around and laughed. "You know its gonna wind up looking like scrambled eggs." "Yeah true. It tastes the same though. I'll just make alot, in case anyone else wants some." Enya stretched her achy neck and shoulders. "Please put eggs on the list." Hunter returned. He stood behind Enya and massaged her shoulders, commenting with a grin. "My fault?" A sigh escaped her mouth, followed by a guilty smile. Mayne looked at her in disbelief. "Really?" "Really, what? Kettle, Black?" Both Raine and Sage smirked, in synch. Hunter smiled at Mayne, shook his head and went back into the living room. "I'll be inside if I'm needed." As he walked past the stairway, Mia came running down, stopping short upon his presence. Hunter smiled. "Enjoy the ride, Mia." She found his comment suspicious and watched him walk into the living room. She proceeded back to the kitchen. "Ok, I'm ready." Sage pleaded in dismay. "But I just made alotta omelets. Don't you want some?" Enya laughed. "No thanks. I ate a donut." Mayne looked at Enya with a blank stare and pulled the keys from her pocket "Follow me. I gotta get the helmets." She walked to the closet, next to the side door and pulled them out. "This one should fit you. Put it on." "This is heavy." Mia had trouble fastening the buckle. "Come here." As she adjusted the buckle, she watched Mia closely for signs of Enya's spell and slowly put on her own helmet. "Ya ready?" Mia nodded. "The bikes in the front. Come." As they walked through to the living room, Enya leaned in, over the kitchen table and eventually followed them from an unnoticeable distance. Looking straight at Hunter, Mayne walked into the living room first, with Mia a few feet behind. Hunter was watching the TV. As Mia passed by him, his attention went to her. Mayne uttered as she passed him. "We'll be back before dusk." As Mia approached the door, she began to experience an old familiar feeling. She began to feel apprehensive and her cheeks turned crimson. Her breathing became erratic and she began to feel the effects of anxiety. She turned to look at Hunter when she began to feel overwhelming heat throughout her body. "Is this you? Are you doing this to me?" "No, Mia. What's wrong?" Mayne grasped the doorknob and watched her as she opened the door. Some of the images from her last dream began to flash in her mind. As the door slowly opened, the light of the sunny day beamed across the floor, causing her to squint. Thinking of the baby Blue Jay and how much she wanted to go for this ride with Mayne, she fought the negative and fearful feelings with every ounce of strength. Mayne held the door opened. "Mia. Lets go!" Her loud voice made Mia jump. Leery eyed and tense, she looked up at Mayne and then proceeded towards the door. Mayne looked at Hunter, then back at Mia and walked out. Mia stood at the entrance of the door and watched her as she approached her bike. Her excitement and will to go had dissipated. Instead, an overwhelming fear of leaving seemed to take over her thoughts. "Come on Mia, let's go!" Mayne shouted at her again. Mia felt a rush of anxiety, spiraling throughout her body. While the feeling of anxiety was similar, she could not explain the reason behind this particular episode. It seemed to be fed by a fear of leaving. She felt herself beginning to lose her psychological battle. The tears fed off of her anger and frustration. She fought with the two images of the Baby Blue Jay: one fighting with its own fear and the one, succeeding. She wanted so much, to be the latter of the two.

Mayne sat on the bike, glancing back at Mia while she revved its engine. Mia pushed the door opened and took a step past its seam, squinting from the Sun's glare. The rays cascaded everywhere within her panoramic view. She gazed at the Sunbeams from sky to ground and watched as their erratic rays visually defined themselves before her. The glaring sting lessened as the seconds passed by, making clear what needed to be revealed to her. Her eyes followed their waves as they flowed through the air and bounced off of the ground, exuding into effulgent columns. The soothing warmth felt as if dawn itself, had taken up residence on the front lawn. A sudden icy chill ran through her body. She was immediately torn away from her Zen feeling when she realized what had come into view. The crystal columns from her dreams had now, in waking state, slowly emanated before her eyes. The mere presence of these columns turned her face white with fear. She now knew what they had represented. Mayne shut the ignition off and walked to the front door. "What the hell is going on with you?" With tears in her eyes, Mia stared blankly at the columns. She ran inside, passing Hunter and opened the side door. The columns were there as well. Sobbing out loud, she ran into the kitchen, passing Enya, Sage and Raine and opened the blinds on sliding doors to the yard. The columns were also there. She stood with her hands and forehead against the glass door and wept. Mayne walked into the kitchen with Hunter. They looked directly at Enya, who held a sate grin on her face. At first, no one said a word and just quietly observed her. She knew that the columns meant imprisonment, however, she was unknowingly bewitched by Enya's powerful spell and inevitably succumbed to her fear, choosing to remain the frightened baby Blue Jay. With her eyes swollen and tear filled, she turned around and looked at Mayne. "I can't go." Mayne looked at her with flared eyes and then glanced over at Enya. Raine stepped over to her and swiped Mia's hair away from her face. "What's wrong Mia?" She shook her head and cried silently. She slid the door opened and slowly walked up to the crystal columns. They protruded along the inner fringes of the yard, parallel with the fencing. She placed her hands on one of them. As Raine followed her into the yard, she saw her hands touching something unseen to her. "What are you doing, Mia?" The wind was gusting against her back in an Eastern direction, her hair, veiling her face and partially obscuring her vision. Searching for a hidden message, she observed her surroundings, as well as the orient of the wind. Its direction would determine its message to her and then redirect her attention, her true North, guiding her ability to reason with her inner cognitive conflict. As she began to recognize this, she thought of the lion and the fight that he had referred to and realized that her battle was about to begin. "Mia, do you hear me? What are you touching?" Mia looked at her own hands and tightly grasped the column.

"My fear."

CHAPTER 19

THE WEAKEST LINKS

Hunter stepped out into the yard and approached Mia. He stood beside her, placed his arm over her shoulder and tried to get her attention. He followed the direction of her gaze and then slid his hand along her arm. She watched his hand glide down to her forearm, stopping at her wrist, for a brief moment. He turned to face her, slid his hand over hers and onto the crystal column. She followed his hand as it grasped the column. Her speculative thoughts ran rapid, trying to decipher his awareness of the very thing that her hands held onto. When Raine saw that Hunter's hand mirrored Mia's, her curiosity peaked. She reached over to where their hands were, waved her hand, mimicking the position of theirs and felt nothing. Observing this, Mia's eyes began to tear. When Raine looked at Hunter, he was already holding a grinned stare at her. At that point, Raine knew something was in fact there and perhaps not meant for her eyes. She glanced at Mia, placed her hand on the small of her back when she noticed a tear rolling down her cheek. She experienced the depth of Mia's anguish and absorbed her melancholic aura. Like Mia and Sage, she shared empathic traits as well. She decided that for the time being, it would be best to hold off on her questions and returned back into the house.

"Lets go inside, Mia. You can spend the day with me instead." Hunter grasped her wrists, sliding them off of the column and led her back into the house. As they entered through the kitchen, Enya was leaning against the refrigerator, looking directly at her. Mia saw an open newspaper on the table and the bold print from an article seemed to jump out to her. It read "ALIVE". The word struck a cord within her subconscious mind. As she neared Enya, she saw her expressionless stare. Her eyes were glassy, dark and enigmatic. Mia stopped in her tracks, inevitably stopping Hunter as well. Standing inches from her face, Mia peered deep within her eyes, searching for relative clues. "Why do you stare at me, Enya?" Enya didn't respond. The silence among them grew uncomfortable, leaving Mia to search further into her own theories. The sudden loud engine of Mayne's bike distracted and startled everyone, particularly upsetting Mia. Mayne was now leaving without her and there was now a burning sensation deep within her stomach. She hugged herself and silently wept. Hunter grasped Mia's hand and led her to the living room. She released his hand and walked up to the window, watching her as she sped off. "Come sit next to me." He placed a pillow on his lap and lifted his legs up onto the table as he surfed through the channels. With a disheartened expression, she dragged herself over to the couch, sat near him and gazed mindlessly at the television. Hunter patted the couch between them, gesturing for her to lie down. "Would you like to discuss your perception of what has happened?" "No." She paused for a few moments. "I wanna hear yours." "Ask your questions." "How did you know about the columns?" "I've already answered that question, Mia. I see what you see. I walk in your dreams and you have yet to recognize me in them." "Are you the lion?" "Sometimes." "Why are those crystal columns out there?" "For the same reason they surround you in your dream. When you realize who you are and why you belong here with us, your answers will then, be revealed to you." "I wanted to go with Mayne. Why was I not able to go?" "You have not learned how to fly, Mia. Your fear occludes your courage." She stared at him as he spoke, listening intently to his mysterious words. He pulled her closer to him. "When you piece everything together you will." She felt a mild headache beginning to emerge. She lay her head down on the pillow, nested on his lap and closed her eyes. Focusing on her fears, recent and past, she realized that she had somehow left behind the one thing she had always done to aid and protect herself. The Full Moon was approaching and she knew that the items that she needed could be found in Enya's room. Mia knew that these things had no bearing on her Magick without her acceptance, focus, courage and silence. Although unclear in the details, she also knew that the next Full Moon to rise would bring forth the battle of her life. It will be of slow, steady and strong ascent. It will belong to her, solely. From her current state of dormancy, she will rise like a Phoenix fire. With this Moon, all will be revealed to her and those around her.

It had only been about twenty minutes since Mayne had left. The psychological, burning sensation in her stomach had somewhat dissipated, replaced now by a sense of abandonment, in Mayne's absence. Sage entered the room to check on Mia and sat on the arm of the couch, next to her feet. "Hey?" She pointed at Mia, greeting Hunter, inquisitively. He nodded. "She'll be fine, Sage. Would you mind fetching me a mug of coffee? As you can see, I can't get up at the moment." "Sure. Mia, would you like some too?" "No." She whispered. He pointed over to Sage's end of the couch. "Toss that blanket over her, please." Sage gently draped it over her and left to get his coffee. As he focused on the movie, he continuously ran his fingers through her hair to keep her relaxed. The anesthetic, tingly feeling radiated through her, leaving her feeling serene. Her mind was clear and free of angst, allowing her to focus on the messages from her previous dreams. Her first priority was to subconsciously distort their view of her thoughts and dreams. For this, she would need assistance. She knew what she had to do however this ritual would have to wait until she was alone. As of now, she knew that all of the pieces of information that were fed to her via her dreams or in waking state, as well as the sporadic verbiage from those that surrounded her, needed to be re-identified and interlocked in order for her to understand the whole picture. At that point she would be able to move forward. The near-endless list of variables overwhelmed her but she knew that the start of any journey always began with the first step.

She recalled seeing a notepad in the kitchen and needed to somehow excuse herself from his presence, grab the pad and go off on her own in order to begin. Mayne's room would serve as the perfect setting. She shifted herself and sat upright to face him, holding a morose expression. "I need to use the bathroom." "You know where it is."

Upon entering the kitchen she spotted the notepad, a pencil and a tiny sharpener on the kitchen counter, slipped them into her pants and proceeded to the bathroom. After wallowing for a few minutes, she flushed and turned on the sink in case he was listening for her and returned to the living room. Still holding the same facial expression, she asked for his permission to go upstairs. "Can I please go sleep in Mayne's room?" He smiled. "Do you miss her?" She answered, knowing that she was only telling a partial lie. "Yes." "Come. I'll escort you there. I needed to get up anyway." He paused the movie, stood up and held his hand out to her. As she walked with him, she held her other arm against the pencil and pad to ensure that they didn't slip down into her pant leg. In the back of her mind she hoped that he wouldn't linger too long. At the foot of the staircase, he released her hand and stood behind her. "Hold on to the bannister." She proceeded up the stairs and he followed behind her. As they approached Mayne's room he reached for his keys and unlocked her door. She walked inside, lay on her bed and crawled under the blanket. "I'm locking the door, so that no one disturbs you. You can come back downstairs later, if you like. I'll be back to check on you later."

She pulled the notepad, pencil and sharpener out of her pants and remained in the bed for about ten minutes, in case he returned.

Hunter stopped by Enya's room and knocked on the door. "Who?" "It's me." "Enter." Upon opening the door he saw Gwen sitting on the bed. Her face lit up at the sight of him. "Hello Gwen. Listen girls. Mia is sleeping in Mayne's room. Keep your ears open." "Will do. The girls are in Raine's room." "I'll let them know as well." He shut the door behind himself and proceeded to Raine's room. The girls were chatting and trying on clothes when they heard a knock on the door. Faeryn quickly slipped into one of the dresses that she was trying on and then Sage ran to open the door. "Ladies." He paused for a moment and smiled. "Hi Hunter. What's up?" "Is this a bad time?" "Not at all." "Mia is sleeping in Mayne's room. Keep your ears open, but don't disturb her." "Sure. Is she ok?" She'll be fine. She misses Mayne." Sage smiled.

Mia heard a set of footsteps and held her breath until she heard them fade away. She waited a few minutes longer, listening for any new possible visitors, then sat up, propping the pillows behind herself and began to write notes. Her thoughts traveled backwards, lightly visiting each clue. Beginning with the most recent of events, she listed everything in an effort to decipher them.

Failed bike ride with Mayne =
Hunters words = I don't know how to fly because my fear occludes my courage.

Crystal columns =
Hunter's words = They exist for the same reason that they're in my dreams. When I realize who I am, I'll have my answers. Do I bind myself or did someone bind me with their spell? It's Both. It was Enya. That's why she smiled! Aithusa erroneously showed this to me. I am strong enough to bring these columns down.

Dreams =
Hunter, Mayne, Enya and Aithusa can see my dreams and are sometimes in them. Why don't I recognize them? They hide and sometimes present themselves in harmless forms.

Sunbeam rays that turned into the columns =
I thought this was my fear but it feels like something is holding me captive. The direction of the wind as I held onto the columns was East. = East/Air/communication/Air can destroy anything in its path = This is telling me that I'm strong enough to carry out the fight that the lion had communicated to me.

Blue Jays
Mother and baby - Are they representative of the Goddess?
I'm not the frightened Blue Jay! I can fly! I will fly! Is she trying
to teach me to fly solo?

Why can't I control my emotions and their outward effects?
Flickering Lights = Me - why?
Yard and chandelier lights
Why can Hunter control me when I do this?
At the peak of my emotions, if I can't act on or release what
I feel, they exude from me in another form. Can I control
and direct this?

Bruise/Bite mark = blue frog with onyx eyes = Onyx doesn't
reflect light = This is Mayne!
The other frogs represent the other Witches. Why did she
bite me in my dream and again in waking state? Blue Frogs
are poisonous. How does this relate to Mayne? -= She's sometimes toxic. I can change this. I soothe her rage. I need to be
careful when I do this so that I don't get hurt.

Lion that sheltered me from the rain and the threw me into
the lake = This is Sebastian - He is a Witch = Why didn't he
tell me? He is protecting me and trying to shake me, awake.

Lion's fists, drawing the Sundial and triple phase Moon = The
time for me to fight is approaching with the next Full Moon.

The bizarre rain storm = rain pelting me from all four directions. This is a msg. from these points of direction.

Still waters run deep = The Frogs in the water showed me that
many Witches were aware of me. I remember suffocating.

Why??? Lion is Sebastian, showing me that I'm being held captive by these columns and that I can break free from this prison. The occasional singular cooled crystal column = There is a way out.

I had told Mayne that I don't play with fire. I control it. Then she said no one can control fire. I said I know, but it could be guided. Why does this conversation stand out in my mind? = Am I going to be guiding an uncontrollable entity? ME?! Yes I am!

ALIVE = I saw and heard this word twice.
I saw this word on the newspaper that Enya was reading. It seemed to scream at me. The other time was when Aithusa said it to me in my dream, when both had our fingers in the candle flame. = means?? Their Spells worked.

Aithusa in my dream: White kitten, frog with pearl eyes, candle, cone and altercation with her when I woke up. She lured me, in the form of a white kitten then she turned into a frog. = Cats can walk in and out of sacred circles. Frogs can travel between worlds. She said to me; "Am I what I seem?" What does this mean? = She is not what she seems! How was she able to make me put my finger into the candles flame and why, with hers? I fed my fear into this candle and told myself that I'm the flame. When I did. she said; My spell is ALIVE. = She cast a spell on me, however she had also broke the Pyramid by telling me that it was alive. How did she tear down my cone? = I let her. She knew that I was watching her. She felt my fear. This was a dream within a dream! The Lions fists - Was Sebastian telling me about my altercation with Aithusa? = Yes!

The ride back in Hunters truck with Lucius They sung a song about learning to fly and Hunter stared at me while he sang. I wasn't talking to anyone. Hunter made me take a bath, asked me several questions and pointed out a few things to me. When he held my finger, his hand felt unusually hot and I felt him pulling on my spirit. He and Mayne admitted to being able to see my thoughts and intervene within my dreams.

Mia sharpened her pencil and glanced at the braided bracelet on her wrist that Enya had made for her. She recalled the things that Enya had been doing in her presence on that night.

She continued writing her notes.

Enya's newspaper word - ALIVE!!! This bracelet has something to do with her spell!!!! <u>What the H. E. double hockey stix kind of Spell did she and Aithusa cast on me?</u>

Enya claimed to be healing my wounds. This was when she put this bracelet on me. The candles flame, flickered. Enya asked me to lie on her bed. She walked around the bed a few times. There was smoke. Mayne was there too. = Enya = All these things were inclusive of her Binding spell on me! How do I remove this bracelet without it having a negative effect on myself?

<u>Group ritual?</u> I remember drums. I was weaving through them as they stood around the table. Then I crawled on top and lay on it staring at the Moon through the ceiling's skylight. At the end of this ritual, they had all touched my face and hair. I never let people touch my hair unless I know and trust them. CRAP! Joint effort spell?!

There was an iridescent green frog in my dream prior to this ritual. I held this frog on my chest. The crystal columns were there. It jumped off of me, hopped through the fence, stared at me and left. The lion and his frog showed up. The lion sat me on the bench and then, they left me there. = The green frog is Enya - They were showing me that I couldn't escape.

Lucius and the Magick that I did with the tree branch
= I broke the Rede by doing harm to another. I pointed twice, with negative intentions towards Lucius. How did Hunter know what I was doing and sway the branch? = He knew of my thoughts and did it with his Magick. My Karma returned to me = Hunter broke my finger. Why did he go to this ridiculous extreme only to heal me? He knows what I can do. He needed to stop me from doing this in a reckless manner. He could have just told me!

The barbecue on the night before the Full Moon
Mayne really pissed me off that night! She pointed a gun at me. My fear caused the lights on the bar to flicker. I blacked out. Hunter discussed the flickering lights with me. Then later, Mason harassed me. He provoked me on purpose, to test me and show me how I affected the lights. My rage caused the lights to flicker.

The aftermath of stealing Mayne's bike
Hunter returned early. He and Mayne healed me. The lights flickered violently from my fear of not knowing what they were doing. I felt bizarre vibrating waves of warmth when Hunter touched on my wounds. I saw the rare essence of tranquility and compassion in Mayne's eyes. They chanted. How did they heal me??? He answered my questions in riddles. I'm aware that the flickering lights were caused by my fear. He also said that the answer to how they healed me is in the

Pyramid and he used the four words that represent it, to explain this.

The wolf dream and bike incident
The dream prior to stealing her bike - I drove the bike alone, on a highway and saw the Full Moon. It was cold. I saw the "DON'T STOP" signs. The Song lyrics encouraged me to slow down. = This dream showed me not to stop at Gwen's bar when I stole Mayne's bike. Why didn't I recognize this ??? I remember that I was so thirsty and hungry. I couldn't focus. = The wolf was Mayne.

Blue Jay was in the back yard yelling at me as I stared at it through the sliding glass doors. = Goddess again? The way out was being revealed. She must want to smack me at this point!

The night before, I did a Full Moon ritual within my thoughts because Hunter was in the bed with me and I couldn't physically do it. The curtains blew and the wind blew over me. The bed wasn't even in the direction of the window. = Both were the Goddess. She wanted my attention to show me that a way out was revealing itself to me. Bike - Naturally, I screwed that up! dammit!

Hunters wall Pentacle
Hunter pointed out to the Pentacle and Frogs on his wall, compared it to my necklace. Then he embraced me, just like the lion did in my dream = In the dream prior to this, there was a pond strewed with Frogs on lily pads. Each frog had different colored eyes. When I ran from them, I crashed into the Lions chest. = This lion was Hunter. The Frogs were all the Witches surrounding me.

The sound of jingling keys startled her. She shoved the notepad in-between the mattress and pretended to be asleep. Hunter opened the door and walked into the room. Mia listened to his every footstep as he drew near, anticipating his eventual touch. The blanket was partially covering her face. She kept her breathing steadied when she had felt him lift the blanket to look at her. He sat on the bed beside her and lingered for a while. Within her thoughts, she was panicking because she had thought that he was trying to see into her dream and may figure out that she wasn't sleeping. She thought about the words; *"Dream Weaver"* and then had her solution. To distort her dreams she needed to simply change the story. She knew that this wasn't an easy task. She had once attempted to trick him before and the results were traumatizing. She knew that this visual illusion had to be flawless. She lay still, envisioning this fake dream and implemented her meditation method, inclusive of all of her senses. This would enable him to visualize exactly what she needed him to see. Her sole intention was to show him what he wanted to see. Something simple. She pictured the lion and frog sitting at the lake's bank beside her. She focused on that image for a few minutes, trying to imagine the surrounding smells and the scenes colors as well. The easiest simulation in thought was her olfactory-induced memory of fresh cut grass. She gazed across the lake, taking in its cool freshwater scent and then focused on the cascading ripples across its surface. She stared into the amber eyes of the lion and held a serene expression on her face. She then focused on intertwining the emotion that she felt for Mayne and the bike ride and then straight into the emotion behind her next simple thought. "I belong." As she repeated her next two words, the wistful memory was so surreal that her intense focus enabled her to generate teardrops from her eyes. If Hunter were now in synch with her mind, she would know by the reaction from the lion. She retained eye contact with him, while maintaining pseudo dream control over her thoughts. If she could master this then she should be able to do this in her dreams. She heard him inhale and then felt him touch her hair. When she felt his touch she shifted herself closer to him. At first, he stared back at her in a peculiar manner. She focused on her bewitching thoughts, the act of believing in the falseness of this vision that she wanted him to see and thought of the two vital words to reflect this. "I belong." Another tear fell. As she waited for the Lions reaction, she envisioned him embracing her and once again tapped into her memory of the feeling of his fur on her skin. She felt as if she were living twice at once. She realized that she was now traveling between both worlds, like a frog. "I belong." She thought, once again. Another tear fell. She waited for the lions reaction, closed her eyes and within her thoughts she yearned for his embrace.

Hunter knew that she was, in fact, traveling in-between both worlds and not just within her paradoxical sleep, however, his perception of what she was trying to show him, remained somewhat distorted. He assumed that she was demonstrating her newly discovered trait, in an innocent way and also felt that she was simply playing with him, in the interim. She led him to believe that she had finally come to terms with the fact that she belonged with his Coven. He smiled, kissed her on the forehead and gave her the hug that she desired. When she felt the Lions fur against her skin, without delay she returned his embrace, remaining focused on the feeling of security and serenity that she felt from Mayne's hugs.

Hunter slide off of the bed. She listened to his footsteps and waited for the sound of the closing door. The sound of the jingling keys and the lock's click, followed suit. She once again waited until she could no longer hear his fading footsteps and then added a few more minutes to that waiting time in case of his possible return. When she sensed that the coast was clear, she rolled off of the bed and reached in-between the mattress for her notepad. The smile on her face reflected her satisfaction with both Hunter as well as the giant step of achievement towards controlling her dreams and mastering her trait. She forged on with her notes.

Mason
The dream of a wolf, standing on an incline with the West wind blowing onto him while he perused the area.

= This wolf is Mason and this wolf was searching for me in my dream. He courted me in deception by not telling me that he is Hunters brother. Full Moon that night = Ritual
He drugged me on the beach with the damn blue smoothie!!!
The lights flickering on this night were a result of my rage.

The night at work with Sebastian
At work, I remember the odd feeling of someone tapping into my spirit. The text from Hunter - How was he able to find me??? There was a dream the night before, of shattered glass. = As Hunter carried me out, I saw that very same shattered glass window. Hunter was also pulling on my spirit in the truck. I had performed two Moon rituals. Why didn't they work? =They did work. I was able to escape. The dream did warn me but I didn't recognize the wolf that was Mason.

Dancing around the bonfire
My dream of the rising Phoenix with blue pupils, the night before?? Sage invited me to their Full Moon gathering at the beach. They danced around the fire and she made me join them. They performed a Full Moon ritual. I remember seeing the bonfire's flames in Hunters eyes and he wasn't even facing them! I felt the pull on my spirit this night as well. They drugged me and brought me back to their house. Two nights prior to this, when I was walking on the beach. I met Sage for the first time. The next evening I saw her again with the others. Hunter approached me. He introduced himself as Hunter and told me that his real name was Theron. How did I not recognize him from the Samhain party????

The Samhain party and Aithusa
This is where all this evil sorcery began!!!

I met Ceridwen and Faeryn at a fair. I remember a Blue Jay. I held my finger up and it flew down onto it. = This was my first encounter with the Blue Jay. Was this the first message from the Goddess? They saw my necklace, approached me and invited me to their party. This is when I had my first related dream. It was vague. I saw people but not their faces. This is where I started dreaming of the lion and frog. = They hid themselves from me in my dream!! My next dream was about the lion and frog again. I was drugged again! I remember being somewhat coherent and feeling the lion mirroring Hunters touch. When I blocked the lion from touching me, he roared and I woke up. Just before the Samhain ritual, Hunter was stalking me. I was drugged! I recall seeing a candle and then I saw the continuum of that flame in Hunters eyes. This happened twice and this was the first time!!!
I remember waking up and finding myself in Aithusa's room. She drugged me! When I woke, I heard a thunderstorm approaching and drew from its energy. I managed to drug her and escape. This was the first time that I had freed myself from them. There was a song stuck in my head. My interpretation was similar to Sebastian's. These people and events surrounding them are not as they seem!!!

Mia's jaw dropped. She stopped writing. *"What the fuck?"* She thought to herself. *"These freaks believe that I'm one of them. Even if I were, why have they gone to these ludicrous extremes to keep me here? Why am I so important to them? What trait could I possibly have that they deem superior to their collective traits?"*

There was noise in the hallway. Mia snapped out of her train of thought, quickly slid the notepad in-between the mattress and returned to her pretend sleep-state. She lay on her back and focused on calming her breathing to a steady rhythm. The sound of the keys unlocking the door followed as anticipated. This time she had heard two sets of footsteps entering the room, one of which ended and sat beside her. The other ceased at the foot of the bed and leaned on the footboard. The person sitting beside her gently lifted Mia's hand and entwined their fingers with hers. She determined that this person was female. She remained motionless and attempted to create scenes within her mind to block them from her true thoughts, however it was futile. The person who was holding her hand, distracted her ability to focus. She decided to simplify, by creating a singular scene - a field covered in snow, inclusive of cascading flakes. She tuned into her memories of serenity from the white noise that was always present during a snowfall. The only feeling that she was unable to hone in on was the chilled feeling of this very scene. The female holding her hand placed her other hand on Mia's cheek. Her hand was ice cold. Mia jolted from her touch, erroneously opened her eyes and saw that it was Enya touching her. The coldness of her hand and the manner in which she looked at Mia had confirmed that Enya had known of her thoughts. Leaning at the foot of the bed, was Hunter, staring at her in the same manner. They made her feel as if they knew that she had been doing something naughty and had been caught in the act. Mia remained silent and expressionless, even within her thoughts. Hunter grinned. "Are you cold Mia?" Mia's eyes widened. She felt somewhat victorious in knowing that they saw the vivid thoughts of her wintry scene. Somewhat. Something else seemed awry with them. Mia swiped Enya's cold hand off of her face and tried to read her. Her eyes remained as cold as her touch. Hunter stepped over and stood beside her. "What are you hiding underneath the snow?" With strict diligence, Mia thought of only the snow. Although she had heard his questions, she remained within her pseudo-meditative state. She would not allow her mind to process the answers. Enya touched her cheek once again. This time, her hand was unusually warm and now held Mia's full attention. "When the snow melts, all that you hide from us will be revealed." Mia's eyes widened once again. Without missing a beat, she reverted back to her relentless, wintry thoughts. Hunter's baleful laugh haunted her. Mia watched them as they exited the room. When she could no longer hear their footsteps, she then slid out of the bed to use the facilities. With her elbows leaning on her thighs, she rested her forehead against her hands. "How do *they know that I'm hiding something? Did my subconscious idea of blanketed snow, tip them off?* She washed her hands and stepped over to door leading to the hall, with her ear against it. The hall was soundless. She shuffled back to the bed, pulled her notepad out and sat down.

The window behind the bed was opened. Someone was playing music.

♪*...Her name is what it means...*♪

She realized that each person had a peculiar name. Beginning with Enya, she jotted each of their names, with the intent to look up their meanings. She perused the room in search of a laptop or tablet. She found a tablet in Mayne's nightstand and turned it on. The screen displayed a four-spaced entry point for a password. *"Dammit!" Think hard Mia! What would her damn password be?"* She typed in Mayne's license plate number. That wasn't correct. *"Think! Think!"* She glanced over at the closet. She thought of the box that Mayne kept her stash in and typed 0420. *"Yes!"* She smirked. *"Stupid password, Mayne! Were you high when you made this choice?"*

One by one, she researched the meaning to each name and then followed up with their known traits.

Enya = Fire
★ Strong Witch / Psychic / Dream Weaver / Dream Interpretation / Light Worker / Visionary
Theron = Hunter / Untamed
★ Strong Witch / Psychic / Dream Weaver / Dream Interpretation / Light Worker / Visionary / Empath / Medium / Telepath
Mayne = Powerful / Brave/ Hard Strength
★ Strong Witch / Psychic / Dream Weaver / Dream Interpretation / Light Worker

Mason = Stone Worker / Steadfast / Ritualistic / Speaks in wisdom
* Strong Witch / Psychic / Dream Weaver / Free Mason / Visionary
Sage = Wise / Calm / Protector / Heroic / Healer / Knowing
* Witch / Psychic / Light Worker / Empath
Raine = Queen / Wise Ruler
* Witch / Psychic / Empath /Intuitive / Spiritual
Emery = Brave / Power
* Witch / Psychic
Lucius = Light / Bringer of Light
* Witch / Psychic
Zephyr = West wind / Strong
* Strong Witch / Psychic / Dream Weaver / Visionary
Gwen = Celtic / White / circle / Merlin's wife's name
* Strong Witch / Psychic / Visionary / Mystical
Ceridwen = Simple sorceress / Celtic Goddess / Poetic / Inspiration
* Witch / Psychic / Empath
Faeryn = Of Fairies / Adventurous / Mischievous
* Witch / Psychic / Empath / Fairy
Aithusa = White Dragon of Flight
* Witch / Psychic / Dream Weaver / Visionary / Empath / Medium
Sebastian = Revered / Exalted / Honor / Respected
* Witch / Psychic / Empath / Dream Interpretation
My name = Mia God Like / Mine / Leader / Independent / Free
* Witch (They seem to think that I'm a strong one) / Psychic / Dream Interpretation / Dream Weaver / Light Worker / Empath / Visionary / Telepath

CHAPTER 20

THIRTEEN

The plethora of information that had been stagnant, deep within the back of her mind, was now staring her in the face. She recalled every relevant word that he had spoken to her and now had a clearer perception on Hunter's collective questions and riddles. She knew that there would be additional possibilities that had yet to present themselves. Now that she was aware of them, her perception of all that had happened, had now changed. Things were never as they had seemed. The pieces to this puzzle were interlocking before her eyes. Several proverbs came to mind. *"Still waters run deep."* Mia whispered this one, several times. *"Things are not as they seem."* She questioned herself. *"Am I what I seem?"* *"If I have to ask, then obviously not."* *"You attract what you send out into the Universe."* *"This is why they surround me. As powerful as they are, I believe that they need me more than I need them. Do I need them?"* In regards to all that has occurred, she decided to change the way that she viewed these facts. *"Life is ten percent of what happens to you and ninety percent of how you react."* She questioned whether or not she had reacted in the correct manner, each time that something negative had occurred. She noticed that there were three sheets of paper remaining in the notepad. On these pages, she would write her final summation of all this information and then try to create an algorithm that will lead to her answers. She slid off of the bed for a drink of water, splashed some on her face and caught a glimpse of herself in the mirror. *"Why me?"* She asked herself. *"Why would it take a dozen Witches to find, lure and capture me? … A Dozen?"* Her eyes lit up. She shuffled back to the bed and one by one she scribbled their names in her notepad, assigning a number to each of them.

1 Hunter 2 Enya 3 Mayne 4 Sage 5 Raine 6 Lucius 7 Zephyr 8 Emery 9 Mason 10 Ceridwen 11 Faeryn 12 Gwen 13 Aithus

She thought to herself. *"If memory serves me correct, a coven is usually inclusive of at least three members and some could also be inclusive of nine to thirteen members. Thirteen is the number of Esbats within a year. Can some have more? Counting just the first eight people would leave a spot empty. Adding the others would make thirteen. Mason lives West of here and the other three have their own coven. So that leaves eight. How and why do I fit into this equation? I'm not leaving Sebastian for these freaks! They want something from me. I know they are afraid of me because they try to keep and contain me on several levels."* She had remembered Hunter saying to get the answers that I seek and that I had to ask the right questions to obtain them. *"The key question that I need answered is; Why do they want me here?"* She searched around Mayne's room for items of divination that she could use to assist her. She knew that Enya had a broad spectrum of Magickal tools, from the most common items to the most elaborate. She even knew where she kept her beloved tarot cards but she couldn't go in there at the moment and this form of Divination was not her forte anyway. *"Ask the right questions."* She repeated to herself. This thought struck a nerve. *"The most straight forward Divination is the pendulum. This can answer simple questions!"* She searched around Mayne's room for something that she could use as a pendulum. She searched through the items on top of her dresser and nightstand, checking inside the drawers as well. There were a few crystals and stones in the corner of her top drawer. She shuffled through them and came across an oblong shaped blue stone that looked exactly like the Lapis Lazuli stone she had at home. She searched Mayne's closet for a pair of sneakers, pulled the lace out of one of them and tied it to the stone, then took a glass tray from the dresser and sat on the bed. There were two pieces of paper remaining in the note pad. She tore out one piece and placed it on the frame. Then tore out the other piece and began to jot down her questions. She slid the tray in front of herself and grasped the lace, dangling the pendulum above the paper. With her elbow on her knee, she held the Pendulum by the cord above the tray. She lowered the Pendulum onto the tray and then lifted it up slowly and watched it sway. Now she needed to establish the Yes, No, Maybe and unclear directions. She whispered to it. "Show me – yes." The Pendulum swayed indeterminably for a few moments and them steadied its sway in an up and down direction. She drew a line horizontally wrote Yes on the top and bottom of the paper. The Pendulum continued to sway as she drew each of these dividing lines and their labels. "Show me – no." It spiraled for a few moments and then steadied its sway once more in a side-to-side direction. She drew a line vertically and wrote No on the left and right side of the paper. "Show me – maybe." It swung in an oval motion for a few moments and steadied its sway in a diagonal direction. She drew that diagonal line, labeled it and completed the diagram with remaining diagonal direction, titling it - Unclear. She took a deep breath and began the Divination, writing down the answers, as they were shown to her.

Do I possess a trait that the people in this circle lack? Yes
Am I aware of this trait? Yes
Have I used this trait before? Yes
Have I always practiced this trait? No
Have I just recently practiced this trait? Yes
Do I need to practice this trait before this battle? Maybe
Is this the reason that they hold me here? Yes
Is this the only reason that they hold me here? No
Are they afraid of my traits? Yes
Can I fly on my own? Yes

Her perception was once again, evolving, as a result of these answers. This unknown trait was the entity that set her apart from them and she now knew why they were apprehensive of her. Thinking of the times when she became most emotional in a violent manner, she remembered how they had dealt with her. *"They had diffused me with drugs!"* A look of utter disgust reflected across her face. *"Why couldn't they just try communicating with me, tell me, show me, cut to the damn chase instead of holding me against my will and forcing me to learn in this ludicrous manner? What a fucking concept, huh?"* She laughed at her thoughts.

The most un-common denominator of these traits was telepathy. The only other Witch that shared this trait with her is Hunter. She crossed out that one and continued, speculating about what this neoteric trait of hers could be. She re-read her notes to see who had similar traits and which trait was held only by a few of them and crossing them out as she reviewed them.

The strongest of the Witches held the least common of the traits, which are Dream Interpretation and Dream Weaver. She compared the notes about herself and saw that although she had the trait of Dream Interpretation, she lacked the Dream Weaver trait. She had a strong feeling that this new trait was linked to this genre of traits. What she had recently practiced had now become clear. She whispered the answer. *"Dream Control! I just did this for the first time! This is the reason why Hunter and Enya had both came in to check on me! They knew! How did they know that I could do this before I was aware of it, myself? This is why they keep me here! This is why they fear me!"*

She checked online to see when the next Full Moon would occur. The website reflected that she still had a few days. She needed to practice her newfound trait and prepare for this battle as well. She thought about the lion, whom had stressed the imperativeness of this particular approaching Full Moon. She glanced back at the webpage and saw the list of Full Moons for the current year and smiled. She saw that it was the second Full Moon in the month, which makes it the Blue Moon. *"This Full Moon will be my Moon! After all, Mia means mine!"* She giggled as she whispered its new name to herself.

"Mia's Moon!" Envisioning this battlefield, she felt that perhaps the beach, just outside the house would serve her best because the Elements had always embraced her there. Her questions began to emerge once more. She grabbed her notepad and wrote the questions on her last piece of paper. She then slid the picture frame with the Yes/No diagram page onto her lap and grasped her make shift pendulum.

> Should I hold this battle where three of the Elements reside? Yes
> Should I plan for this battle? No
> Will they use drugs to stop me? No
> Will I know how to fight when this time arrives? Yes
> Will the Element of Fire be present? Yes
> Will I be capable of controlling myself? Unclear
> Will I guide the Elements to my advantage? Yes
> Will I survive this battle? Yes
> Will I win this battle? Unclear
> Will they win this battle? Unclear

Mia now realized what part she played in all of this and now knew who she is and what she clearly represented to them. She also knew that each one of them had betrayed her. In a whispered voice, she recited the Rede. She knew it by heart and honored it, always.

The Rede
Bide by the Wiccan law ye must
In perfect love and perfect trust
Eight words the Wiccan Rede fulfill
An' ye harm none, do what ye will
What ye set forth comes back to thee
So ever mind the law of three
Follow this with mind and heart
Merry ye meet and merry ye part

She felt her resentment and anger growing. She knew that each and every one of them had broken the Rede. She would speak no words to them from this moment, forward. *"The conversations end now."* She thought to herself. Since the pendulum advised her that there would be no need for her to plan for this battle, she had decided to bide her time until the day of the Full Moon: Mia's Moon. She untied the makeshift pendulum, returned the stone where she had found it and re-laced Mayne's sneaker. She took her notepad and the pendulum diagram and searched for a secure place to hide it. It would be too vulnerable in-between the mattress. It needed to be in a place where no one would look. She scanned the room. The large dresser would be foolproof, however she knew that she was not strong enough to lift it. She spun herself around and spotted the next best thing: the nightstand. With the exception of the lamp, she placed each item onto the bed in the same exact order that it was arranged so that she would know where to return it. She placed the lamp onto the floor, slipped the diagram into the notepad and placed it on the floor. She tilted the night-stand and slid the notepad underneath and centered it. She didn't realized how heavy the nightstand was until she lowered it back down. Those in the adjacent rooms as well as the floor below heard the bang. She knew someone would be coming. *"Time to practice again!"* She slid onto the bed, on her stomach and steadied her breathing. Her arms and legs were separated, as not to touch one another. Without moving a muscle, she steadied every nerve throughout her body until she felt the stillness and numbness of the meditative state that she so well mastered, long ago. She knew that she was at this state when she felt the same sensation that one would feel as if their foot fell asleep. She focused her thoughts on one Element; Water. She recalled the dream with the pelting rain and relived that memory within her mind. She walked through he rain and stood behind the tree, hidden from sight. She focused on the sounds of the endless heavy downpour and fixated on its hissing sound. The sounds from those present became white noise to her ears. She heard someone grasp the doorknob, but did not respond. She remained unresponsive and disconnected from the out-side sounds, within her meditative world. The door didn't open. She heard a knock on the door and then heard Raine's voice. "Mia, are you ok in there? The door is locked." Mia didn't answer. Sage stood by the entrance of Raine's door and spotted Enya and Hunter walking up the staircase. "I heard a loud thump. It sounded like it came from this room, but the door's locked. I knocked but she's not answering." Hunter grinned. "We've got this." He unlocked the door and stared at Mia. Enya walked in and stood at the foot of the bed. He shut the door, stepped over to Enya and whispered into her ear. "She's doing it again." Enya smiled. "I see. It's rain she uses this time." "The bang?" "We'll talk in my room." Hunter gestured for Enya to wait. He stepped into the bathroom and took a towel and an umbrella. He placed them on the foot of the bed, took a piece of scrap paper and a pen and wrote a note for Mia, showed it to Enya and placed it in-between the towel and the umbrella.

"The next time that you choose to brave the Elements, travel prepared. Hunter."

Enya read the note and smiled. They left the room. Hunter locked the door behind them and followed Enya into her room. Enya faced Hunter and whispered. "She hides something and we need to find it." "I know what she was doing. She was writing and she hid what she wrote within that room. It was either hidden high above her reach and she jumped down or she hid it under something heavy, hence, the bang. She's on the verge of knowing herself and is now aware of her trait. As you have seen, she's honing her trait very well. I'll fill Mayne in on everything when she returns. She'll find it." "Do you think that she has deciphered anything else?" "Yes. We'll know where we stand when Mayne brings those notes to me."

Mia stretched her muscles, sat up and looked at the clock on the wall. She knew that Mayne would soon return. Her method of practice was once again, successful. For now, she needed to keep herself grounded. She focused on a set of core guidelines, derived from her beliefs. Her intention is to keep these thoughts in mind at all times and use them as a tool in her future decisions, regarding this battle.

The Thirteen Goals

1. *Know yourself.*
2. *Know your Craft.*
3. *Learn.*
4. *Apply knowledge with wisdom.*
5. *Achieve balance.*
6. *Keep your words in good order.*
7. *Keep your thoughts in good order.*
8. *Celebrate life.*
9. *Attune with the cycles of the Earth.*
10. *Breathe and eat correctly.*
11. *Exercise the body.*
12. *Meditate.*
13. *Honor the Goddess and God.*

Her stomach began to grumble, however, she was hesitant of going downstairs to get something to eat. She needed to prepare herself for those who may be present, downstairs. Within her mind, she would only reflect what she wanted them to see. She slid out of the bed and placed her ear to the door. She unlocked it, opening it just a crack to peek towards Raine's room. Raine's door was ajar. The sounds of the ongoing usual chatter echoed into the hall. She glanced in the opposite direction and saw that the stairway was clear. As she made her way down the staircase, she maintained an impassive expression. At the base of the staircase, she heard male voices emanating from the living room. She walked towards the living room and stood at its entrance with a valiant expression. In unison, Hunter, Zephyr, Mason and Lucius turned their attention to her. She glanced at each of them. The fixed and simple image within her mind was of a field of tall weeds, flowing with the gale forces of the wind. Hunter paused the television and stood up. He stared directly into her eyes until he held her attention solely, on his. Without moving a muscle, she pierced his eyes with hers, while focusing on her tempest imagery. She knew he could see what she was showing him and decided to toy with him. The thrashing weeds ignited. Hunters steely eyes widened. Mia channeled into the feel and essence of blazing heat, picturing the flames crackling, the weeds disintegrating into ash and sending embers fluttering into the air. The wind increased. Storm clouds rolled in and the pelting rain followed, snuffing out the fire. The intense passion of her thoughts reflected on her face. She feared no one and made that clear to him. Emery slithered up, behind her and slid his hands over her waist. Before he could get a tight grip around her, she elbowed him in his stomach. Her focus was so intense, that her arm was the only thing that she needed to move. Remaining in place, with her eyes locked on Hunter, she smiled, turned and proceeded to the kitchen. Emery was nursing his ribs. "What the fuck was that all about?" Hunter grinned and replied. "She's testing her new-found talents on me." Mason chimed in. "Or is she challenging you?" Hunter nodded. "She is." Lucius stretched his legs and snickered. "My little lamb is evolving into a lion." Deep in thought, Hunter returned to his seat and gazed at Zephyr. Zephyr spoke with an eerie tone. "Something wicked brews in this house." Hunter's baneful laugh emanated through the house.

Mia stood at the kitchen's entrance and watched Enya standing at the sink, washing dishes. She waited quietly, for her to notice her presence. Enya knew that she was there. Mia stared at the back of her head, maintaining a singular thought. "*I KNOW.*" Mia envisioned herself standing within a blizzard, looking at Enya through the bands of spiraling snow with these two words echoing from within her mind. She sustained this disciplined daydream, allowing no other intruding images or thoughts to enter her mind. Enya turned the faucet off and held onto the edge of the sink, staring at the wall. "*Show me what you know, Mia.*" Mia continued her pattern of thought, changing only the words. "*I will.*" Enya turned to face her and stood face to face. Mia held her steely-eyed stare. The sounds of the gale winds within her minds storm grew louder, reflecting Mia's anger. Enya spoke in a reticent and austere tone. "*How dare you challenge me. My wrath is not to be tested.*" Mia's dauntless expression perturbed Enya. Mia remained silent. She released her stare, opened the refrigerator and perused its contents. She took jelly, cream cheese and bread and placed them on the table. She returned to the refrigerator, for milk and chocolate syrup and placed them on the counter. Enya watched her in silence. Mia reached for a glass, prepared her drink and returned the perishables into the refrigerator. She sat at the table and made her sandwich. With each bite she glanced at Enya. By the third bite, she stared at her with a grin. Mia's thoughts now reflected her standing in a snow-covered field, staring at Enya. Mia knelt down and gathered the snow, formed it into a ball and threw it at Enya. It struck her arm. Mia laughed and then took a sip of her chocolate milk. Enya pulled up a chair and sat across from her. *"You're playing with fire, little girl."* Mia smirked and continued eating.

Zephyr walked into the kitchen to grab a few bottles of beer. He kept his eyes on Mia as he took the bottles from the refrigerator. Mia decided to toy with him as well. Mia watched him as he placed the bottles on the table before her. He pulled up a chair and sat next to Enya. As she sipped her drink she focused on the bottle in his hand and then held a poker-faced stare on him. He glanced at Enya and then back to Mia, addressing Enya as he stared at Mia. "My dear Enya, do tell what's going on in here?" "Mia is playing a dangerous game with me." "Is that so, Mia?" Mia remained stone faced. "I think I'll stay here and watch. If there's wager being taken, my money goes on Enya." He stared at Mia and laughed. Mia paid him no mind. As she lifted her drink to finish it, she saw the braided bracelet on her wrist. The thought of its meaning and purpose caused the anger to seethe within her. She thought of the time when Mason had antagonized her and remembered the result of her emotions - the flickering lights. She tested her theory in a different manner. Through the corner of her eye, she focused on the bottle in his hand. He cracked open his beer and its contents spewed out of the bottle, all over his hair and clothing. Mia's mischievous smile was as wide as the Cheshire cat. Zephyr was furious. He knew that she was responsible. He huffed and walked over to the sink to clean himself. Enya's was livid because she had just finished cleaning the kitchen. She shouted at her. "You're gonna to clean this damn mess! Get up!" With the flickering lights in mind, Mia once again, toyed with Enya. She pushed her plate and glass across the table, gesturing for Enya to put them in the sink and clean them. Enya's eyes widened. She grasped Mia's hand. "Get your ass up, put them in the fucking sink and clean everything now!" Mason and the flickering lights came to mind. She directed her anger at the dish and glass, deciding to do as she was told. The dish and glass slid off of the table, nearly missing Zephyr and shattered in the sink. Mia flared her eyes at Enya, slid off of her seat and returned to Mayne's room. Zephyr clenched his fists but chose to restrain himself. As she approached the stairway, Hunter was on his way into the kitchen. "Mia, what was that crashing sound?" She stopped for a moment, looked at him with a brattish attitude and continued on her way without responding. He grasped her arm and yanked her in as she passed him. "I've just asked you a question!" She pursed her lips, pulled her arm out of his grasp and ran up the staircase, slamming the door behind herself. Hunter proceeded into the kitchen and saw Zephyr cleaning the shards of glass from the sink area. "What happened Enya?" "Her eminence has learned a new trick." Enya filled him in on all that had happened. "Did anyone get hurt?" "No." Zephyr was still annoyed about his wasted beer. He directed his anger to Hunter. "She needs a fucking attitude adjustment!" He grinned and handed Zephyr another bottle. "She'll be getting one very soon." Hunter glanced at the sink. "Use the hand-vac for the shards." He entered into his quarters to retrieve his cell phone.

"Mayne, what's your E.T.A.?" "Why? What's up?" "Things are progressing with Mia sooner than I've anticipated. I'll explain when you get here." He disconnected the call, tossed the phone on his nightstand headed upstairs.

He knocked on Raine's door. "Who?" "It's me." Sage opened the door. "What's up?" "I want all of you to steer clear of Mia." "Why?" "She's beginning to understand herself, however, she's also angry and has become aggressive with this knowledge. I don't want any of you do be in her next line of fire." He saw Aithusa grinning. "Don't test her! I'll handle this. Am I understood?" He looked at each of them and they answered in synch. "Yes." He left the room and opened Mayne's door. Mia was sitting on the bed against the headboard, surfing through the television channels. She pursed her lips and muted the television. He stood before her at the side of the bed and leaned in, face to face. "I'm not pleased with your behavior. Out of respect for me, Enya and Zephyr chose to restrain themselves in regard to your recent shenanigans. I assure you that you would not have survived their wrath, unscathed." Within her mind, she stood with legs spread in the field of snow and threw a snowball, point blank, at his chest. She grinned through the entire thought process. He returned the same grin and then sat on the bed beside her. He held his malicious smile for a few moments and then grasped her neck, pushing her against the headboard. "I've had enough of your shit! Your evasiveness is unacceptable. By tomorrow evening, I will know all that you hide."

CHAPTER 21

RESPECT YOUR ELDERS

Hunter returned and approached Enya. "I'm calling her now!" Enya's face turned pale. He entered his bedroom and made the call. Enya grabbed her cell phone and called Mayne. "Where the fuck are you?" "I just pulled up!" Enya hung up, ran to the front door and met her outside. Mayne had just taken her helmet off and was walking to the house. "What's going on? Hunter called me too. That's why I rushed home." As they walked back into the house, Enya filled her in on all that had happened. "Did you get hurt?" "No." "Where is she?" "She's in your room. Don't go in there until you speak to Hunter." "Where is he?" He's in his room, on the phone with her now." "Are you kidding me? Is he really calling her?" She threw her helmet on the couch and ran into his room without knocking. He held his hand up to her, gesturing for her to be silent as he was still conversing with the woman on the other end of the line. She sat on his bed, listening while she waited in angst. He closed the conversation. "A car will be waiting for you." He hung up.

Mayne stared at him in awe. "Is she really coming here?" "She'll be here at noon, tomorrow." "I can't believe you've called her." "Has Enya filled you in?" "Yes." "There's a change in the air. You'll feel it when you see her. She speaks to no one and you may very well be inclusive of her silence as well. Don't allow her to pull you into her distorted thoughts. She'll test you. Be ready." "What's she hiding?" "We'll know, tomorrow. Follow me upstairs."

He paused at the top of the stairway. "Be mindful of your thoughts. Only show her what you want her to see." "Fine, but how the hell did she go from the pathetic mess she was before I left, to this shit?" "The answer is in what she's hiding. In a nutshell, she's deciphered something or perhaps, everything. If I were to guess her state of mind, I would say she's filled with rage, however, rather than react in her usual ways, she's merely testing herself and her theories, beforehand. I'm certain that her plans are building up to something extensive." Mayne reached for her keys and looked at him. "Are you going inside with me?" "No, I'll wait here for the time being."

Mia heard the sound of approaching footsteps in the hallway. When the doorknob turned, she kept her eyes on the door, ready for her next possible challenge. Mayne slammed the door open and closed it just as forceful. She glanced at Mia and tossed her keys on the dresser. "Miss me?" Mia replied, smiling like a Cheshire cat. "Immensely." Mayne went into the bathroom to freshen up. When she returned, she headed to her closet and grabbed her stash. "Move over." She hopped onto the bed and rolled a cigarette. She lit it, took a few puffs and passed it to her. Mia pushed her hand away. Mayne smirked. "Suit yourself." She swiped the remote from Mia's hand and channel surfed until she found something to her liking. "What was your malfunction with the bike ride?" "You tell me." "Nope. But here's my question. Why do you speak only to me?" "If I wanna speak, I will." "Your evasiveness is cute. Are you trying to be like me, when you grow up?" Mia was silent. Mayne picked up her cell phone and called Enya. "Hey, what are you making to-night? I'm hungry." "Emery just left to pick up a few pizza's. He should be back soon." "Call me when he gets here." Mayne lay back, placed her hands behind her head and closed her eyes. She waited for the lucidity to set in and began her own dream. Knowing that Mia was waiting for this, she planned to play her game and challenge her endurance. Since Mia was supposed to go on a bike ride today, she pictured the scenery that she had passed on her way home earlier and continued riding through this scene until she felt Mia's presence tapping into her thoughts. Within her daydream, Mia sat on the back of her bike, tightly holding onto her waist. She accelerated. The blaring sound of the bike's engine pulsated through their bodies and the wind caused

Mia to hide her face against Mayne's back. At every highway curve, Mayne angled the bike close to the ground, to scare her. The road remained straight for a long stretch. The Sun had just set. There was a tiny glow emanating in the road's horizon. Mayne was generating this light. As they grew closer, she purposely reduced her speed so that Mia would notice and look up. The glow began to reveal itself and it was now obvious to Mia that this light was a fire. Mayne kept her speed at a minimum, to lead Mia into believing that she would either stop or change direction. The smoke of the fire irritated Mia's eyes and its emanating heat began to waft around them. Mia saw the fire's embers cascading through the air and tightened her grasp around Mayne's waist. Mayne knew that Mia was now experiencing the effects of anxiety and would now challenge her endurance. She accelerated. She could feel Mia's pulsing heartbeat against her back. They were less than a mile from the blaze before them. Mayne displayed a bold thought within her mind for Mia to see.

"You wanna be like me? Then show no fear." The bike accelerated and Mia felt its terminal velocity. It was now evident to her that Mayne was going to drive through the fire. Within Mia's panic ridden state, Mayne's message stood out in her mind. She knew that she was challenging her. Rather than hide her face behind Mayne's back, she lived by her own previously spoken words. The phrase *"I can guide it."* filled her thoughts. Her eyes followed the road up to the base of the fire. With malicious intent, her vision fixated on the center of its blaze. She called upon her recent and trusted dream Element, adding Enya's melting snow threat to the mix. As the bike approached, she projected the avalanche of snow, needed to part its flames within the path that they were about to drive through. The snow snuffed the flames, melting upon impact. Mayne skidded the bike sideways and stopped. They both turned to look at the fire. The flames remerged where they had parted. Mayne quickly swayed her hand and the fire was extinguished. She kicked the bike's stand outward and slid off of it. She was unable to hide her mischievous smile and Mia returned the same expression.

Mayne's phone rang, immediately disengaging them out of this dream realm. "Speak." "Foods here." "Great." She sat up and glanced at Mia. They held the same nefarious smile as was in the dream. "Lets go eat." Mia followed Mayne downstairs. Faeryn stood at the entrance eating a slice and Mayne smacked her ass as she passed her. "Hey Fey." "Yeah, Hey! Cut it out, asshat!" "You like it." "Whatever. Hi Mia. Grab a slice. It's delicious!" Mia smiled at her. Everyone engaged in his or her conversation, with the exception of Hunter, who stood against the refrigerator eating a slice, with his sole focus on Mia. Mia took a slice and stood in the center of the room, across from Hunter. She ate, challenging his stare. Enya disengaged from her conversation with Gwen and observed them in silence. It was clear to Enya that there was a prescient standoff between them. It was Mia's obstinate attitude that perturbed him, most. She grew weary of the staring contest, reached for one of the plastic cups on the table and poured herself some soda. With the Full Moon approaching, she helped herself to another slice and left them to sit in the yard to gaze at it in solitude. Hunter gestured for Mayne to follow him and he walked into the living room.

"What happened upstairs?" "I engaged her into my own version of her game." She filled him in on the details of the fiery bike ride. "I didn't think she'd have the courage to follow through, but I pushed her to the limit and she held her own." Hunter frowned. "She may think she's ready for flight, but if she attempts this before she understands, she'll put herself in imminent danger." "We just need to hold off on extreme reactions with her, until tomorrow. When our High Priestess arrives, we'll know." "Until then, we'll let her go about her little secretive shenanigans, with only mild intervention." "Since she's in the yard, lets give a heads up to everyone so that they are aware." "Agreed."

As the evening progressed and the Moon ascended above her, Mia felt the events of the day, taking its toll on her. She yawned, struggling to hold her eyes open. She didn't want to go to bed just yet, so she went inside to get coffee and a sugary snack to sustain her for a little longer. She found it odd that no one was in the kitchen. Someone had always kept an eye on her. She placed a pod in the coffee machine. With the exception of a container of chocolate frosting, the refrigerator's contents lacked of sweets. She took a spoon and scooped a heaping spoonful of it. Their absence peaked her curiosity. She took her coffee and proceeded to the living room, licking the spoon of frosting as she walked through. Mason, Lucius, Zephyr and Emery were playing a game of Cards Against Humanity with Ceridwen, Faeryn, Sage and Raine. Mason saw Mia standing at the entrance, licking the icing off of her spoon. He sucked his teeth, staring at her in a salacious manner, but refrained from lewd commentary. Sage frowned at him. "Mia would you like to join us?" She gesturing her disinterest and left the room. She removed her shoes and crept up the stairs. Her intention was to remain reticent as she approached any occupied rooms. She leaned near Mayne's door and heard nothing. When she opened it, no one was inside. Enya's door was also closed. Mia knocked. No one answered. She took advantage of her absence and swiped a few items that she needed. She stashed them in her pockets and headed back to Mayne's room to hide them. Underneath the nightstand was a shoebox collection of bootleg dvd's that had collected dust. Careful not to shuffle the dust, she stashed her items underneath them and dusted her hands off. She returned downstairs to seek the whereabouts of Hunter, Enya and Mayne and Gwen. There were only two unchecked rooms remaining: Hunter's and the basement rooms. She remained silent, as she approached the base of the stairs and turned sideways so that those in the living room would not be aware of her presence. She slipped into the large room that led to Hunters quarters. No one was in there. She knocked on his door. There was no answer. She went into his bedroom and stood at the foot of the bed, gazing at the pewter symbol on the wall. She held her necklace up, once again, comparing its quinary similarities. She touched it and one of the pewter Frogs below it as well. Hunters cell phone vibrated, causing her to jolt. The caller's number displayed on the screen titled as HP. She succumbed to the temptation of curiosity and answered. "Hello." There was a moment of silence before the caller spoke. "Hello Mia." "Who is this?" "You'll meet me in your dreams tonight. Until then, blessed be." The caller hung up. Mia threw the phone on the dresser and stared at it. Her breathing became erratic and was quickly followed by the adrenaline rush, a collective feeling she knew all too well. It was the feeling of someone trying to dominate her, once again. When she began to feel constrained and lightheaded, she turned to sit on the bed and saw Hunter standing in the doorway. She fainted. He knew that when she felt his presence, it would send her over the edge. When he saw her faint, it was evident that he could still maintain control over her. Hunter stood before her, staring at her, slouched against the foot of the bed. He lifted her up, placed her on the bed and checked his cell phone. He saw the display and knew why she had come undone. He grinned and left the room to return the call.

The chilled sensation of ice against her neck and forehead brought Mia back into consciousness. She squealed from the unexpected shock. Hunter was sitting beside her, holding a small bag of ice just above her face. He took a swig of beer and smiled at her. "Welcome back." The confusion reflected on her face. "Do you remember what happened?" Mia stared at him. "You fainted just as you saw me." He smirked. "You answered my phone. Who was on the other end, Mia?" She sat up and stumbled into the bathroom to splash cold water on her face. As she stared into the mirror, she could still hear the woman's enchanted voice, haunting her. Her words spiraled within her mind, repeating them over and over. She realized that this woman, whom she had never met, was going to invade her dreams tonight. Tonight, she would have one shot to master her trait. Failure was not an option. Having no idea what she may be up against, what she looked like or what form this woman may take in her dream, she would have to be ready to react without missing a beat.

She exited the bathroom and walked out of the bedroom, making no eye contact with him. Although it was getting late, she needed to stay awake a while longer. When she entered the kitchen, she saw Raine and Emery arm wrestling. Raine's attention diverted and she lost. "Hey Mia." Mia acknowledged Raine with a simple smile. She made herself a cup of coffee and went into the yard to think. The warm breeze wafted around her, embracing her like a favorite blanket. The scent of the night air enhanced by the clear sky was so inviting. She sat on the edge of the pool that faced the Moon and waded her feet in the pool while savoring her coffee. Reverting back to the results of the pendulum, one by one she recalled the questions and its answers in an effort to help guide her. Like a puzzle, she applied the answers to the possible variables that she may face in her dream. She recalled Hunter's inquiry about the caller and realized that he had known who it was. It was obvious that he had been talking to this woman about her because of the specific words that she had chosen to say to her. *"The pendulum said that they're afraid of what I can do. How does this woman fit into this? Did he call her to help him?* She couldn't wrap her head around the fact that he would need help. Her perception of Hunter, Mayne and Enya, were that of powerful and fearless Witches.

The first of the pendulum questions came to mind. It became clear, that this answer was what tied this woman to her. *"They can weave into dreams and guide what happens just as I can guide Elements. They can't control dreams. I can. Can this woman do this? Is that why he had called her?"* The result of first of the unanswered question's now concerned her. *"This unanswered question was now answered. It foretold this woman in my dream tonight. She will be the one who challenges me, next."* Mia stared at the Moon once again. There was no fear, just curiosity. The pendulum's answers reaffirmed her confidence.

Mia heard the sliding door and turned to see who was there. With a drink in hand, Enya stared at her as she walked to the bar and sat on a stool, facing her. Mia turned to face her and returned her stare. Enya's expression was hostile. Her demeanor attested to the fact that she knew of this woman's intentions as well. Mia intentionally reflected the opposite expression. Without losing eye contact, Mia stood up and walked slow-paced, toward her. She watched Enya as she shook her glass, swirling the ice in her drink. Mia stood inches before her, arrogantly pursed her lips and spoke in a detesting tone. "Each one of you has challenged me. Each one of you wants a piece of me." She turned to Enya and continued. "Be careful of what you wish for, Miss Enya." Enya raised her eyebrow. "Are you threatening me, Mia?" "That wasn't a threat. It's a promise."

Hunter stood at the door, listening and noticed the heated static between them. As Mia headed into the house, she spotted Hunter standing at the door. He slid the screen door open for her. "Are you turning in for the night?"

Mia stopped and slowly turned to face him. "Sweet dreams, Hunter." Mia knew that she had struck a nerve with him when she saw his smile. He laughed out loud.

Mia ran upstairs. She needed to meditate intently in order to fall asleep. With no time to lose, she switched on the nightstand's light, opened the wooden box in Mayne's closet and helped herself to her homegrown sleep aid. Although her rolling skills left much to be desired, she did the best that she could. She shrugged her shoulders, smirking at her finished product. The clothing that she wore was uncomfortable for sleep. She sifted through Mayne's drawers to find something loose fitting. Although long fitting, the tank top that she found, worked just fine. She changed her clothes, pulled the blanket halfway down the bed and sat on the edge. The smoke began to fill the room. She paced herself to allow a gradual effect. She ground out the remains in the ashtray and situated herself on the bed, with no parts of her body touching the other. As her meditation commenced, she focused on relaxing every muscle. She focused her thoughts on the proverb; *"Still waters run deep."* and envisioned the serene waters of a pond. Every muscle in her body was as still as the water. She waited for the familiar relaxed sensation to set in. She conceived this feeling to be the separation of body and spirit. She arrived. Her spirit was present with one foot on each side of the realms: dream and waking state.

Hunter and Mayne went upstairs to check on her. Mayne opened the door, making no sound as she turned the doorknob. They crept in. The distinct aroma within the room wafted like backdraft into their faces. A few faint smoke waves were still visible. They saw her lying on the bed, in a deep and tranquil state. Mayne pointed to her wooden box, wide opened, on the floor. She closed it and returned it to her closet. Hunter knelt over her to listen to the rhythm of her breathing. The rapid movement of her eyes indicated her depth of her trance. They didn't know if Mia was aware of their presence. In fact, she had anticipated their eventual arrival and had assumed that Enya would have accompanied them. She remained in a pseudo-state of suspended animation. No one knew that she was now proficient in existing between both realms and Mia knew that having this edge, would keep her a step ahead of this woman. Hunter stepped into the bathroom to call the High Priestess.

"She waits for you, M'Lady." "Show her to me, Hunter." He stepped out, holding the phone for her to see live feed of her sleeping. He stepped over to the far end of the room. "Would you like me to stay with her?" "Not necessary. I want no outside entities to change the course of my intentions." "Understood. I await your call." He hung up and exited the bathroom, gesturing for Mayne to follow him into the hall. The closing door signified to Mia that what lies ahead was about to begin. Choosing her usual playing field, within her mind, she returned to the lake where she had always found the lion and stood in the center of its grassy field. She looked around to ensure that all the usual landmarks were in place. The lake was to her left, the bench, to her right and just ahead, stood the tree where she had witnessed the baby Blue Jay take its first flight, were all in place. She kept her eyes fixed on the tree in front of her while maintaining attention to things within her peripheral view as well. She kept her arms an inch from her body and her fingers separated to feel any subtle change in air movement. Her feet were inches apart, in a comfortable and balanced stance. Nearly full, the Moon was shining bright, emitting its effulgent beams and casted shadows that danced through the tree and onto the grass. The silence that surrounded her seemed as dormant as she was. She knew that she was being observed and that this entity was merely waiting on her first move. A familiar, gradual warmth emitted throughout her body. She recognized this feeling from past experiences with Hunter. She sensed the woman's presence and could feel her eyes upon her. Her attention was averted when a sudden blurred streak of white light ascended from the tree and into the bushes behind it. Mia's eyes widened. With fingers flared, she remained vigilant, ready to take on and thwart any challenge that may present itself. The bushes were still and the unceasing silence returned. Being an impatient one, the unnecessary waiting was not one of Mia's strong points. She decided to take control. As she walked toward the bushes, she noticed an abnormality in the grass. In this dream realm, it was nighttime and there were dandelions protruding above the grass, with their tiny petals opened as if the Sun were shining. She knew this was the woman's doing because these flowers close at nightfall. One by one the heads of each flower, popped off and fell onto the ground. The wind blew across the field, towards the bushes, combing the blades of grass along the way. The detached dandelion flowers transformed into mice, following the direction of the wind. Their faint squeaks were heard as they ran across the field and invaded the bushes. The squeaks ceased and the silence returned. Mia worried that this woman may have harmed them. The squeaks were quickly changed to a bizarre vibrating sound accompanied by faint sporadic chirping. The sounds grew louder. A flock of hummingbirds emerged from the bushes and flew towards Mia then coursed over her head and disappearing into the sky. The silence returned once again. Frustrated from the quid pro quo exchange, Mia was no longer going to work with the Elements just to lure her out. She peered at the bushes and communicated an insistent telepathic message to her. *"Come forth or be gone, woman."* Knowing that Mia didn't know who she was, let alone the hierarchy seat in which she held, she gave Mia a free pass on her disrespectful command. The bushes rustled. Mia saw a light reflected from a set of eyes. A blue eyed, white Bengal tiger emerged and sat on the grass in front of the bush. Mia flared her fingers once more, but held her ground and showed no emotion. *"Show yourself."* The tiger stood up, made a few growled sounds and advanced towards her. Halfway across the field, the tiger leaned back as if it were going to pounce her. Mia flinched. The tiger stood on its hind legs and transformed into her true self. Her hair was as white as the tiger and her long tresses swayed with each step. She stood nearly a foot taller than Mia and her voice was soothing and amiable. The woman stood before her and smiled. "Hello Mia." "Mia nodded her head and smiled, half heartedly." "You need not fear me. I'm here in peace." Mia listened and observed intently, but remained wary of her. The woman extended her hand. "Walk with me, Mia." She nodded her head and kept her hands to herself. "What do you fear about me?" Although she heard her question, Mia refused to put thought to the answer because doing this would have given her a gateway into her mind. She remained alert, focusing only on the woman's presence and her own surroundings. She waited for Mia's answer.

"Speak to me, Mia." Mia whispered a generic answer. "I fear nothing." The woman stared into her eyes, trying to hold Mia's attention. Snow began to fall. Having not created this precipitation, Mia's eyes widened at the sight of it. She knew that she had done this on purpose. As the minutes passed, its density increased and the snow began to accumulate. "If you wish to see what I hide Mia, then change the snow." "Why do you test me, woman?" "Humor me this one time. I wish to show you something." The snow changed to rain, revealing the dandelions, restored to their original state. Mia glanced at them and then looked back at the woman.

"Look at the dandelions again. Mia." The flowers closed their petals before her eyes. "Hold out your hand, Mia." The woman extended her hand: palm closed and placed a mouse into Mia's hand. Mia was now distracted from her own self-protective state. She stared at the tiny white mouse as it wiggled its whiskers. "Look at me, Mia." Mia looked up at her. "Now look at the mouse." "The mouse transformed into a white frog. It sprung from her hand, landed onto the grass and fused back into a closed dandelion. Mia thought about this woman and her strengths and had come to a quick conclusion. If Hunter called her for help, then she must be a stronger Witch then he.

"I know that you're a Witch. Who are you and why do you show me these things?" "I'm a High Priestess. I am like you, Mia. I can do all that you can, and more." "And what is it that you believe I can do?" "What trait has just been revealed to you?" "You tell me." The woman smiled. "I will show you." She reached out to touch Mia's cheek. While intrigued by her, Mia remained on guard, ready to control this dream if need be. The woman smiled. She reached out to her with both hands. Just before her hands touched Mia's cheeks, the woman saw the brilliant flash of blue light in Mia's pupils. It was this very moment that that the woman had been waiting for. Mia disappeared from the shared dream realm.

CHAPTER 22

HIGH PRIESTESS

Mia felt the isometric pressure of the bed against her body. She pressed her palms onto the bed to feel the softness of the sheets. These sensations, inclusive of the familiar scent of the room were a cumulative indication that she had returned. She lay motionless with her eyes closed. Her senses set on high. Any change in air movement would signify the presence of people in the room with her. Although she felt nothing, she remained cautious. Upon opening her eyes she saw the woman that she had intentionally deserted in her dream, standing beside her. At eye level with Mia, Mayne squatted beside the woman, next to the nightstand. She looked ahead and saw Hunter at the foot of the bed grasping the footboard. To her left, stood Enya. The woman sat on the bed beside her and smiled. "Welcome back Mia." The woman paused for a few moments and smiled. "Do you understand what has happened?" As Mia listened, she felt the collective eyes of the others, fixed on her. "We've both controlled your dream. I set the stage and with some subtle persuasion and I let you lead." Mia rehashed the events of the dream while staring at her like a feral cat and then slid back, against the headboard to distance herself. "Mia, I'm impressed with your conscious ability to exist between both of these realms. It's these traits that set you and I apart from those who live here with you." Mia knew that she was using a correlated method in order to get her to speak. Mia wasn't buying into it. She glanced over to Hunter, saw the seething expression in his face and knew that her reserved behavior irked him. The woman shifted herself closer to Mia, her eloquence, reassuring and serene. "I'm going to put my hands on your cheeks. Don't be afraid of me, my little baby Blue Jay. I only want to help you fly." The High Priestess chose wisely. Mia's eyes teared. Her words eased her preconceived notions while distorting Mia's intuition in order to gain her trust. Mia now questioned her original perception of the Blue Jays. As she reached to her, Mia inhaled sharply and flinched, grasping and digging her nails into the pillow beneath. She placed her palms on the sides of Mia's face, her enigmatic eyes piercing through her mind and soul. Mia froze. She realized too late, what the woman was doing. She tried to fight her hypnotic invasiveness but was unable to focus long enough to block her. Each feeble attempt to conceal her thoughts seemed to be intercepted.

"Show me what you hide, child." Tears fell from Mia's eyes. The feeling of being trapped and unable to control her situation triggered the affects of anxiety. The woman's grasp tightened. Mia watched her changing expressions and struggled to pull her eyes away from hers. She felt her hidden secrets surfacing to the forefront of her mind. As her anxiety increased, the faint light in her pupils grew bold. She retracted her tight grasp. The woman's hands slid to Mia's shoulders, and followed down her arms. Mia trembled as she felt her fingernails gliding down them. She continued to hold Mia's eyes captive while holding her hands within hers. With tears in her eyes, Mia pleaded to her. "Release me."

She rose from the bed and approached Hunter. Distraught and violated, Mia leaped out of the bed and ran downstairs. She lost her balance, nearly falling of the last few stairs, but managed to break the fall by holding on to the bannister. When she caught her breath she sat on the bottom step and cried. Raine and Sage ran in from the living room when they heard the noise. Sage looked at her with a perplexed expression. Mia looked at Raine. Raine pursed her lips. She didn't let Mia's watery eyes affect her. "Mia. At this point, there should be no tears. What have I taught you? Don't let me see this side of you again. Suck it up, cupcake. Counter-attack, dammit! Go forth, plot and proceed."

The woman returned to the bed and patted the bed. "Sit." Enya and Mayne sat beside her and Hunter pulled a chair over. "She hides herself from you... all of you. She hides things from you as well. In an effort to decipher what she did not fully understand, she has written detailed notes and analyzed them. All that she now knows and all that she has planned is reflected in this notebook. There is a drawing of what one would use for Divination - pendulum answers. It's imperative that you find this book. It's hidden, but resides within this room. Look where the light source rests." She looked at Hunter. "You need to prepare. She is strong and she will fight you. She'll emerge and test every fiber of your strength. I know that you have her contained within this property, however, at some point she will free herself. This is when your battle will begin."

Mia dried her eyes with her sleeve and proceeded into the kitchen to feed her current mood. Raine's words had reset her, however, what felt most unnerving was the fact that this woman was now revealing to the others, what Mia had concealed from them. She shuffled through containers of left-over take-out food and other odds and ends and spotted a package of sliced cheese. She took the cheese and two slices of bread, settling on making herself a grilled cheese sandwich. She didn't feel like making it the usual way, since that would produce dishes that would need to be cleaned. Instead, she placed the bread into the toaster, relying on the warmth of the toast to melt the cheese. Since chocolate milk was her drink of choice, she made that while waiting for her toast to pop.

She remained torn about her Blue Jay comment. *"If this woman came to me as the mother Blue Jay, then why go through the hassle of approaching me in this manner?"* She sat at the table and ate, disregarding her never-ending self-inquiries. She heard splashing and looked through the sliding door and saw Gwen, Aithusa, Faeryn and Ceridwen in the pool. She had thought that they had left and had forgotten about them. The sound of footsteps emanated from the stairwell. Hunter and the High Priestess appeared at the bottom of the stairway. He peeked into the kitchen and then continued escorting her to the front door, where a car awaited her just outside. Zephyr emerged from the basement. He and Mia glanced at each other then he walked into the living room. Mia heard their voices but couldn't make out what they were saying. Their talking ceased. Hunter and Zephyr returned upstairs with Mayne and Enya following behind them.

Mia finished eating, grabbed a can of soda and went into the yard. The girls stopped what they were doing and looked at her. At first, she made no eye contact and took a seat at the far end of the yard. She cracked open her soda and then glanced over at them. They were whispering amongst themselves. She spotted Emery at the bar. He stared at her while talking on his cell phone. She chose not to participate in his staring contest. The cold can touched her stomach and she flinched. As she took a sip, she saw the braided bracelet and was reminded of the tasks that lie before her. She placed the can on the ground and closed her eyes.

"What did she say about these notes?" Zephyr inquired. Hunter reiterated her words. "She said it's in this room and to look where the light source rests." Mayne climbed onto her bed, searching the seams of the windows and then shuffled through her dresser, searching for her large flashlight. Hunter watched her and grabbed one of the drawer handles. "Pull the drawers out completely. It may be hiding behind them." Finding nothing, Mayne became frustrated, blurting out threats. "I should just drag her ass up here and make her show me where it is!" Hunter laughed. "That wouldn't be prudent at this juncture." Mayne looked at Zephyr and threw her hands in the air. "Really? He's got jokes for me now!" She threw herself on the bed. Her head lay near the edge of the mattress facing the nightstand. "This is pissing me off. I need to smoke or I'm gonna snap!" Hunter slid the last drawer back into its slot. "I need you clear headed right now." Mayne punched the mattress. Enya paced the floor repeating the woman's words. "Where the light source rests…."

Mayne looked at Enya and sighed like a child. "What are you twelve...? ya cranky brat!" Mayne ignored her and glanced backwards at the ashtray on her nightstand, yearning to smoke. She sprung from the bed and everyone turned to look at her. She searched under the lamp cover and then pulled the drawer out and emptied its contents onto the floor. Under the stand was the small box of DVD's, where Mia had stashed what she had stolen from Enya's room. Seeing no paper protruding from it, she placed the box on the bed. She stared intently at the lamp and then placed the ashtray and the lamp onto the bed as well. She knelt in front of the nightstand and tilted it. "I found it! Where the light source rests! It was next to me the whole fucking time!" She handed the notepad to Hunter and darted to her closet for some much needed, Zen paraphernalia.

He sat on the bed and perused through the pages. His eyes widened as he read through her notes, stopping to comment when he deemed it necessary.

"She has a keen memory. Her level of perception is phenomenal. She knows just about everything. Each of us is mentioned throughout these pages: some, more than once. There is an outside entity that helps her. I believe that person is Sebastian." He returned to the notes. He began to read the list of their names with the information that she had written beside each one. "She has done her homework." He paused momentarily and smirked. "Within these notes, she is trying to figure out one of the most elementary things. She knows that we are a coven, however, she doesn't seem to understand the number of people permitted in one." He glanced at Mayne and laughed. "The other thing that she has not fully deciphered is you, Mayne." "Oh you got more jokes for me? That's ok. That's because I don't need what you have, to do what you do." Hunter laughed. "Touché!"

He read on. He read through a list of questions and answers and then turned the page to find another list. The last page was a simple drawing. He realized this was the page that the woman had spoken of. He reread the questions and answers. "As anticipated, every word that our esteemed guest spoke of was on point. "Each one of you will read this in its entirety, now! I will go downstairs to fetch the others. When you have all finished, meet me in the big room."

Sage and Raine had joined the girls in the yard. Sage was sitting on the edge of the pool when Lucius and Mason walked into the yard. They had been working together, restoring an old motorcycle and were filthy from head to toe. Lucius scooped some water out of the pool to splash himself. Sage screamed at him. "Lucius! That's disgusting! Go hose yourself off and take a shower, you filthy animal!"

He and Mason laughed. Lucius decided that it was time to harass Sage. He held his grease-ridden hands open and slowly walked towards her. She screamed and ran to the other side of the pool. "Don't even think about it, jackass!" Mia watched him chase her around the pool. She waited for him to return to her side, stood up, tripped him and pushed him into the pool." Sage howled. When he emerged to the surface, he spotted her standing near the edge of the pool, bullying him with her steely eyes. He smirked, then waded to the edge and lifted himself out of the pool. Mia held her callous stare and spoke in an icy tone. "It would be in your best interest to back away from me right now." She stared him down without as much as a flinch. When Hunter appeared at the door, Mason approached him. He glanced at Mia, whispered into his ear and retreated back into the house. Mason knelt at the edge of the pool and reiterated the message to Raine. He whistled to Lucius and waited for him by the bar next to Zephyr. Mia watched them intently. They disappeared into the house. Mia glanced over to Raine and saw her talking to the girls. Raine dried herself off and disappeared into the house with Sage. It was now evident that they were conspiring together. Gwen, Ceridwen, Aithusa and Faeryn remained in the pool for the time being and eventually followed suit as well. Mia glanced up at the nearly Full Moon and went inside to make herself a cup of coffee. No one was around. She swiped a pack of cigarettes that someone had left on the counter and returned to her chair in the yard.

The lighter was turned up high. Mia took its blaring flame as a sign. She lit a cigarette, took a drag and then sipped her coffee. When she took a second sip, the braided bracelet scraped her cheek. The sign meant it was time to begin. With no one around she began with the bracelet. Simply removing it would not free her from Enya's spell. She put the cup down and ran back inside for paper and a pen. She returned and began to write a reversal spell for the bracelet. Mia realized that she may not be aware of the exact verbiage that Enya had spoken as she braided it, however, she recalled the word ALIVE and the words just began to flow.

When she finished, she turned her chair around to face the Moon. The image of the lion punching through the crystal columns came to mind. She smiled, glanced at them and sat down. She unclasped the bracelet. Line by line she recited what she had written in a whispered tone while simultaneously unweaving each level of the braid.

> By the knot of nine I bide my time
> By the knot of eight I open this gate
> By the knot of seven This spell will lessen
> By the knot of six This spell is nixed
> By the knot of five I come alive
> By the knot of four I open a door
> By the knot of three My Spirit is free
> By the knot of two I walk through
> By the knot of one The spell is undone

Mia took a deep breath before she stood up to look. She looked at the Moon, rose from the chair and sighed in elation. The crystal columns were gone. She ran to the fence and stood on a crate, peering over it and crying tears of joy. She knew that she could just walk out of the yard at this moment, but they would find her. She needed to end this the correct way. She glanced up at the Moon once more and thought of the lion, the Moon phase and Sundial that the lion had drawn. Tomorrow night she will fight for her life.

She shoved the untangled cords into her pocket and went into the house to get a jacket to conceal her wrist, since the bracelet was no longer on it. She entered the kitchen and passed through it to go upstairs. Hunter's outer door was closed. She could see only faint shadows of people through the frosted glass. She crept upstairs. Mayne's door was closed. She listened against the door. When she heard chatter she decided to go into Raine's room to grab a jacket. She found a hooded fleece jacket on her bed, slipped it on and returned to the yard. She took a sip of her coffee and wound up spitting it back into the mug because it was cold. Back inside she went, to make a fresh cup. While the coffee was brewing, she grabbed a few cookies to snack on and peeked at Hunters doors. When she saw the shadow of two people standing close to the frosted glass of the doors, she ran back into the kitchen. She shoved a cookie in her mouth and made an unavoidable mess of sugar and milk on the counter as she rushed to return to the yard before they came back out. She shoved the milk back into the refrigerator and when she grabbed the door to close it, it wouldn't move because Hunter had his hand on it. He waited for her to step out of the way away and closed it. "Were you eavesdropping on us?" She ignored his question and continued on her way. He cracked open a bottle of beer and watched her through the door.

Mia stepped behind the bar to get an ashtray and saw a box of fireworks resting on the bar. She sorted through it, found a pack of sparklers and slid it into her pocket. She took the ashtray and returned to her chair. She withdrew a sparkler stick and lit it. The waves of light from the sparkler emitted lingering, brilliant designs through the air. She looked at the Moon and traced the Moon's circumference with the sparkler several times and then drew stars against the night sky. A thought came to mind as she drew them. The sparkler was almost finished. She lit another one and began drawing invoking Pentagrams in the air. The first was for Air, beginning at her right and going left. The second was for Fire, beginning at the top, right and going down. The third was for Water, beginning at her left and going right. The Forth was for Earth, beginning at the top, left and going down and the fifth was for spirit, beginning at the bottom, right and going up. As she drew these, she whispered words of protection and requested the most benevolent outcome for tomorrow night. Hunter watched as she drew each one. By the second one, he had caught on to what she was doing and approached her. "Mia, it's getting late. It's time for you to come indoors now." Perturbed by his intrusion, she turned her head slowly to look at him and sat up, with her feet on the ground. She returned her attention to the sparkler as it spewed tiny flares of light and cast her response to him, into the air.

"NO"

Hunter's scowl made her grin. His request didn't affect her in the least. Since the serenity of the Moon kept her mind at ease, she had decided to sleep under the Moon tonight. She stuck the handle of the sparkler into an opening of the chair's metal frame, ran inside and dashed up the staircase, into Mayne's room. She swiped a pillow and blanket from the bed and proceeded to return to the yard. Hunter was standing in the kitchen with her mug. She walked around him and slipped into the yard to situate her sleeping arrangement, then returned inside to make a fresh cup of coffee. "Mia, sleeping outside was not the option given to you." His stern words were once again, ignored by her. Hunter was standing against the door's frame, when Mayne entered the kitchen. She looked at Hunter with a puzzled hand gesture. "Mia wants to sleep in the yard tonight. In fact, she has your blanket and pillow out there." "Nice! What the hell am I supposed to use, Mia?" Mia shrugged her shoulders and walked outside. Hunter waited until she was outside to break the news to Mayne. "She's not sleeping outside alone. I'll stay with her while you go get something to sleep on. I'm sure there's an extra air mattress in the basement." The utter disgust on her face resembled a child about to throw a fit. "ME? What the fuck, Hunter?" He grinned. "My window will be open. If I hear anything, I'll come right out." "Fine!" She threw her hands in the air. "Just let me get some stuff that I'll need." "Take your time. I'll be in the yard waiting for you." "Great!" Hunter retrieved his cell phone and cigarettes and went into the yard. He sat behind the bar, made himself a drink and looked over at Mia. She knew Hunter was watching her, but continued drinking her coffee and playing with the sparklers. She had two left, but grew weary of them. She yawned, walked over to the bar and turned on the radio. She nudged Hunter's leg over and knelt down to find a station that she liked. "Not too loud, Mia." A car-insurance commercial aired, followed by a concert ticket giveaway contest. She left the station on, stood up and spotted his pack of cigarettes on the bar. She swiped one and lit it with his lighter. Mayne slid the screen door, slipped the air mattress through and carried it over her head. Mia watched her place it next to her chair. A song began to play. She listened as she watched Mayne return into the house. The lyrics were cryptic. He observed her as she listened to the song.

♪...shows his face then disappears...♪

He stared at her and laughed, clanking his glass against the bar. She knew that he was trying to intimidate her. She returned to her chair but instead, decided to try out the air mattress. Mayne returned, dragging a small cooler and a bag of other items. Hunter smirked. "Camping supplies?" "Oh, you got jokes again, Hunter?" Mayne pursed her lips and glanced back at Hunter. He smiled. "Looks like she's jumped in your grave." Mayne parked the cooler behind the mattress. "Off!" Mia returned to her chair and wrapped the blanket around herself while Mayne unpacked her things and sat on the mattress. As she reached into the cooler, she caught Mia watching her. "What's your malfunction?" "What's this about?" Mia pointed to the mattress. "Since princess wishes to sleep out here tonight, I have been appointed to stay out here with you." Mia flashed her middle finger at Hunter. He was tempted to walk over to her and grab her finger, but given the current circumstances, he chose to let it go and went inside.

She watched Mayne light up, anticipating the sweet scent of it. Mayne smiled and sat beside her. She took a toke and moved closer to Mia's face. Mia grinned and let her blow the smoke into her mouth. Mia swiped her beer, took a swig and handed it back to her. "Who was that woman?" Mayne

laughed. "I can't believe that you don't know her. Everyone Knows her."
"We'll, I don't." "She's appeared to you often, in the form of a Blue Jay."
"How did you know that? I didn't share that with you." Mayne relit the cigarette and smiled. "A coven can have as many members as they want." Mia
pursed her lips. "You found them, didn't you?" Mayne's sly laugh mocked
her. "Did you read everything?" "Yes." "Was I correct about what I wrote
about you?" Mayne didn't respond. "What can you do? Show me?" Mayne
took another toke and stared into her eyes for a few moments. "You've seen
some of what I can do." Mia stared into her dark, esoteric eyes. She could feel
Mayne pulling her into the arcane path of her mind. "Stop it!" "You asked.
You like when I do that. You're curious." "Show me something that I haven't
seen." "You show me something and I'll outshine you." Mia's eyes were fixed
on her cigarette, because she had wanted more. It had snuffed out again. She
focused on the end of it and closed her eyes. Her diligent discipline allowed
her to tap into the spirit of Fire.

She envisioned the flame dancing on a candlewick and felt its heat grazing
her finger. She opened her eyes and the cigarette began to smolder. "Nice."
Mayne took a toke and held it in front of Mia. "Now watch it." The smoke
thickened and wafted in the air. Mia watched its waves as they swirled against
the midnight blue sky, forming into the three letters of her name. Mia smiled.
"Do you remember when you told me that I can't control fire? I told you that
I knew that, but that it could be guided. This is what I meant." Mia took it
from her hand, lay back on her chair and indulged. "Would princess like the
beer that I'm drinking as well?" With a devilish smile, Mia held out her hand.
Mayne handed it to her and cracked open another beer. "I did the quid pro
quo thing with High Priestess, in my dream." "Oh yeah?" "I knew that she
was challenging me. Tell me about her." "Why didn't you ask her for yourself,
when she was here?" "Why did he bring her here and what did she say about
me?" "Same answer." "Because I..." "You were afraid of her." "No." "She's
the last person that you should be afraid of. She was here to help you and always has been, in spirit and in your dreams." Mia was silent while she stared

at the Moon. She thought of the woman and everything that Mayne had said as well. She took what she had said with a grain of salt. With heavy eyes, she felt the drowsiness set in. She yawned and closed her eyes.

Tomorrow loomed. She knew that she needed to rest to be ready for what may come. For tonight, she knew that the Moon would watch over her and protect her like a dream catcher.

CHAPTER 23

SETTING THE STAGE

The sweet scent of morning dew caressed Mia's senses, gently waking her with the assistance of the Sun's emerging brilliance. She opened her eyes and immediately squinted, to block the Sun's strong rays. The rhythmic sound of the cicada's synchronized chirps, foretold of hot and humid weather. She turned to see Mayne sleeping beside her, lying on her stomach. The faint ocean breeze did little to cool her off. The heat had already begun to affect her. She wiped the sweat from her forehead. With a naughty grin, she glanced at the pool and then at Mayne, weighing the possible repercussions of a cannonball jump into the pool. For a few minutes, she watched her as she slept, thinking of how peaceful and serene she looked. The idea was as tempting as it was entertaining, but she decided to leave her be as it may be the last time she would see her in this peaceful state. She slipped her shorts off and sat on the edge of the pool, wading her feet to test the water's temperature. The squawk of the seagull's singing along with the cicada's periodic chiming, added to the morning's peaceful harmony. She slid into the pool. The water's cool embrace encompassed her body and felt as invigorating as the affects of coffee. She swam a few silent and graceful laps, first forward, on her stomach and then pushed her feet against the side of the pool to glide backwards. She floated on her back for a few moments, watching the tiny birds flying overhead. A larger bird flew over her and landed on one of the bar chairs. It was the Blue Jay. She waded over to the bar's end of the pool and whispered to it. *"What do you want to tell me?"* It remained still, perched and silent. Mia recalled the day at the fair just before she had met Faeryn and Ceridwen. She held her finger up just as she did on that day. The Blue Jay glided onto her finger. *"Are you her? Are you the High Priestess?"* The Blue Jay stared at her for a few moments. It cawed loudly, vigorously fluttering its wings. Mia's eyes widened. Mayne assiduous stare had been fixed on Mia and the Blue Jay, the entire time. She was amazed by the communication and trust that they had shared. Mia assured reply to the Blue Jay, soothed its ruffled feathers. *"I know. I know. It's time for me to fly on my own. I will, tonight."* The Blue Jay was still. Mia smiled. The Blue Jay voiced its pleased fluted tweet and flew away. When Mayne saw the bird soar past her, she pretended to be asleep, squinting while watching her. Mia dove underneath the water and swam back to the other side. As she emerged, she saw the shadow of a body at the surface. When she emerged, she saw Mayne, kneeling at the pool's edge. Mia wiped the water from her eyes and held on to the side. "Sorry for waking you. I tried to be quiet." Mayne smiled. "The Sun's glare woke me. I don't usually sleep outside." "Did you sleep out here with me because he told you to do it?" "Yes." "Do you always do what he asks of you?" "Most of the time." Mia pursed her lips, grasped Mayne's wrists and pulled herself closer to Mayne. "Did you really want to?" Mayne sighed. "Question time, again?" "Funny." Mia lifted herself up and sat on the edge. "Aren't you hot? Sit next to me and put your feet in." Mayne sat beside her. "I was going to go make us some coffee." "Thanks. It can wait." "Are you gonna ask me more questions?" "No." Mia kicked her feet to splash her on purpose. "Cut it out." Mia laughed. "It feels good, though." Mia slipped her hand behind Mayne's back and pushed her into the pool. When Mayne surfaced, she was a bit flustered. "You think you're funny, huh?" Mia giggled. Mayne stood still for a few moments, swishing her hands across the water's surface and then darted at her. She picked her up and threw her into the pool. Mia screamed. When she reemerged, she shouted at her and then laughed. "You suck!" Mayne grinned nefariously. "So I've been told." "Asshat!" Mia waded over to her, vigorously splashing her and then sprung upward and held her in a headlock. Mayne didn't budge. Mia dangled off of her shoulders as if she were hanging onto a tree. Mayne laughed at her. "Is that all you got, princess?" Mayne slid her arm under her legs. "Now, I'm dunkin' the both of us." "No fair...Nooooo!" Under, they went. Mia coughed as they resurfaced. "Now we're even." Mayne waded to the edge, carrying her and Mia rested her head upon Mayne's shoulder. "We're never gonna be even, Mayne. There will always be a challenge." "Is that so?" "Yes." Mayne placed her on the edge of the pool and stood in front of her. "You've got balls. I'll give you that." Mia held her arms up and flexed her muscles. "Never underestimate me!" "I'll try to remember that." Mayne smirked. "Can I get us coffee now, or do you want me to harass you some more?" Mia put her hands on Mayne's shoulders. "I want you to know that I know about you." "Yeah...and what's that?" Mia smiled, grabbed a towel and went into the house without responding. Mayne jumped out and followed suit. She turned the coffee machine on while Mia used the facilities. Mayne shouted out to her. "Mia. How do you want your coffee?" "Really?" "Look, I just woke up, princess." Mayne paused for a few seconds. "Oh, Cream and sugar. See? I remembered. What's takin' ya so long? Did ya fall in?" Mia stepped out of the bathroom, giggling. "Jackass." "Take your coffee." Mayne sat on the far corner of the table and sprawled across the bench. "So, what's your plans for today?" Mia was silent at first. "I'm relaxing for most of the day." "And tonight?" "I don't know. I'll just ride the waves to where they take me." "Good way to live. I live by that, myself." There was silence for a few seconds. "Aren't you going to ask me about my plans?" "I already know what your plans are. I suggest you do the same as me, today." "Oh, yeah? Why? I don't even know what I'm doing." "Tonight is the Full Moon, which means that there will be some sort of feast here, this evening. More than likely, you will be running food errands for Enya. Enya will be cooking with Gwen and the girls will help her set up the yard. Hunter and the guys will do whatever it is they do." Mayne chuckled. "Oh yeah...? And what'll you be doing?" Mia took a sip of her coffee and looked up at her with an enigmatic gaze. "Observing and supervising." "So, you'll be sitting on your ass, just like the princess that you are." Mia giggled. "When this day is done, maybe I'll be taking a ride on your bike. You can sit behind me, if you wish." Mayne's eyes widened. "Oh you think so, huh?" "For now, I'm gonna go to your room, take a shower and pick out some clothes to wear from your closet. Then, I'll lounge on your bed and watch TV until everyone wakes. Fetch me when breakfast is ready. Peace, out." Mia pushed her mug to the center of the table. Mayne's jaw dropped. "Hey, princess. While you bathe, I'll polish your throne and when our royal breakfast is ready, I'll carry you downstairs and gently place your precious little ass on it. How's that?" Mia grinned. "Make sure the chair's pillow is fluffed to my liking. When you're finished with that you can go wax your bike for me." Mia rose from her chair and as she walked away, Mayne slammed her mug on the table and chased her, stopping at the bottom of the staircase. Mia screeched and ran upstairs.

Mia made a sour face as she entered Mayne's room. Since the room was unoccupied last night, it was hot. She turned the A/C on, full blast and shuffled through Mayne's closet and dresser. Mayne's jeans didn't fit so she opted for the yoga pants and would just have to roll them up. She found her beloved "gas, grass or ass no one rides for free" T-shirt and made her way into the bathroom. The sudden idea of a bath, enticed her. She plugged the tub's drain, ran the water and slipped into Enya's room. Careful not to wake her, she crept into her room and searched for a few items. Remembering where Enya stored her Magickal items, she perused through the drawer until she found what she had needed. Enya had so many things, some of which she wasn't familiar with. She took only what she recognized and understood.

Sage - For clear vision and cleansing of negative energy.
Dandelion - for Divination, calling spirits and favorable Winds.
Star Anise - For psychic and spiritual powers.
Thinking of the lion's eyes, she took an Amber stone - which changes negative energy into positive and also protects.
A Calcite stone - For centering, grounding and calming fear.
A Clear Quartz stone - For intensified energy.

Recalling the Onyx eyes of the frog from her dream, she also chose an Onyx stone - for emotional balance, self control, binding and protection, especially against someone else's Magick. She needed a candle as well, however, with the tub filling, she had no time to look for a specific color. She grabbed a small white candle, because she knew that this color was sufficient for universal purposes.

She crept out of the room and returned to Mayne's room. The tub was nearly half full. She placed the candle on the sink and lit it, then dropped the other items into the bath water. She shut the light, undressed and slipped into the tub. Today she would ask the powers that be, for nothing, as she knew that on the night of a Full Moon, it was all about the Goddess. The candle's ambiance cast dancing shadows around the room. She closed her eyes, allowing the water to soothed and calm her thoughts. She focused of only her departed cat and the good memories that she shared with Sebastian.

Mayne had rested her head on the kitchen table and caught herself dozing off. She glanced up at the clock, wondering why she was awake at this hour. Then she snapped her mind back into alertness, remembering that she wasn't supposed to leave Mia alone. She jolted up the staircase to find her and hopefully catch some more Z's. As she tracked her way up the staircase, Raine was on her way down. "Hey! Fucknuts! What are you doing up?" "I'm not. I'm going back to sleep. Princess just went in the shower and I'm not supposed to leave her alone." "When she's done, come back downstairs with her and help me get the yard ready for later. Sage is helping too. She should be down in a few minutes." Mayne looked at her with a sour expression. "Uh...no."

Sage pranced down the steps and when she saw Mayne, she stopped in her tracks. "It lives at this hour?" "Fuck off, Sage."

When Mayne walked into her room she saw the bathroom door ajar, with the lights out. She turned the light on and saw her in the tub. "How nice. Would princess like a glass of wine?" She blew the candle out. "Don't you know how to knock?" Mia swatted the stones underneath her legs. "It's my room, so, no. What's with the candle and the Dandelion's?" Mia smiled, nervously. "Oh, is it question time?" "Where did you get those? Did you take them from Enya's room?" "I'm sorry but PRINCESS is not taking questions at this time, however for the time being, I will permit you to go take a nap on your bed. If I need you, I'll ring a bell." Mayne clenched her fists. "Wake me and I'll shove the bell up your royal ass!" Mia howled. "WAIT, WAIT...!" Mia tried to catch her breath. "I'm sorry. I'm not really gonna ring a bell. Like you, I'd just like to be left alone for a little while. When I'm finished with my ROYAL fucking bath, I'll wake you gently, so that you may give me my ROYAL foot massage." Mia could hardly hold back her laughter. "You got jokes, Mia?" Mayne turned the showerhead on with just the cold water running and then left the room. Mia shrieked. She maneuvered away from the spewing cold water and shut it off.

Gwen made herself a cup of coffee and joined Sage and Raine in the yard. "Hey guys. Good morning." Raine handed her a clear plastic bag and tossed in the empty beer cans and bottles. "Hi Gwen. Thanks. What are you doing up so early?" "I promised Enya I'd stay for dinner and help her out. We're leaving after that. I need to get back to my bar. They need me." "Aww. Can't they survive without you for one more day?" "Well that's just it. I was supposed to have returned yesterday. My people are good, but I don't want to take advantage of their generosity. They have lives too." "Well at least we'll have you guys here for one more day. Where are the girls?" "Faeryn is in the shower and the other two are still sleeping." Raine tossed in the last can. "I don't know why I bothered to put a blue trashcan out here." She took the bag from her and brought it to the front of the house. Gwen sat at the edge of the pool, stuck her feet in and sipped her coffee. Sage folded the blankets and then took the pillows to bring them inside. "I'm everybody's servant. These people think everything just Magickally finds its way back to where it belongs." Gwen laughed. "Here's a tip. The girls know that I won't clean up after them. The reason why this doesn't happen at my house is because they know that their stuff will be thrown out after a few days." "You throw it out? What happens if it's clothes or something important?" "Gwen held her hands up and made the quotation sign. It still disappears...for a while, then I sneak it back in their room at a later date." "That's not gonna work with garbage though." "The solution for that is to fill the garbage bag and put it in their room." Sage smiled. "Ahhh! Ok. I'll give everyone a free pass today."

Mia dried herself off and dressed. She peaked out of the door and saw Mayne out like a light and snoring away. She brushed her teeth and ran the comb through her hair. As the tub drained, she picked the stones and herbs from the water and stashed them in her pocket. She looked in the mirror and grinned. *"Time for your payback, Mayne."* Mia crept out of the room to get a cup full of ice. When she entered the kitchen she saw Raine making coffee. "Hey, Mia." Mia said nodded with a smile. She reached into the freezer, filled a plastic cup with ice and darted back upstairs. She sat on the edge of the bed, behind her and remained still for a few moments. Her snoring stopped for a few seconds and then resumed. She lifted the back of Mayne's shirt, poured the cubes in and jumped off of the bed. Mayne sprung upright. "What the fuck!" She saw Mia standing by the dresser. "Feels as cold as the shower, huh?" Mayne shook the cubes out of her shirt and chucked them at her. "You better run, NOW!" Mia backed away from her. "But…but…its time for my royal foot massage." "Oh, I gotcha royal foot massage, right here!" She propelled off of the bed. Mia shrieked and ran downstairs.

Enya was woken by Mia's scream. She ran to Mayne's room, saw Mia running down the stairs and Mayne standing at the entrance. "What the fuck did you to her now?" "ME! She threw ice cubes down my shirt while I was asleep!" "One of these days I'm gonna beat the both of you!" Mayne shut the door and went back to bed. When Mia was at the bottom step she saw Raine passing through. "I heard you scream. Why are you smiling?" Raine grinned. "What did you do, Mia?" Mia held an elfish smile and walked into the living room. She lay on the couch and flipped through the channels until she found something interesting.

Faeryn walked into the kitchen and saw Gwen sitting, poolside. "Good morning all." Gwen turned her head. "Good morning Sunshine. How did you sleep?" "Very well, thank you…and you?" "Great." "Is Kerry awake?" Faeryn smiled. "I wouldn't know. She slept downstairs last night." Gwen grinned. "Naturally." "Well, they like each other. You can't blame them." "I know. I wish I had the courage to have snuck into Hunter's room last night." "Why didn't you? "No guts, no glory, Gwen." Sage glanced into the kitchen and saw Hunter standing at the screen door. She giggled. Hunter slid open the screen door and approached her from behind. He massaged her shoulders and whispered into her ear. "You should have." He walked back inside to call Gwen on her cell phone.

When her phone rang she freaked out. "Oh my Goddess! It's Hunter." "Well answer it!" "Hello?" "It's not too late. You know where I am." She turned her head and saw him walking away from the screen door. Her jaw dropped. Faeryn saw her flushed face. "What did he say?" "Fuck! Sage, he heard everything I said. Did you see him at the door while I spoke?" She nodded. "Why didn't you say something?" "How was I supposed to know what you were gonna say?" Faeryn was riled up. "What did he say?" "Never you mind!" She giggled and disappeared into the house. "OK then…" Faeryn paused to laugh. "Since it's our last day here, I thought I would make everyone breakfast. Do you have pancake mix, Sage?" "Why thank you, Faeryn! Yes, its in the cupboard above the coffee pods." "Coffee! I think I'll have some of that, now."

Enya strolled into the kitchen, leaned against the counter while waiting for Faeryn to finish making hers and then made herself a cup. "Good morning Faeryn." She grabbed a notepad and pen. "What are you writing?" "I have to go to the supermarket for a few things for dinner." "Do you need help? I'll go with you." "Thanks. I'm already taking Gwen with me. You stay here, hang in the pool and enjoy yourself." "Umm…" "What?" "Gwen is unavailable." "What do you mean?" She pointed towards Hunters Room. Enya looked toward the direction that she had pointed, rolled her eyes and smirked. "Ok, I'll take your offer." They both laughed. Enya heard the television. "Who's in the living room?" "I think Mia is in there." She grabbed her coffee and went to look. Mia was lounging in the recliner. She sat on the couch nearest to her. "Where is Mayne?" Mia pointed upward. "I know that you were in my room earlier. I watched you fishing through my drawer. What did you take?" Mia glanced at her and then went back to watching the program, without answering. "I heard a clicking sound when you put whatever you took, into your pocket. Did you take stones?" Mia didn't respond. She kept her focus on the television. Enya stood before her and leaned on the armrest of Mia's chair. "This is not how things work in this house. We respect each others property and ask before we take." Enya left the room and went upstairs to Mayne's room. She knocked on the door several times but there was no answer. "I'm coming in." She found Mayne sleeping on her stomach and nudged her. "Wake up." Mayne rolled over. "What?" "Mia is downstairs in the living room. She was in my room earlier and I watched her taking a few stones and what-not's from my drawer." "For what...and why didn't you stop her?" "I don't know and you know why." Mayne huffed. "Can you just keep an eye on her so that I can take a shower?" "Fine. Make it quick."

Enya returned to the kitchen. Mason, Lucius and Hunter were indulging in the breakfast that Faeryn had made and the girls were eating their breakfast, poolside. She greeted everyone. "Good morning all." She gave Hunter a cagey stare. "To what do I owe that look for?" "You know what you did. Where is she?" Hunter bowed his head and smirked. "She's recovering." "I'll bet. Why is everyone up so early?" Mason chimed in. "We smelled the food." "Naturally. Speaking of food, Faeryn. When you're finished, we'll leave. I just have to wait for Mayne to come downstairs." "I'm almost done. I'll put the food in the fridge and leave a note for those who are still sleeping." Hunter looked up at Enya. "Why is Mia by herself?" "She was with Mayne. She's in the shower and will be down in a few. I'm going in there now." "Never mind. You run your errands. I'll go." "Hunter. FYI: Mia had snuck into my room earlier and took a few things. She thought that I was asleep." "Duly noted." Hunter stood up and placed his dishes in the sink. "Enya, before you go, please wake whomever is still sleeping. We'll discuss this evening, when I return."

Mia heard the echo of footsteps emanating from the hall. She glanced over the edge of the couch and saw Hunter and Mason approaching. They seated themselves on opposite couches and Mason questioned her. "Cara Mia. What are you watching?" "Mia didn't acknowledge him. "Mia, you're behaving rudely." Hunter laughed at him and looked at her. "For some reason, she thinks that she can do as she pleases. Mia. What did you take from Enya's room?" Mia pursed her lips and increased the volume on the television. The tone of Mason's vicious laugh sounded disturbing to Mia. She glanced at him for a moment and saw the anger in his eyes. Zephyr had been standing at the entrance and heard both Hunters question and Mason's laugh as well. Mayne showed up and stood next to Zephyr. "What's going on?" Hunter stood up. "Mia is behaving in a disrespectful manner." "What did she do?" "She's not answering our questions." "Princess only speaks to me." Mia flipped her middle finger at her. Mayne laughed. "Don't push me Mia. I still owe you for the ice cubes!" Mia quickly turned to face her. She gave her the finger once more and Mayne punched the wall, in an effort to release her own anger. Zephyr strolled past Mia, parted the curtains and glanced out the window. He spoke with his back to them. "Leave her with me." Hunter nodded and whispered into his ear. "Find out what she took from Enya's room." He nodded. Hunter grasped his shoulder. "Join us in the kitchen when you're finished." Zephyr remained at the window until they left the room and then squatted in front of her. He placed his hands on her knees and tightened his grip to ensure that he had her undivided attention. He grinned. "Mia. We're going to play a game." He stood up and walked behind her. She watched him. "Face forward, Mia." She held a sour expression. He rubbed her shoulders to throw her off, then ran his fingers through her hair and plucked a few strands from her scalp. Mia hissed and swatted at him, trying to retrieve her strands from him. "No worries, Mia. I'll give them back to you, shortly." He hid his hand behind himself, pushed the table in front of her with his leg and knelt on the floor, across the table from her. He cleared off the table, spread out a tissue and placed it in the center. She watched him, intently. He placed the strands onto the center of the tissue. She stared at him. The sharp blue color of his eyes beguiled her. "This game is called: The question. You don't need to speak to play. Are you ready?" Mia stared at him without responding. He placed his palm on the strands. His eerie and steady voice, enunciated every word, burning each phonetic sound into her ear. "Where are the items that you took from Enya?" His unexpected question caused her mind to think of her pocket. Her eyes flared. She was not prepared to block him from her thoughts. "Hand me the contents of your pockets." She froze. "I'm not going to harm you. I will give them back." His manipulative verbiage convinced her to hand them over. He placed the stones and herbs across the span of the hair strands, covered the items with his hand and closed his eyes. Tuning into the items aura, his vision first mirrored its previous presence within a body of water. She didn't understand what he was doing and was leery of his silent game. She grew impatient with his shenanigans, reached out and placed her palm on his hand. He lifted his head slowly to look at her and opened his eyes. The color of them had changed to veiled, indigo. His facial expression was hollow. He seemed to look right through her. Although he frightened her, she showed no fear. Instead, she grew angry, despite of how he made her feel. She clenched his hand and stared him down. He licked his lips and grinned. "I have my answer, Mia. Now it's your turn. You decipher what my question was." He pushed the tissue towards her side of the table. "You see. There was no need to speak and I've returned your things." He stood up and left the room, leaving her to fester in the mystique puzzle of his game.

He returned to the kitchen and approached Hunter. Enya stood up. "She took Sage, Dandelions, Star Anise, Amber, Calcite, Quartz and Onyx stones and used them in her bath."

Enya anxiously addressed Hunter. "Do you know what she was doing?" "Yes I do. She's getting ready." "I need to go to the store. Fill me in when I return. Lets go Faeryn." "Will do. Everyone else, follow me into the yard. Mayne, you go inside with Mia. I'll fill you in when Enya and Faeryn return. Enya reached for her keys and proceeded to the front door with Faeryn. As she passed Mia, she stopped to look at her for a moment and then spotted the items that Mia had taken, laying on the table. She glanced over them, one by one while Faeryn stood at the door. Enya held an impassive expression while Mia watched her. The anticipation of her reaction kept Mia on edge. She looked at Mia once again and then proceeded on her way.

Mayne went into the yard to get the cooler and returned to the kitchen. She reached into the freezer to grab the three water balloons that she had stashed there, an hour earlier, leaving them in the freezer long enough to chill, but not freeze. She tossed them in the cooler with a few bottles of beer, grabbed her cigarettes and went into the living room. Mia was reclined in the chair when Mayne arrived. Mayne propped the pillows and lay across the couch, with the back of her head facing Mia. "Annoy me and you'll wish you hadn't." Mia saw her comment as a reason to do just that. She continued to watch the program until she thought of a way to harass her. She glanced back at her and watched her as she drank her beer, then glanced at the cooler, sitting on the floor beside the couch. With a mischievous smile she whisked over to the cooler, pulled it back to her recliner and rested her feet on top of it. Mayne heard the sliding sound and sat up. She saw the cooler beneath Mia's feet along with her nefarious smile. "Not even ten minutes and you're already bustin' my balls!" She knelt before her, with her hand on Mia's feet. "Comfortable? Would you like me to put a royal pillow under your feet? Perhaps you'd like that royal fuckin' foot massage now." Mia burst out, laughing and then had the audacity to nod yes, in regard to her sarcastic offer. Mayne's menacing laugh fooled her. "Let me just grab a beer princess and I'll get right on it." She stood up and opened the cooler, just wide enough to pull out one of the semi-frozen water balloons. She slammed the balloon on Mia's head, catching her off guard. Mia shrieked from the shock of the ice-cold water. She reached into the cooler to get a hand full of ice and instead grabbed one of the other balloons. Without delay, she slammed it, point blank into Mayne's chest and then held her middle finger up. "Ha! Check-mate, bitch!" "FUCK! Mia, you're so fuckin' dead!" Mayne grabbed the last water balloon and slapped it against her back. Mia howled. The chill of the air conditioner added to the cold feeling, sending shivers throughout her body.

Mia decided to go out into the yard to let the Sun warm her, and dry her clothes. As she walked away, she grinned holding her fingers up, flipping the peace sign to Mayne. Mia stopped short when Hunter entered the living room, placing his hands on the entrance border and blocked her from leaving. He was relieved to see that the noise was not the result of the negativity that he had expected to walk into. "The scream?" Mayne pointed to Mia, holding up the remnants of the water balloons. "Princess doesn't like to reap what she sow's." Mia ducked under his arm and went on her way. "You better dry everything before Enya returns." He pointed to the coffee table. "I hope the water doesn't stain the wood. Bring the fan in here and use ash to dry the watermarks on the table." "Ash. Good idea."

Mia walked in on the conversation between Gwen and Sage. "Where's Enya?" She went to the store with Faeryn." "She's gonna kill me. I was supposed to go with her." Sage chuckled. "I'm sure she understands." Mason chimed in. "My sweet Gwen. When given a choice between grocery shopping and the euphoria of passionate sex, the latter wins. I would have made the same choice." Gwen blushed. "There's no need to be embarrassed. Enya would have made the same choice." Raine carried a tray of plates and utensils over to the table next to the bar. "We all would have."

Mia dragged one of the tall bar chairs into the Sunlight and sat with the Sun facing her backside, listening and observing them. Mason leaned against the side of the house, doing the same to Mia. He watched her wavering demeanor as the others compared their experiences of past pleasures, painting glorious images with their fevered words. Mia placed her arms around the back of the chair and rested her chin, staring at the ground and tuning them out. Mason saw that she had disconnected from them and strolled over to her. He grabbed a fold out chair, sat in front of her in the same chair position and looked up into her eyes. "What's wrong, Cara Mia?" Mia stared back, with no response. "You look at me and yet your eyes are so far away. Talk to me." Mia sat upright and scanned the yard, taking it all into her memory, knowing that this scene would no longer exist, after tonight.

Enya returned to see Hunter patting the couch with towels and Mayne swishing ashes around on the table. "What happened here?" She walked over to the couch and touched it. "Why is the couch soaking wet and who wasn't using coasters?" Hunter laughed and Mayne rolled her eyes. "We got this. Never mind." "Oh yeah? Well this has your name written all over it, Mayne! What ever happened in here had better look like it didn't, when I return!" Hunter tapped Enya's shoulder as she passed. "Enya, please come back in here when you've put the groceries away. I want to catch the three of you up, before the cooking commences. It won't take long." Enya nodded. She and Faeryn went into the kitchen. Lucius was seated at the kitchen table eating and texting. "Good. Lucius, with the exception of the ribs and wings, please put the other items where they belong. I need you to marinate and boil the ribs. Call Emery in her to help you. She put the other perishable items away and returned to the living room.

"What was spilled, that called for the use of a fan?" Mayne replied, rolling her eyes once more. "Its just water. Let it go, already." Enya pursed her lips. "Mia's sitting next to Mason. Lets talk before she decides to come back in here." Hunter sat on the couch and patted it, gesturing for them to sit. "Based on Mia's pendulum notes, we know that she's planning some kind of battle. She is going to use her traits and will also be working with the Elements. She will essentially begin what she may not be able to control. As you have all read, the pendulum results did not provide the answers critical to the midst and ending of what we may be facing. What we don't know is who her target is. It could be all of us. It could be just me. We also do not know just how strong she'll be. If we anticipate her strength to be equal to ours, we will not falter. Use your best judgment and if in doubt, step back and follow my lead. No one is to put themselves, or Mia for that matter, at risk." Mayne smirked. "I can diffuse her. You know this." Hunter spoke in a stern tone. "Your arrogance will result in failure! This is not going to be like anything you've experienced with her. You need to be prepared for the unknown factor. Think before you act. Your actions could wield a negative result." Enya stood up. "I've already done what was needed, last night. I read through her notes and based what I did, on her interpretations." "Good. From this moment, forward, we need to be ready. Understood?" "Yes." Mayne nodded. Faeryn raised her hand. "Have you spoken to Aithusa? She's sort of like Mayne. No pun intended, Mayne." "Yes. I've addressed her just the same." "I'm not sure how late we will be staying tonight. If Gwen says we are leaving and nothing has happened as of then, will you need us to stay?" "We'll be fine. It's up to her. She may want to stay, however, she may reconsider if she feels that this may not be safe experience for you and the girls." "Ok. I'll speak to her. I'll respect her decision, either way." "Very good." Enya pointed into the kitchen. "I need to go make sure the kitchen is in one piece. Lucius and Emery are in there unsupervised, prepping the wings and ribs." Hunter nodded. "Carry on."

An image of the lion's Sundial merged into Mia's thoughts. She glanced at the Sun and noticed that it had already begun its afternoon decent. She saw Raine eating and suddenly felt hungry. Mason had remained in front of her, but turned to face the pool. She slid off the chair and went inside. The table was slowly becoming populated with food for later. There were two large bowls of salad; one filed with fresh cut fruit and the other with vegetables. The kitchen was humid from the boiling water. Mia peaked into the pot to see what was cooking and saw the ribs. She wasn't a fan of them so she searched through the refrigerator for something else. Enya closed the refrigerator door. "New food doesn't appear in there when you stare into it. You're letting all the cold out. If you're hungry, there's salads on the table and Lucius is outside making wings." Mia huffed and took a plate. She picked out of each bowl, choosing only what she had found appealing, took a bottle of water and went into the living room. Mayne was sitting on the recliner and Emery was sprawled across the larger couch. She sat on the floor in front of the table and ignored them. She spotted the remote and pressed the info button to see what movie was playing. Emery sucked his teeth. "Please don't change the channel. The movie is almost over." When the info displayed on the screen, she saw the title. The movie was about aliens invading the earth. She had no interest in it. She looked in her bowl and realized she had forgotten the salad dressing but didn't feel like going back into the kitchen. She ate all but the lettuce, sipped her water and then lay on the smaller couch. Emery's eyes were fixed on the movie. She watched him, recalling her first memories of him. It was on the beach with Sage and the others. His silence on that evening led her to believe that he was shy. To her, he was as shady then as is, at this moment. His steely grey-blue eyes and his quiet demeanor hid his true essence. Her second memory was just the opposite. Her anger grew at the mere thought of that horrific night. She realized that she had never retaliated for what he had done with Mayne on the day that she had stolen her bike. She felt the heated animosity grow within her. He caught her staring and returned the same stare. His attention threw her off. She didn't realize that she was staring at him so intently. He sat up and continued with the staring contest. He tossed his ponytail behind himself. "Why do you stare at me, young lady?" With a vindictive grin, Mia decided to toy with him. She crossed her hands behind her head and waited in ardor, for his opening trick. The anticipation along with his elongated hypnotizing stare and devious grin held her attention. She was primed for what ever he had up his sleeve. With an effortless wave of his finger, he changed the channel, without losing eye contact with her. "What the fuck!" Mayne shouted. He changed it back. Mia yawned on purpose. "Did that bore you?" Mia sat up, shifted closer to him and pointed behind her-self at the television's screen. The screen mirrored Zephyr's live image at the angle that Mia viewed him. He grinned. "Touché." Mayne hissed. "Would ya leave the damn TV alone!" Mia returned the screen back to the movie. She released her stare and directed it to Mayne's cooler. It slid across the carpet and stopped beside Zephyr's feet. He smiled. Just as he pulled out the bottle, its cap popped off. "Thank you, Mia." "Hey, that was my last fucking beer!" Mia grinned at her and pointed to the screen once again. Mayne enunciated the letters on the screen as they revealed themselves.

"IT SUX TO BE YOU."

Zephyr roared. Mayne paused the movie. "You're fuckin' funny, Mia!" She huffed and darted into the kitchen to get more beer. Zephyr yawned.

"You play with Magick and write in starlight. What message do you have for me, young lady?" His tone was as sinister as her response. She pointed to the television. The writing on the screen began to appear. "LETHARGIC?"

His eyes flared. He glanced at his beer and then back to her. "I see that you've upped the stakes and chosen to play hard ball with me. I know where you're going with this. I'll see you in my dreams." He kept his eyes fixed on her until he could no longer keep his eyelids open. Mia sat next to him against the arm of the couch, rested her legs across his lap and watched as he slipped into a paradoxical sleep. Mayne returned with an armful of beer. As she sat in the recliner, she noticed them sitting together. "Zephyr?" He didn't answer. "What's with him?" Mia shrugged her shoulders, pulled the pillow from behind his back and propped it behind her own head. She closed her eyes and began her meditative ritual. With steady focus, she relaxed every muscle and nerve, until she felt the familiar feeling of numbness. The deeper she slipped into her own mind, the clearer Zephyr's realm appeared to her. She spotted him sitting on a graffiti painted boulder, within the confines of a baseball field dugout. She walked toward him and leaned against the fence. "That was a clever thing that you did to my beer. You've certainly caught me off guard. I'm impressed. Had I known, I would have taken it up a notch." Mia pursed her lips. "I haven't forgotten what you did to me. That was my gentle version of fucking you, from the inside." As he recalled the event, his scowling expression changed to a perverse grin. "There's no need to be gentle with me. Bring it." He stepped in closer to her. Mia glanced over the baseball field and then waved her hand, outward. "Perfect setting for a game of hardball, Zephyr. I believe it's your move." "Would you like to pitch or swing?" He grinned, perversely, again. "Since it's your turn, I'll swing, my Witch of the West wind." Mia giggled. "Batter up, baby girl." They stood a short distance from each other, much like a standoff in an old western movie. He raised his arms above his head, remaining still for a few moments, knowing that Mia's curiosity would peak from the delay. When she saw the spiraling movement of his hands, she knew that he had chosen to work with the air. A gentle wind began to flow around her. As it grew stronger, her hair flowed into her face and distorted her vision. His ruse was an aberration to catch her off guard, just as she had done onto him. The ground's vibration skewed her equilibrium, further distorting her vision. She grasped her locks in a ponytail and saw him holding his palms against the grass. His pupils were like burning flames. Before she could react, the ground sunk in beneath her and she fell into its depths. The dirt spiraled upward. Mia lay bruised and dazed against the walls of the pit. Zephyr stood at the edge and looked down at her. The eerie, hiss of his voice sent chills through her body. "You will stay here until I am released from your delusional dream prison." He walked away leaving her to fester within the hole she had dug herself into. Mia panicked. She realized that she hadn't put enough thought into the length of time that her Magick would keep him in sleep mode. She stared at the Sun's receding timeline against the pit's wall. Anxiety set in because she knew it wouldn't be long before the Full Moon's ascent and she needed to be present in realm of waking state before nightfall. Unfamiliar with his realm, the long silence that that surrounded her only added to her anxiety. The faint sound of a panting animal emanated from above. As it grew near, she recognized it and smiled, releasing a faint sigh of relief. The lion hovered over the pit's opening and stared down at her. He held his paw up, gesturing for her to fight. She held her hands up, desperately reaching for him. Her confused expression was obvious to him. He extended his paw and with swift movement he waved, inward. A gust of frigid air flowed into the pit, chilling her to the bone and causing her teeth to chatter. She hugged herself to keep warm until the chill faded. He jolted his paws upward and then with his claws extended, he lowered them to the ground and dug them into the dirt. Dark clouds eclipsed the Sun, emitting bolts of violent lightning across the sky. The ear-piercing sound of thunder followed its lead, catching Mia off guard. She jolted like a terrified cat. The hissing, heavy downpour soaked her. She looked up at him with tear filled eyes wondering why he would want to drown her. He extended his paw inward, once again, reminding her of the frigid blast of air and then scratched the side of the pit's walls. She recalled one of her recent acts of Magick and knew what to do. It was time to change the dream. She closed her eyes and changed the rain to snow. When she felt the frozen flakes touching her face she opened her eyes.

The rapid accumulation mirrored the speed of the heavy down pouring rain, enabling her to climb out of the pit. When she was in arms reach of the lion, he grabbed her arm and pulled her out. She cried tears of joy and hugged him as tightly as she did, when she hugged Sebastian. Although she was free from the confines of the pit, she was still not free of Zephyr's realm. The lion released her. He locked eyes with her to hold her attention. She watched his face, noticing that his lips were slowly parting and revealing his fangs. He took a deep breath and released a deafening roar. Mia froze, staring into his mouth. The sound resonated through both realms.

Mia fell off of the couch, panting in a cold sweat. She turned to see if Zephyr was still on the couch. He was already sitting up with his arms behind his head, staring at her and grinning. "Riveting, Mia!" Mia said nothing to him, glanced at Mayne and left the room.

The downstairs restroom was occupied. She ran upstairs to Mayne's room to use hers. The clock on the bathroom wall displayed four-twenty PM. The restlessness set in. She held her forehead in her hands and whispered to herself. *"Everything changes in a few hours. Everything."* She thought about how simple her life had been, prior to the fair. She pictured that very moment within her mind, when the Blue Jay had landed on her finger and wondered how she could have been able to foretell that the spiraling road ahead, would lead up to this day. It had all began with that particular Blue Jay, veiled as the High Priestess. She couldn't fathom any possible reason to why this woman led her through this bizarre labyrinth. She flushed the toilet, washed her hands and face, then threw herself onto Mayne's bed to meditate and clear her mind of her defaulted, what-if thought pattern.

Zephyr went into the kitchen to get his cigarettes. He shook the pack and saw that there were two remaining. "I'm going to the store. Does anyone need anything?" He dangled his bike keys. Enya realized that she had forgotten to get ice for the coolers. "Take Hunter's truck and get a few sleeves of ice." "Sure." Hunter tossed his keys to him. "Hey, what was that sudden nap all about?" Zephyr detailed the events that lead up to their shared nap. "I've kept her static until I was able to decipher the reversal of her adorable little enchantment. When I had realized what her intentions were, I decided it would be best to contain her, rather than giving her free reign to manipulate my dreams." In jest, Hunter pointed to his temple. "Kidneys." Zephyr laughed and peeked into the yard. "Where is she?" "She's upstairs using the bathroom. This one was occupied." He pointed behind himself. "Where's Lucius?" " He's in the yard, cooking." "Good. I'm hungry."

Mia wandered to the end of the hall, opened the window and peered outside. The house resided on a dead end street and the wooded area had a dirt road that lead to the beach. She looked down and saw the cars, bikes and trucks, belonging to those within the house. When she spotted Gwen's truck, she realized that the may be leaving soon and wanted them to stay long enough to witness the events to come. She shut the window and slipped into Enya's room. She had a vague memory of a spell that Enya had done onto her and searched around the room for those items. They were no longer on the table. She opened the nightstand and found the jar of honey and unscrewed the top. At the bottom of the jar was a small piece of paper. She stuck a pencil in and scooped it out. After gently swiping off the excess honey, she saw that it was a skewed picture of her own face. Her eyes widened. She remembered that Enya had also made the bracelet for her on that very night as well and was now aware of some of things that she had done to keep her bound to the property. She searched through her drawers and closet for a photo album. At the top of the closet was an old shoebox. She pulled up a chair to reach for it and sat on the floor rummaging through it until she had found a photo of each person. One by one, she cut their faces out and placed them into the jar, whispering words to bind them until she saw fit to release them. She returned the box on the closet shelf and dragged the chair back to where she had found it. She returned the honey jar to where Enya had left it so that it would be hidden in plain sight.

She returned to the window to ensure that Gwen had not left. She opened it and peered outside once again and heard the sound of a loud truck in the distance. Moments later, she saw Hunters truck pulling up and parking just below her window. Zephyr stepped out, spotted her and looked up. "Don't jump. Mia. You don't know how to fly." She flipped him the finger and closed the window. When she turned to face the stairway, she saw Aithusa standing at the doorway of her room with her hands perched against either side of the doorframe, holding a speculative look. Mia leaned against the wall, across from her and returned the stare. Aithusa gently slid her hands down the door's frame and paced towards her. "Whatcha doin' baby?" Mia's poker face revealed nothing to her. She placed her palms against the wall, above Mia's shoulders and whispered in her ear. "I saw you walking out of Enya's room." She felt Mia's pockets in an inappropriate manner. Mia grasped her shirt, slammed her against the wall and pinned her hands above her head. Aithusa's perverse laugh irked her. "If you didn't take anything, then what were you doing in there, Mia?" Mia retracted her arm and lunged her fist at Aithusa's face, stopping within an inch of her jaw. Aithusa flinched, her evil laugh, playing down Mia's physical threat. With a sadistic stare, Mia released her and walked downstairs. When Mia realized that Aithusa was following behind her, she walked faster. Aithusa followed suit. Midway down the stairs, Mia grasped the bannisters and stopped short, causing Aithusa to bump into her. Mia turned to face her and pierced her eyes with hers. She looked up at the chandelier and made the lights flicker. Aithusa smiled. "I'm not afraid of you, Mia." Mia replied in a wicked tone. "You should be."

Mia walked into the living room, taking account of each person's presence on the ground floor. She saw Mayne, stretched out on the couch and Emery doing the same on the recliner. She turned to see Aithusa and walked around her. Upon entering the kitchen she saw Enya, Gwen and Faeryn sitting at the table. She walked past them, grabbed a mason jar from the counter, slid the screen door open and browsed the occupancy of the yard before stepping outside. Hunter was sitting at the bar directly across from the kitchens entrance. Standing next to him were Zephyr and Ceridwen. Lucius was finishing up at the barbeque and the girls were sitting at the other end of the bar. Everyone stared at her. Enya broke the silence when she, Gwen and

Faeryn made a beeline to the table, with the food. Everyone flocked, except for Hunter. He and Mia remained still with eyes deadlocked on one another. Mia walked to the edge of the pool, glanced at the sky and then back at him. Feeling a bit impish, she walked over to the table, grabbed a plate and rudely cut the line. She returned to the far end of the pool, placed the jar beside herself and sat with her feet in the water, picking off of her plate. Hunter remained in his seat, analyzing her every move. "Did anyone call Mayne?" Enya called out to her through the screen door. "Mayne! Food!"

Mia waited for everyone to be seated before testing the waters, so to speak, with her opening act. Her intentions were not meant to incite negativity, but to simply set the stage. She watched them nonchalantly, while maintaining her peripheral view of Hunter and his undivided attention on her. A cool breeze wafted over her. She closed her eyes and absorbed it, as if it were the queue of beginning orchestral notes for an opening scene. She glanced at the sky once more, noticing the prismatic sunset. It had already passed the peak of the house and the yard was now shaded. Mia raised her right hand, and waited for her spirit animals to fill the void between her palm and the cement. A cat slipped underneath the fence and strutted towards her with the swagger of a panther. It took its place under her hand, beside her. The caw of a Blue Jay echoed in the distance. She lifted her left hand and extended her index finger. It landed and took its place on her shoulder. All eating and conversations ceased amongst everyone. They watched in awe. Ceridwen and Faeryn looked at each other, recalling the Blue Jay at the fair, on the first day that they had found her. Mia picked up the jar and lowered it into the water. Then Hunter watched her lift it out of the water and place it beside herself. Sitting inside the jar, was a green frog. There was a growling sound just outside the beachside gate. Mia lifted her left hand. The wolf propelled itself over the fence and took its place under her hand. In anticipation, Mia took note of those who had appeared in her dreams in another form and waited for these spirit animals to take their devout places before her. Hunter rose from is chair and Mayne walked over to him and stood on his left side. Aithusa stood on his right side and Enya sat on the edge of chair, behind him. Mia looked over to those at the bar and grinned, pleased with the collective vehemence reflected in their eyes.

She knew that Hunter was on edge. She stared at the pool water, taking in a panoramic image of it into her memory and then closed her eyes. She focused on the scents that surrounded her and connected her spirit with the Element of Water and Air, as well as the presence of the Cat, Blue Jay and wolf. The animals remained as still and silent as the water in the pool. Mia whispered to herself. *"Still waters run deep."* She extended her arms forward, hovering her hands over the pool water. The water began to move deosil/ clockwise. The rippling sounds of the Water increased. Its progressive speed caused the water to seep over the pool's barrier, creating a strong circular current that evolved into a whirlpool. She felt the old familiar feeling of Hunter's spiritual pull, sensing that he was penetrating her thoughts. This time, she chose to allow him to enter her mind. Aware of his presence, she waited for him to communicate with her while keeping her minds eye, focused on the spiraling water. His words were weaved with the spectral sound of his voice. "What are your intentions, Mia?" She responded in the same esoteric tone. "All will be revealed." "These pieces of Magick that you continue to use are just that, pieces. There is a bigger picture that has yet to present itself to you." Mia's response fed off of his words. "…And all these pieces will fall to my wish." Mia's eyes opened when she felt him release her. The look within her eyes vexed him. He walked towards her, remaining vigilant in his approach. She returned her attention to the whirlpool, closed her eyes and extended her arms over the water, once again. Her hands swayed, wielding the water into the form that she chose to bring into extant. The water rushed inward, emitting the mighty sounds of raging rapids. The upsurge formed into a Phoenix. With her hands on the wolf and cat, she watched as it developed into the turbulent splendor, depicted from her intentions. She perused the faces of all those surrounding her, taking pleasure in their speechless awe. The lighting in the yard flickered and dimmed, transitioning its hues from white into red and illuminating the figure in perfect light. Hunter was silent within his speculative thoughts, glancing back and forth between Mia and her Phoenix.

"Remarkable, Mia." He walked to the opposite end of the pool and her Phoenix spiraled to follow him. Its mouth opened and spewed streams of red and white illuminated water onto him to simulate a fiery breath. He faced her Phoenix and then stared into the water below it. A dark figure emerged, rising within the dimensions of her Phoenix. The torrent black water surged downward over its red and white wings, dissipating her Phoenix into the pool and revealing the darkest of fire dragons. It lowered its head towards her and Mia remained still, staring into the dragon's red eyes with steadfast hostility. "I know this effigy is you. It would be in your best interest to step up your game, Sorcerer." Her sharp sarcasm was noted. With eyes locked on one another, they remained in an eerie never-ending reticence. The unearthly tension between them was ghastly. Enya, Mayne and Aithusa stepped out from behind him to get a closer look, enthralled in the anticipation of Mia's next course of action and eager to see Mia unleash her Magick traits. Mia turned her attention to the bar. The ear-piercing buzz of the speakers caught everyone off guard. When she held their undivided attention, the speakers transmitting a specific melody of her choice.

♪...my freedom I hold dear...♪

As the music played, Mia knelt, petting the wolf and cat. She stared into thier eyes, sending each of them a telepathic message and then kissed them. When the song had ended, she looked directly at Hunter and chose another tune.

♪...flames from the dragons of darkness...♪

The songs lyrics depicted what was to follow. When the song ended, she chose no more. The radio volume lowered and it resumed regular programming. Hunter slid his hands into his pockets. "Mia. I grow weary of your elementary bullshit." Mia grinned. "Do I bore you, Sorcerer?" His eyes flared. Gwen hissed in astonishment. "Is she certified?" Lucius howled. "Mia! You're fucking audacious!" Hunter shouted across the pool. His deep spectral voice instilled fear in everyone but Mia. "Sorcerer?" His derisive laugh, setting the tone for his vicious response. "Disrespect me once more and your brazen little ass will not survive the night! Let this be your final warning!" Mia grinned, knowing that she had struck just the right nerve to arouse his fury. She glanced at the sky, noticing the darkness taking over as the Sun's last glimpse of light sunk into the horizon. The stars took their rightful place in the midnight blue sky, enhancing the Full Moon like curtains drawn on a stage, indicating the start of a main attraction. With persuasive intent, she replied, addressing Hunter with the ultimate derogatory title to assure that he would be provoked to the edge of vehemence. "Your threats, Warlock, they mean nothing to me."

Lucius' jaw dropped, astounded by her insolence. With eyes of fire, Enya rushed beside Hunter and screamed at her. "MIA!" Hunter extended his arm to catch and hold her back. His despicable laugh was a sure sign of his imminent wrath. "Warlock." He uttered. He stood with his hands behind his back and took a deep breath. Mia knew that he was impeccable at maintaining an even-tempered disposition, under any level of pressure. She also knew that the more placid his demeanor, the more enraged he was. His dark dragon plummeted into the pool with a wave of his hand. He replied with malicious intent. "I'm going to briefly discuss the word, Dare, in regard to the Pyramid. In our many encounters, I have shown you many sides of me. You have shown your knowledge of; Know, Will and Silent. Dare, is the entity that you have only experienced in low-grade practice. I will show you the true meaning of Dare, with which you challenge me. Every facet of myself will be revealed to you, in one true form. There will be no turning back. If your strength endures and your mind survives this, then I will silence you." Mia listened intently; taking heed to his every word, however, her perception interpreted his intention of these words to be nothing more than a mere intimidation tactic. She knew that he had chosen these words to play on her anxiety affliction. She had no fear of the unknown. The pendulum reinforced this. The what-if perception no longer played a role in her life.

"You talk too much. Perhaps I should Silence you."

Although short-lived, the reticence was unnerving.

The Blue Jay blared its aggressive shriek and soared onto the peak of roof, facing the beach. The cat growled and hissed, revealing its fangs. The energy from its roused spirit caused its blue eyes to glow. It climbed the tree behind her and perched itself on a branch facing the beach.

A germane tune played on the radio. It's lyrics were a telltale sign that the time had come to prove her worth.

♪*...And it's time you should be going*♪

Gwen tapped the bar table. "Girls! Get your things. We're leaving now." With what she had just witnessed she felt that the girls were not ready to experience what may lie ahead. She was most concerned with Aithusa, given her wild-child demeanor. Just as they rose from their chairs, Mia raised her arm and pointed at them. "NO ONE LEAVES!" Mia's will, forced them back into their seats.

"It begins now!" Hunter demanded, spiraling his index finger, gesturing for the others to follow him inside. Mia remained, watching them flow into the house and curious as to why they would suddenly leave her there, unattended. Within minutes, they returned to the yard wearing their cloaks, just as they had at the restaurant. With her hand still on the wolf, Mia stood and faced them. The wolf growled, revealing its fangs, its eyes, raging and fixed on Hunter. Mia and the wolf looked at the Moon. The wolf's prophetic howl signified to Mia that it was time to begin. Mia turned to face the locked gate, leading to the beach. With a swift sway of her hand, the gate's hinges arched, its frame contorted and opened a pathway wide enough for her and the wolf to walk through. She freely walked out of the yard, unchained to its domain. The wolf followed, beside her. She stood at the edge of the beach's' cement walkway and knelt before the wolf. She hugged the wolf and kissed its forehead, then proceeded onto the sand. Mia looked at the Moon and stared into its vibrant white light. She stood with her feet apart and raised her arms above her head. Her eyes were filled with her glow. She allowed herself to become one, with her Moon. A body of brisk cold air encircled her. As she allowed the Goddess fill her, she felt a strong tingly sensation in her hands that traveled throughout her body. She knew that she was not alone. She summoned the attendance of Elements. The gentle cool wind spiraled around her, making her aware of its presence. She raised her arms once again to allow the Element, Air to encompass her. The high tide enhanced the tempest wrath of the oceans crashing waves. She turned to face the most powerful version of the Element, Water, inhaled, taking in its rich, salty scent. Her toes wiggled in the soft grains of sand, physically reconnecting herself with the Element, Earth. A few feet away, were a few dry-rotted logs. She closed her eyes and filled her thoughts with spirited images, recapturing the true emotion of moments when the rage she had felt, exuded from her body. She opened her eyes and pointed at the driftwood. The torrid memories fed into her quiescent anxiety, slowly erupting into a controlled rapture of Fire and completing the collective presence of the four Elements.

CHAPTER 24

ONE BY ONE

Hunter stood at the edge of the sand barrier beside the wolf, assessing all that Mia had induced. He recalled the words of warning from the High Priestess. Her words were transpiring, verbatim. Mason, Zephyr and Mayne approached Hunter. They watched his eyes as he stood in silence, knowing that his reticence had always been the prerequisite to his next course of action. Mason placed his hand on Hunters shoulder and glanced at the unflinching wolf. "Why do you stand beside the wolf?" "For the same reason that the wolf remains beside me. We are opposing magnets with the same allegiance." "She's putting on quite a show for us." "This is not a show. She's summoning, requesting and inviting. To her, all the pieces appear to be falling to her wish." Mayne grew inpatient. "What are we waiting here for?" "We wait for her to draw the starting line. Where are the others?" Zephyr turned to look. "Enya, Emery and Lucius are a few feet behind us and the rest stand behind them."

Mia stood in front of the fire, facing them. The sparks of crackling embers shot through the air behind her. Defined by the glow of the pyre, her silhouette defining her repressed rebel yell. She took several paces towards them and stopped, studying their faces. "You look at me in awe, yet each one of you are the collective reason as to why we stand here." She paused, taking a panoramic view of their facial expressions. "Your curiosity and anticipation seem to battle one another." Hunter grinned. "I admire your self confidence, Mia, however, your eloquence delays the inevitable. I will break you." "Sorcerer, You can't break me. None of you can. In fact, the only thing that you and your coven of freaks have managed to break is the Rede. When you write your story in starlight, you leave your version vulnerable to change. Tonight, I will change your story. In the end, it is I, who will be sitting on your precious throne. I am Karma."

She returned to the pyre and held her arms at her sides. "This Moon is titled Hunters Moon. I'm changing it. It's mine." She raised her arms to the Moon. The wolf howled. Its vociferous howl frightened Ceridwen and Faeryn. Aithusa and Raine laughed at them and moved a few feet closer to beach. Mia chanted into the night sky, requesting the presence of the Winds and summoning the presence of storm clouds. Lightning flickered in the distance, chasing the evolving thunderous clouds, which were in turn, chasing the wind. With her finger pointed toward the sky, she wrote Ceridwen and Faeryn's name in starlight. She then, pointed at them. "Come forth." Gwen stood in front of them and commanded that they return to the house at once. As the girls ran, Gwen darted over to Aithusa. Mia pointed once more. A bolt of lightning struck just a few feet before Gwen. Its energy thrust her into the tufts of beach grass. Sage and Enya ran over to her. Aithusa's name reflected against the sky with the most enticing words. *Come play, Aithusa.* It didn't take any further coaxing on her part, since she had been waiting for this moment all along. Hunter reached out and blocked her. Aithusa shouted. "No!" She struggled to push his arm out of her way. "I got this, Hunter! You and Gwen are always holding me back. I'm not a damn eggshell. I can take whatever she dishes out. You know this!" He grasped her wrist. "You have only merely toyed with her. That's the extent of your experience. If a precarious situation becomes evident, I will intervene. Understood?" "Yes... yes!" Filled with elation, Aithusa walked onto the sand, circling Mia like a starved panther. She found it peculiar that Mia didn't spiral to follow her. As Aithusa returned to face her, Mia slid her hand around her waist and held her body, flush against her side, to face the bonfire together. She slid her hand down Aithusa's arm and cupped her hand. She enunciated her words in a spectral tone. "Do you remember the candle flame, my sweet white dragon?" Mia guided her hand to mirror hers and pointed at the flames, luring and angling them outward and brushing their index fingers in trice. Mia led their hands in a pivoted motion, tracing a three-foot ring of fire to encircle them. "Do you remember my cone? Bring this one down with the correct intentions and I'll set you free." Mia knew that the key to her success was to recall the fluctuating emotion from that night and direct that negativity into the most benevolent outcome. Nevertheless, she would give her the benefit of the doubt, if she failed. Her sole intention was to show her the meaning of *"Harm None"*. If Aithusa used negativity, she would fail. Aithusa grinned. Mia read the excitation within her eyes. "Mia, if you set me free, I will not return the favor." "Do as you Will. Know that the cone will not come down until you see as I do." The inferno's waves of heat were felt by all that stood along the edge of the sand barrier. Within the circle, it remained cool. Gwen limped over to Hunter, screaming in a panicked voice. "She's in there with her! Why did you let her go?" "I am watching, Gwen. She knows that I have her back." "What is she doing?" "She is testing her limits with the same challenges that Aithusa had used on her." "What challenges?" "Speak to Enya."

The wind revolved around the outskirts of the unyielding flames, veering and swaying with its momentum. Aithusa moved close to Mia, slid her hands through Mia's hair, grasping the sides of her head and whispered into her ear. "I will bury you." The lightning streaked across the sky, emitting a boisterous, cracking sound. Mia stared into the depths of her eyes. "You will fail." Mia's words angered and challenged her. Aithusa smirked. "You seem so sure of yourself. Do tell." "Because there are always two paths before you and you always seem to choose the wrong one. Prove me wrong. Choose to see this through my eyes. When your perception changes, so will your results." "I choose the road that excites me. It always leads to my desired results." Her insidious words disheartened Mia. Aithusa took a step back and raised her arms. "This will be elementary, Mia." With her palms held vertically, she spiraled slowly, lifting the sand into the air. She lowered her arms and the wall of flames contorted, enabling those outside the circle to see them. The fire pulsated on an angle, shooting its flames both inward and outward within the circle. Mia watched the sand brushing around it. Mia raised her arms slowly, guiding the fire to raise itself. She watched as the isometric pressure began to take a toll on Aithusa. She struggled to snuff out the fire into the sand but the flames would bend no further. Mia stepped closer to her and clutched her face. "Your time is up." With a sway of her hand, Mia snuffed the circling inferno. The smoke and ash supervened in the path of the diminishing wind. She pointed at Aithusa's face and then lowered her finger to the ground. Aithusa became unstable and collapsed at Mia's feet, crying tears of frustrated defeat. "The flames that I've created fed from you, Aithusa. They gave back the same emotion that you had fed into them. Negative begets negative." She held a fixed stare on her and pointed to where Hunter and Gwen stood, waiting for her in angst. "You're dismissed."

She perused the lot of them, for her next adversary. Hunter slipped his hood over his head. Emery, Enya, Lucius, Zephyr and Mayne followed suite. Mia grinned. "Your cloaks intimidated me at the restaurant. I'll give you that. As for now, they give you no power over me, however, if I make it drizzle, at least your hair will be protected." Lucius held his middle finger up to her. Mia laughed. "Do you wish to be next' Lucius?" "Oh, I'm ready, little lamb!" "As you wish. By the way, I was looking forward to a match with both Ceridwen and Faeryn at the same time. Do they hide in the house?" No one answered. "That's ok. I forgive them. After all, they only followed the orders of your Sorcerer." With a brassy grin, she looked directly at Hunter. She pointed to him and blared her words. "I take orders from no one! I follow no one! I can fly alone and I can fight alone!"

Lucius valiantly approached her, speaking as he walked. "You better bring it, little lamb, cause' I'm not holdin' back." The lightning streaked across the sky. She recalled the prerequisite to her broken finger and quickly pointed the very same finger to the lightning, directing it to the ground a few feet before him. The loud humming sound from the bolt's unyielding current caused his heart skip a beat. He tried to run from it but the subliminal blindness cause him to trip and fall. Emery ran to his aid. She looked at both Hunter and Mason with a Mona Lisa smile, knowing that they had forbade her to point.

With an alluring smile, she set her sights on Zephyr. "Come forth, Witch of the West wind." Zephyr held his arms out as he approached, as if he had intended to hug her. "I thought you had forgotten about me." "Why no, Zephyr. We play well together." The lightning splintered, striking its vigorous and jagged current into the ocean behind her. She pointed behind herself and lashed forward. The lightning bolt followed her will, striking the ground behind Zephyr, and continuing its scorched circular path around him. He looked down at the charred sand that surrounded him. "Lightning again, Mia? Have you no other tricks?" Mia smiled. "I do." With a twisted wave, Mia swayed her left hand and whispered words to summon the presence of the West wind. The clouds swiftly converged. The sounds of the progressive gusts howled through its black winds, whipping across the beach and generating lightning strikes across the sky. Within the seconds that followed, the thunder crashed with such mighty force that is vibration resonated with the parallel strength of an earthquake. The sand imploded where Zephyr stood, leaving a deep, wide crater. Mia walked to edge and peered into its depth to see Zephyr lying dazed, within the darkness of the pit. She spoke to him in a hostile tone. "I should bury you." Hunter approached and spoke with gritted teeth. "You've gone too far!" Mia looked at him and replied in a vengeful tone. "I haven't even begun, Sorcerer." She peered into the pit, staring at Zephyr with merciless animosity. "This time, you will stay here until I choose to release you."

With the exception of Hunter, those that remained, stood above the pit, quietly debating on how to safely extract him. With keen focus, Hunter watched Mia pacing behind them, stopping only to choose her next opponent. She slid her hand into Enya's hand and whispered into her ear. "Come, my sister of the Moon." Enya turned to face her with eyes as steely as Mayne's were on the day she had found her at Gwen's bar with her bike. With vengeful grip, Enya clutched Mia's hand and yanked her to Mia's makeshift, ground zero. When Mayne saw Enya with Mia, she shouted in a fit of rage. "If my sister doesn't bury you, I will!" Mia looked back at her, smiled and replied in an arrogant tone. "Your turn will come soon."

Enya threw Mia's hand aside and grabbed her jaw. "I have had enough of your shit! How dare you even consider challenging the likes of me! My Magick will always trump yours. You had better be able to take what you dish out, sweetheart, because I intend to return it, times three!" She released her jaw and shoved her backward. Mia smirked. "Oh, Enya. You can't. But don't be afraid. My intention is not to harm you." "Oh, I can't? Why is that?" "I'll show you." The lightning crashed across the sky once again. To Mia, the veined, incandescent streaks were the collective fingers of all Deities. The distinct sweet aroma of ozone caressed her senses. She raised her arms, accepting the gift of energy from the lightning and thunder's pulsing magnetic surge. Its spellbinding drumfire seduced her, keeping her focused and primed. The gale winds and raw scent stimulated every nerve of her body. Mia swung forward with her palms facing Enya and the wind followed her directive, seizing Enya and knocking her off of her feet. Enya covered her face to block the sand from going into her eyes. She spiraled around in an attempt to counteract Mia's action. When she pushed her palms outward, nothing happened. Mia observed Enya's continuous, failed attempts, never once lessening the winds strength. Enya's endurance grew weak. She stood helpless, with her back to the wind, unable to fight her. Mia eased her hands downward and the wind ceased. She walked over to Enya and extended her hand to lift her. "Déjà vu, Enya?" Enya gazed up at her. "Déjà vu what?" "I recall being in this very same predicament with you at Gwen's bar, however, the roles were reversed." "Yeah...? Touché' bitch!" "Enya. This situation hasn't even come close to a Touché' yet. But it will." Bewildered and out of sorts, Enya stood on her own. "Oh, will it, now? What novice, bullshit Magick did you do to me?" Mia reached into her pocket and pulled out the three black cords from the spell-weaved bracelet that Enya had put on her wrist. "Do you remember these cords?" Her eyes widened. "You little bitch! You undid my spell! So, this is how you were able to leave the property!" "Freudian slip, Enya? Perhaps you meant, Witch, not bitch. Well with that said, I suggest you go to your bedroom. Under your pillow is a poppet. If your Magick trumps mine, then you'll be able to undo what I have done. Now, it's Touché'." Enya grabbed Mia's arm. "Did you bind me?" Mia pointed to the house in reticence and Enya pursed her lips. "This is far from over, sweetheart!"

As Enya walked away, Mia peered over to her remaining opponents. Mayne's stance clearly indicated that she wanted to be next. "What the fuck did you do to my sister?" "Her Magick has been suspended, for the interim. She needs to learn that she should not cast spells on others without their knowledge, unless of course, the intention is for healing or protection." "How the fuck did you bind her?" Mia held her hand up to her face. "You should know better than to ask that of me. The Pyramid. "Fuck your Pyramid!" Mayne slapped Mia's hand and stood face to face with her. "I'm next, princess!" A tear ran down Mia's cheek. "Patience, Mayne. I'm familiar with your fury and I intend to tame it, tonight. It will be worth the wait." Mia stared at her, quickly switching her temperament to that of mischievous intent when she spotted Mason standing beside Mayne. She maintained eye contact with him as she paced backward to return to her sacred fighting ground. Her deceitful smile and open arms easily enticed Mason's attention. With his alluring grin, he walked to her. "Cara Mia. I know that you're up to no good. It has been a long time since you've welcomed me with opened arms." "That's just it, Mason. Lets forget about all that negativity that we shared and focus only on the memories of our beginning." She slipped her arms around his waist and rested her head upon his chest. "Mason, please say that you still see the Moon in my eyes." She lifted her head. Her eyes slowly followed the trail of the opened buttons on his shirt. She grazed her fingers along his chest and gazed into his eyes. "Mason, do you still cherish that night on the beach?" The sincerity in her voice captivated him. He slipped his hands around her waist. "Yes I do, Mia, to both of your questions, however I remain skeptical to the reason behind them. What Magick will you be challenging me with?"

She released him, stepped back and pouted. "How can you say that to me, Mason?" Even now, his seductive green eyes consumed her. "How can I not, given the current situation. Tell me what you want." "What I want is for us to walk away from this situation and pick up where we left off. I want that night again, Mason. You said that you would protect me. Before you took me into your arms that night, you had asked if I was sure. Are you no longer sure?" The crocodile tears trickled down her cheeks. His bewitching green eyes pierced her soul, bringing to mind the bittersweet memories they had shared. If she didn't know better, he would have captivated her once again, with his beguiling charm. "Take my hand, Mia." He pulled her close to him and embraced her. His inviting essence nearly threw her off of her intended course. His scent was so alluring and nearly impossible for her to resist. She nudged him toward the shore with gentle persuasion and seductive body language. "Please, let's go." He smiled. The dominion that she now held over him was evident. She knew that he had to some extent, fallen victim to her melancholic symphony of words. When they arrived at the shoreline, she let him lead. His grip on her hand was tight. She kicked her sneakers off to walk barefoot in the flowing waves. "How far do you want to go, Mia?" She stopped in her tracks and stared into his eyes. "As far as you're willing to take me." Her sincerity hid her dark deception. He took a deep breath and searched within her eyes, intrigued by her double meaning. Mia stopped when the distance from the others, was sufficient. She stood before him and stuttered her words. "Take me... there, as you did that night. This time, it ends different." "Different?" "Without your deception, Mason." When he saw her pouted lips, he rushed in on her, grasped her face and kissed her fiercely. Caught off guard, she struggled to keep her focus. Her mind was on track, but her body's reaction to his impassioned touch and otherworldly aura communicated, otherwise. Although a part of her wanted him, she knew that she had to fight this urge. There was no turning back. She needed to remain adamant with her intention. He grabbed her backside, reining her in against his body. His unbridled fire challenged her endurance. She pulled off his shirt and pressed her body against his. His kisses were relentless and unyielding. It was all she could do to try to breath. She had to force herself to stop reacting to his bewitching charms. Her feelings of empathy were quickly replaced with apathy. Her every move became automated, following his lead and feeding into his lustful hunger with parallel intent. He eased her down onto the sand and only stopped kissing her for the seconds that it took to pull her shirt over her head. For her, his heated passion was a battle within itself. He nudged her onto her back, straddled over her and pinned her hands beside her head. His sensual green eyes were inches from hers. She could feel the vibrations of his heart pounding against her chest. She knew that she couldn't control his fiery Element. Her intentions were to ignite, feed and guide his fire. Then she would follow through with the rest of her plan. "Mia amore... I assure you that I wont hold back this time." His sensual voice, tempting her, bending her will to fight him. Her alluring smile aroused and encouraged him. She chose her kindled words, wisely. "Neither will I, Mason." She grasped his arms and quickly jerked her body to throw him off balance and overthrow him. Her fingers, tightly entwined into his dark, silken locks, along with her iniquitous expression, gave her a feeling of empowerment. "I'm driving this time, Mason." The Moonlight reflected his teeth-gritted grin. He growled at her like a starved wolf revealing its fangs. "Oh, are you, now?" With her inhibitions in close check, she began to release her Magick. The fervency in her kiss was as potent as the vengeful ferocity that filled her heart. The sand beneath him shifted imperceptibly, beneath the lower half of his body. He slid his hands onto her backside and wrapped his legs around hers, struggling to push her pants off of her derriere. When Mia felt the sand shifting faster, she kicked her legs out of his clutch and planted her knees on the stable sand on either side of him. By the time he noticed, Mia had sprung upward. She stood above him and watched as he sunk. The pressured hold that the sand held against his body was unyielding. When the grains ceased its movement, his head and neck were all that remained above ground. She would do no harm to him however her sole, malicious intention was to seduce, betray and instill fear in him, just as he had done onto her. His vicious expression contradicted his soft but threatening, words. "WHEN...I emerge from this...YOU will know my full wrath. There will be no mercy! You will reel from the pain." She stepped out of his direct vision to reveal the ocean's rising tide. "Mason, you are hardly in a position to threaten me. However, as justifiable your words may seem to you, know that this is how I felt when you betrayed me. "Enjoy the view, Mason. The tide is rolling in." She knelt down to stare at his face, touched his cheek and whispered her sweet words of revenge. "Mason, I see the Moon in your eyes." She laughed and strolled back to her makeshift battleground, where Mayne and Hunter impatiently awaited her return.

Mia's brazen grin infuriated them. Hunter stepped in and stood face to face with her, looked down into her eyes and spoke in a vicious tone. "Where is my brother?" She smiled at him. "He is safe and will remain that way." Her attention turned to Mayne. "It's time for you to ride with me." Mia turned, gesturing for her to follow, "Oh Yeah? Lets do this, princess!" Mayne clutched the back of Mia's neck. Mia shouted. "Get your hand off of me NOW or my plans for you will change!" Mayne swung her around to face her and clutched Mia's shirt. "I don't give a single fuck about your plans!" Mia gently pulled Mayne's hands off of her shirt. "It's imperative that you banish your negativity right now." Mia stood before her, reflecting the serenity that she longed to see in Mayne's spirit. "What the fuck is your malfunction?" Mia pursed her lips and spoke softly. "Please stop cursing." Mayne became antsy. "Aren't you gonna fight me with your princess Magick?" "Stop mocking me." She stood before her, searching within Mayne's eyes, sensing and feeling her every emotion as she always did, before. This was the one trait that she some-times hated. Feeling what others felt when they spoke to her had always taken a toll on her heart. She knew that her anxiety was partially derived from this empathic trait. "Mia why are you looking at me like this? Tell me what you want." "I did. Did I stutter? I said you ride with me this time." Mia walked to the opposite side of the pyre and returned, carrying with a long wooden post with both hands. Mayne laughed, stepping backward with her hands in a defensive position. "So your princess trick is to beat me with a stick?" Mia took a deep breath and sighed. "What part of my sentence did you not un-derstand?" Mia held the pole up to the Moon with both hands and chanted words of change to the Winds. Mayne watched her bury the pole into the sand. When Mia gazed up at her, Mayne's jaw dropped. Mia's pupils were a lucent, blue. She pulled the pole from the sand revealing its significant transition. Mayne laughed so hard. "What are you going to do...sweep the beach?" Mia's stone cold stare was a clear indication to Mayne that she wasn't in the mood for her jokes. Mayne simmered her laugh. "What?...Ok. Talk to me, princess. What's with the broom?" Mia repeated herself, once again. "You ride with me, now. Get on." Mia placed the broom between her legs and waited for her to get on. Mayne struggled to hold back her laughter. "Mia, are you fucking kidding me with this shit? You can't fly." Mia refused to let her dispiriting words avert her focus. "Shut up. Get on. Believe in me for once in your life." Hunter had been watching. When he saw that Mayne was about to saddle herself onto Mia's broom, his deep, wicked laughter emanated his own dissuading opinion of Mia's ability. Mayne pursed her lips and held up her middle finger. Mia stared into the midnight blue sky. The spellbinding brilliance of the Full Moon was rapturous. "You may want to hold onto my waist." A brisk gust of wind blew against their backs, blowing the sand into the air. When Mayne opened her eyes, they were airborne. She reeled in her senses, astonished by the unforeseen strength of Mia's craft and will. It nearly took her breath away. The view of ocean from above, especially at night and under a Full Moon was entrancing. Its glistening waves enhanced its veiled surface. Mayne held on tightly to Mia's waist. They soared a few feet above the ocean onto a small craft, moored a few miles out. Their sudden decent caught Mayne off guard and jogged her equilibrium. They landed, stern-side and the rough landing teetered the boat. "How did you do this?" "The wind, she carries me and guides me." Mia glanced at the Moon. "So am I walking the plank to my demise? Is this how you fight me?" "I'm not fighting you, Mayne. I'm protecting you." "From what?" "Yourself. I'm fighting Hunter next. I don't want your actions to have any affect on the outcome. I can't be distracted." "Mia, how do you expect to fight Hunter when you can't even fight me! He'll bury you!" "First and foremost, I don't want to fight you. Secondly, why do you doubt me again? Did I not just prove myself to you?" Mia held up the broom and Mayne rolled her eyes. Mayne laughed nervously. "Mia! Do you even understand his level of hierarchy? Why do you think he is, who he is?" "… And I am who I am. This is why I was kept here. So, what does that tell you, Mayne? Maybe I'm as strong or stronger than him?" "No! You're not! Listen to me now and heed my words! You have a few traits that none of us have and you needed to be molded to fit into our coven!" "Coven of what, Mayne…Deception, lies, drugs, sex and Black Magick? Wrong answer. I practice White Magick! I'm Solitaire and I intend to stay this way! I know that you found and read the papers that I wrote. So did everyone else. With that said, I don't know if I will win or lose this battle. Either way, I will have succeeded because I know now, who I am. I believe in myself and I'm not afraid!" "I'm not letting you fight him!" "Why?" "Because I know how this will end." Mia was speechless. Touched by her words, she stared into her eyes and shed a tear. "What are you afraid of, Mayne? I know the answer, but I want you to tell me." "I'm not doing this with you, princess. It's not me! You know this." Mia's speculative smile put her on the spot. Mayne threw her hands up. "What!?" Mia giggled and stepped closer.

"You like me… You're worried about me, aren't you?" Mayne failed to hold back her smile. "Fuck off, princess!" "You even have a pet name for me! With all the one night stands that you live for, Why me?" "Once again, I'm not doing this!" Mia giggled. "Do you want me to be your princess?" Mayne grabbed her by the shoulders. "Do you want me to throw you off of this boat?" Mia pursed her lips. "…and if you did, you'd dive in to rescue me." As Mia knelt to pick up her broom, Mayne grabbed her arm. "I said we're not going!" Mia lowered the broom and pulled her arm out of her grip. "No… we're not. I am." Mia quickly turned and soared into the night sky, leaving her on the boat."

CHAPTER 25

THE MERIDIAN

Her march toward Hunter was bittersweet. With each step taken, she recalled every memory of him. One by one, the images that were burned into her mind came to light, feeding her rage and transmitting its affects within and outside of her as well. Her intention was to become everyone's karma. Although different in each approach, her battles with the others were singular in their sense of Magick. With him, her fight would be inclusive of all that she knew and all that surrounded her. All but Hunter had been served and now her biggest challenge stood before her.

Vibrating echoes of rolling thunder emanated from the distance. It's sound foretold the strength of the impending surge of pure energy, requested, summoned, called and stirred, by Mia. He watched her intently as she approached. The blue in her pupils grew brighter as she neared him. Behind her, the ocean's crashing waves followed the queue of the increasing winds. To her right, the bonfire swayed with the rhythm of the wind and ocean. She stopped a few feet before him and saw the pyre's glow, mirrored in his eyes. The flame in his eyes seemed eternal. She walked behind him and he spiraled to follow her. As she had suspected, the flame that burned within his eyes, was his own. She felt herself become entranced by him and his familiar spiritual pull. The sudden crack of lightning jolted her and snapped her mind back to the here and now. As she returned to her ground zero, he followed beside her. They stood facing each other on a timeless plain of imminent Armageddon. The raging ocean rose in allegiance and the thrusting pressure of its crashing waves depicted the opposing tension between them.

"Tonight, I hide nothing from you. So, who will go first, Warlock? ...Or should I just lead you to your demise?" His wicked laugh mocked her in every way. "First...? I am first and last." "I have no time for your riddles, Warlock! However, I assure you that you will be the last of your kind.". He reached out and clasped her throat, breathing his hissed rage through his gritted teeth. "My demise? ... Last of my kind? ... WARLOCK? You cannot begin to perceive the imminent danger that you have chosen to put yourself into. Suffice to say, I will be the one to clean up the aftermath of your elementary challenge. You had better not fail, my sweet Witch. If you do, I will take away each and every one of your traits and they will only be given back to you as I fucking see fit! I will shred the fire within your heart and consume your spirit. When I'm finished with you, I will watch you writhe on the ground, weakened in mind, body and spirit." The lightening's warning signs gave no warning to the delayed, ominous and deafening thunderclap. Mia felt her heart skip a beat. She gasped for air as she dug her nails into his hands. Her blushed face exhibited her nearly oxygen deprived state. She reached inside her soul to release the pent-up, raging energy derived from his actions and words. She pushed her hand forward against him, releasing her pent-up energy and propelled him backward and onto the ground. The wolf ran to her. The telepathic connection that they shared was strong. His boisterous howl clearly indicated to her, to not take this time for granted. Using his down time to her advantage, she backed away from him to commence the heart and soul of her epic battle. With her arms to the sky, she stared into the Moon's white brilliance, drew down the energy from her and called for her presence. She knew that she owned this night. This was her Moon: Mia's Moon. With swift motion she extended her arms outward, parallel with the ground. In the spiritual presence of the Moon: her Goddess, she summoned the Elements and requested the collective presence of the four Winds. The assuring sound of her spirit guide's howl and her Familiars, the cat and the Blue Jay watching over her as well, eased any sense of fear for the endless plight that she now faced. Hunter stood up and dusted the sand off of his cloak. He raised his arm and with a swift sway of his hand, the wolf was silenced. Mia was furious. He smiled. "Your wolf is fine. I've only silenced him. Now face me, my sweet little Witch and lets get on with your feeble attempt to silence me." She clenched her hands and held her index finger to her mouth. "Shhh. You talk too much, Warlock. My Magick will speak for itself."

The interweaving Winds enhanced the oceans climaxing waves. The behavior of its cresting white caps was depictive of the influence of multiple storms approaching from different directions. The sand sifted like snow through the air. Mia's seamless directive of all these respective entities was like that of a tenured maestro leading a ghastly orchestra. The reckless and wild flames of the pyre wielded itself like a child that desperately wanted to play. With precision and grace, she weaved her finger over the perimeter of the fire and it's flames danced with the rhythm of her motions. His unearthly voice echoed through the chaotic noise that surrounded them. "You've honed your traits well, however there's something that you've failed to factor in to this equation. The collective energy of this Magick that you wield will become its own powerful entity. You won't be able to control it. You are still the baby Blue Jay." She remained silent as his condescending words and laughter irked every nerve within her body. While she knew that he might be correct, she was content with the pendulum's answers and chose not to be concerned with his discerning words. "Warlock, What you have taken from me, I'm now going to take back, times three. Do you recall that first night when I said this to you? My words, they are now real. The time has come for you to receive your karma." His seething, merciless words flowed from his gritted teeth. "Yes, I remember your feeble threat, sweetness." He grinned, lewdly licked his lips and continued with his impeccable words. "I remember every detail, every dream, every thought, every curve of your sweet body, every tear that you shed and every ounce of fear that I've instilled within you." A gentle gust of wind swept the fabric of his cloak, enhancing the picturesque effects of the burning flames within his eyes. Mia clenched her hands, loathing his supreme eloquence. "Fuck you and the broom you flew in on, Warlock!" His face lit up, brighter than the bonfire beside him and his resounding laugh emanated through her like the vibrations of an earthquake. "Ahh. There you go again with "fuck you". I am starting to sense that the Warlock thing is just your way of sparking my fire and that this battle is your version of foreplay. I had thought that we've sufficiently addressed this activity. I'd be happy to indulge, however, don't you think that we should wait until you've finished beating me up before we engage in this activity? Although your endurance level will have been depleted, I will be happy to pick up the slack, as you are personally familiar with my stamina. What say you?" His sinful grin burned through her soul. Mia answered him with the unified assistance of earth's creatures. The rolling thunder brought forth the most orphic sound. With a fixed stare on him, she raised her right hand and pivoted it in the air. An unusual humming sound vibrated through the night sky. As it drew nearer, its perplexing presence peaked Hunters curiosity. This pulsating collective entity glided along with the fluctuating winds of the night sky, forming into various shapes to signify its intent and meaning to Mia. The echoing sound was preceded by a swarm of fireflies, emitting their Luciferian bioluminescence as if they were bringing forth a procession of royalty to Mia's playing field. Following behind them were a fierce army of cicadas. Their unnatural presence aroused Hunter's curiosity. He had recalled that the seventeen-year brood had only just occurred last year. He watched as they collectively formed into various Pentagrams, each depicting its meaning. The first symbol formed was in the direction of an invoking Air Pentagram to represent its communication of awareness and divination to Mia. The second was an invoking Fire Pentagram to signify the presence of Mia's passion, desire, courage and transformation. The next symbol was a banishing Fire Pentagram to remove negativity from interfering in her quest. The next symbol was an invoking Water Pentagram to increase psychic energy, emotion, intuition and cleansing. The last was an invoking Earth Pentagram to bring forth the growth of the most benevolent outcome. Mia watched in awe as the entities that she had brought forth, echoed their allegiance in light, sound and message. Their exhilarating ardor roused her courage to no end. She knew exactly what the illustrated messages depicted, while all the while knowing that Hunter understood only their basic meanings because their true messages were veiled and not for him to see.

The bright eminence of the oceans plankton enhanced the ambiance of the night. Its glow lit up the shore as if to announce the anticipation of a theatre's main attraction. The Winds changed direction to an Easterly flow. The crashing waves foretold of the wrath that was about to be released on the shores. The sound pitch of the cicadas changed with the fireflies sudden descent, cueing the dawning of Mia's Moon. No one but her Goddess could stop her now. She fixed her steely eyes on him. She held her arms just above her shoulders, while she whispered words to summon the Element of Fire. The fireflies plummeted toward Hunter with fervent speed, leaving a streak of light in their wake, within the night sky, to lead the cicadas to their target. They dispersed just before reaching him, ceasing their glow to indicate the final target to the cicadas. The cicadas pummeled into him with tempest furor, encompassing his body and blinding his vision in order to distract him. With a wicked grin as lethal as her rage, she watched in bliss while every detail of her plan unfolded before her eyes. The sparks in her hands evolved into palm-sized pyres. In timed repetition, she catapulted each fiery blaze directly at him. When one palm was discharged, the other reloaded. Just as the fifth one was thrown, she noticed a bizarre change in the air. The airborne blaze slowed in its path, obstructed by the Magick of two veiled, opposing forces. The circumference of its flames tightened like the eye of a hurricane. The trees bent violently as if they were bowing to him. The flare stopped mid-air and was pulled into a vortex, disappearing into the void that Hunter stood within. She noticed a glow of red light emitting through the swarm of cicadas and could no longer see evidence of his body through the flying chaos before her. The Sand whipped around him, its grains piercing the Cicada's like a machine gun filled with glass shards and driving divisions of lifeless cicadas to the ground. Two hands parted a seam through what remained airborne and the remaining cicadas plummeted to the ground. Mia was frozen with fear when the source of red glow revealed itself to her. She realized that the fire that she had thrown had inadvertently fueled his now relucent eyes. Recalling only seeing his pupils in this manner, she had never before seen the white of his eyes filled with such feral rage. He stood before her with his hood draped over one side of his face, piercing her eyes with his. With his biceps extended outward like machine guns, he raised his arms, sucked his teeth and hissed his words to her. "My turn... sweetness. Fire, you use first... fire, you lose, first." The Magick that fed the bonfire mysteriously lost its energy. The chill of the night air encircled Mia, causing her to shiver. Laced with frost, her breath became more and more erratic, clearly indicating her state of mind to him. When she noticed the darkness that now surrounded her from the nearly snuffed, fire, she realized that he had also decreased the natural oxygen level that surrounded both her and the pyre that she created. As she crouched downward, he watched her gasping for air. She could barely get the words out through her hoarse voice. "Not fair!" His vile and merciless laugh haunted her, chilling her to the bone. Tears fell from her eyes with every desperate gasp. She sat on the ground, no longer able to hold herself up. He knelt down before her and pointed. "Follow my finger and watch closely, my sweet Witch." He stood in front of the dying bonfire and pointed to the ground beside her. The oxygen level suddenly increased and a backdraft behind him blazed in all its glory, blowing his cloak in the wake of its torrid waves. As Mia began to catch her breath, she felt the waves of heat from the flames and watched the sand sifting beside her, at his will. A misty vapor rose from the sand that he had pointed to, evolving itself into sparks which in turn, fueled the enigmatic fire that now burned beside her in the sand. Hunched over and holding herself, she watched as the small, brisk and fiery entity began to trail its course, growing in height and encircling her within a kindled cage. Before she could catch her breath, she was trapped. The unyielding flames originally fed by the bonfire and now guided by him, were now being fed from her. The higher the flames grew, the weaker she became. The Element of Fire that she had summoned and absorbed was dissipating within her and now being summoned and absorbed by Hunter. The seething heat and dense air consumed her. Tried as she did, her hands, when raised to reclaim her Magick, emitted only a few faint sparks. She sat against her calves, crouched over and covered her head. The light from flames directly in front of her, lessened. When she looked up, she saw a dark blur of color and had thought that the fire was dying. Hunter stood amidst the flames, unaffected, as if he were one with the Element. His eyes were filled with the flames of his unceasing desire for victory.

He looked down at her and laughed. His disparaging words sent a sharp pain in her gut. "Fetal position, already? GET UP NOW YOU PATHETIC VERSION OF A WITCH!" Tears ran down her cheeks. She gritted her teeth and managed to push herself up on all fours. Her body trembled. Her fingers clenched the sand while her faint cries of fury, desperation and anxiety battled within her. Her will to fight was not strong enough to kick-start her body into motion. The flames continued to grow higher and higher, blocking her Moon from her view. She gasped. Although her mouth was dry and voice, hoarse from coughing, she managed to conjure up enough energy to cry out to a single word to her Goddess. "Why?" She collapsed. She lay on the sand facing a wall of fire. As she stared into its fervency, she recalled the candle flame and her experience with Aithusa. She searched within her memories of all things said between them, as well as the images surrounding the Magickal aspects of that night. She recalled the notes that she had written about Aithusa's traits. When Mia looked beyond all the negativity that surrounded that very night, she realized that Aithusa was, in fact, trying to show her something. She showed her how to recognize the true foundation of her fear and to focus her mind on the other side of this fear. It was then that Mia was able to put her finger into the candle's flame. There was no pain because Mia was, in essence, on the other side of her own fear. She realized that she had been living on this very side of fear, during her entire tenure with Hunter and his coven of Witches, within this realm. Of all the Magick that had occurred between them on that night, it was the Element of Fire that carried its message through to her in the here and now. She now knew that the requisite Element needed to defeat Hunter was the Element of Fire. Mia had always feared and respected this Element, however now she knew that her fear was not real. Her respect for this and the other Elements had always been aligned in the utmost, respectful allegiance. She knew that she had always worked honorably with this and the other Elements. Her fear was generated by the results of other's misuse, greed and distortion of her own religion. They, in essence, bent the rules to justify and satisfy their own needs without giving heed to Karma. The results of their dark Magick led them to believe that they were successful, however, the harm that Mia witnessed returning to them, was the negative side of Karma's threefold law. As elementary as this law is, she knew that it was just as imperative as the Rede and the Thirteen goals. Although this realization now cleared the path for her, giving her the answer to what she needed to now do to defeat him, she also knew that most of this required strength that she now lacked. It was time to get it back.

Her Moon, the Solitary source of strength that she needed, was just above her, illuminating the beach and waiting for her to draw from its source. She shifted herself onto her back and raised her arms to her Moon, drawing down her energy as best she could. The effulgent rays caressed her face like the touch of a warm blanket, embracing and recharging her spirit. She grasped the sand in her palms and shifted onto her stomach. As she raised her head she slowly shifted herself closer to the firewall and extended her arm. She envisioned Aithusa on the opposite side of the flames, mimicked the Magick of the candle from that night with her and inched her finger into the base of the blaze. The flames displayed an invasive disconnect and just as the firewall separated, the roar of the lion echoed throughout the beach. From where she lay, she could see the sound waves of his roar, resonating in visual vibrations of blue hues and bouncing off of the sand. She raised her head and saw the lion standing before her with the wolf howling beside him. The energy of the wolf's howl roused every muscle in her body. She managed to push herself upright, onto her knees. The wolf stepped in front of her and bowed his head. She in turn, did the same and their heads touched as a gesture of their kinship. The wolf stepped beside her to assist her in standing. Elated over the wolf's restored voice, she looked up at the lion and thanked him. She knew that he had done this. The wolf returned beside the lion and howled once again. She continued gazing at the lion in awe. He pointed to the Moon and held up his paws. At that very moment she recalled one of her dreams, which mirrored this exact moment in time. She smiled because she now knew its meaning. Her dream foretold of her most crucial battle and her source of courage, strength and protection had always been her Moon. The lion snarled as he turned to look at Hunter. She knew his elongated grumble had always been the prerequisite to his blaring roar. His sudden roars had always startled her but this time his blaring sound was oracular. Its pulsating effect oscillated through her and held her mind within a suspended state. She felt stilled in time, floating above everything that surrounded her. The wolf's howl summoned the presence of the other wolves from his pack. One by one, their howls returned their unyielding and undivided alliance. As they each took their place, the whites of their fangs projected their seething stamina to her. Their collective energy rejuvenated her. Like a Phoenix Fire, she proudly rose, piercing Hunter's eyes with her own and stood inches from his face. She grinned and smirked at him. "As you've just witnessed, things are never as they seem, Warlock." He grinned and repeated her word. "Warlock." He laughed. His sinister eyes displayed his brewing rage. "Did I push a button…again…Warlock?" She licked her lips and laughed at him.

She stepped back, raised her arms and slowly clenched her hands. She summoned the Elements of Water and Air. The clouds quickly merged above them. Mia felt the plunging cold air rush in around her legs and her hair reacted from the incoming storm's charged static. A large lightning bolt streaked through the sky and struck the ground nearby her. It continued its magnetized path through the sand, sending up a smoking sand geyser. The sound of its vibrating, powerful current was almost as deafening as the thunder that followed. Mia was fully charged. She watched Hunter as the relentless, freezing rain soaked him from head to toe. She raised her arm and swirled her hand. The rain changed to ice. Thick hail pummeled the ground. Hunter slipped his hood over his face and walked over to her while covering his eyes. She swayed her hand once more. Crackling sounds echoed. The beach was now a frozen tundra. She looked at Hunter and smiled. He was frozen in place. With a wave of her hand, the hail ceased but the cold air remained. She walked up to him and encircled his body, sliding her finger along the ice that incarcerated him. She faced him and peered into the glassy ice. His eyes returned her stare. She grinned and then proceeded to enunciate her words loudly, so that he could hear her. "Ahh, my tall glass of Warlock. I think I'll keep you on ice." She kissed the ice. Shivering from the brisk wind, she embraced herself and walked a few yards away from him. She summoned warm air, allowed it to encompass her body and thaw her tingly fingertips. She sat on a nearby, beached log and sifted her hands through the tiny granules of ice that had already begun to melt. She scooped up a handful, looked at Hunter and smiled snidely, as she sprinkled the hail back onto the ground. Her smile quickly turned into a frowned curiosity, when she saw the faint glow of red light emanating from his eyes. She panicked and ran to him. The cold air had sunk and dissipated. The ice that imprisoned him had begun to sweat. As she reached to touch the ice near his face, he was grinning. His odious expression sent chills down her spine. She had thought that she had taken back the Element of Fire from him but now knew otherwise. Popping sounds emanated from his weakening ice coffin and its grading sounds sent her into a full-blown panic. When he caught her looking at him, he glared at her, holding eye contact and imprisoned her within his mind. She saw his chest expand, but was unable to run. The ice shattered, sending deadly chunks in every direction. Mia lay unconscious. A shard of ice had left its mark just above her eyebrow. Blood trickled down her forehead and into her hair. Her wolf ran to her side, prodding her and licking the blood off of her face.

Mia's thoughts floated pendulously, deep within her paralyzed, subconscious state. The pungent smells of blooming Spring flowers wafted within her minds olfactory senses. Its scent awoke her. She lifted her head when she felt the sensation of fingers running through her hair and saw that she was now beside the old familiar lake, with the lion sitting beside her. He patted the grass and as she situated herself, she felt a sharp pain on her forehead. He lifted her chin with his claw to observe the opened wound just above her eye, slid over to the banks edge and pointed into the water. When she looked into the water, to where his claw was pointing, he touched, just above the gash on her forehead. He pointed to the water once more. Images of the results of her last fight displayed on the waters surface. Holding her forehead, she gazed up at the lion and cried profusely. He snarled and his Amber eyes widened. He swiped her hand off of her face and covered her wound with his paw. When she felt the heated sensation, she realized that he was healing her. Her memory flashed back to a similar time in waking-state, when Hunter had done just the same, but in Mayne's presence. Her speculative thoughts ran wild. There were times in her dreams when she knew the lion was her advocate, however, there were also times when she believed the lion to be Hunter. He pointed to the water, once more. The gash was gone. She expected to see nothing less. The lion grabbed her arm and stood. He pointed to the tree. On the ground, were the Blue Jays, from her previous dream. The Mother fed the baby and flew onto the branch above them. Mia had remembered that the baby had struggled to take flight on its first attempts. She observed, listening the mothers loud and summoning caw. The baby fluttered its wings and in one attempt, it soared effortlessly onto the branch. The lion nudged Mia's chin to face him. He pointed to the Full Moon, picked her up and cradled her in his arms. As he turned to face the lake, dazzling orbs of blue light began to emerge to the surface and floated pendulously into the air. Mia touched a few of them as they passed by her. She managed to catch one of them and held it in her palm. As she stared into its glow, she noticed that it was cool to the touch. The lion growled. She felt his grasp tighten on her body and then felt him sway her. Just as she looked up at him, he threw her into the lake. As she plummeted into its depths, the orbs of light followed in her path.

When she opened her eyes and saw them encircling around her, their touch now, warm and comforting against her body. Time seemed to have stood still for a few moments and her need for breathing seemed to hold no significance to her own life force. The brightest of the orbs floated within her peripheral view. She watched as it took its place in front of her. Its radiance summoned the other orbs and one by one, they detached from her body and merged into one. Mia watched in awe as the orb expanded. The circumference of its evolving size grew as wide as she was, tall. As she stared into it, she could see the smaller orbs circulating within the sphere. Small pockets of hot air began to expel from tiny perforations on its pressurized surface and its outer layer began to weaken. In anticipation, Mia quickly swayed backward. The orb exploded, propelling her backward with potent force and transporting her through a spiraling waterfall. In the blink of an eye, she lay on the sand unaware of how she managed to land, uninjured. When she looked around, she realized that she had been in a dream state. The lions actions came to mind and this time she was able to easily decipher his actions.

As Hunter approached Mia, the wolf's vicious, tooth-gritted growl grew louder. With fixed eyes on Hunter, the wolf clenched his fangs around her wrist, tugging and prodding her to bring her back to a sentient state of mind. Hunter stood above her and stared into the wolf's eyes, snarling with gritted teeth to incite a challenge. The wolf knew that if he fed into Hunters lead, he would be silenced and unable to protect Mia. He instead remained adamant, clenching his fangs tighter as he continued to nudge her. The wolf's sounds stimulated her mind and the sensations of his teeth on her wrist along with the wafting salty scent of the ocean, roused her sense of being. She opened her eyes, smiled and caressed the fur on his face. As she rubbed behind his ears, his eyes squinted, enjoying the brief massage. She knew he liked when she did that because all of her animals did as well. She knelt before him, smiled and kissed him between his eyes. She whispered her thank you, to him. With his help she managed to balance herself and stood up to face Hunter.

"As you can see, I've risen, once again, Warlock. Perhaps your Magician's ass-hat is faulty. You may want to exchange it or maybe even consider joining a circus." She smirked. Her brazen words made him smile in the most malefic manner. "And you, my Witch, shall be my circus pet. When I say jump, you say how high, just as we do now." Mia flared her eyes. "Oh, you think so, huh?" He laughed. "No sweetness, I know." Mia stared at him with steely eyes. "No one tames me, Warlock." He raised his eyebrow as if she had challenged him to do just that. He stood an inch from her and lifted her chin with his sharpened, lengthy fingernail. "I will have you kneeling at my feet within the hour." Mia held his stare for a few moments, their eyes locked on each other in silence. She inhaled through her nose, smiling at him. In one swift move, her teeth clenched his finger with a taut grip. She released him just when she knew that she had broken skin and stepped back, wiping her mouth. "Warlock...the first elementary rule in taming is to never put your finger near the mouth." He shook his finger, staring at her with malicious intent. "Is that so?" He laughed and continued. "Here's what sets us apart, right now. I would not have released my bite, until I've broken bone."

CHAPTER 26

FULCRUM

With her back to Hunter, Mia faced her Moon, with her focus steadfast, in allegiance with her brilliance and all she stood for. She closed her eyes and focused on the image of the pendulum, her fulcrum, swaying in tune to her thoughts and answers. It was time for her to reset the course of this distorted train of Witches, driven by this Warlock. Mia's true strength would now be tested to its full extent. Failure will not an option and fear will not be the choice. Within her mind, she put forth the image of herself and became this very image: The Phoenix Fire. The pendulum's answers returned thoughts of the lion's valor, the baby blue jay's determination and the wolf's resolute endurance. These collective entities filled her mind, body and spirit with thoughts of dominion over the myriad of possible challenges he may throw her way. She knew all that she needed and needed no Magickal tools. Everything needed was always there: As above, so below, as within and so without. She knew that the five Elements had always surrounded her at all times, throughout her life and she knew that she was well protected.

She took a deep breath, lifted her head and opened her eyes. Her Moon, her Goddess was as bright as her own life force. "I call on the Lady and Lord. Guide me in accordance to your will, your Rede and your Laws. I ask for your steadfast protection." She looked across the ocean and then down, at the sand. She projected her thoughts to the fire behind her and turned to see it in a blazing pyre of Magick. With her eyes fixed in its infernal rage, she whispered her fervent words, just as she had done with Aithusa and her candle. "I am everything that I allow to surround me. I can change what I wish to control and what no longer serves me will be dismissed." She swayed her hands apart, her fingers extended to the sky. "As above." Her arms descended. "So below." She placed her hands on her heart and then extended them outward. "As within…So without." Beginning with Air, she faced East and began to summon each of the Elements, respectfully. "I summon the Element, Air. Send me your tempest intellect and Divination. I Know." She faced South. "I Summon the Element, Fire. Allow courage and transformation to ignite within me. I Will." She faced West. "I summon the Element, Water. Permit the surge of psychic energy to flow through me and purge what is negative. I Dare." She faced North. "I summon the Element, Earth. Allow my actions to heal, my intentions to emerge and grow in love and light. I keep my Silence."

Mia watched as the fireflies danced in the heat of the night. In their wake, their collective pirouettes caused streaks of trailing light, like sparklers on the fourth of July. Their glow streaked across the horizon, creating symbols from ancient alphabets and Sigils created by and known only to Mia.

In the order in which they were called, the Elements began to create a symphony of energized Magick. Their orchestrated union followed Mia's harmonious directive under the illuminated glow of her Moon. A plunging gust of cool air touched Mia's ankles and sent shivers through her body, indicating the start of her Elemental concerto. As she stared into the sky, she envisioned musical notes flowing within the air, dancing on the clouds and riding the distant flashes of lightning. A warm breeze tepidly traced the clouds, encompassing their collective mist and materializing into a spiraling bouquet of Magick. The warmth of the air combined with the oceans mist, caressed Mia's face, duly noting the respective manner in which she had summoned its presence. She briefly closed her eyes, inhaling its briny essence. The sweet serenade of the increasing Winds whistled into her ear as its strength fed into her spirit. The gusts of eclectic waves provoked her rising courage to levels of unprecedented heights. The rolling thunder grew nearer. Its rumbling sounds vibrated within all that was in contact with the earth. At full tilt, an unusually large bolt of lightning snaked across the oceans surface, subdividing its jagged veins and discharging them into the ocean. Mia jolted from its haunted, pulsating current and nervously laughed at herself for doing so. She felt the uplift of the air's voltaic fields, her hair flowing with the static. She covered her ears in anticipation of the thunders crash. Its deafening clap echoed in her ears, haunting the atmosphere with its ensuing and resonant baritones. The ocean proudly crested its white-capped waves in acknowledgement of her summoned respect. Lightning crashed once more, redirecting its potency into the bonfire and causing its pyre to glow in a fury of White heat. Its fire rose and accelerated the pyre's fiery mass, spewing out its crackling embers at her feet in acceptance of her respected protocol of its summoned presence. She noticed that only three of the four Elements had shown their echoed response. Earth had yet to rise up to meet her, however, she knew that this would happen in its own time.

Encompassed by the three collective surges of energy, she stared out into the oceans distance, raised her arms and drew down the Moon. Its eternal light flowed through her, filling her with love, light and unprecedented resolute. With her back to Hunter, she blared his name, his real name. "THERON!" She turned to face him with her arms behind her. His eyes were as red as the bonfire. At first glance, she noticed that his body seemed taller and larger. She kept her focus. The lightning streaked above them, its lucent bolt, static, for a few long seconds, showed the outlining of his true form. Mia now knew with whom she was up against. His expression was as heinous as his intent. She knew that he was trying to instill fear within her. He held a deadpan expression. She would not allow herself to be deterred by his intimidation. The lightning's veined fingers channeled toward her, connecting with her fingertips. Mia's eyes flared, her face was now as nefarious as his. With the grace of a blue jay and the stealth of a lion, she swayed her arms forward and aimed her fingertips at his eyes. The voltaic surge streamed its extreme, unyielding fury, encompassing his body and nearly claiming his life force. Mia's hatred was now relentlessly feeding into the current, directing its stimulated pulse with such malice, that she could feel her suppressed Grey side taking over and turning darker and darker by the minute. She could no longer control this unfamiliar side of herself. The seduction of darkness was overtaking her.

The air mysteriously thinned and Mia struggled to catch her breath. He smiled while watching her wheeze and cough. Fed by a mysterious back draft, the pyre blazed wildly. As she caught her breath, she felt the change in the air. She knew this was all derived from him. He saw that her hatred was now feeding into the pyre. He had summoned her dark side, the side of her that she had always quelled.

Lightning struck onto the sand beside them. The familiar sound of Hunters laugh merged with the rolling thunder that followed. The combined sound was equivalent to a thousand tribal drums, pulsating its melody of sibylline rudiments. She allowed its rhythm to hypnotize her, seducing every cell of her body. Resistance was futile. She now craved this darker shade of herself. She wanted to defeat him, to destroy him, to end him. In the process, her hatred had blurred her conscience and she lost sight of the Rede. Hunter grinned. All the pieces were falling to his wish. His deep, seething tone, ensnared her into his world.

"Now you are as dark as I am. Let my darkness feed into you. Feed into it, my littlest Witch. Don't fight it."

His eyes flared at her. He raised his forearms, flexing his guns and tearing them from the webbed tentacles of voltage that had held them captive. He raised his right arm, redirected the current that had flowed through his body and channeled it through his hand. The current arched, the ebb and flow running solely between their hands. They held their steely stare at each other, one no fiercer than the other. He held is hand steady, while staring at her and grinned once more, his teeth reflecting the light from the bolting energy. With a sway of his hand, he grasped the surging streak of lightning as if he were in a tug of war challenge. The sudden sound of clanking steel distracted Mia's focus. She watched as the lightning bolt evolved into a searing, white-hot chain, it's links, pulsating with high voltage energy. He gritted his teeth, grasped the fiery chain between them, whipped it upward and then slammed it to the ground, pulling Mia with it. Her body torqued violently, following the chained lightning within its path. She hit the ground hard and the wind was knocked out of her. She managed to block her fall to protect her face, however, her wrists were badly sprained and her elbows and knees were throbbing. Her gasps further accentuated the pain. She held her ribs, feeling the pain with each breath. She collapsed onto the ground before him, writhing and moaning, unable to scream. He grasped the chain, lassoing its links around her wrists and slowly dragged her listless body to his feet. He grasped her arm, pulled her up to eye level and released the chain. It dropped onto the ground and dissolved into the earth. With a merciless grin, he stared at her war torn expression. Her face was strewn with tears, sweat and smeared blood. Squinting through blurred vision, she felt her body flush against his, his body as hot as the seething heat from the bonfire. She held onto his wrists, clenching her nails into his skin. The heat of his hand on the back of her skull was unnerving. He pulled her face closer to his and hissed his words with malicious intent. "When will you learn, Witch? Whatever little Magick tricks you choose to employ from your ever-inept mind and use against me, will be manipulated and used against you. I know. I have always been. Those foolish enough to challenge me have all met their demise." She gazed up at him, clenching his cloak. "Why do you choose to keep me alive? End me, as you did the others, if you think you can." His wicked laughter seared through her body. "You belong to me." Utter disgust was evident in her expression. "I belong to no one." She paused to clear her throat. "By the end of this battle, you'll belong to me and I'll choose your fate. The souls of those that you've destroyed, wait for you in the shadows and I intend to hand you to them, ALIVE!" He grasped both of her arms, painfully clenching her biceps. Her feet dangled while she writhed, trying to break free. "Your

Delusions of grandeur never ceases to amaze me." He released her, mid air and she fell onto the ground. Bruised and battered, Mia sat upright, holding her knees and nursing her wounds whilst diligently trying to shake off the combat fatigue. She watched as he opened his palms. One by one, the chains links reformed in his hand before her eyes, reconstructing its fiery sequence. The lightning struck, splitting its veins and jolting the last of its searing circuit. The chains chiming, discorded rhyme caused her to flinch in fear. He whipped the chains in the air, just above where she sat and its sibilated sound caused her to cower. She ducked and lay in a fetal position with her hands wrapped around her head. He slammed one of the chains on the ground, beside her head. She screamed, quickly sliding away from it's unraveled, scorching heat. Panting like a frightened cat, her face was almost as pale as the white in her eyes. He approached her, standing inches from her knees. His long black nail hooked under her chin. He knelt, lifted her to face him and sucked his teeth as if he were about to feast on her. She rose onto her knees, fearful that he may cut her with his sharp, talon-like fingernail. The tone of his voice was deep and not of this world. "Here you are, once again on your knees, before me." She hissed as he dug his nail into her chin. "Allow me to save you time and suffering, by telling you how the remainder of this bullshit will play out." She struggled to hold back her tears but her body language was evident to him. "I will break you, tear you apart until you are a shadow of the Witch that you thought you were. When you're spirit clings to its last glimmer of life and you are begging me to save you from the pain, it is then that I'll spare your life. Then I'll do whatever it takes to revise and reawaken your thought process to ensure that you become the Witch that I need you to be." He pulled his finger from her chin and held his nail in front of her face. A droplet of her blood, dangled from its tip. He slowly drew his finger to his mouth, licking the blood from his nail in a vilest manner. He sneered, licking his lips whilst holding her attention. He whispered. "Sweet." Mia cringed. He lashed the chains, one at a time, immediately drawing her attention to them. Unsure of her next move, she sat against her calves and stared at the Moon, waiting for an answer. Her mind became lost in thought. She closed her eyes and went within, as a means to protect herself for the moment. She thought of her last glimpse of his chains and was now aware that he was the last link, the last in this line of her binding captors. Within the domain of this Coven, and with the exception of Mayne, she had severed every link up until now. All that Hunter had done in response to her Magick had inadvertently given her the answers that she needed to end this. The remaining Element would be key to her victory. The image of a scorched earth, burning what no longer serves, followed by its regrowth, provided a clear and precise perception of what would be. The missing Element was intended to be absent until now, until she understood that the other three are derived from this one. Water makes up approximately seventy percent of earth's surface. Fire resides within its core and plants, born of the Earth, produce Air. Earth heals itself. She recalled Hunters exact words and reiterated them as she stared at him with an evasive smile. She stood and approached him, whispering her words, her riddle, to him. "Earth is first and last."

She focused on his chains, certain that his darkness would die by the very sword that he used. She stood intrepid in her demeanor, maintaining steadfast, disdained focus on the eye of her target. He lashed the chains in the air and its bullwhip sound echoed its fierce allegiance. She caught the ending links and held them tightly. With her focus fixed on its lengths, she invited the spirits of an untapped Familiar to her playing field. She held the ends of the chains to her face. The lucent blue energy in her pupils fed into it, pulsing its frosted blue light through each link, hissing and smoking like dry ice, from the swift change in temperature. It stopped just halfway through the last dangling link. This sole weakening link, battled between two opposing thermal degrees. In a swift motion, she raised her hands, snapping this weakest links and severing it from his hands. The chains soared into the air, thrashing its renewed allegiance to her and dropped onto the ground. Her eyes, still glowing, she continued to feed her Magick into its live extant. She stared into the brightest depths of her Moon and directed her Familiar spirits to proceed with her intentions. The Grounded ends of the chains began to writhe and rise up. The steel began to change into various hues of Green, expanding and evolving into two solid entities. The chain's ends formed into jaws, revealing its species. The serpents rose, each standing on either side of her as still as a tree and waiting to be queued by her sway of hand, to strike. Hunter keenly watched their precarious and subtle sways, keeping an even closer eye on their lethal fangs. He moved himself one step toward her and was forced to stop dead in his tracks. Bizarre bursts of steam emitted from the ground beneath him. He sifted the sand with his foot and noticed a faint, sulfuric scent wafting through the air. "How very crafty of you, sweetness, given the fact that there are no earthquakes or dormant volcanoes here." She moved her arms back, placing her palms on the serpent's stomachs, alerting them to be ready. The ground beneath him began to vibrate, causing him to rebalance himself from the affects of vertigo. Just as he took a step toward her, the rapid onset of seismic waves caused the ground to split, cascading the sand into the depths of the crater. He lost his balance and fell inches from its edge. With his attention distracted, she slid her hands along their scales, stopping at their throats. She lifting her arms outward and the serpents latched onto her arm, dangling from her biceps. As she swayed her arms forward, they propelled into the air and over the crater. The serpents slithered behind him, undetected. The surging heat from within the craters depths spewed tiny lava bombs, one nearly missing his hand. He slid away from it and jumped up. Standing at the edge, he peered inside the fiery pit, amazed at what she had summoned. He laughed loudly. "Your visual affects are quite impressive, in fact they're almost believable. I see what you are doing. You're not strong enough to see this through. Wielding is not your forte."

His insults didn't affect her in the least. She stepped to the craters edge, inviting him to do the same. She stared at the ground beneath his feet, froze the image in her mind and closed her eyes. With her intent, steady within in her thoughts, she pointed at the ground beneath his feet. Upon opening her eyes, she blared his true name, queuing one of the serpents. It lunged at his thigh, sinking its fangs into his flesh and seeping its lethal venom through his veins. The other serpent thrust itself into the air and clenched its jaws into his neck. His muscles weakened and he fell to the ground, gasping for air. He watched the serpents spring and glide into the air, returning to

Mia. They lay flat on the ground at her feet. She knelt and thanked them, then slid her palms over their heads and they reverted to their original steel-linked form. With a piercing stare, she kept her eyes fixed on him and grasped the chains. "How does it feel to be at my mercy, Warlock? This is what you get when you try to bring out my dark side. When justified, the results will always only be a darker shade of Grey, at most. Black is a very dangerous emotion. Since you wish for me to be heartless, then for you, I will. It's justified. For the record, I will not be sparing your wretched life. You will die by the distorted sword that you've used." The animosity in her expression was evident. "My darkness, Warlock, can be defiant. Do you remember this finger?" She held up her index finger, the one that he had broken. Ensuring that she had his undivided attention, she reiterated her words, louder. "DO YOU REMEMBER THIS FINGER?" She grinned and quickly switched to her middle finger. "Go to hell!" She pointed her finger to the unstable ground beneath him. The sudden upheaval shifted the ground transversely. His darkness held on long enough to pierce her eyes with his hell bent stare, in an attempt to instill fear in her one last time. Unable to control his muscles from the venoms affects, he plummeted into its depths, his body slamming against the crater walls and submerging into the spewing magma. Once again with a sway of her hand, she summoned the other three Elements to assist in sealing his grave. Relentless gusts of gale wind blew in from the West, whisking the sand into the pit. The ferocious Winds swelled the ocean's crest, surging its merciless waves onto the shore. The raw and collective energy filled Mia's spirit with irresistible, euphoric vigor. She raised her arms to her Moon in sheer delight, continuously drawing down its effulgent rays. Lightning streaked across the sky, dividing and subdividing its jagged scepters just above the oceans surface. The West Winds blew, filling her spirit with unprecedented elation. She watched, intently as the rolling thunder chased the wind, cracking and echoing its rumbling blare. Her eternal love of apocalyptic thunderstorms had always reflected in the Delphic look in her eyes. She couldn't resist this animated force of nature and always surrendered to the seductive lure of their energy.

The cloudburst streamed its wind driven downpour, releasing its pent up moisture, inundating the sand and weakening the ground surrounding the crater. The winds violent upward flow, vacillated hot and cold air, producing a hailstorm and filling the crater with its crystal orbs. Layer by layer, the watery ice pellets sealed his grave. Piping hot steam plumed out of its depths and its thick clouds swiftly diminishing with the storms gusts. She continuously pushed her Magick to the edge, challenging herself with boundless ardor. The gravitational affects of the Full Moon peaked the tide, creating a swift upsurge over the beach. Mia paced backward, watching the affects of her intentions come alive. The ocean cascaded into the crater like a waterfall, filling every nook and cranny.

The climax of these collective forces made her feel as if she were riding lightning. Her spirit was filled with adrenaline overload. She was astonished at the level of Magick that had always been within her. Distracted by her own valiance, she lost sight of what was still occurring around her. She began to panic when she realized that she didn't know how to wield this energy and return it to its source and now knew what Hunter had meant. The symphony of eclectic Magick was now in a state of anarchy and had become an entity in and of itself. In a panicked state, she had realized that she had fallen off of her path by bending the rules and the Rede that she followed. She knew now that she had misused her traits by trying to become Karma. She had fed off of her own suppressed darkness, submitting Willfully to its false enticement. She realized that Hunter was winning this battle, by simply setting the stage for her. What she had done was unnecessary and nothing short of overkill. Her impatience was her downfall.

The oceans undertow caught her off guard and pulled her under its surface. Its pull was much stronger than her endurance. She believed that Karma had found her and that she was going to die by the sword that she used to destroy him. The echoed acoustics of the oceans reverberations enhanced her fear, causing her to further panic and release some of her lungs remaining oxygen. Her muscles began to spasm. She knew that she was facing imminent death. Her conscious state was slowly depleting. She sunk deeper, within her mind, succumbing to the powers that be. Her spirit was now at ease. As she slipped into a semi-conscious state, she saw a faint glow in the distance. As she waded with the current, its details began to reveal itself to her. As the source of the light took shape, its edges radiating a cylinder shaped beacon. Her body spiraled closer to it, with each influx of current. Within its circumference, she saw various shades of color, each vivid shade presenting itself to her in a singular pattern as if to communicate a message to her. She knew the meanings of each color, but couldn't decipher the collective message. The colors ceased, leaving a black hole in the center. She could only see the cylinders pearly bright edges. Its perimeters were in arms reach. With heed, she touched its edges and the lights flickered. Its circumference was wide enough to wriggle her body through its opening. She grasped the edge with one hand and pulled herself up, high enough to peek inside. Feeding into her inquisitive mind, she pulled herself up closer to its opening and peered into its depths. The current began to sway and she struggled to hold onto its edge. The darkness within the portal was changing to a brighter shade of Grey. She watched its shaded center continuously evolve into lighter hues. A blurred, brown entity slowly emerged from within the portal. She watched as it came closer into her view. Stronger flows of current pulled against her, each wave, stronger than the last. She held onto the edges with her fingers and was quickly losing her grip. The last wave ripped her hands from its edges. With the portals opening still in sight, she caught a glimpse of the enigmatic entity, materializing and reaching out to her. It grasped her arm and pulled her through the portal's luminous vortex.

The sounds of the nocturnal creatures and the gentle waves of the ocean synchronized its harmonious melody to the flickering glow of the stars. Mia's listless body lay cradled against the lion's chest. He caressed her face with the back of his paw, occasionally nudging her body whilst waiting for her eyes to open. Her wolf stood beside her, whimpering every so often in an attempt to wake her. The warm breeze cascaded off of the oceans surface, gently awakening her senses. She heard the rhythm of his heartbeat and knew that she was safe. Her hand slid across her chest and grasped onto his arm. She inhaled sharply and opened her eyes. She smiled. A distraught tear ran down her cheek. Her wolf nuzzled his nose against her neck and licked her face. She giggled, pulled him closer and hugged him. She gazed up at the lion and cried. He touched her nose, pointed to the Moon and held his fist high. She smiled and did the same. His roar echoed across the beach, inciting the wolf to howl. Mia placed her finger over her lips and whispered to them. "Shhhh." She giggled and grasped onto the Lions shoulder to pull herself upright then pulled the wolf next to her and howled at the Moon with him. An unusual sound echoed through the night sky. Recognizing it, she held her hand up and extended her finger, paralleled to the ground. The fluting and cawing sounds grew louder. Both mother and baby Blue Jays soared above them. The Mother landed on her finger. Mia lifted her other hand and watched as the baby Blue Jay soared like an Eagle, gliding along with the waves of the wind. It landed on her finger and Mia cried and laughed with tears of joy. She whispered to it. "We did it, baby. We finally did it."

The lion stood. She slid out of his embrace and stood before him. The Lions eyes flared and Mia stepped back, in fear. He raised his front legs and extended his claws. The color of his golden fur darkened before her eyes. The fur on his arms lengthened and his body slowly transformed into a larger and darker form of himself. He raised his arms, and spread them outward, exposing his immense, dark wings. The Moon's brilliance highlighted every curve of his body, shining its effulgent rays along the edges of his dark wings. She gazed up at his face, terrorized by what she saw. She whimpered his name. "Hu…Hunter." A rush of adrenaline surged throughout her body. She trembled with fear, screaming his name once more, his true name. "Theron!" Her voice echoed. He uttered her name. "Mia…" She quivered and became distraught. He waved his wings, snapping them behind his body and spread them outward, shrouding her from her Moon, the sky and all that surrounded her. She could only see the darkness of him. He encompassed her body within his dark wings. Her breathing became erratic. She felt lightheaded.

Just before she lost consciousness, she heard the whispers of someone's voice. "Take my hand and I will show you how to fly through this." She fell against his chest. He caught her and wrapped his wings tightly around her, seizing her mind, body and spirit.

CHAPTER 27

MIA'S MOON

The florescent lights unpleasantly greeted her eyes as she came out of her unconscious state. The sounds of high- pitched noises startled her. She felt someone's hand on hers and as she regained her focus her eyes widened. She wanted to scream but couldn't. She recognized him. Barely able to speak, she was only able to force sounds from her mouth. "S…sss." She hyperventilated, but was calmed by his soothing voice. "Mia" He cried. The tears rushed down his face. I'm here." "Sss…Sebastian." She managed to whisper his name. "We're all here." She raised her eyebrow. "Who?" She felt the touch of several hands, turned her head slowly to see to whom they had belonged. She panted nervously, at first sight of them. The entire Coven of Witches surrounded her. She gazed downward, to the person who held her feet and saw Mayne. Mason and Enya stood beside her. Sage and Raine sat on the bed next to Sebastian and smiled. Zephyr and Lucius rose from their chairs and stood near the foot of the bed. To her left stood Gwen, Faeryn, Ceridwen and Aithusa. She felt a warm hand touch the left side of her face. She turned her head slowly and saw Hunter. Her jaw dropped. She was speechless. He sat on the edge of the bed and kissed her forehead. He whispered into her ear. "My Phoenix Fire." She tried to speak. He placed his finger over her mouth and whispered once more. "Shhh."

She silenced herself for the moment. Tears seeped from her eyes as she once again, took a panoramic view of everyone that surrounded her. Until now, she had thought that she had been victorious and then bits and pieces of her memory began to fill the void, inclusive of the last of the events, prior to losing consciousness. She vaguely remembered the feeling of drowning. Hunter moved his arm over her shoulder to pull the blanket over her. At that moment, she saw a fleeting glimpse of his dark wings and recollected the events leading up to her imminent failure to wield. Her thoughts, laced with unjustified thoughts of what may follow. She wailed her words. "WHY... Release me!". Hunter sat on the bed beside her and held her quivering hands in his. "Mia, please listen to me. You are just like us. You are a Witch. You are also an Empath and a Dreamweaver. We collectively have traits that vary amongst our Coven members. What sets you apart from us is your ability to control dreams. You have always been a rainbow, hiding in the dark. For most of your life, you've always practiced as a Solitary Witch. Until you've met us, you practiced nothing other than low-level, simple Magick. We brought you into our Coven, not only to enhance its power, but to also show you that within the collectiveness of our Coven, you can stimulate and strengthen your suppressed traits so that you can reach your true full potential and see who you really are. Together, this Coven is stronger. You need to accept this."

She remained unconvinced of the true intentions of her inclusiveness in this circle and their thirst for her to accept her place among them. She wiped her eyes and stared into his for a few moments. Then, one by one she stared into the eyes of each and every one of them. Nothing had changed. She could still sense the Greyness within their souls. Their malicious intent could no longer remain hidden from her. She took a deep breath, falsely portraying her calm and accepting demeanor to them. "I want everyone to come closer to me." They gathered around her, some sitting on the bed, and some leaning over others, who sat beside her. She smiled. "I know who I am. I'm the Sentinel. I see and feel everything. I know. I see your true colors of Grey and Black Magick. I know of your sole intentions. You may think that you have found me, however, it is the Goddess who has brought me to you. I know why I'm here. I don't need you. You need me. I'm here to either reprogram this Coven or banish it. I am the sentinel."

She realized that nothing was, as it seemed.

Even at this very moment, it wasn't.

She felt a change coming in the air and knew that her perception was about to change…

Connected Perception

When I see clouds, especially the whispy cirrus ones, my first thought is about how they are connected, always, in different stages, at different times, different seasons, different strengths, shapes and sizes. They are forever changing form, separating and merging together to create their own perfect symphonies. Everything, every single molecule comes from the Earth. There are 5 Elements. 4 of which are essential for life on Earth. Earth, Water, Air and Fire. These four Elements are 4 of the most powerful entities. In addition, 2 imperitive and powerful entities are The Moon and the Sun, which guide everything.

There may be times throughout a person's life where they feel disconnected. If you pull a plant out of the Earth, it withers. If you take a fish out of the Water, it also withers. When one is taken out of its natural habitat, it has difficulty adapting or surviving. Animals are always truly connected to the Earth. They always follow nature's plan, season after season. They recognize atmospheric changes and know when the weather is changing, before humans do. They sense Earthquakes and storms before we are aware and automatically take cover. They are always on track and never lose sight of what is important. Humans tend to disconnect from whats important.

Often, when we feel disconnected, we sometimes find ourselves at a beach, walking barefoot. Your feet are touching the ground and or the Water.

You usually feel better afterwards. This is because you have physically reconnected with the Earth, so, naturally, when you reconnect with the Elements, you feel more in tune with the Universe and as you do this, you are essentially releasing negativity.

Every living thing is connected to each other and the Elements. Everything, every single molecule comes from the Earth. Never forget where you came from. If you feel disconnected, always go back to the beginning. Mother Earth.

> PS: The 5th Element is your higher power.
> Molly-Keet

Acknowledgements

To my Familiars – My Sentinals - Jax/Sean/Bella/Geo/Tigger/Princess/ Prince
Your united, ever changing & everlasting Spirit lives with me forever. I love you.
Jax - Your feral demeanor fed this book.

To Mommy - My Spirit guide. Every time I hear of the song Magic by ONJ, I think of you. You are my eternal flame. I will always miss you.)O(

To my 7 siblings
For torturing me (with love) and inevitably asking for my wrath of endless reciprocity. You may now bow to me.

To Speed / K.V.L.)O(
For always resetting me & keeping me Grounded, my Sister of the Moon

To Mark & Richie)O(
For your guidance, your Magick & for showing me how to socialize with) O(others)O(
Thank you for hosting your yearly great Balls of Fire.

To 13Moonstorm13)O((Paul Croft)
For finding me…again, banishing my fears, guiding me through this journey & flying with me, always & forever. ……ps: hands you a mad frog……

To Rose Angel
The most elegant flower veils itself until its Magick is ready to open its petals and rise like a Pheonix Fire to reveal its hidden Faeryn to the Universe. PS: Puppycats rule!

To Elaine Diaz
For being my Beta Reader & for being my cheerleader throughout this journey.

To Brian Portaro
For your encouragement, coffee, lottery & pizza !

To J.N.
For your guidance & assistance. Thank you …hands you a large coffee.

To B.R.
For your technical & Twitter guidance…Steers clear of your dragons.

To Steven McCole for your phenominal and entertaining editing, in depth knowledge of this genre and my kick-ass epic book cover design! You are the "Highlander" of editors and your art has ALL the Magick of the 4 Elements. whelk7@aol.com - Artist & Editor

To "IT" / The Turch – My caffeinated buddy of mahem & madness & my website designer.

To my friends – You know who your are. Thank you for being my friends.

To Jyn - Write that damn book drummer chick !

To COFFEE – YOU RULE !

<u>TO ME ! YOU DID IT – FREAK !</u>

About the Author

NYC born and raised
I love the beach especialy on a Full Moon night
Thunderstorms – They feed my Spirit
Coffee
Rock 'N' Roll & Metal
Snow
I love writing, reading, playing my drums & bicycling
Animal advocate forever – Please consider adopting a stray or shelter pet
Caffeine enhances everything… Just sayin'

If you have enjoyed this book, please consider posting your kind review.

The Hunter – Available on Amazon, CreateSpace & Kindle

Hunters Moon – Summer 2016
Mia's Moon TBA
The Moon Writer TBA